REVENGE
OF THE
Mistress

Also by Cydney Rax

The Reeves Sisters

A Sister's Secret

The Love & Revenge Series

Revenge of the Mistress

My Married Boyfriend

If Your Wife Only Knew

My Daughter's Boyfriend

My Husband's Girlfriend

Scandalous Betrayal

My Sister's Ex

Brothers & Wives

Reckless (with Niobia Bryant and Grace Octavia)

Crush (with Michele Grant and Lutishia Lovely)

Published by Dafina Books

REVENGE
OF THE
Mistress

CYDNEY RAX

KENSINGTON PUBLISHING CORP.
www.kensingtonbooks.com

DAFINA BOOKS are published by

Kensington Publishing Corp.
119 West 40th Street
New York, NY 10018

All Kensington Titles, Imprints, and Distributed Lines are available at special quantity discounts for bulk purchases for sales promotions, premiums, fund-raising, and educational or institutional use. Special book excerpts or customized printings can also be created to fit specific needs. For details, write or phone the office of the Kensington special sales manager: Kensington Publishing Corp., 119 West 40th Street, New York, NY 10018, attn: Special Sales Department, Phone: 1-800-221-2647.

Dafina and the Dafina logo Reg. U.S. Pat. & TM Off.

ISBN-13: 978-1-4967-0144-2
ISBN-10: 1-4967-0144-5
First Kensington Trade Edition: February 2017
First Kensington Mass Market Edition: October 2018

eISBN-13: 978-1-4967-0143-5
eISBN-10: 1-4967-0143-7

10 9 8 7 6 5 4 3 2 1

Printed in the United States of America

Acknowledgments

Many thanks to everyone who supported me, including my coworker Steven Burns (you have a mastermind underneath that innocent face), and my other colleagues who willingly shared their knowledge and insight. I'm grateful to Officer James Stanley for the CSI details (for some reason he likes to sing a Motown song and put my name in the lyrics. Thanks for the laughs.).

Shout-out to my humble beginnings: Cass Tech High School in Detroit, and the written communications program at Eastern Michigan University. This is where my interest in writing was initially birthed. Of course, after reading a Terry McMillan novel, the desire to write fiction grew stronger. I'm grateful for every opportunity.

Kudos to the literary team: my agent, Claudia Menza, and former editor Mercedes Fernandez, who acquired the novels in the Love & Revenge series. Mercedes, thanks for collaborating with me and being the best possible advocate of my works. You will be missed! To my new editor, Esi Sogah: Let's do this! And to the Kensington production editor Rebecca Cremonese, and the book cover folks, Kristen Mills for the marvelous covers, and George Kerrigan for the photography: I love what you do in support of the books. Also special thanks to Lulu Martinez, publicist extraordinaire, and the marketing team. Thanks for going above and beyond. You rock!

To the faithful readers who've been there from the beginning, and to the new ones who've just discovered the novels and have reached out to me—I hope you get a huge thrill out of *Revenge of the Mistress*, which I found to be both a challenging and amazing experience to write!

Let me know what you think about the books. My twitter is: @neecee48204

Cheers,

Cydney Rax

When Karma comes back to punch you in the face,
I wanna be there . . . just in case it needs help.
—Unknown

Prologue

Only five-feet-two, the little man suddenly appeared at the warehouse door. He pointed a semiautomatic at Rashad. With a second to spare, Rashad took off running. But the shorter man was faster. He whizzed past him, threw up his legs, and kicked Rashad in his back. He crashed into a mountain of boxes filled with heavy material. His kneecap got banged up, and he cursed and yelled while spread out on the dusty floor.

The man quickly stood over Rashad. He aimed the pistol again. Rashad stared at the weapon and struggled to lift his hands. "What did I do? What do you want?"

The man said nothing. He gaped at Rashad with no visible emotion.

"Hey, man, I'm talking to you. You want money? You can have my debit cards, my credit cards."

"Don't want money. But you are who I want."

An electronic voice changer made his attacker sound peculiar. A low, evil-pitched tone that uttered frightening words. Rashad's mouth felt dry as he shouted, "Why are you doing this? Who are you?"

"Just call me Death."

"W-what?"

Rashad then realized this wasn't a simple robbery. It was something much more sinister. The man was so short and slight that Rashad thought he could take him. His attacker noticed a metal folding chair nearby on the ground. He pointed the pistol at Rashad and ordered him to pick it up and sit down. Rashad started to obey him. But on a whim, he reached for the leg of the chair. He yelled with all his might and swung at the guy.

"You motherfucking asshole!" he screamed. He bashed him in his temple. His attacker was temporarily stunned and rocked on his feet. Then he fired a wild shot; a bullet pierced Rashad's leg.

Blood poured from his left calf; his dark slacks turned red. Rashad yelled, "Fuck. Ugh!" The pain was excruciating.

The attacker set the chair upright and pointed at it. He motioned at Rashad, who immediately responded. Wincing in agony, he lowered himself onto the seat. It felt uncomfortable as hell. He moaned as he tried to stop the blood from spilling. His hands turned red and felt sticky. He removed his jacket and placed it over the wound.

The man moved to stand next to Rashad; he calmly pressed the steel tip of the barrel against his head.

"You are Rashad Quintelle Eason. And a woman asked me to send a message to you."

"A woman?" he asked, his voice trembling. Blood oozed and drenched his shoes. This was unbelievable, and he could barely think. "W-what are you talking about?"

The man's piercing black eyes blinked rapidly.

"She said to ask, 'Why did you let Satan use you like you did?'"

"What woman? This is crazy. I-I don't know what you're—"

"She said you should know everything that she's talking about."

"But who is *she*?"

"Shut the fuck up. Right now."

The little man skillfully duct-taped Rashad's hands securely behind his back. Rashad was losing more blood; he slumped in the chair. It felt like he was about to keel over on the floor. His mind was foggy, his tongue thick. This was his worst nightmare.

Rashad tried to take deep breaths, but it was hard. His heart pounded like he'd just run twenty miles without stopping. He badly wanted to get the hell away, and he struggled to loosen his hands from the tape.

"Please, sir, please."

The man ignored him. He reached in the rear pocket of Rashad's blue jeans and removed his wallet.

Then he wound a wide, dark piece of cloth around Rashad's eyes. It felt tight and unmerciful. He felt like a blind man when everything went dark. His shirt was cold and wet against his skin. Was this some type of joke? Was someone trying to scare him just to make a point?

He sat in horrid anticipation. Soon he felt his mouth being pried open with tiny, rigid fingers. A thick sock was stuffed inside his mouth. It took away his saliva; he tried to cough but couldn't. The fibers from the cloth absorbed all the liquid from his mouth; the dryness made him want to vomit.

This was the most uncomfortable Rashad had ever felt in his life. He could not conceive what was happening. *Who is this guy? Am I about to die?*

As Rashad grew weaker, he recalled the man referring

to a woman in his life. For a moment, he felt sorry . . . sorry for things that were too late to change.

The black steel pistol was shoved harder against Rashad's temple.

Rashad slumped in his seat.

I wish I could . . . I wish I could get my . . . my cell phone . . . make a call . . . talk to the people that I . . . my kids . . . the family that I love.

But Rashad knew those wishes might not ever come true.

Beeva. Mama.

He knew his mom was crazy about him. And she'd be brokenhearted.

Nicky. My ride or die. Oooohhh God.

A weird animal sound escaped from his mouth as he silently sobbed in front of the man he could no longer see.

The man only laughed.

Rashad wanted to open his mouth and scream. But the darkness grew darker. He stopped crying.

Jesus. God, help me.

Seconds later a loud blast sounded in the hollowness of the room. The pain in Rashad's head made it feel like he was going blind, it hurt so terribly. Instantly, a fountain of blood poured from his head and formed a dark red pool on the ground beneath him. He fell over in a heap with the chair still attached to his body.

Rashad lay on the floor and took his last breath. He nursed one thought as he transitioned into eternity: *Why?*

Part 1

Love Is Stronger Than Revenge

Chapter 1

Nicole Kelly Greene marched into the church foyer wearing a floor-length Afrocentric gown. Her sequined heels clicked across the stone surface. She abruptly stopped and adjusted her selfie stick. "Mmm, gorgeous." She took a few shots until she was content.

Nicole had never looked more stunning in her entire life. It was Saturday, March 12, the day she was going to wed Rashad Eason, the man to whom she'd been engaged since last fall.

Nicole resumed walking and scampered into a tiny room for last-minute preparations. Shyla Perry-Fallender, Nicole's matron of honor, raced behind her. The two women huddled in front of a wide mirror and waited for the ceremony to begin.

"By all outward appearances, you look fine." Shyla carefully examined Nicole's fabulous dress and makeup. "And not too long ago, girl, I remember thinking I was flawless on my wedding day. But inside I was a bundle of nerves."

Nicole *did* have jitters, but she wasn't about to totally admit it.

"So, my friend . . . how are you really feeling?"

"Booya!" Nicole shouted.

"Excuse me?"

"Sorry to disappoint you, sweetie, but you won't find a bundle of nerves inside this woman. It's all pure, positive energy. In fact, I feel like I'm in a freaking Tyler Perry movie, or some romance novel. I want to weep with happiness, to laugh because I know I'm winning, to dance like I'm in a Chris Brown video."

"Why are you sounding so different and weird? You don't even talk like that."

Nicole sashayed back and forth and swung her arms around in jubilation.

"Oh, really? All of that?"

"I'm talking different, Shyla, because I *feel* different. Nicole Greene getting married? This is surreal. And you want to hear something else? I'm floored at the way everything turned out at the last minute—because you know we were on some ridiculous CP time trying to pull this wedding together. And I honestly don't give a care if you think I'm acting weird. Don't try to catch me because I'm floating on a cloud . . . a very high cloud."

In some ways Nicole wasn't lying about her jubilant feelings. The fact that she was about to marry Rashad Eason was nothing short of a miracle on a biblical scale.

"Think about it, Shyla. Years ago, I came this close to marrying Ajalon."

"Yeah, you told me all about your little drug-dealing ex-boyfriend. Good thing that situation didn't work out."

"I know, because even though Rashad isn't perfect, I think he's perfect for me," Nicole concluded.

She opened her cell phone and reviewed the most recent photos she had taken of Rashad.

"Look at this handsome-ass piece of chocolate."

"Mmm-hmm," Shyla murmured. "He looks good enough to eat. Yum!"

Nicole giggled. "I dodged a motherfucking bullet, because the smartest thing I ever did was to dump Ajalon and convince Rashad to make me official."

"If you say so."

"Girl, when I compare those two, hell, there is no comparison. I mean, I was happy when I learned that my ex-boyfriend left Birmingham to come find me here in Houston."

"But didn't it feel awkward, since you were, like, *living* with Rashad?"

"Well, yes, but still . . . a teensy part of me was curious about Ajalon."

"Yeah, you told me." Shyla frowned. "You were as curious as a nosy little cat. And you allowed yourself to get caught right back up with your ex. I still can't believe that shit."

"Girl, I needed to be sure." Nicole frowned, too, feeling a little ashamed of the fact that she'd briefly snuck around with Ajalon. But when he came back around and made her feel wanted again, she was so tempted. She couldn't forget how good he used to love her before he'd messed up their lives by getting himself locked up.

And when Nicole made up her mind and found the courage to dump Ajalon one last time, she'd hoped that Rashad was still feeling her enough to marry her. And last October, when Rashad had agreed to be her husband, with Shyla's help, the two ladies had coordinated her wedding in record time.

"And look at me now, here in the church, about to do it up," Nicole said.

She stepped away from the mirror and calmly observed her surroundings. They were in Fifth Ward Houston, inside a stone church that had a huge cross and stained-glass windows.

"First of all, I'm glad we are getting married in a house of God and not at the justice of the peace, or worse, in Las Vegas. Doing it in this building gives me the confidence I need to believe I'm making a solid decision for my future."

"I'm glad, too, boo. This place feels more real. Much more spiritual," Shyla told her.

Being in church was soothing to Nicole, yet she felt a little guilty, because she'd knowingly slept with Rashad when he was still married to her boss, Kiara. And as Nicole stood there in the church, it seemed like she'd been offered another chance. And that opportunity helped to ease her conscience.

"I have no idea what the Lord even thinks about me. He has been good to me, because as bad as things have been they could always be worse. I could be a single mom for the rest of my life. Not that there's anything wrong with that, but I want to raise our child with Rashad. And I want God to know I take my vows seriously," Nicole said. "I am not playing with nobody's pastor."

"Nobody's pastor? Dang, that sounds like you don't even know the man who is marrying y'all."

"Of course I don't know him personally, silly woman. But does it really matter? As long as the Lord knows him, then that's cool with me."

"Ha! That's completely obvious," Shyla said jokingly. She was happy for her friend, but at the same time, she felt some kind of way about how perfectly everything had ended up for Nicole and Rashad. A frequent jokester, Shyla grew surprisingly thoughtful. "This is truly a great day for you, Nicole. Yet, as a newly married woman myself, Nicole, I wish y'all could have at least gone to marital counseling a few times so you would truly understand what you're getting yourself into." She thought of her own marriage to Wesley Fallender. He was a good man, but that didn't keep their relationship road from being bumpy. He liked his space, whereas she preferred to be up under him all the time. And when unexpected bills came their way, so did the loud arguments and slamming doors.

Shyla gasped with great emotion at the painful memories. "Counseling helps you to put everything on the table and forces you to discuss potential issues that are hard to talk about, or things that can cause you to have hurt feelings. But it looks like you ain't got time for that . . . you found you a nice little bootleg minister who only cares about—"

"Shhh, don't say that. This preacher man might not be Joel Osteen, who was my first choice, but it's alright. It has to be. And forget a marriage counselor. We don't need anyone trying to tell us how to live our lives. We got this." Nicole shut down the subject. Shyla was giving her a weird vibe, but she concluded it didn't really matter what the woman thought. Nicole was minutes away from getting legally yoked to Rashad, premarital counseling or not.

"Change of subject, girl . . . do I really look alright?"

Shyla could not lie. "What can I say? You're a beautiful bride. When he sees you, you're going to make Rashad very happy."

Shyla smoothed back a flyaway piece of Nicole's hair and returned it to its place. Nicole's hair was upswept and secured by floral hairpins. Her fresh manicure consisted of a beautiful gel nail color. For once in her life, Nicole felt like a princess, and she couldn't wait to begin her new life without any problems.

"I'm so nervous I could scream."

"Wait till the honeymoon, boo."

"I know that's right." Nicole hugged herself. "Can you believe my family is out there waiting on me? They're going to die when they see me looking like a beauty queen. I hope their jealous asses enjoy themselves, because this woman is marrying up and they never thought it would happen."

"Some families can be such haters, but they'll get over it. Have you enjoyed them visiting you so far?"

"Yeah, it hasn't been too bad at all, especially since Rashad was nice enough to pay their airfare and hotel expenses." Rashad had flown in her mother, Evelyn, and younger sister, Mimi, and set them up at a Marriott for several days. "Rashad didn't have to do that, but he did. He's a good man. I feel like the most blessed woman in the world. I'm not even used to amazing things like this, and sometimes I can't believe it."

"Mmm-hmm. You're starting off real good, girl." Shyla moodily stared into space. "On the real, the average newly-weds lack the funds to do what you're doing, Nicole. They are struggling to pay for the wedding, let alone having a nice reception and a decent honeymoon. But, child, I'm assuming you won't have any worries when it comes to all that. There's that luck of yours again, working out every detail for you." Shyla gave Nicole a sad expression that disappeared quickly as she decided to play off her resentment by touching up her own makeup.

"I know, right. Plain dumb luck."

Poverty was a condition that Nicole had suffered from during her formative years. Her mother held down two jobs and hustled to provide for her family. But just because you grew up with financial struggles didn't mean you had to keep living that way.

"I'm telling you, Shyla, I'm not used to having money to pay for the things I want. Shit, my mother used to put furniture, school clothes, birthday presents, and Christmas toys on layaway. I always had to wait months to get the stuff I wanted. It would just kill me. And all while growing up, the struggles were real. Sometimes I wore my cousin's hand-me-downs. Mama couldn't even afford to send me to my prom or our graduation trip to Nassau. And I resented not being able to participate. It hurt like hell when my classmates showed me photos of their pretty gowns. And on the night of the prom, some of my friends even got the works: They rented Hummer limos, ate at nice restaurants, or rented luxury hotels for all-night parties." Nicole's voice caught in her throat at the painful memories. "But I can't forget how I was stuck at home that Friday night. My mother was working that night, Mimi and my cousins went skating, and I sat alone on the front porch watching my friends drive down the street with their prom dates. They looked like they were having the time of their lives. They even blew their horns and waved at me. When I couldn't stand it anymore, I went inside the house and started watching *Good Times* reruns."

"Are you serious, girl, or are you joking, because if it's true, then it sounds completely messed up." After hearing Nicole's sob story, Shyla felt ashamed of herself for even feeling a little envious of her friend.

"Yeah, all of it is true! And it perfectly explains why I'm so very happy today. Every woman wants to know how it feels to be Cinderella. I don't deserve it, yet I am so blessed."

Shyla's feelings of compassion rapidly disappeared.

She could not forget that Nicole had slept with a married businessman and that's probably why she was so-called blessed.

"Um, are you serious?"

"Shyla, because of how I was raised, it was normal for me to dream about how it would feel to win the lottery . . . be a millionaire . . . and now I know."

Shyla had had enough. Her friend's new fortunes were almost more than she could bear. "Wait a second, Nicole! Sorry to burst your bubble, but I simply cannot believe that Rashad is a millionaire. I mean, how can he be, when he's fresh off a divorce with two babies by his ex-wife, plus another daughter from his baby mama? Isn't he paying some baller-type child support?"

Nicole laughed, then sighed. "Girl, stop. Rashad was a little bit hurt financially by the divorce, but no, he's not flat broke."

"But still, Nicole, he gotta be paying his ex a grip."

"Look, he's not like that silly Ochocinco with his four baby mamas, or that ridiculous Ray Lewis with his six baby mamas. My man's got a good head on his shoulders; he's generous, but he also knows how to manage his money, even with the child support he's forced to pay. That much I know."

"Or else you wouldn't be marrying him?"

"Oh, goodness, Shyla, really? Look, I'm marrying Rashad Eason because we are soul mates." Shyla uproariously laughed, but Nicole ignored her and continued. "And I truly believe that with his smarts and strong work ethic, my man will rise up and do even better than before. We're a team. I consider myself part-owner of Eason and Son. And with my PR background, I can help promote the company the way it should have been done years ago. I've got huge plans for us, regardless of ex-wives and baby mamas and any other type of drama."

Shyla quietly listened to her friend as she went on and on about her goals for her soon-to-be husband. "I hope your plans include all three of his children."

"Ouch, that stings."

"It should. You're only twenty-six, and you've already had stepmama duties before you could even say 'I do.'"

"You ain't ever lied, girl." In truth, at times Nicole wished she could forget Rashad had two kids with his ex-wife, Kiara. There was his oldest, Myles, who was almost nine, and eleven-month-old Jazzy. And she couldn't forget Hayley, the three-year-old daughter of her coworker Alexis McNeil.

"You know what, Shyla? I could let all the baby-mama drama make me completely avoid this man. But nope, I won't do it. I mean, look at us. I feel like I'm winning already, because we are about to be official. As far as I'm concerned, we can all live together and have a good time—me, Rashad, and all of his kids. So yeah, they all are definitely included in my master plan."

"You have a game plan. Good for you, Nicole, but I still haven't heard you say that you are deeply or hopelessly in love."

"Shyla, don't even go there. You of all people should know that I love me some Rashad with a deep passion, and I have felt that way almost from the beginning. From the time we met, Rashad treated me like a person and not just a piece of ass. When he came to my house to do my renovation work, he acted like he cared about me as an individual, and he made me feel like much more than just a client."

"Mmm-hmm, from what I've heard, he sure did." Shyla rolled her eyes and cackled.

"Stop playing. We were friends, genuine friends, long before we started smashing."

"From friends to bed buddies, from bed buddies to spouses. Wow!" Shyla gave Nicole a knowing look. "And the fact that this man already had a wife didn't seem to faze you one bit. Did it?"

"Look, I am not a home wrecker."

"Ha, says the home wrecker." Shyla laughed uncontrollably, unable to help herself.

Shyla was Nicole's friend, but she wasn't going to sugarcoat the situation. Plus, she felt that Nicole should be honest about what she was getting herself into and see things from a different perspective.

"I'm suddenly getting a nasty vibe from you, Mrs. Perry-Fallender, and I don't get it. Why are you saying such crazy shit to me on my wedding day?"

"Look, I am happy for you, baby girl, but you gotta consider that you are about to marry someone that you *know* had a couple of affairs on Kiara. And you better hope that what you did to his wife is not something that may get done to you. That's just keeping it real."

Nicole threw up her hands and sighed. "That's the past, alright?"

She looked into her friend's eyes, and for the first time ever, she saw they resembled the appearance of a green-eyed monster. Nicole knew that some women would begrudge her marrying Rashad, but she didn't want to think that her closest friend could feel that way.

"Why are you predicting that bad things are going to happen in my marriage? Whose side are you on, Ms. Matron of Honor?"

"You already know I'm on your side, boo, that's why I'm giving it to you straight. A person who did not care about you for real would tell you the fairy-tale shit that you want to hear. But that type of thing only lasts for so long. And if you want to make it for the long haul, you got to look at things the way they really are, and not just the silly way you hope they will be."

"Ouch. Well, damn." The truth really stung! Nicole felt as if a knife had just dug into her soul.

Temporarily speechless, she wiped away a tiny tear that formed in the corner of her eye.

"Oh, great. Now it looks like the Blind Boys of Alabama applied my makeup."

"Let me fix that."

Shyla expertly touched up Nicole's mascara until she looked perfect again.

"Don't pay me any mind," Shyla told her. "I'm shooting off at the mouth because, hell, I'm nervous, like I'm the one who's about to get married. Weddings always make me unhinged." She let out a hearty laugh. "And I'm sorry for sounding shady as hell, Nicole. But it's coming from a place of love. Because I really am glad for you in spite of everything, or else I wouldn't even be here."

"Ha!" Nicole sniffed. "Your ass is here because you are as nosy as that talk show hoe Wendy Williams, and sometimes you're as cruel as her, too."

"Talk show hoe? Not *host*?"

"I said it how I meant it. Talk show hoe!"

"Oooh, that's so cold. I love Wendy. Yet"—she giggled—"you are so right. We are both some nosy-ass, opinionated bitches."

The women fell out laughing, giggling until they both felt better, till their hearts felt lighter.

"Aww, I know the whole thing may sound nuts. Yet I know you want what's best for me, Shyla. And I can admit

I've traveled a rocky road to get here. So I've already asked God to forgive me for doing anything that might have hurt Kiara."

"*You* seriously asked *God* to forgive *you* for all the hell *you* put that woman through?"

"'All the hell,' Shyla? You're exaggerating. It really wasn't that much."

"Hmm, I guess going around the office bragging about your boss's husband and being openly happy about getting pregnant by him wasn't 'that much'?" She smiled as she tossed her wild accusations.

"Not really." Nicole's voice grew shaky. "Not to me."

"Nicole, let's get real. If it was enough to make those folks get divorced, how can you think it wasn't 'that much'?"

"Alright, since you wanna go there, in my opinion, it's *not* that much, because those two were already in trouble. Remember, Rashad had another baby mama long before I came into the picture, so you cannot blame the failure of their marriage entirely on me. I didn't steal Kiara's man. She *gave* him to me. And *that's* the truth, whether you want to accept it or not. Another thing: Stop acting so concerned as if I fucked *your* husband. I did not, so shut the fuck up."

Shyla gasped and nearly fell out. She quieted down and then meekly attended to the bride's makeup one last time. She whipped out an eye shadow kit and asked Nicole to close her eyes.

As Nicole stood there and let Shyla re-create her smoky eye, all the talk about her affair with Rashad did sting, but she refused to feel guiltier than necessary. Sure, she could admit she might have toned down her fascination of being with Rashad. But, hell, what did Kiara expect? It wasn't like she'd gone after a married man on purpose. Nicole could still remember how she'd arrived in Houston with no friends or family. She would go to work at her job at the

Texas South West University, put in her eight hours, and then come straight home. And that summer nearly two years ago, all she had was the warm enthusiasm of Rashad each day when he came by her house to do his job fixing up her dreadful kitchen and outdated bathrooms. He did his work and engaged her in warm conversation. His charm and humor made her want to get to know him better. And so she did. The fact that their personalities instantly clicked and they eventually fell in love wasn't planned. In fact, if Nicole could do it, she'd go on Twitter and start a new hash tag: #SideChicksMatter. She felt the world needed to understand that these situations weren't always the "other" women's doing. The wife played her own part, as well. A lot of times the husband complained that his needs were going unmet. But the wives did not want to hear that. Nicole knew that some wives would only offer their husbands an obligatory blow job on his birthday, on major holidays, or on their anniversary—other than that, forget it! Or some wives would eventually be unwilling to meet their husband's other basic needs, such as cooking a full-course meal, cleaning the house, or doing whatever else she needed to do as his partner. Some wives still wanted their needs met, but eventually they did not care about their husbands'. Nicole did her research. She read advice columns. She took copious notes and was determined to not be a modern-day slacker wife who took her spouse for granted. Now, mind you, some husbands were trifling and did not deserve the royal treatment, but she hoped that Rashad would not be one of those men. And that's why Nicole planned to be a much better wife than Kiara ever was. She knew marriage would be hard work. But working hard until Rashad knew that she really was his ride or die was what she pledged to do.

After Shyla finished Nicole's makeup, she could not

help herself. "Look, keep Wesley's name out of your mouth. I'm pissed that you'd think I'd ever be worried about you and him hooking up. You're a hooker, but you ain't a damn fool. Are you sure you're even worthy to be a man's wife?"

Nicole helplessly threw up her hands. She lacked the patience for one of Shyla's ratchet speeches right now. Nicole began to march around the tiny room wringing her hands. The start of the ceremony was drawing near. She began to sweat underneath her beautiful gown and she worried it would stain. She felt short of breath, almost like something was pressing down on her nostrils and making it difficult to breathe.

She inhaled, exhaled, and opened her mouth to speak.

"Shyla, of course I'm worthy." She was almost in tears. "My past is over, and I will not walk down that aisle unless it is clear in my heart that Rashad and I are free to spiritually and legally unite." Nicole gasped and reflected on everything that had happened up till that point. The sneaking around with Rashad, the confrontations with Kiara, the pain of having a baby with her boss's ex-husband. Who was she kidding? She almost wanted to sit down and think some more.

"What's wrong with you, Nicole? You don't look so well. Are you sure you want to do this?"

Suddenly frightening thoughts made it difficult for Nicole to think rationally. She felt like she was in a war zone of hostile territory.

But Nicole was a fighter if nothing else.

"I absolutely will go through with this," she concluded in a quiet, determined voice. "You know my mother, Evelyn, and sister, Mimi, are waiting out there, right? Girl, when I told my mother I was getting married to a rich man, she nearly called me a liar. Do you know how much that

hurt me? I-I've had to prove a lot to her. After we got engaged, I made Rashad get on the phone with my mother so
she could hear his voice; I had to text my sister so she
could show my mama multiple photos of me and Rashad in
the same room. Mama was on some BS at first, but now
that she is here and sees it's for real, she can barely open
her mouth to speak. This shit is real, Shyla." Nicole broke
out in a nervous, angry laugh that made her eyes wet again.

"I went to school, and I put myself through college
without Mama's financial help. By the time I turned nine-
teen, she was doing better, making more money. She told
me that she couldn't cosign any student loans for anybody,
not even family. Can you believe that? And now Rashad's
money is my money, and I don't need her stupid-ass loans
anymore." Nicole enjoyed her moment of triumph. "Shyla,
I love you like a sister, but please leave me alone with all
your finger-pointing about how I did this and that to
Rashad's ex-wife. I did nothing. Everything that happened,
Kiara did it to herself. 'Cause we keep forgetting that her
scandalous, vindictive ass almost got knocked up by another man. And I guess that's my fault, too, huh?"

"All righty then. Calm the fuck down," Shyla pleaded
with Nicole. "All this time, I was just messing with you,
girl. I wanted to see how determined you were to go
through with this, because once you make this decision,
there is no turning back. It takes a lot of balls to get married these days and stick with it for more than a few minutes. So actually, I'm happy to see that you've got your
head on straight about this major life decision. Booya! Be
free to do you, all right?"

Nicole silently nodded. The ladies stood in reflective
silence for a moment, and then they heard the organist
begin playing soothing music.

The sounds of love were in the air, and Nicole was eager to get caught up in the spirit of the wedding.

Shyla stared at Nicole's face, and noticed that her friend's eyes were alit with joy. She knew in her heart that Nicole was sincerely fond of Rashad and that she wanted to be his wife more than anything.

"As the woman whom you chose to share in your honor, I am hereby shutting my mouth and from now on will focus on the positive. Because, you know what? Your ass is glowing like a Fifth Avenue Christmas tree. You look like your finger got stuck in an electrical socket."

"Aww, shut up, my nutty-Wendy-Williams's-acting best friend."

They laughed together and rocked each other in a tight hug. Someone came and knocked on the door. The beautiful bride started for the door but twirled around to face Shyla.

"If I've never told you this before, I'm saying it now. Thank you for being my friend." Nicole was serious for a change. "I don't always click with women. But you and I hit it off from the beginning."

"That's because we're a lot alike."

Nicole smiled with happiness. "Today I feel complete. I feel like every tragic thing I've ever gone through in my life was because one day I'd end up with all of this. Shyla, girl, I have the man of my dreams. I am the mother of a healthy, beautiful baby girl. There's no turning back now."

With that, Nicole slipped her arm through Shyla's, and they both headed for the sanctuary.

Chapter 2

The energy in the church could be felt by all. Nicole nervously stood at the double doors that led to the sanctuary. The guests sat on the edge of their seats, craning their necks when they knew the moment had finally arrived. When the marching music began, little Hayley trudged down the aisle first. A crown of baby's breath was clipped to her hair. And she clutched a wicker basket filled with flowers between her tiny hands. Hayley smiled each time people waved and took photos of her. Nicole proudly noticed that she did exactly as she'd been instructed: petal toss, smile and wave, petal toss, smile and wave.

Her new stepson, Myles, looked handsome in his gray tuxedo. His eyes sparkled in amazement as he carried the ring bearer pillow a few steps behind Hayley. Right before they reached the front, they happily marched side by side, grinning and nodding at every clicking camera.

The music suddenly changed. Mimi and Nicole started down the aisle alongside each other. Nicole squeezed her sister's arm in a tight grip, feeling amazed that any of this was actually happening.

Moments later, a beaming Nicole joined Rashad at the front. She hadn't seen him in twenty-four hours. He calmly nodded at her and gave her a lopsided grin.

Together they turned to face the pastor.

As the ceremony proceeded, it took Rashad several tries to state his vows.

"You are the flame that lights . . . that sheds light on . . . um . . ."

He cleared his throat and asked if he could start over.

"Are you nervous, son?" the minister kindly asked.

"Do I look nervous?" Rashad rocked backward on his heels and almost slipped.

Jerry, his employee and best man, held up Rashad by his elbow.

"You all right, man?" Jerry whispered.

"I-I'm straight."

Nicole fanned herself with her floral arrangement. The smell of liquor hit her nose, and she nearly gagged. Why was her man smelling like a roadhouse bar? It wasn't even three o'clock yet.

Rashad tried again and managed to recite his vows.

The minister asked Nicole to speak her part. She cleared her throat and loudly said, "Two flames—"

Shyla burst out laughing.

"Sorry, I will start again," Nicole murmured. "Two flames, one light. Rashad, I offer you this ring as a sign of life and myself as your . . . as your wife . . ." Nicole felt so emotional her legs almost caved in, but she got through it and within minutes, they were married.

An ecstatic Nicole kissed Rashad. He kissed her back with sleepy-looking eyes, but she barely noticed.

* * *

The wedding party and guests relocated to the social hall in another part of the church. Nicole changed into a lavender cocktail dress and was feeling good.

The DJ played "Here" by Alessia Cara. Nicole sang at the top of her lungs. And she was thinking of Ajalon Cantu as she mouthed the lyrics. She couldn't believe how close she'd come to losing Rashad by foolishly letting herself get involved with him.

"Bye-bye, my sexy Afro Italian," she sang as she swayed to the music. The next club banger was specifically requested by Nicole: "Do What I Want" by DJ Carisma. The happy bride laughed, clapped, did a two-step, and broke it down to the ground. Everyone surrounded Nicole, cheering her on as she danced her ass off. The music was loud and booming, and the guests were having a grand time.

Nicole's mama, Evelyn, mostly stood around staring listlessly at everything. Nicole stopped dancing and went to have a few words with the woman.

"Are you all right, Mama? Is everything okay?" Nicole kept asking. But she didn't care about her mother's stunned appearance. Evelyn looked like she was going to be sick, and Nicole knew exactly why. She knew all her mother saw were dollar signs when she looked at the lavish decorations, the stylish clothes, the line of limos waiting out front, and the large spread of food.

Usually when her mama saw this type of spread, it was because someone important had died and she had to cater the event; as a popular cook, Evelyn had actually prepared meals for the mayor of Bessemer, which was where Nicole had lived until she was twelve. Evelyn raised Nicole, Mimi, and two other nieces in a one-story, one-thousand-square-foot house that had only one bathroom. The best thing was that they had a huge lot with enough space for the kids to run around barefoot whenever they wanted.

But most of her other memories were troubling. Nicole vowed not to forget where she came from. She hoped her mother was happy for her and knew she'd come a long way.

"I'm just so relieved for you," Evelyn uttered. She beamed at her daughter. "You made life work out beautifully for yourself."

Nicole was stunned. Her mother had never said such flattering words before to Nicole.

"I beg your pardon?"

"Your dreams came true, daughter. You're doing better than I ever did . . . at least for right now. Let's hope that you can keep it up."

Ouch, Nicole thought. "Mama, I don't see why things won't be kept up."

"You never know with a marriage. But at least you're starting out great, daughter. You got your education. Finally got that college degree."

"Without any help from you, but yeah, I still got it."

"Please, Nicole. Let's not go into that. You seem to think that I never wanted to help you. But to be honest, I wasn't always in a position to help out. My credit was jacked up. Back then I couldn't get a loan to buy a DVD player. I struggled to pay the mortgage on that little piece of land we had. Doing it alone was hard. That's why I pushed you to get your education, find a good job, and be independent. Why I told you from an early age that you needed to work, pay your bills, and be responsible. I know you thought I was being hard on you. But the world we live in is tough and unpredictable. I tried my best to prepare you for the future. And I was hoping you wouldn't repeat all of my mistakes."

Nicole stared at her mom through a different set of

eyes. In the past, the woman was always so quick to say "no" that she'd assumed the lady was mean-spirited.

"Mama, when you told me you didn't have money for my prom, I thought you were just being cheap or hateful."

"In truth, Nicole, I *wanted* to save up and send you to prom, but we were two payments behind on our mortgage. I had to choose between having a place to stay or sending you to an expensive one-night party. As a single mom, which would you have chosen?"

Nearly being homeless was a serious matter. And Nicole felt ashamed to realize she had misjudged her mother all those years. "Of course I would choose the house. But Mama, you never told me any of this before."

"Because you're not good at listening when it comes to certain things. There were a lot of things happening all at the same time when you were in twelfth grade. I told you, but you wasn't hearing it."

"What are you talking about?"

"After I got caught up on the mortgage, I was thinking it would be nice to try and do something for you for prom, even though I did not agree with how pricey everything was. I had secretly put a dress on layaway for you."

"You did?"

"Yes! Everything was cool at first, but then things got tight. You asked me again if you could go to prom. I told you very specifically that it depended on how many hours I could get at the restaurant. And you slinked out of the room before I could even finish. I was trying to tell you that a lot of spring weddings were on the calendar and I could do a lot of cooking and make enough money to buy you a nice dress. But you heard 'it depends' and that was it for you, young lady. You take one little word and run with it, and once you started thinking all that negative stuff, I could not do a thing with you. I just said forget it and I got back my deposit on that dress and paid a bill."

"Really?" Nicole asked, feeling even worse. It was hard for her to pretend like the past did not matter. The past made her see herself for who she was, and that realization made her embarrassed. "I acted like that? Well, I was a kid. I didn't know any better."

"You were a kid then, but even today you are set in your ways. You moved away to Texas without even caring about my opinion. That's why I barely called you on the phone these past couple of years. I decided the only way for you to learn a lesson was to go through hard times on your own. See how it feels to be a real woman who has to work hard to get what she wants. It hasn't been easy raising you girls, but I did my best."

"I know, Mama—"

"And that's why I backed off the way I did." Evelyn shrugged. "I loved you from a distance. I prayed. It was the only thing left for me to do. And it must've worked." She stared at her darling oldest child recognizing the woman she had become. "Again, congratulations."

"Thanks, Mama." Nicole's voice was a sad, empty whisper.

"And now that you've spread your grown-up wings and made it big-time here in Texas, I suspect I won't hear from you anymore after today. I hate to say it, but somehow I think you made sure I got here in this church so you could rub your good fortune in my face, and that's fine. But after this day, I wonder if you'll share any more of your happiness with me. So I wish you the best, sweetie. And I love you just the same."

Evelyn Greene had spoken her peace. She moodily stared at her daughter, then discreetly walked away from Nicole.

The new bride stood in disbelief. She grabbed a glass of

champagne and took a long swallow that did not stop until all the liquid had trickled down her throat. She burped and wiped her top lip. Then she picked up another glass and repeated the process.

"Eat, drink, and be very happy, Mama." The music was so loud that Evelyn didn't hear Nicole. "You no longer have to worry about me again. You don't ever have to pray for me, either. I'm going to be just fine."

Nicole triumphantly held up her empty glass. She gazed at the crowd that had come to share in her and Rashad's happiness. She grinned hard and waved at her guests as if she was extremely happy, but in truth she wanted to sit down and cry. She wished that the past could've been reversed so that the things her mother revealed didn't feel like a sledgehammer to her head. Raw truth always hurt Nicole. She was a pro at telling other people about themselves, but she could barely stand it when the truth was pointed out about her.

The DJ was playing nineties music. Shyla was dancing, until she stopped and approached Nicole with a cosmo drink. Nicole set down her empty glass and smoothly grabbed the one her friend handed to her.

"I shouldn't be drinking this much, but, hell, if not now, when?" Nicole took a large gulp, then got up and danced about like she had no worries, feeling eager to forget any bad thing that had ever happened to her.

Shyla watched Nicole and assumed she was in a celebratory mood. She raised her own glass.

"Now that it's all over, girl, I'm slowly starting to believe this was the right move for you. You put in the time and you finally got your man. I can't hate on that. Cheers to us married ladies. We don't have to whore around anymore. Oops, rather, *you* don't have to whore around anymore, Nicole."

"I can't be mad at you, because you're right. I whore no more." Nicole winked. "My sex life is official now. What God has joined together, a bitch better not try to break apart. And I swear to you, he and I are united until death us do part. I mean that."

"Let the church say 'amen' then." Shyla clanked her glass against Nicole's, and they sipped on their teal and lavender cotton candy cosmos and took a few more photos.

"Before he and I got married, I owned only the few things that I had to my name. My Mustang, my clothes, some DVDs, and a trunk that I got when I was in college. But now that Rashad and I are joined together, what's his is mine." Nicole beamed at Shyla. She wanted to forget every damning thing her mother had just told her. The old Nicole was dead. The new one had a fabulous life to live.

"I know you're pumped, girl, but I must warn you. You gotta play it smoother, Mrs. Eason. Although you now have money, you still want everyone to think that you're used to having it. You're not quite nouveau riche, and I hope you don't act nigger rich," Shyla informed her. "Old money acts real unbothered about their millions or billions. And that's because they were born in it. And I admire their low-key attitude."

"Oh, so are you saying that when Rashad bought me my new Jeep, I went overboard trying to show it off?"

"Pretty much, Nicole. Put it like this: when is the last time you've seen Bill Gates show off his Rolex? Now that crazy Chris Brown loves showing off his fleet of Lamborghinis. And Justin Bieber's young ass flosses his wealth, too. Look, I'm not mad at these folks earning their paper, but if you gotta flaunt it, in my book that's what you call nigger rich."

"Justin Bieber is—?"

"Look, silly woman. Buying expensive shit and showing it off to people who you even don't care about is tacky. It's the N-word, and yeah, white folks can act that way as well as blacks. You don't wanna be like that, Nicole."

"I disagree with you about me being the N-word," Nicole replied with a sparkle in her eye. "Because now that I'm married, from now on, when it comes to the N-word, it's going to mean *nice*."

"You, nice?" Shyla smirked.

"Yes, don't laugh. I really am trying to change for the better. I will do my best to get along with Kiara and Alexis. I have no reason to feud with them, not when I now have everything I want."

Shyla could only laugh and down another mouthful of her liquor, for she knew her friend very well. She knew Nicole wanted to forget her negative past and be a better woman, but she doubted the girl would be successful.

"I mean it, Shyla. This wedding is intimate and joyous and just what I envisioned."

"I'm glad you have had a nice wedding with the bells and whistles, and even the nice little write-up you'll probably get in the *Houston Chronicle*," Shyla told her. "Hey, you might even go viral on Vevo. But when this reception is over with, are you going to have a healthy marriage?"

And she turned and walked away.

"Hey, Mr. Eason." The reception was in full swing. Nicole took a break from socializing with her guests to happily greet Rashad in a little hallway near the restrooms where they could enjoy a moment to themselves.

"How you doing, Mrs. Eason?" Rashad slurred his words and nodded at her. He struggled to stand flat on his feet. He kept holding on to the wall and wondered why it seemed to keep pulsating. Rashad wasn't a regular drinker, and the little bit of vodka he did have impacted his blood-stream.

"Have you been boozing it up a little too much, babe?" Nicole asked.

"Nah," he said. "It isn't too much. In fact, it's not enough. This party is just getting started. I'm about to go fill up my glass."

Nicole heard that he'd been drinking a lot last night. And Jerry pulled her to the side right after the ceremony and informed her that Rashad had also gotten smashed mid-morning. Nicole was shocked at the revelation. She wasn't fond of Rashad's behavior at all but attributed his unusual deeds to nervous jitters. But now she wanted to have a serious conversation with him.

"I've been thinking, Rashad. Don't you want us to start our marriage off right? Like, shouldn't we set up a nest in a different house? I want Emmy to know what it's like to live somewhere with a backyard big enough for a couple of dogs to run around."

"Sure, yeah, whatever you say," he said and slumped against her with his eyes all red and beady-looking. She took one look at her husband and asked him to excuse her for a second. She quickly came back and handed him a fresh glass of ice water. She took care to pat his beaded forehead with a soft towel.

"Looks like I'm fulfilling my nursing duties for my husband already," she said. Nicole remained next to him and talked sweetly.

"You need to sober up a little, Rashad. We can open a few of those gifts on that gift table that I've been dying to see."

"I don't care about any of that."

"But I do. And I want you to be there with me. Just to take photos with a few of the items."

"Okay, Nicole. Whatever you say."

"You do want to make me happy, don't you, babe?"

"Of course I do."

"Then drink all of that water please, and don't swallow any more liquor. Promise me right now."

"I promise. I do. I will. Happy now?"

"We'll only be here a little while longer, and then when it's over, you can get some rest. I know you're tired. I see your male friends are here helping you to celebrate, and I'm just happy that people came out to support us."

"Yeah, it's all good in the hood, babe." Rashad sipped on his glass of ice water. He was beginning to feel slightly better than he had when he'd woken up that morning.

"Speaking of the hood," she said. "I was thinking we need to start looking to move. I am ready to see what is out there since the market seems to be doing well in the Houston area."

"Huh? I feel like I have a headache."

"I'm sorry, babe."

"So we can talk about doing all that eventually."

"What's wrong, Rashad?"

"Nothing's wrong. But can you please lower your voice?"

"I'm not even talking that loud."

"But you need to still lower it."

She made sure he drank lots more water and waited until he seemed more alert.

"Okay, now, getting back to us buying a house right away," she sweetly told him. "When can we move?"

"Nicole, let's stay in the other spot till the lease is up. No need to waste any money by losing the deposit."

Her eyes burned with disappointment, but she tried to hide it.

"Rashad. We've got to move. It would be a big mistake to stay there."

"Why is that?"

"Because, babe, to be honest, I still think of that house as 'my' place. I've read on the Internet that when a man lives in a home that was originally owned by the female, she could throw her weight around and act very bossy and territorial."

"Easy solution. Don't throw your weight around. Think of the place that we live in now as yours and mine. Can you do that for me please?"

"Rashad, I could pretend like that house is ours but the bottom line is we're just leasing. What if old boy wants us out of there just because?"

"He can't do that legally. That's what leases are for and we aren't doing anything criminal to make him want to evict us."

"Well, maybe we ought to do something criminal so he can evict us," she told him sarcastically.

"You ain't no criminal, Nicky, don't even try it."

Feeling frustrated, Nicole lowered her voice. "Regardless of all that, I'm ready to move out, and I just think we'd feel much happier once we find something that we can call 'our' place."

"Look, Nicky, too many wives out here act like they have a penis. But I'm the one who was born with a dick, not you. That means I am the head. I will lead our household the way I think it should be done."

Before Nicole could make a rebuttal, her new husband quietly reclined against the wall, closed his eyes, and was unmovable for a good twenty minutes afterward. Nicole felt embarrassed as people kept coming by and asking if everything was okay. The photographer they'd hired even took a few photos of Rashad thinking they'd make a great gag. She shooed him away and asked him to have respect.

"Is Rashad all right?" Shyla pressed her as she came by looking for Nicole.

"Everything's great. He had a little too much to drink and is trying to come down. I learned that my husband is terrible at handling his liquor, so we're getting sobered up now. We're going to be just fine."

As Nicole prepared to go and open a few wedding gifts, she resumed feeling excited. Her last conversation with Rashad had bothered her. But right then it really didn't matter. Nicole had finally captured her man.

The next day, the Easons began honeymooning in Harbor Island, Bahamas, where the beaches consisted of pink sand and the Atlantic Ocean was a pretty aqua color when the sunlight hit it.

They enjoyed a cab ride that transported them to a water taxi, and after paying the fare they checked in at their hotel.

Nicole entered the Ocean View Club arrayed in a pretty off-white dress and wearing loads of bangles and dangling earrings, a surprise gift from Shyla.

"Oh, wow. Everything is just so beautiful," she cooed as they walked through the lobby. "I feel like I'm in that movie *Why Did I Get Married Too?* Remember that scene when Janet Jackson's character and Jill Scott and the gang arrived at that hotel?"

"Nah, not really."

"Aw, boo, then we need to stream that movie while we're here, okay?" She swung her hips and Rashad could not help but feel proud that they were finally taking a real vacation together.

He beamed at her and laughed. "You're a little too excited."

"You damn straight I am. I got the right to turn up. And you do, too."

"Oh, really?" That lopsided grin of his looked too damn sexy.

Nicole suddenly turned around and planted an unexpected wet, sloppy kiss on him. Then she reached down and grabbed his package, rubbing his dick through his shorts.

"You are getting me hot, Rashad." She nibbled on his ear right there in the lobby.

"Whoa, whoa." Rashad laughed and tried to duck.

"Whoa? Really? On our honeymoon?"

"I'm just saying, time and place for that. Remember the baby?"

"Oops. Oh yeah."

Nicole turned around and continued pushing Emmy's stroller. Nicole never thought in a million years that she'd be spending her first honeymoon with both her husband and their only child. But in reality, no one else was available to care for Emmy. So Rashad insisted that Emmy join them. At first Nicole was horrified. It was supposed to be just the two of them getting the chance to be alone in the right way since they'd met each other. Then, when she really thought about it, she grew ashamed and realistic.

"You're right," she'd told Rashad. "Emmy's part of the package. If it was Jay-Z and Beyoncé, they'd definitely take Blue Ivy with them. We will bring Emmy with us and still have a damn good time."

After finding their room, they settled into their suite, then dressed down to swimsuits. They took turns, one of them would watch the baby and rest on the beach while the other swam and enjoyed having fun in the ocean. And when they both had enough of the crystal blue water, they sat next to each other in chairs on top of the sand and gazed in awe at the beautiful sky.

Nicole surveyed her surroundings. "Can you believe we're here?"

"No, not really."

"Your ass does look like you're still in a daze. You've had that look ever since yesterday. And that was fine for then, but babe, you gotta snap out of it. Soon."

"Yeah," Rashad agreed. He was silent for a minute, watching the gulls soaring above them.

The sound of the waves splashing felt relaxing.

"I kind of predicted all this, though, didn't I Rashad?"

"What are you talking about?"

"Remember, not long after we met, you drove me to Galveston Island. We went to the Bolivar Ferry and we spent time together. I remember feeling like it was a prelude to a honeymoon. Don't ask me why I did, but I did."

"Oh, did you, now?" His familiar lopsided grin stretched across his face.

"Yes, I did. It's okay to dream, isn't it?"

"Sure, Nicky. Nothing wrong with dreaming."

"Dreams are great. They help me forget the past I've left behind and make me feel hopeful about the future."

Rashad squeezed her hand. "That is true, but sometimes you wake up from something that you've enjoyed dreaming about," he said in a careful tone, "and then you have to sit up, get up, take a piss, brush your teeth, and wash your crusty ass."

"All that? Really, Rashad?"

"I'm just saying. Dream over!"

Nicole yelped with laughter. "Oh, alright, thanks for letting me know what I have to look forward to every day for the rest of my life. I think I should be able to face the realities of this marriage. I know it won't be totally perfect, but it'll be damn near perfect. You've got the experience already from you-know-who," she said, referring to Kiara.

"And I'm going to believe you've learned any lessons from any mistakes made with her."

Rashad calmly listened to Nicole, but he couldn't believe her audacity. She'd helped him to deceive his wife. How soon side chicks forget.

Nicole joyfully gazed at her paradise surroundings. "And even though it's my first time getting married—and my last time—I feel like I can deal with your realities. That's why I'm somewhat glad that we lived together before we made things official. I like to 'test-drive' the car I plan to drive." She winked at him.

"I hear you, and I know, Nicky." He closed his eyes and felt like he wanted to fall asleep. Plunge fast into a deep sleep that never ended. It felt surreal to be there with Nicole. With their darling daughter resting in her portable crib next to the both of them, on a beautiful beach in the Bahamas.

The white sand drifted in between Rashad's toes as he dug his feet deep into the fine grains. He felt a world away from his normal reality.

Finally he uttered, "What are we doing? Nicky, what the hell are we doing?"

"We're starting over again. The both of us. We're taking this journey together, as husband and wife, and we are going to stay on this road and see where it leads us."

"There's nothing else that we can do," he told her.

Once they were done swimming, they retreated to their room and fed Emmy. They enjoyed a room-service meal, then Nicole told Rashad she wanted to snuggle in bed and watch movies.

"We'll start off with that Tyler Perry movie I was telling you about, and then we gotta also watch one of my favorites called *Jumping the Broom*."

"Another wedding flick?"

"Yes, but this movie has special significance. I first saw it when I was twenty-one. And I remember how much it inspired me and planted a dream inside of me."

Rashad smiled at his new wife, happy to see her so excited.

"How did it inspire you?"

"I loved how Paula Patton's character wanted to be with her man, but she had to go through so much hell before she got what she wanted. And in the end, despite family drama, she had the wedding of her dreams. She made me want to have that, too. A wonderful man, a beautiful ceremony, and a great life. And look at me now."

"Yeah, look at you. You're shining so bright ain't nothing I can do to dim it."

"You got that right."

She removed her clothes and crawled in bed along with her husband and they started watching the film. Around halfway through, Nicole announced, "Okay, that's enough." She flicked off the power and she and Rashad quickly got cozy, wrapping their arms around each other.

Unexpectedly, Nicole bounced back up. "Rashad, hold up a sec."

She went to her suitcase, unzipped it, and pulled out a small mattress cover.

"Get out the bed. I need to do something." He quickly obliged.

Nicole unstripped the bed and laid the mattress cover on top.

"What's up with that?" asked Rashad.

"This is a nice hotel, but they may have had some nasty guests in here before we checked in."

"Oh. Is there anything in your past that makes you know about those kinds of things?"

Her face turned red. "Um, let's say I have had some experience checking in and out of motels."

Rashad gave her a curious look. "Are you talking about
your boy Ajalon?"

"Babe, please. This has nothing to do with my ex. He is
the past. You are right now."

"As in 'Mister Right Now'?"

"Jesus. No! As in you, Rashad Eason, will be my husband until death us do part, okay? I am not thinking about
any other man except you."

"Are you positive?"

"Are you kidding me? We're on freaking Harbor Island. Do you understand how surreal this is? I never in my
life thought I'd get to this point. So yes, I'm positive that
you're the only man I'm thinking about. If you were the
man who got me here, no way in hell I'm about to fuck it
up with another man."

"Okay, just checking. Lighten up, Mrs. Eason."

Nicole calmed down.

Although Rashad seemed like he wanted to continue
talking, Nicole took one look at him and shook her head.
"We are on our honeymoon. Let's act like newlyweds."

She crawled back on the bed with her ass pointed high.
Looking back at him, she smiled and began to make her
way toward the headboard. Rashad followed suit. She let
him kiss and lick her from behind until she felt nice and
wet. He built up a nice rhythm and made her squirm and
moan in pleasure.

When she felt Rashad press his dick against her vagina,
she imagined he was like a race car driver, revving up and
wanting to break loose. He poked against her several times,
and when he felt hot and hard, like he was ready to plunge
recklessly inside of her, she asked him to hold up. She made
him strap up with a condom. Then she told him to lie on his

back. He instantly obeyed. With her breasts bouncing, Nicole straddled Rashad and pulled him against her chest so that they were face-to-face.

"I'm yours—you believe me?"

His eyes glazed over. "I believe you."

They held each other and gazed upward through a skylight; it looked like millions of stars were sprinkled across the midnight sky.

Nicole was hot and couldn't stand it anymore. She jammed his penis deep inside of her.

"It's the first time we're doing it the right way, as husband and wife," she sighed. They rocked together, holding each other tightly as if they were addicted to each other. She couldn't feel him like she wished she could, due to the condom, but still, he felt great inside of her. She hopped up and down on him. The more it hurt, the better it felt. He seemed to be into it, too. She watched him close his eyes, grunt, groan, and jerk and move his hips in sync with hers.

"I love you, Rashad."

"I love you, too."

"And, babe?"

"Yes."

"If you ever even think about looking at another woman, I will cut your motherfucking dick off."

Rashad instantly stopped moving. He opened his eyes. His penis grew soft.

"I hope you're just joking." His voice sounded cold and unloving. "You'd better pray you were just joking, or I will—"

Nicole froze. Maybe she'd gone too far. She never would want him to cheat on her, even though that was the way she got him.

Nicole leaned over and tried to kiss Rashad on his lips. He turned his head away. Her lips ended up on his neck.

She fell into her husband's neck, aware of the hurt she'd caused. She wished she could snatch back the words that had carelessly flown out of her mouth.

When Rashad did not respond to the kisses she gave to his neck, she rolled off of him and lay on her back next to him. She stared at the ceiling.

"Okay," she said in a tiny voice that was barely audible. "Maybe I went too far with that joke. I-I was in a weird type of mood just then. It will never happen again. I shouldn't have threatened you."

"You shouldn't have."

"But you couldn't have taken me seriously, right?"

"I took it how you said it, Nicole." He sounded furious. That made her scared. She tried to hold his hand, but he snatched it back.

Her heart pounded wildly inside her chest. The abrupt disconnect felt frightening. It was much too soon for her dreams to end. How could she fix this?

"Babe, I'm so sorry. I apologize. I know that I should think before I speak. I know that if you said something like that to me, it would hurt my feelings." A tiny cry escaped from her mouth. "I do not want to hurt you, babe. I never, ever want to hurt you, Rashad. Shit, I love you. I *love* you."

She begged Rashad to believe her, but stiffness emanated from his body. She began to imagine the worst. What if he didn't forgive her? What if the rest of their honeymoon was filled with tension?

"Rashad, we all say things we don't mean."

"I don't."

"I'm sure you have at some point in your life. Maybe you've done it and forgot about it."

"I don't say stupid shit like that, though. That wasn't cool."

"I know. But as my husband, you've got to forgive me.

I'll admit I messed up. I will probably mess up again. But I didn't mean it, I swear. I hate knives anyway, so can you imagine me trying to slice off a dick—especially one as big as yours?"

It took Rashad a long while before he spoke again.

"It's cool, Nicole. My guess is that you were trying to say, in a really awkward and bad way, that you don't want me hooking up with any Nicole Greenes."

"Oh, Rashad, c'mon." His words hurt her so much that she could barely think. She never wanted him to continue thinking of her as a woman he'd cheated with.

"If Nicole Greene was that bad, why would you marry her?"

"Don't ask me that."

"But it's an honest question. Answer it."

"I ain't doing that. And don't be demanding with me. You started this shit by threatening me. I've never taken threats well. So, before you get on my case, think about what *you* did to get us to this place."

Nicole knew that if she wanted him to forgive her, then she'd have to forgive him, too. His biting words hurt like hell, but she had to start somewhere.

"Alright. Fine. All I was trying to say is that I want us to have a really strong relationship in which no cheating ever happens, because I don't want that for us. It's just you and me in this relationship."

"I get that."

"And?"

"I *get* it."

"Rashad, I-I do expect you to be faithful to me and not do anything shady with another . . . Nicole Greene."

"I do not plan on doing anything shady with anybody."

"Alright. Good. It's settled. Discussion is over."

"It's definitely over."

His choice of words made Nicole feel uneasy. She gnawed on her fingernails until she realized what she was doing.

A hit dog will always howl, but she didn't want him to think of her as that type of animal.

"Look, I'm ready to move past this, but hear me out one more time. I'll admit I shouldn't have let my insecurities or your past ways make me think anything negative about you. Rashad, from the bottom of my heart, I hope you eventually forgive me. We are supposed to be enjoying ourselves."

"And we will. Just relax a bit. Things will be alright. So far you have gotten everything you've wanted."

"Except a new house."

"I'm sure you will figure out a way to get that, too."

And he turned around so he could get some sleep. Lots and lots of much-needed pleasurable rest.

Chapter 3

On the Sunday afternoon when the Easons were vacationing, Kiara, Eddison, Alexis, and Varnell were in southwest Houston at a crowded buffet.

"This is freaking unbelievable," Kiara said aloud. Alexis, who was standing behind Kiara, nudged her boss from behind.

"I'm with you on that one, Kiara."

"I feel like it's Emancipation Day. The 'massa' has gotten the message that the slaves are free to go. And they are grabbing everything they own and getting the hell off the plantation."

"Damn, Kiara, was being with Rashad *that* bad?"

Alexis felt a little embarrassed asking her boss such a personal question. She wanted to think that their awful past was behind them, that they could now function as grown women who'd had kids by the same man.

Maybe Alexis was being naïve. After all, how many women would go out of their way to befriend their ex-husband's mistress? "I don't want to completely diss the father of my children. I really don't. But the fact that he had the guts to marry that woman tells me that he's moved on."

Eddison paid for their meals and even for Varnell Brown's lunch. It was their first double date, and it felt good to be out and about on a beautiful Sunday afternoon. Kiara adored her children, Myles and Jahzara, but she also enjoyed having a moment in which she could be around adults and not have to deal with baby spit or her energetic son.

Kiara found a corner spot by the window. She set her purse on her chair and watched Eddison take a seat across from Varnell.

"You ladies go ahead and fix your plates. We'll watch your purses."

"You do that, sweetie." Kiara looked cute and relaxed in a pair of blue jeans and a cowl-neck knit shirt.

Alexis followed behind Kiara, who started out deciding which meats she wanted to load on her plate.

"I just hope that Nicole doesn't feed Rashad to the sharks while they are on their honeymoon," Alexis said jokingly.

"Amen to that. If your troublesome significant other asks you to go with her to an African safari, or to take a relaxing cruise, watch your back."

Alexis giggled. "But Rashad is doing exactly what he wants to do."

"Correct. He's grown," Kiara told her. "And whatever happens at this point, it's going to be all on him."

"Oh right. You did tell me that you warned him not to marry Nicole."

"I dropped a million hints. But I didn't outright tell Rashad not to do it because he'd assume that I still care about him."

"And you don't care, right?"

"Not in a romantic way. But hey, I can't wish bad to happen to him. Sometimes I want to kick him in his balls for the crap he's put me through. But if I did that, he'd think I still loved him. I'm damned if I do and damned if I don't."

"It's complicated," said Kiara and Alexis at the same time. They burst out laughing. It was amazing to Alexis that after all they'd been through, they could discuss such sensitive matters in an open and honest way.

"Well, pardon me for saying so, Kiara, but I had to learn to stop being angry at what I couldn't control. If I could apologize to you a million times over for the pain I caused you, I would do it. But I know you've already made peace with what happened."

"Yep. You're good. Don't even sweat it." Kiara proceeded to pick out a couple of pieces of baked chicken and fish, and then spooned vegetables onto her plate. There. That was a good amount to start with.

Kiara returned to their table and was pleased to see Eddison and Varnell engaged in bits of conversation.

"Yeah, man," she heard Varnell say, "I just hope the Texans can pull it off and make it to the play-offs next season."

"How 'bout them Cowboys?"

"Oh Lord, not football talk." Kiara smirked.

"Okay, babe, do you prefer it if we talked about politics, war, religion, or death?" Eddison studied her reaction.

"Truthfully, none of that sounds good. Tell you what." Kiara sat down next to her man. "Stick to football. How 'bout that?" Eddison jumped up and grabbed Kiara into a friendly hug. She stared into his eyes. At that moment, any negative thoughts she'd had regarding her ex-husband completely disappeared. The past was insignificant.

The men went to get their food, and soon everyone sat together talking and eating like longtime friends.

This was the good life, Kiara thought. Living in the moment and staying clear of drama. She felt so content that she never wanted that good feeling to leave her. Problem was—she really didn't know how to ensure that her current happiness would last forever.

"What are you thinking about, Kiara?" Eddison nudged her as he buttered his wheat roll.

"Nothing!"

"I can tell when you aren't being real with me, Kiara."

"Can you? Okay, I'm busted. To be honest, I-I was kind of wondering how my ex's marriage will impact all the kids."

"Ahh, the truth emerges. If I were you, I wouldn't worry too much. Those things have a way of working themselves out."

"You think?"

"I do. Just relax and enjoy the current season of life that you're in. Which, by the way, I wanted to share my good news. Remember that wonderful piece of property that I showed you a while ago in Fort Bend County?"

"The big empty lot in Katy?"

"That's the one. I bought it. It's mine."

"Eddison, I'm so happy for you. Congrats. What do you plan to do with it? Hold on to it until someone makes you a million-dollar offer in ten years?"

"That would be excellent. But I'm sure I'll do something really good with it long before then." He winked at her and grinned.

She truly was happy for him. Eddison was a good person. And good people deserved good things to happen to them.

* * *

A woman who claimed she'd never dreamt about living life on a grand scale was a woman in denial. What average woman who's worked hard all her life has never wanted to make it big?

Nicole Greene Eason was no exception. The day the newlyweds returned from their four-day honeymoon, she quickly got down to business. They arrived in Houston at 10:15 a.m. on that Thursday. Nicole contacted a Realtor and began setting up appointments. Rashad came home and crashed, then later woke up and went into his office and was gone until late evening.

The following morning, Nicole made a light breakfast of scrambled eggs, sausage, and grits. She fed her daughter, got showered, and dressed. Her husband was anxious to get back to work and headed out before the sun rose.

It didn't bother Nicole one bit that Rashad didn't accompany her on her little excursions to master planned communities. She got Emmy all dolled up, and wrapped a pretty wide bow around her thick curls. Nicole sat in her Jeep in front of her house with the engine running. She typed various street addresses into the map app on her smartphone. She put the vehicle in gear and drove for miles and miles. She drove and chatted with her daughter and had a good time doing it.

"You are a princess, Emmy," she yelled behind her. Eminence Forever was securely bundled in her car seat. Since she was seated diagonally across from her mom, Nicole had the perfect view of the girl. "If you're a princess, then I'm a queen, and your daddy is the king. We are a royal family. And it's time we started living like one."

Nicole arrived at a model home that was hosting an open house for its subdivision. Her mouth began to sali-

vate the second she parked her Jeep in front of the beautifully extravagant house.

"Curb appeal. Check. Exquisite landscaping. Check.
Stone and brick. Check."

Nicole wheeled Emmy in her stroller and made notes
and concurrently snapped photos. Her heart began to pul-
sate with every step that she took inside the house. The
cleaner it was, the fresher it smelled, the more perfect it
looked, the more she began to tune out the person giving
her a tour.

Nicole began to daydream. The more she saw, the more
she knew exactly what type of dwelling she was looking
for.

Feeling pumped up, Nicole left the open house and
continued her home search mission. And later that day, she
parked her Jeep in front of a different brick house. She was
waiting to meet a Realtor named Joy.

Nicole got out of the Jeep and quickly observed the ex-
terior. Goose bumps tingled underneath her skin. Moments
later Joy arrived.

"Hey, Mrs. Eason. Sorry that I'm late. There's always a
lot of traffic on Highway 6 around this time of the day."
Joy came over to shake Nicole's hand. "As you probably
already know, Riverstone is a very popular subdivision in
all of Fort Bend County. So if you're ready, let's go take a
look."

Nicole remained unusually quiet as Joy inserted the key
and they entered the two-story house. When they walked
into the foyer, Nicole's eyes rested on the wooden spindle
staircase that led to the second floor. The walls were
painted in a soft beige tone that seemed elegant and felt
tranquil.

"The owners aren't here, so we are free to stay as long
as we want." Joy explained the different features of the

home while Nicole followed her down the long hallway. They advanced to the kitchen, which was an open area that included a family room with wooden beams in the ceilings. The place looked and felt extravagant yet homey. It was unlike any place she'd ever lived before.

"I come from Alabama," she explained to Joy. "And I've seen some good days, but I also know what it's like to go to hell and back. Life's been a little rough, but it's getting better. I want so bad to live and feel like a normal woman." Nicole continued pouring out her heart. "Ever since I was in high school, I wanted to know what it was like to live in a big, beautiful house. I was raised with my sister and two cousins all under one roof. Very crowded but filled with love."

"That's pretty normal."

"Anyways, as an adult, I want a different type of normal—one with good things happening all the time instead of just *some* of the time."

"I see. I will help you achieve that. Ain't nothing like living the American dream."

Nicole continued to take in everything with a breathlessness that made her feel dizzy. The study with built-in shelves, the second-floor game room that overlooked the living room, and that kitchen was a chef's dream. Something whispered in her heart, *This is it. This is my dream house.*

From the kitchen Nicole could look through all the windows and view the spacious backyard.

"I can see Emmy running around the backyard. Her and Myles."

"Oh, you have more than this cute little fuzzy-muzzy here?" Joy playfully nuzzled Emmy's plump cheeks.

"Um, yes. Lots of stepkids. Tons."

"No problem. This house has four to five bedrooms."

"Yeah, we'll need every single one of 'em. I love a house full of kids."

"Hmm, good for you. Let's check out the master retreat. By the way, there are two master bedrooms on the first floor."

The women ventured inside the first suite. The more Nicole saw, the more she wanted.

"I have a good feeling about this one," she told Joy.

"Well, Nicole," Joy told her. "I think you'd want to know that the current owners have been here less than two years and the property is in immaculate condition. The only reason they are moving is because the husband's job was unexpectedly relocated to Florida. And this would be a quick sale, which sounds like something you'd be interested in."

Nicole listened on with eagerness as they returned inside and did another complete walk-through.

"Joy, how's this for quickness? I am ready to sign a contract immediately."

"That's a great idea, because this house won't stay on the market another day. Tell you what, Nicole. I can get the paperwork. We can meet up at my office."

"Hold on a sec." Nicole suddenly remembered she was a wife who needed to consult with her husband. "Let me get real. How much is this place?"

"It's listed at four twenty-nine."

Nicole didn't blink an eye.

"That price is a real bargain when you consider everything you'd be gaining."

"I agree. How much would we have to put down?"

"Um, let's go back into the kitchen and I can pull out my mortgage calculator and play with the numbers."

The two ladies tirelessly went over figures and interest rates and possible down payments.

"I'd say that your mortgage could be between two thousand and twenty-five hundred a month. You think you could handle that?"

"My man is doing very well. A twenty-five-hundred-dollar house note is a drop in the bucket for him."

That was all the Realtor needed to hear. Joy and Nicole smiled knowingly at one another, shook hands, and went their separate ways with Nicole promising to get back in touch real soon.

That night Nicole knew exactly what she wanted to do the next time she saw Rashad, but she didn't want to overdo it. She had to plan carefully.

When Rashad finally made it home around six thirty that evening, Nicole had dinner ready and waiting.

He washed his hands, settled down at the head of the table, and took one bite of his Salisbury steak. He immediately spit it out.

"What's the matter?"

"This meat tastes raw."

Nicole took her fork and turned over the steak. She grimaced at the bloodstained piece.

"Yeah, you're right about that."

"Well, what happened? Why isn't it done all the way?"

"I've been having problems with this stove. There's something wrong with it. It's just not acting right these days."

"I'll have to look into it."

When Rashad piled some rice on his fork, he took one big bite and soon spit that food out, too. Bits of rice splattered all on top of the table.

A toothless Emmy started grinning and banging her fist on her high chair. Then she made little spit bubbles with her mouth.

"Like father, like daughter." Rashad gave the baby a sympathetic look.

"Maybe you can eat Emmy's baby food, because to be truthful, anything being cooked on that stove over there won't taste right."

"Did you eat any?"

"Nope, I had to settle for a peanut butter and banana sandwich."

"You're serious? Call a handyman. Get him over here and get that damn piece of junk fixed. I won't have much time to do it myself. Why are appliances always breaking down around here?"

"The place is old, Rashad. I will call a handyman, though." Nicole nodded in agreement. "With the number of hours you've been working, sweetie, I know not to bug you about issues that are going on around the house. No husband wants to deal with problems twenty-four-seven when he already works so hard." She stood up, then walked over to Rashad and crawled into his lap. She was relieved he'd returned to his normal friendly self since they'd gotten back from Harbor Island. Nicole lovingly placed her arms around his neck. As she inhaled his scent, she moaned. Rashad smelled so good and rustic. She pouted and gave him a tongue kiss. When Nicole pressed her lips against his, at first Rashad didn't pay attention to her, but as she hungrily inserted her tongue into his mouth, he began to respond. He could feel the love emanate from her. He hungrily kissed her back.

Nicole kissed him until he could barely breathe. She finally let him come up for air and she stroked his penis.

Rashad started getting an erection and was ready to remove his pants.

But when he tried to stand up, Nicole stopped him. Her thick thighs held him down and she stared into his eyes.

"Baby, I wanted to talk to you about something."

"What's that?"

"You know I've been looking around for another place to live." She kissed him again on his lips and sucked them for a hot minute. "And," she said in a breathy tone, "I think I found our mansion today."

"A mansion?"

"Well, not quite. It's a little over four thousand square feet. Spacious, but not overwhelming."

"Is that right?"

"And so, baby, I am very ready to make a move." She kissed Rashad again. "I want to break this lease." She rubbed his penis and felt it getting plump with stiffness.

"I want to sign a contract for the new house. Make the sellers an offer."

He moaned as she licked his dick over and over.

"Ahhh." Rashad arched his neck and shuddered. "Keep going, Nicky."

"Did you hear what I said about the house? I'm ready for us to buy."

"I don't know about that."

She took her mouth off Rashad and tried hard to hide her anger and disappointment.

"Oh, c'mon, babe. It's amazing. And once you see the house for yourself, I just know you'll think differently."

"No."

"Please, baby?"

He sighed. "Where is it?"

She grabbed his penis and started toying with it. Her

hands were like a violinist. She strummed her fingertips across his delicate skin and performed other sexy maneuvers that aroused him. His penis stuck up like it was saluting her. Soon Rashad was ready to penetrate her. But even though his dick had gotten bigger and harder, she wasn't ready for him to do it just yet.

One thing Nicole loved about Rashad was his size. His penis reminded her of an eighteen-wheeler during rush-hour traffic. It was big, bulky, noticeable, and always seemed to be in the way.

Nicole began to lick him and was pleased when he began to moan.

"The dream house is in Sugar Land . . . Not too far from where Myles lives." She licked him again. "Don't you think it's better to stay somewhere close to Myles and Jazzy than way over on this side of town?" She kissed the tip, then licked it like an ice cream cone. "Your kids, I mean, *our* kids will love the beautiful park and clubhouse. And they have tennis courts, biking trails, and you know how much Myles loves to run around and play."

"Ohhh, Nicky. Let me put it in."

"We're not done talking about the price yet."

He grunted. "How much?"

"That's the thing, babe. It's a lot higher than my rental house." She made sure to sound as sweet as possible. She moved from his torso, up, up, and across his body. She nibbled on Rashad's ear, totally covering it with her mouth. She blew hot air in it and kissed it. Nicole knew he loved it when she did that. After she teased his other ear for a while, she returned to his penis to see how it was faring. Not surprisingly, Rashad was so stiff it pointed at the ceiling. She knew she'd worked her magic and the house was as good as hers. Nicole had always been told a man was hard when he was soft and he was soft when he was hard.

"Baby, the mortgage would be about twenty-two hundred. Something like that. And I can help with some of the expenses. I really, really want this house." She could close her eyes and still envision herself living in that space. "I've been dreaming about this for years, Rashad. I've never known how it feels to live in a place other than an unremarkable one-story that lacks storage space. But you've already experienced the finer things in life. While other folks can only wish and hope and pray . . . please, Rashad. Please make my dream come true." Then she placed his ear inside of her mouth and licked and sucked on it until he began moaning and wiggling around, enjoying everything his wife was doing to him. He loved the way she made him feel. And she always knew just what to do.

The next thing he knew, Nicole removed all her clothes and made him take off his slacks and his drawers. She grabbed his penis and rubbed it against her vagina, teasing her husband over and over.

"This," she said, "is what you'd have every single day in the new house. I will fuck you from the foyer to the refrigerator. Would you like that, babe?"

He nodded his head vigorously.

"Is that a yes?"

"That's a yes."

She squealed and let her husband enjoy her body. He ravished her, stroking every crevice with his hands and mouth, enjoying her moans. Nicole grabbed him around his waist and pulled him tightly against her. He plunged deeply inside of her, marking her as his.

Seeing Nicole's face light up gave him joy. And right then he knew he wanted to do whatever it took to make his new bride happy.

"Nicole, you know. You don't have to try to convince me the way that you do. I don't need you to plead your case like that. Just be a decent wife, stay on top of your business, and good things will happen."

She relaxed and thanked him the only way she knew how.

The next afternoon, Rashad skipped lunch so he could pick Nicole up to go look at the house. By two o'clock that afternoon, he'd completed the sales contract and agreed to sign on the dotted line.

Joy shook both their hands and said she'd be in touch.

"If all goes well, you will be in the new house very soon."

"Thank you very much," Nicole exclaimed. "I look forward to hearing from you. I have a good feeling about this. I have a good feeling about everything." And Nicole gave her husband a big hug. "Thank you for making every single one of my dreams come true."

Rashad told her no problem but as they drove away from the house he wondered what he'd gotten himself into.

Chapter 4

The next evening Shyla came by Nicole's rented house to help her open the remainder of the wedding presents. It was Saturday night. The women were tucked away in Nicole's tiny dining room surrounded by boxes large and small. The table was completely filled with silverware, lingerie, "Mr. & Mrs." pillows, china, and lots of scented candles.

"Mmm, girl. Where are you going to put all of this stuff?" Shyla asked.

"That's what I was wondering. I may have to store some of it in the attic."

"Hmm, you know what happened the last time you hid something in the attic." She was referring to the time when Nicole hid her ex-boyfriend in the attic one day when he came by to visit her. Nicole had told her friend what happened and Shyla still couldn't believe all the drama she'd gone through trying to juggle two men.

"Where is Ajalon, by the way?" Shyla asked.

"Hell, I don't know. We don't stay in touch anymore."

"Literally, huh?"

"Oh, girl. There you go." Nicole paused. "Why did you

have to bring up my ex? I'm for real, Shyla, there is no more fooling around, sneaking around, none of that. Ajalon had such a strong influence on me back then. And that's why I had to shoot him the deuce once I got engaged."

"You've blocked him from calling you?"

"Sure have."

"But it's just as easy to unblock someone as it is to block him."

"Are you saying that I will get weak and let him back into my life? Not on your life, girl."

"Alrighty then. I was just checking."

"Trust me, I got this. Even though Rashad and I have only been married a few days, I'm completely about this life." Nicole laughed. "For example, when we got back home from the Bahamas, I was in the laundry room sorting the clothes that needed to be washed. And um, Rashad popped his big ol' head in the doorway. He took one look at me and I could tell right away that my man was so happy that he had someone to wash his clothes. Ain't that a shame? So I did my thing while he stood and watched me. But then he became annoying. He starts giving me instructions about 'don't do this' and 'don't put that one in the dryer' and 'make sure not to put bleach on my shirt,' and finally I had to tell him to back off and slow his roll. He was shocked I spoke up for myself; he realized that though I love him, no, I won't let him boss me around. We got into an argument all over the stupid laundry. Do you know he nearly cursed me out?"

"I'm not surprised. Rashad can be a little hothead."

"I know that, but I didn't expect him to cop an attitude right after we returned from our honeymoon. I got so mad at him that it could have gotten physical. But when I asked him if I was Kiara would he be acting like that, he straightened his ass up and apologized. Then I got him good. I told him I needed some new spring dresses and Nordstrom was having a sale. And you know what? That amazing man handed over his Amex card just like that. I was like, hmmm, I could learn to like this."

"Well, Nicole Eason, I'm glad you got it like that. It sounds as though you think the answer to a successful relationship is to pick fights with your husband, toy with his emotions, and then get some retail therapy. That definitely won't work for all married couples, but hey, if that works for you, at least you'll get to build yourself a brand-new wardrobe, huh?" she asked teasingly.

"No, no, not really," Nicole replied. "Rashad is pretty generous if he's in the position to do so. And I know I can get every material thing I can think of . . . without the petty fights. There's still time." Nicole laughed and wanted to hug herself. She couldn't believe that only a few years ago she was a broke college student, counting dimes, dollars, and quarters, and feeling underneath the couch cushions, hoping to find extra spare change.

Shyla's voice interrupted her thoughts. "Marriage is way more than the ability to use someone else's credit card when you want to go shopping, or even having a man to sleep beside you every night. No, it's the fusion of two individual souls, two spirits knit together as one. Compromising, giving in, and doing the irritating shit that he wants, especially when you are not even trying to hear it . . ."

"And I'm really not trying to hear you, Mrs. Perry-Fallender. Like I said a dozen times, I'm good. Now. Let's keep opening these boxes and checking out all these cool gifts."

The ladies continued reviewing the various items. Nicole asked Shyla to type a list of names and addresses of the guests, and to e-mail the file to her so she could print mailing labels for thank-you cards.

"Will do."

Right then Myles walked into the room, bouncing a basketball across her wooden floor.

"Where'd he come from?" Shyla asked, almost yelling.

"He's spending the night with us."

"Okay, you actually look like you're fine with that."

"Why wouldn't I be?"

"I thought you—"

"Shhh, don't be rude." Nicole wasn't sure if Myles could hear them, he was so involved playing with his ball.

"He's my child now. I'm fine with him visiting us. He's a good kid."

"Oh, alright, glad to hear that."

"Hey, Mom. May I get something good to eat? Something sweet?" Myles asked.

"Sure, darling. I will get you something after a while. We have a little project going on right now, but as soon as we're done I—"

"But I am hungry now. Like, my sweet tooth is aching and if I don't eat something—"

"Myles, you gotta be joking."

"No, I'm not. So, can you please make me a cake?"

"A cake?"

"Yes. A chocolate cake."

"No, Myles."

"Why not? You did it before. You did it the first time I spent the night over here. Why can't you do it again?"

"Because!"

Shyla stared at the two of them going at it, and for once she could not talk.

"Back then I was just Rashad's girlfriend. I wasn't a wife yet."

"What does that mean?"

"It means that I wasn't as busy back then as I am now, Myles. Wives have lots of things to do. All of the time. We hardly ever get a break. And once we get started on something, it's hard to stop. Now, I did not say I *wouldn't* get you something to eat. But it will have to wait a few minutes."

"Ms. Nicole."

"What did you say?"

"I mean, *Mom*, I don't know if I can wait a few minutes. I'm really hungry. So, may I please walk to the store?"

"Absolutely not, Myles, you know better than to ask a question like that. This is not a good neighborhood."

"It's not a good neighborhood?"

"No, it has crime around here. Sometimes. Not all the time. That's why I ask you to play in the backyard and not in the front yard."

"This sucks. I want to go to my other house. It has good food, a bigger backyard, and no stupid crime. I hate it here." He stormed out of the room, bouncing his ball.

Nicole's hands were trembling. She held them up for Shyla to observe. "See what he does to me?" she whispered.

"Wow. Just, wow."

"I don't mind him at all. He really is not too much trouble. I love his energy. But he wears me out."

Myles popped back into the room. "Mom?"

"Yes, Myles."

"We talked to each other for such a long time that you could have made me a cake. That's how long we talked."

And he left the room, bouncing the basketball, until she couldn't hear its sound anymore. But what she did hear was the complaints of an Eason man inside her head.

* * *

When Rashad showed up outside Alexis McNeil's front door, she was surprised to see him. She cautiously stepped outside.

"What are you doing here? Why didn't you call first?"

"I was at a job in the area and thought it would be nice if I could pop in and see Hayley real quick. I wanted to call you but my battery died."

"Oh, really? You can't charge your phone in your car?"

"I tried but it didn't hold the charge, so now I'm here."

"Fine, Rashad."

"Is it okay if we go inside, please?"

"Um, that wouldn't be a good idea."

"Why not?" Rashad peered at the vehicles parked in her driveway and in front of the house. "I don't see your boy's pickup."

"It's not Varnell that you should be worried about. It's—"

Abruptly, the front door flew wide open. Mona Hooker stuck her neck outside, gave Rashad a brutal look, and slammed the door shut.

"Damn, what's up with your mama?"

"I think she's getting sick of my shit."

"What shit?"

"The grandbaby, you, everything."

"What do you mean, the grandbaby? I thought she loved Hayley."

"Oh, she's crazy about the girl, but she's not always in the best mood to try to take care of her just because I ask. And, um, basically I ask a lot."

"That's not a good sign. I know what it's like not to be wanted at your own house." He hesitated. "You could always come and stay with us—"

"Ha-ha. Very funny. Shrek Eason would never go for

anything like that. You're asking to get yourself, and me, killed."

"Hey, I was just trying to be funny."

"Well, try harder, because that joke was weaker than month-old iced tea."

Rashad grinned at Alexis and instantly reminisced about their good old days—the sweetest of days, when no one knew the two of them were lovers. People had no idea that a married man had fathered a daughter with Alexis McNeil. Back then Rashad was oh, so smooth. The lies rushed from his mouth with ease, and Kiara was clueless about his double life. He'd surprise Alexis with all kinds of jewelry that she loved and cherished. But now, Rashad was lucky if she let him buy her a cold bottle of water. He hated that things had changed between them, but he was glad he and Alexis had managed to come to an understanding.

"Hmm," he muttered. "I feel like an unwanted Jehovah's Witness standing outside the house."

"Ha! Tell me about it." Alexis paused, feeling bad about her mom's attitude. "Rashad, I'm sorry you wasted your time coming over here. Hayley is stuck right now at a playdate. I'll pick her up in a couple of hours."

"Oh, alright. Tell her that Daddy said hello. I guess I'll go now."

"No, wait. Actually, I am glad you stopped by. We need to talk business."

"Wait. Let me guess. How much you need?"

"Stop it. Everything isn't about money. But seriously, I do want to claim Hayley on the tax return. I've been busy and haven't filed yet," she explained. "But I plan to do it soon."

Rashad said nothing.

"You got a problem with that? You don't look so happy."

"If it ain't one thing, it's another."

The door popped open again. Mona Hooker held the door ajar with her back as she plunked an apple-green folding utility crate onto the porch.

She quickly disappeared, leaving them alone again. Rashad blankly stared at the crate.

"What's all this?" he asked.

"That's the remaining part of my jewelry collection. I hawked most of the stuff a while ago."

"What? Why?"

"Because. It was time for a change. Anyway, the stuff in that crate is the least-expensive bracelets, rings, and earrings and a couple of pricey and sentimental pieces."

"Your mom is seriously trying to put you out?"

"Seems that way. My mother has been giving all kinds of hints the past few weeks. And I see right now she's doing her best to try to embarrass me in front of you. I don't understand the woman. I hope I never do to Hayley the things she does to me." A rare tender lump formed in Alexis's throat. "Whatever happened to compassion, or patience, or at least trying to understand what a person is going through?"

"You two had it out?"

"Somewhat. She bitches and moans about me, but why can't my mother admit that I have made some progress? Hell, I work every day. I'm taking care of my child, and I am trying real hard to get my life together. Because my mama made it clear she didn't want me messing around with worthless married men anymore."

"'Worthless'? Ouch."

"And so I luck out and hook up with Varnell Brown. Great guy."

"I don't believe it, but go on."

"And because he is a great guy, I want to take time to hang out and bond with him. He's busy a lot of time working at the airport. So when we can do things together, we plan it real quick and try to make it work. Some of the activities include Hayley, but some do not. So, of course, I ask her grandmother to watch the baby for me. She says yes, but I can tell she has a little attitude. I try to enjoy my date, but I can't. The lady has learned how to text, for God's sake. And my date night gets cut short. I rush home to see what the problem is. My mama yells at me, and accuses me of things I haven't done. She gets frantic, because she says she can't find Hayley's belongings, but there they are in plain view. Either she is lying or I think my mama could be losing her mind. That has to be it. Because the crazy stuff she does makes no kind of sense. I am not a bad person . . . am I?"

Alexis's eyes pleaded with Rashad for warmth and concern.

He placed one arm around her waist and gave her a hug. "You, Skillet, are definitely not a bad woman. I can tell you some stories about bad women." He expelled a low whistle. "I know one thing. With your ass being put out on the curb like it's trash day, you are reminding me of me more than I ever thought."

Rashad chuckled so loud that Alexis was ready to punch him in the gut. But she assumed he was referring to that horrid time when Kiara got sick of his shit and asked him to leave their home and never come back.

"I remind you of you, huh? I don't think so." Alexis hoped he wasn't gaining pleasure out of her sorrows. Right then she decided that pouring out her heart to Rashad was a bad idea. She needed to regroup. "I better go now, before my clothes and purses get thrown on the street. I really need support right now and yes, money will help. Rashad, will you please let me claim Hayley?"

"Go right ahead. Don't even sweat it."

He told Alexis good-bye and advised her to keep a low profile. She thanked him for wanting to check in on Hayley, then she went back inside the house thinking about how she wanted to spend her tax return money.

Chapter 5

Joy contacted Nicole while she was at work with good news: The seller had accepted the offer. "Get all your financial paperwork in order, based on that list that I gave you. You can also sign some additional documents, and once all that is finalized, a closing date can be set. We're almost there, and things are looking good."

Nicole thanked the Realtor and said she'd be in touch. As soon as she ended the call, she raced around her office emitting tiny screams. Being approved for such a magnificent piece of property was the biggest miracle that had ever happened to her.

She and Shyla had agreed to meet for a quick lunch so Nicole could share her good news. They both had a taste for fried chicken and decided there was no better place to go than Frenchy's on Scott Street. They drove over to the spot, ordered, and sat down to wait for their food.

"Yeah, girl," Nicole said. "It's a done deal. I'm about to own my very first house."

Shyla's eyes widened. "Hmm, that man must really love

some Nicole. I just can't believe he'd move to that large of a house so fast."

"Why not?"

"Because even when he married Kiara, I doubt they moved into a big-ass pad that soon after the ceremony. Am I right?"

"I don't know, and honestly I don't care how fast or slow he did anything with her." Nicole sounded annoyed. "I don't care about shit that happened a million years ago."

Shyla quickly viewed the photos of the house that Nicole was showing her on her smartphone. "I'm sorry, girl, but your dream house looks very similar to our boss's."

Shyla knew what Kiara's house looked like because she had gone out of her way to find it on the Internet.

"Oh, but it isn't like hers . . . Kiara's crib is nice, but mine is much more superior. The only thing missing is a private swimming pool."

"Hmm, the only thing missing is a wife who is really in tune with her partner."

"Say what you're really trying to say."

"If I were you, I would never put that type of financial pressure on my brand-new husband. He just paid for the wedding, reception, trip to the islands. Did you contribute any money toward those expenses?"

"Shyla, why would you even care? It's not like we spending your money."

"I know, but—"

"But what? I hate to say it, but I don't like all this shade you're throwing at me. You're my girl. You're supposed to have my back. Share in my joy. Not being in your feelings and throwing my ass under a bus every time I tell you something good that's happened for me and my man."

Shyla lapsed into giggles in an attempt to defuse the situation. "Girl, stop. You know I'm happy for you. I can't wait to go shopping with you when you go to furniture showrooms."

"Hmm. I don't know if I believe you. In fact, if you really are a jealous-ass bitch, please let me know right now. Because if it's not that, then what else could it be?"

"Nicole, stop. I am glad for you. I'm actually trying to seriously watch your back, since you're too blind to see what's really going on around you. That's what happiness does," Shyla remarked with a shrug. "It blinds you. Again, congrats on the gigantic new house."

"That sounds like a shady-ass back-door compliment. I'm not really buying it, Shyla. Your mouth telling me one thing but your heart is feeling the opposite."

"You're still a newlywed, Nicole. I think your blinders are on big-time, and it seems you cannot see the forest for the damn trees."

"What are you talking about now?"

"I'm talking about how you gotta crawl before you walk."

"Oh, so you've been married a few months longer than me, and now you call yourself on some Dr. Phil shit?"

Nicole stood up. She'd had enough of feeling dumped on. "What's this really about? Is it about the fact that Wesley recently lost his job and now y'all staying with his mama and her man? And you feel embarrassed, which is understandable because you went from living pretty well in that condo y'all had to that rat trap of a place you now live in. I'm truly sorry about how things changed for you. But that's what happened in *your* marriage. It won't be happening in mine."

Shyla, who also was fed up, pointed a finger. "Hold up a sec. Look at who's on some Dr. Phil shit now? Because not even you can predict what won't happen in your marriage, girl. Shit happens. To all of us. And yeah, maybe God is trying to humble me. Because you couldn't tell me nothing when Wesley and I moved into that wonderful condo and bought all that furniture and high-end appliances and curved screen TVs and all types of nonsense we thought we had to have but honestly couldn't afford." Shyla's voice caught in her throat. "So you see, I know what it's like to be on top of a mountain looking down on everyone else who's in the valley. But it didn't stop bad things from happening to me, and you can best believe I never thought it would."

Humiliated and exhausted, Shyla collapsed in her seat. The pressures of life were getting to her, and she'd hoped that Nicole could be a friend who understood.

But Nicole felt that if Shyla was her friend, she'd keep things positive. Nicole believed that she and her husband could conquer any troubles that impacted their marriage, or else why even go through the ceremony? She allowed herself a few moments before speaking.

"Shyla, I don't want to argue with you. And I'm really sorry that you and Wesley are going through a rough patch. But Rashad and I are different."

"Really? What makes you two so different?"

"Because I believe in us. No matter what we face, our love will see us through."

"I'm sure his *first* wife believed the same thing."

"That's a low blow."

"It's the truth. You might not like it, but you can't argue with fact." After an unreasonably long time, their orders were finally ready. Nicole went to the pickup window and was handed their food. She brought the chicken, sides, and drinks over to Shyla, who graciously accepted.

"Thanks, girl. I'm starving." Shyla was so wiped out from fussing all she wanted to do was dig into her meal. The chicken thigh was so huge it looked like it was on steroids. But it tasted crunchy and salty and completely hit the spot. She enjoyed her lunch and engaged in small talk for a few minutes. But then Shyla grew quiet and sullen, almost losing her appetite. Nicole was smiling again, and her voice was filled with excitement.

"Girl, I already have ideas for the kitchen and the family room. I love the smell of fresh paint. Rashad will get some of his workers to come by and do all kinds of touching up and make our house feel like the home I've dreamt of having."

Nicole went on and on. Shyla tuned her out, allowing herself time to think about what she wanted to say next. She knew her most recent actions probably confused and angered her friend. For it had been obvious that Nicole was stunned to see this other side of Shyla: a more contemplative and downright bitter side. But sometimes bitterness was where life led you after happiness and dreams got stolen. Shyla remembered how ecstatic and confident she felt when she first became engaged to Wesley. Life was filled with promise. And she couldn't forget how the "engaged" Shyla Perry looked down on other single women in the office and constantly gave them unsolicited advice, something her coworkers despised. It was as if she'd written the blueprint to a happy married life. But now? The "married" Shyla Fallender felt horribly ashamed at how often she bragged on her relationship. She didn't give advice because she was rooting for other women. She did it because it made her feel better about herself. But these days her proud words were reduced to dust, for she would die if anyone knew that she'd gone from a condo to the ghetto.

She sat and listened and drank a mouthful of her sweet cold lemonade. And when Nicole paused for a few seconds, Shyla spoke up: "Listen, Nicole, if you two are on a great path that'll lead to everlasting happiness because for some reason y'all just so different than the rest of us mere mortals, then good for you. But I can only hope that what happened to your husband and his ex-wife will never happen to you. It's always sad when a couple breaks up because a third party is involved."

"What are you talking about? Why bring that up now? Didn't you hear me when I said that I am not stuck on the past?"

"As the new wife you may not be, but trust me, Kiara is still hurt by it, even though she acts like she's over it."

"Oh. Well, I'm not really worried about all that. Plus, there was no reason for her to be hurt when she turned around and did her own husband wrong. And I think that's why Rashad eventually left Kiara for me."

Shyla nearly choked on her drumstick. "He what? Girl, you are tripping now."

"When you think about it, Rashad picked me over her."

"No. She kicked his ass out, remember? Because he was messing around with you. She didn't want him anymore. That makes you the rebound wife. You're the rebound."

"I am not—"

"Nicole, even Alexis wasn't dumb enough to want Rashad anymore after all the mess he put Kiara through. I'll bet that you weren't even his first choice. No other woman would tolerate his cheating ways . . . except you."

Shyla's words hurt Nicole so much that she closed her eyes tightly to try to wipe out the memory of what she'd just said. Unbelievably poisonous words that could not be retracted. But what if Shyla's accusations were more than jealousy? What if they were true? Nicole wanted to believe that in spite of their extramarital affair, Rashad truly cared for her. He'd gotten used to her. He learned to trust her and accept their love. *After all,* she reasoned, *if he doesn't love me, then why marry me?*

"You know what, Shyla. I've never seen this side of you before, and I just think that because you are all of a sudden going through hell, it makes you lash out at those closest to you. You are taking out your frustrations on me. I get it. But I don't like it. And I'm going to try hard to pretend like none of this has happened. Let's change the subject."

Nicole spoke her piece and was ready to resume eating, drinking, and talking about other topics, pleasant things that suggested she could be and always would be happy.

They ate in silence and observed a mob of people who had waited an eternity just to get their Frenchy's fried chicken.

Shyla watched the people that were standing around. Could she just look at anyone and determine whether they were happy or miserable? Married or single? Did it really matter? At one time looking the right way at all times was something that greatly mattered to Shyla. But life had taken an unexpected turn and placed her on a bumpy path. Shyla looked Nicole squarely in her eyes. "Some days I wonder whether I should return to the single life. I think it was a lot easier than being married, if you really want to know the truth. I might be better off by my damn self."

"Oh girl, please. You're just saying that. You told me marriage wasn't easy, and I know you're not weak enough to give up."

"It has nothing to do with being weak. It has everything to do with the way life is. To be honest, we started having financial troubles almost immediately after we got back from Central America. After going on our honeymoon and trying to pay the rent on our condo, I-I barely had enough money to be your matron of honor. In fact, Wesley advised me not to. He said we had our own bills to think about. He told me everything costs too much to try to support another woman and make her dreams come true. But no, I shut that nonsense down, and I told my husband—my *husband*— that I would be there for my best friend because I knew how important it was for you to have supportive people around you. I-I knew there'd be no one else . . . No one but me, a woman who will hee-hee and ha-ha with you, but when it's time to keep it real and pull you to the side like a true friend should, you don't wanna be hearing what I have to say. You've thrown your hand up at every good piece of advice I've offered. And because of that, I can predict where our relationship is headed. Nowhere! Sooo, Mrs. Eason, now that I know that you will not let me be the supportive friend that I've tried to be to you since day one, starting right now, consider me an ex-friend."

"Wait a second," Nicole sputtered. "Why are you just now telling me about the financial troubles and how you had to fight to be in my wedding? Girl, I had no idea—"

"You had no idea because you are one self-centered bitch who thinks that the world revolves around you and your husband, your daughter Eminence, and your everything. Nothing else matters to Nicole but Nicole. You did anything and everything you could to get a married man. That is why I've never let you be alone with Wesley, not even for a second . . . I was always scared I might be next."

Evelyn Greene had always warned her daughter not to tell all her business to a female coworker. And now Nicole understood why. When Nicole used to tell Shyla about her and Rashad's sex life, her friend would listen bug-eyed.

"So your conscience doesn't bother you?" she'd ask.

"Hell, nah. It's just sex. We're doing things to make ourselves feel good. And if you knew how good he was at licking my pussy, you'd be like 'Wesley who'?"

Shyla would smile and make little comments like, "You go, girl," but now Nicole knew that Shyla was pretending all along. She thought her friend was a shameless whore who'd sleep with anyone's man.

And right then Nicole was astounded at Shyla's disclosure. "You thought I'd seriously fuck Wesley?"

"I sure did. Scared as hell to even let you have my man's number. Women like you might try to sleep with your best friend's man just for the hell of it."

"Hell to the fucking no. Take it back. Right now. For you to accuse me again of doing anything with Wesley is straight madness."

"Is it the truth, though?"

"Shyla, c'mon, we're better than this. We're friends for life. And true friends don't do friends any kind of way. You know I would never do anything like that to you. But I don't know why you're suddenly coming down on me like you're my enemy."

"Maybe because things aren't always as they seem."

Nicole's eyes drew moisture just that quickly. "Shyla, are you trying to say you were never my real friend?"

"I was your friend, but certain things about you made me feel uneasy."

"And now you tell me this? Have you been faking our friendship all along? Girl, I've trusted you with my secrets and all kinds of shit." Nicole's food was tasteless and she'd lost her appetite. Seriously arguing with a woman whom you considered your closest friend felt like pure misery.

"Nicole, I haven't been fake. I was your friend. Your only friend."

"That again. Shyla, just because you think you're my only friend doesn't give you the right to drag me to hell like you have. It hurts."

"I don't care about you being hurt."

"If you don't care whether or not you hurt me, then you're selfish."

"And what if I am?"

"Then you're also one ungrateful bitch."

"Who are you calling a bitch, bitch? If anything, you are the ungrateful one. Who else at that job deals with your stupid ass except me? Everyone else laughs at you behind your back. And no one trusts you around their man, either. I used to defend you, but now I see why other chicks don't like you. You're stupid enough to try anything to get what you want. Now, *that's* the definition of selfish. I hope Rashad wakes up one day and sees you for the tramp bitch you really are."

With animosity on her face, Shyla whirled around and nearly tripped over a little child as she rushed out of the restaurant.

A red-faced Nicole sat down and tried to finish eating. But with every bite, her chicken tasted like dirt. And dirty was exactly how she felt.

Alexis's hands shook as she held the leasing agreement. Varnell peered over her shoulder.

"Go ahead," he told her in a gentle voice. "Sign and date it."

"I know. I will—"

"But?"

Alexis shrugged, took a deep breath, and quickly scribbled her name. She handed the leasing agent a cashier's check as her deposit.

"Thank you, Alexis. We will get the apartment ready and will give it a nice fresh coat of paint and some new carpet. It will be ready on the twenty-sixth."

"That gives me a few days to locate a mover."

"You don't have to even worry about that, sweetheart," Varnell assured Alexis. "I got a big pickup, remember?"

"Yeah, of course. I'm so excited I almost forgot." Alexis stood up and walked alongside Varnell as they approached her Benz.

He opened her door, then he went around and sat in the driver's seat.

Alexis leaned back and sighed. "I'm finally growing up and it's about damn time. It took me a minute to strike out on my own. But I'm finally doing it. I know my mama is counting the seconds till I'm out of her house."

"She may fuss and all, but I'm sure she'll miss your presence."

"She's going to miss that money I've been giving her, but hey, I can't do it anymore. I will have to pay my own rent, pay the electricity, buy my groceries." She gave Varnell a worried look.

"Don't even sweat it, love. You know I'm here for you, to help you in whatever way you need."

"I'm glad you said that. Because you know I want you there with me when the court finalizes the adoption."

Although Alexis McNeil was Hayley's biological mother, after the girl was born she'd allowed her half sister, Glynis, to care for her. But a couple of years later, when Glynis died unexpectedly, Alexis felt ready to legally claim her daughter. She requested full custody, which meant that a judge had to override any previous decisions regarding Hayley. "Wow!" Alexis felt overwhelmed by all of her life's recent changes. "So many important things are going on at once. And the year has only just begun."

Varnell squeezed her hand. "You've been through a lot, young lady. And the best is yet to come."

Alexis beamed at him and relaxed as he started the ignition. They sped off toward the freeway. Varnell agreed to assist Alexis in selecting the furniture she would need for her new apartment. They ended up at a store off the Katy Freeway.

Walking through the front entrance, Varnell wrapped his arm around Alexis's waist. She felt the warmth of his body. She wondered how much longer he would wait with her not being intimately involved with him. Alexis adored sex. She'd lie in her bed at night thinking about sex. But she wanted to do things differently with Varnell and try to hold off as long as possible. Alexis tried to act casual and talk in a light tone as they perused bedroom sets and mattresses.

She saw a queen-size mattress and dashed toward it. She jumped on top of it and attempted to bounce up and down. "What you think?"

"Hey, that's all on you. If it feels good, you need to make that decision."

"Yeah, but maybe one day you would come over to my house after a long day at work, and maybe you'd be good and tired and you might want to lie down and get you some rest. You need to be able to feel comfy in my bed, too."

Varnell shoved his hands in his pockets. "Hey. That sounds good to me. If I'm lucky that day will come, young lady."

"But not anytime soon, right?"

"No one really knows if any day is coming."

Alexis switched subjects. "I think I want to look at a few more sets before picking one that I absolutely want to buy. Seeing that I'm all on my own on this one. Welcome to the life of an independent woman, huh? That's what I get for wanting to be grown-up, right? Can't get no type of help around these parts."

Varnell pulled her off the mattress. He tickled her under her arms until she screamed and begged for mercy. As they calmed down and started acting like civilized people, she realized she enjoyed his gentle way with her.

"I like you, you know that?" she said.

"I don't know anything."

"Oh, you know how I feel about you and you *know* you know."

"Okay, I'm cold busted . . . because I'm feeling you, too!"

They held hands and rounded the corner to see what other offerings the store had, when they ran smack into Nicole.

"Well, if it isn't Nicole Greene."

"That's Eason. Mrs. Rashad Eason." She flashed her wedding ring triumphantly even though Alexis had already seen it ten times.

"That's right. I do remember hearing about a wedding," Alexis said. "Nice rock, by the way."

"It is, isn't it? You want to try it on? See what it feels like to wear a wedding ring?"

"Um, no thanks."

Nicole eyed Varnell with mild curiosity, then started cackling.

"Is that a downgrade or what?" She tried to speak in a low voice, but Alexis heard what she said and calmly asked Varnell to excuse her.

She gently grabbed Nicole's elbow and led her a few yards away.

"Mrs. Eason, please don't act like you're the only woman who sports a nice rock."

"Oh, I know I'm not. But it's pretty sad when another woman can have a man's baby but can never get the man himself."

"Girl, please. Rashad and I are no longer together, but when we were he wanted my ass day and night."

"None of that matters right now."

"And since it does not, stop trying to wave your fake-ass happy marriage, look at your jewelry in my face. It takes way more than silver and gold to make a relationship work."

Nicole grinned. "It feels soo weird to get marital counseling from a baby-mama, single-ass bitch. How should I pay you for your advice? With an EBT card?"

"Watch your mouth. You sound stupid and look even more stupid. First of all, I'm not low income you stupid-ass bitch. And I may not be married right now, but it doesn't mean I haven't felt the love of a man in my life. I've had good love many times. And I will have it again. With a nicer ring than what you've got."

"Who cares?"

"Obviously you do since you all up in my business. I'll have a better life than you one day."

"Dream on, Alexis. You wish you could get a man to do you like Rashad does me. Remember my nice-ass Jeep he bought for me? And that was before he even proposed."

"You are a miserable little soul and I hope you get everything you've schemed for."

"Sounds like the words of a true hater. Don't hate the player, hate the game."

Alexis raised her hand, ready to slap the shit out of Nicole's bragging mouth.

"The game means you got my leftovers," she told her as she patted her hair instead of slugging the woman like she wanted to.

"Your leftovers sure taste good. They taste damn good."

Even though it seemed childish to her, Alexis was tempted to flash a piece of jewelry that Rashad had given her years ago. She still carried it around in her handbag, undecided whether she should pawn it or keep it just because of its pure beauty. Nicole would die if she knew Alexis still had a pricey ring that Rashad bought for her. But Alexis resisted the urge to stoop to Nicole's miserable level. She didn't want to act the fool in front of Varnell and make him think she was ratchet and out of control.

She tried to take the higher road, and told Nicole, "I'm glad you know what good leftovers taste like and that you're enjoying them. And I hope you two will be really happy."

"We are happy and we are gonna stay happy."

Alexis was done. This chick was impossible to deal with.

Nicole flashed her wedding ring again. Then she began to peruse the furniture displays, the marvelous bedroom sets and leather recliners built for a king. When you had money, you could get all kinds of things to make yourself happy. And Rashad had money. She enjoyed every penny he spent on her.

Alexis stood a close distance away, unable to take her eyes off her coworker. Nicole stopped to look at every piece of furniture, touching it and commenting on its beautiful craftsmanship. She acted like she could afford anything she wanted.

But Alexis felt not one twinge of envy.

She knew that people pretended like they had it all when, in reality, they didn't have much of anything.

"Good luck being his wife," she told Nicole. "I really mean that." And she grabbed Varnell's arm and turned and walked away.

That Saturday, Kiara asked Rashad to come over to her house. Their daughter, Jahzara, would turn one during the first week of April, just two short weeks away. They sat at the breakfast table. Kiara offered him some blueberry muffins and breakfast blend tea.

"Thanks for the hospitality," he said. This was Kiara's first time taking a good look at him since he got remarried. Instead of appearing haggard and beat down like she thought he would, he seemed refreshed and self-assured.

"I try to be cordial to all of my visitors, Rashad, so don't get any strange ideas."

"But I'm not just *any* visitor," he reminded her, feeling indignant. "You haven't done with other visitors the things you've done with me." He winked and took a big bite out of his muffin.

"And I hope you haven't done to other wives the things that you did to me."

"Okay, Kiara. Let's not start with all that."

"I'm just saying," she retorted.

"I'd like to enjoy a nice little visit with you, Miss Lady. If I have offended you in any way, either in the past ten minutes or in the past ten years, please accept my sincerest apologies."

Kiara decided to ease up on her ex and get down to business.

"Look, I know you recently got married and I really didn't want to bother you since you're probably still on your little honeymoon and all, but I wanted to discuss Jazzy's first birthday. I believe you should be included."

"That's very thoughtful of you." He munched on his muffin and scanned his surroundings. The place looked the same but felt different. "Thanks for thinking of me. But, um, why isn't what's-his-face here?"

"Eddison does have a life, in case you weren't aware. I told him in advance that you and I would probably plan a little get-together for the baby and that I'd share those details with him later. He was perfectly fine with that."

"Whoa, he sounds like a real gem."

"That he is."

Rashad set down his food. "C'mon, Kiara. You're talking to me. Eddison Osborne is a man. Not a saint; not a knight in shining armor, or anything close to that."

"Are you assuming these things, or do you know them for a fact?"

"I'm just saying," he told her and started eating again. "Every man has flaws. You know all of mine. I'm sure he has them, too."

"Nope, he actually has no irritating personality quirks. He is responsible, attentive, nurturing, we never argue, we have debates but they are always respectful—"

"Stop. Enough. Okay, then tell me this. Does his shit smell like shit, or roses?"

"Funny. He's considerate enough of me to use the upstairs toilet, and from what I can tell, he always sprays afterward."

"Fucking amazing."

"My man is not too good to clean a toilet, which was something you always expected me to do even though it was you who messed it up half the time. In fact, Eddison does a lot more great and wonderful things, and he has no problem doing them—"

"I've heard enough. I really don't even care. But, Kiara, your boy ain't what you think he is."

"And I think you're jealous."

"What?"

"Please, Rashad. You just admitted that I know your flaws. You get jealous if another man gives me attention. Remember when we got engaged? And you thought this man at the tire shop, a man I didn't even know, was trying to push up on me. He saw me in the lobby and he was talking to me while you were in the restroom. When you came back out and saw the guy sitting next to me, you near 'bout had a fit. And later on you started pointing out everything that didn't look right to you about that man—a man you didn't even know."

"Oh, um. I don't remember."

"Well, I do. I knew right then that you have a jealous streak. You hate competition, or is it that you thrive on competition? I don't know. But I do believe your envy of my man makes you look like a sore loser."

"I'm not admitting to being completely jealous, but yeah, he got what used to be mine. And that bothers me."

"Your fault, dude."

"Maybe so. And I think you should keep your guard up, because everything that glitters ain't gold. Sometimes it's scrap metal. A cheap imitation. Made in China."

Kiara laughed like he'd said something hilarious.

"Thanks but no thanks, ex-hubby. I don't want or need your advice. At least not about my love life. Now. Let's talk about the baby's upcoming party."

And Kiara laid out the plans of what she wanted to see happen at the party while Rashad listened, nodded, and nursed his emotional wounds.

"This domestic life stuff really agrees with me," Nicole told her husband. They were shopping at H-E-B, one of her favorite grocers.

"Domestic life agrees with you, Mrs. Eason? Oh, really?" He laughed at her. "You're lucky I have some rare free time on a Sunday."

"Rashad, I know the old you worked almost every Sunday. But I'm hoping this is a new era."

"A new era?"

"I didn't stutter, babe. I don't want you to revert to your old ways. Working way too much and rarely being home."

Rashad stopped in his tracks. "I'm glad you told me this before I signed a big fat contract for a new house."

"Oh, um, wait."

"No. Too late now, Nicky. You can't have it both ways. If you want me at home in your face all the time, then common sense says that's gonna affect the pockets."

"Shit. I-I gotta figure out something."

"Yeah, you figure it out." Rashad quietly stormed away from Nicole.

She desperately wanted to remain calm. And for a second she wished she'd taken Shyla's advice to get marital counseling. She didn't realize how much hard work this relationship would be, and she yearned to be a better wife.

Nicole grabbed her shopping cart and began to push Emmy down the aisle. She hurried along in an effort to catch up with Rashad, who was making his way toward the meat department.

"Honey, wait up. I-I want both of us to figure out things since we are a team now. It isn't always about what I want."

"That's not how you tell it."

"It came out wrong. That's all. We can sit down tonight, lay it all on the table. Okay?"

Rashad pretended to inspect packages of steak. "What? This little packet costs almost twenty-two bucks."

"Shh!" Rashad's loud voice made Nicole feel mortified. She didn't want the other shoppers to think they couldn't afford to buy prime meat.

"Forget this. Where's the chicken?"

"Over there." She walked to a freezer bin and pointed out a family pack of wings.

"Eleven dollars? When Kiara and I were married, these things cost five bucks. You gotta be rich to eat these days."

"Oh my God, Rashad, please don't make a scene." Nicole tried to ignore the curious stares she was getting. "He's just joking," she explained.

"Isn't that the businessman with those commercials?" she heard someone ask. She whisked Rashad away from the large open area to a more private part of the store.

"Look," she told Rashad when they got settled in the coffee aisle. "Try not to stress over things like the price of food. I will help pay for it."

"What?" he said in mock surprise. He knew exactly what he was doing. Some of Rashad's behavior was designed to test his wife. Was she ride or die like she claimed, or was she riding as long as times seemed favorable?

"Yes, babe. I will pay for all of our groceries. You never have to hand me over any cash or a credit card for our meals. It's the least I can do. That sound fair?"

"Hell, yeah. Kiara usually paid for groceries, and I handled the special holiday meals."

"Rashad. You don't have to remind me what she did."

"Well, she did. Don't expect me not to ever say her name again. That's unrealistic. Kiara is the mother of two of my kids. I love them."

"But do you still love her?"

"What you talking about?" He started walking again and left her alone.

"I'm not done talking to you."

When he suddenly abandoned her, Nicole felt disrespected. Where was the love? Although she hated herself for running after him, she did it anyway. She finally caught up with Rashad and felt like bursting into tears. Why did he have to mention Kiara? Just last night he'd accidentally called her by his ex's name. She nearly punched him squarely in his chest. He apologized, but she wondered if he'd made an honest mistake or had he really been thinking about that woman?

Kiara Eason haunted Nicole. Everything that Nicole did she wondered if she did it better than her boss. Nicole was confident that she could cook her ass off. And when she served it up sexually to Rashad, she knew that he couldn't possibly want any other woman after she got through with him. And she tried to stay interested and involved in whatever he talked about: his business, his competitors, his kids, anything.

Those were the good parts. But just then, in that grocery store, it felt like her relationship had hit a brick wall.

Nicole thought for a minute. She walked over and grabbed Rashad's hand and squeezed it. "I love you, Rashad Eason. You believe that?"

He shrugged.

"Wow. Just wow."

"Don't try to read into my mood. I'm actually thinking about the NBA game that's on right now. Warriors versus the Cavs. I wanted to see Steph Curry shoot the lights out the place. But I'm missing it."

"No problem. We can just get a couple of items and go home to watch the game. I'll go shopping for the rest of the items tomorrow after work. On my tab."

"You're too sweet." Rashad finally cracked the smile she wanted to see. He caressed her cheek. She felt much better. The love was there.

As they stood in line to pay for the food, Nicole thought she'd better explain her actions.

"Babe, you gotta teach me what you want, just like I must learn to teach you some of the things that I want." She glanced around and noticed some twenty-something chicks who wore their shorts up their butt in the middle of late March. Even though the temperature was fairly pleasant that day, the girls still stood out and looked like hookers. Nicole frowned when she saw them pose for a selfie.

"Now, look at them," she complained. "That's what I'm talkin' about. That was me only six or eight months ago. My priorities were all screwed up. I feel like the biggest goal of my generation is for someone to get a first like on Kim Kardashian's Instagram. That ain't shit. And that ain't me anymore." She gave her husband a serious look. "I want way more out of life than that. I may not always explain what I want in the nicest way, Rashad, but I mean well. I've come from nothing and wasn't expected to be anything. So achieving success in life is very important to me."

"When you put it like that, it makes you the same as most every other adult in America. I get it." And he gave her a sexy grin.

Rashad's words bridged a gap and gave Nicole the hope she desperately craved. And she was able to leave the store feeling better about her man as well as their future.

Chapter 6

It was Tuesday evening and a little over two weeks since he'd gotten remarried. Rashad and Jerry, his right-hand man, were the last ones at the Eason & Son office building. They'd just locked the door. An elderly, no-nonsense guy with a good heart, Jerry was rushing toward his car filled with apologies. "Sorry, Boss Man. I gots to run to the house and help out my old lady. The grandkids are puking all over the bedroom; they have a fever and don't want to eat anything. We're going to the ER, but I will drive them instead of calling the ambulance."

"No problem, Jerry. Hope everything is okay."

"Yeah, maybe my two little cuddle bugs got the flu. They better not have the Zika virus. I know that much."

"Think positive, man. Take care. See you tomorrow or whenever you get back."

Jerry waved, leaving Rashad alone. This meant that Rashad would be responsible for making the bank deposit. He decided to go to a Wells Fargo near his neighborhood. He drove along the darkened streets, constantly checking the rearview mirror. He did not notice anyone following him. When Rashad reached the building, he brought the vehicle to a stop and turned off the ignition. The parking lot appeared empty. He looked both ways before exiting the car.

Rashad walked up to the depository and punched buttons on the keypad. Seconds later, a large brick caught him on his head. The deposit bag got violently snatched from his hand. Stunned and dazed, he massaged his head and frantically turned around. He noticed a man running. Instinctively, Rashad took off after him. But the thief swiftly rounded a corner and disappeared into the darkness.

"Fuck!" Feeling angry and frustrated, Rashad stopped chasing the guy and started for his vehicle. "Damn, at least I still have my ride," he said to himself, remembering how he had a bad habit of leaving his keys on the car seat.

Right then he decided not to file a police report. Most times nothing ever came of it anyway. Instead he drove on home. When Rashad arrived and found his wife in the kitchen, Nicole's eyes grew large with surprise. She was wringing her hands and pacing the floor.

"What's wrong with you, Nicky?"

"Nothing," she lied. She eyed an ugly red bruise on the side of his forehead. "What happened to you?"

"Get the first aid kit."

She raced to the bathroom and returned in a panic.

"Did you get into some kind of fight? Were you in an accident?"

"No!"

"Then tell me, what the hell is going on?" She ripped open an antiseptic towelette and applied it to his wound.

"Ouch. That stings."

"It's supposed to. I never knew you were such a big baby." She gently kissed Rashad's forehead and placed a

Band-Aid on it. The tension in Rashad's shoulders began to subside. He finally muttered, "Thanks, Nicky."

She handed him a cold beer. He took one sip, then he told his wife what had happened and griped that the robbery had cost him a lot of money. "I might have to start carrying my own fucking gun. I have one, but I don't keep it on me, because I don't do the deposits anymore. Jerry does. But he had an emergency. So I went to our bank right up the way. He could have warned me."

"No, Rashad. Are you trying to blame your boy for what happened? I personally don't like Jerry, but why would you assume he knew this was about to go down? Everything was just a coincidence. But it's also proof that we need to move to a safer neighborhood."

"I guess. If it ain't one thing, it's another. I take one step forward and two miserable steps backward. What's next?"

"At least you're alive and you came back home to me in one piece." She tried to focus on the bright side. "Baby, have a seat. Dinner is ready: meat loaf, mashed potatoes, green beans, corn bread. And my famous sweet tea. How's that sound?"

"Sounds good. Thanks."

"Once you eat and calm down, you'll feel a lot better."

"Are you serious?" he snapped. "How in the hell will eating replace the money that bastard stole from me? I swear, if I ever see that guy again I'm going to sink some bullets in his punk ass. As hard as I work and I still have to pay my crew and my creditors? Shit, shit, shit."

Nicole decided to keep her mouth shut. She quickly arranged his dinner on a plate. Rashad sat down and angrily chewed his food. The meal tasted good, but he kept a sour frown on his face.

"Other than what just happened," Nicole said, "how did your day go?"

He shoved some mashed potatoes in his mouth and glared at her.

"Well, um." She nervously laughed. "My day was good, babe. I finally got around to changing the sheets on our bed. And the new comforter set . . . remember, it has all those pretty pillows? I put that on the bed, too."

He stared at Nicole like she'd lost her mind. She fell into silence and tried to ignore the small tears that formed under her eyelids.

When Rashad finished his meal, he went out to the garage to look for some of his tools. He quickly returned to the kitchen, ready to talk to his wife.

"Why the fuck is the Jeep smelling all nasty and shit? I see smoke rising from underneath the hood like a fog bank or something. Do you know what the hell is going on? That's a *new* Jeep."

Nicole immediately began crying.

"I . . . it was . . . things got busy . . . time flew."

Rashad could barely understand her. "Calm down, Nicky. What happened?"

She took a few deep breaths. "I-I forgot to get an oil change."

"Okay, that happens. But how long has it been?"

"I-I've never gotten one."

"What?" He grabbed his wife by the shoulders and shook her until her head hurt. "We got that car last October and you've never taken it for a lube change? How can you not do that? What the fuck is wrong with you? All you gotta do is remember to change the oil every three thousand miles. Am I expected to take care of everything around here?"

"I know, Rashad. I forgot. I'm sorry. With the baby and everything and—"

"Oh, don't give me that you're-too-busy-with-the-baby

shit. Forgetting important stuff when it comes to the Jeep can cause long-term damage. Surely you realize that, Nicole." He focused on her and suddenly noticed her new layered hairstyle. And the colorful outfit she was wearing was brand-new and made out of costly fabric. He knew Nicole liked to go to work in one stunning outfit and then come home and change into another pretty dress accompanied by some leather pumps. "Nicole, you mean to tell me you can't remember to do something important like get an oil change, but you never forget irrelevant shit like your hair and wardrobe? Get the fuck outta here."

"You're right, I'm wrong. But it's going to be okay, Rashad. I swear I will take the Jeep to get an oil change first thing tomorrow."

"Too late for that. The Jeep probably has to go to the mechanic. That engine needs to be checked for sludge."

"Checked for what?"

"Never mind. Damn, Nicole."

He turned around and started to return inside the house. He paused and faced her. "So you want us to get a new house, right . . . an expensive-ass house that will need all kinds of preventive maintenance. Are you going to forget to keep up with that, too?" Instead of waiting for her answer, he headed back for the garage and slammed the door behind him.

Kiara and Eddison had just gotten in his car and were on their way home from watching an adventure flick at a suburban movie complex. He drove them in silence. Kiara had noticed that he kept leaving his seat while the movie was playing.

"Eddy, are you alright? You are awfully quiet tonight."

"I'm fine. Movie was good."

"How would you know?"

"What?"

"You kept leaving, and so you missed some of the action sequences."

"It's not the end of the world. I can always see it again. Or wait till it comes out on DVD."

"But that's not the point. We were on a date. And you seemed very distracted." She paused and gathered her thoughts. "Sweetie, I noticed your phone kept ringing. You excused yourself, which is nice. But I want you to be available only to me when we're on a date."

"I can understand that. But I-I had an emergency."

"Oh, really? Is everything alright?"

"Yes," he said in an odd light tone. "It'll be alright in time."

Eddison didn't divulge any further information, so she let it go and folded her arms tightly across her chest. This mysterious silence wasn't like Eddison at all. And Kiara couldn't forget how when they were in the theater, he barely held her hand.

The conversation ceased the rest of the way home. When they pulled up at her house, Eddison walked Kiara to her front door. She gave him an expectant look. "Aren't you going to come in?"

"It's getting late."

"That's never stopped you before. I don't understand."

"Look, I have something to take care of . . . some family business."

"Family business?"

"Yes, I will talk to you about it later. It's bothering me, so . . . that explains my odd behavior." He reached over to kiss her. His lips were smooth and warm. He gave her a little bit of tongue, then quickly backed away.

"Go on in, Kiara. I'll wait here until you're safe, then I'm out. I-I love you."

"I love you, too," she said in a quiet voice. She let herself in the house and stood in the darkness of the living room peeking through the drapes. She watched Eddison get back in his car. She watched him pick up his cell phone, then press it against his ear as he began talking. She watched him drive away and leave her questioning what could be happening with her man.

Rashad nervously stood in front of Beeva Reese's front door. He took a deep breath and rang the doorbell. It was a Wednesday. He skipped going to work since Myles's school had no classes that day. He bundled up the kids and took them on a little road trip.

An hour and a half later, he was in Bryan, Texas, pulling up in his mother's driveway. Soon Beeva Reese answered her door and welcomed him with a big smile and a warm hug.

"Hi there, son. It ain't even Christmas and yet here you are to see me."

"Don't start, Beeva. I-I thought you'd want to see Myles and Hayley."

"Hayley?" she squealed. At hearing her name, little Hayley popped out from her hiding place . . . behind her daddy's long legs. She emerged with a shy smile. And when Beeva laughed with joy and waved at Hayley, she rushed out into the woman's welcoming arms.

"Oh my God, you are such a beautiful little doll." Beeva hugged her with moistened eyes. "Thank you, son, for bringing my grandbaby to see me."

"I'm here, too, Grandma." Myles had been poking around

on the side of the house and ran around to the front. Beeva welcomed her family inside.

Rashad took a seat. Being at his mother's felt real good. Before he knew it, Beeva Reese insisted on breaking out a carton of fresh strawberries, chilled whipped cream, and spongy little shortcakes. She happily worked in the kitchen, fixing up bowls of dessert and happily presenting them to the grandkids.

While Myles and Hayley stuffed their mouths with food, Beeva pulled Rashad to the side in a corner of the kitchen and away from the listening ears of the children. Once she knew they were occupied, she took a seat at the table next to her only child.

"How are things going?" she asked, getting right to the point.

"That woman spends money like I'm Bill Gates."

"What do you mean, like you having to pay all the normal bills?"

"Normal bills don't faze me. I consider paying those my job as a man. But it's all the extra stuff that I hate. The stuff she sneaks and buys and won't let me know about until the credit card statements come in the mail. I can't stand that shit."

"Rashad, I hate to ask, but . . . didn't you know Nicole had dollar signs bulging from her eye sockets before you married her?"

"Well—"

"Well, nothing. You knew. And you married her anyway."

"Beeva, hear me out. At first, Nicky was real low-maintenance. But once she got used to me trying to help her out, and especially after we bought that Jeep, she's been slowly flipping out with the credit cards. Twenty-six-percent interest, Beeva. I feel like I work every day for five or six different banks."

"And you do. Bank money ain't free money, and this is what happens when you spend borrowed money impulsively. Bankers will always get their cut."

"That type of spending is about to get cut, too—"

"Look, son. You married a woman whose heart pumps at the thought of riches. Preferably your riches. You should have gotten a prenup. But because you made her legal, her problems, her habits, are now all yours. Hell, she could wreck your credit. And I will not let that hoe bag destroy what your daddy built for you."

"Beeva, that's my wife you're talking about—"

"Son, I'm not trying to be disrespectful. Yes, she is your wife, but right is right and wrong is wrong. And if what's currently going on in your life didn't bother you, no way you would have driven all the way up here."

"You speak not one lie. I wanted your honest opinion."

"And now that you have it, what you gonna do about it?"

A little silence gave his mother the necessary gumption to ask another much-needed question.

"Rashad, since you married her what's done is done, but did you two at least go to financial counseling before you got—"

"No, Beeva. No."

"That's a damn shame. Some of you men are so quick to lie down with a big-booty hoe. Just because you went half on a baby did not mean you had to marry her, Rashad. She ain't the first single mother and she damn sure won't be the last."

He gave his mother a helpless look.

"I honestly don't even think that you are deeply in love with her, either. Are you?"

Rashad rose to his feet. He shoved his hands deep in his pockets. The blood drained from his face and he knew he was in over his head.

"I love her, Beeva." He shrugged. "May not make any sense, but I do."

"You're not making a bit of sense. That's not how I raised you."

"Give me a break. You asked if I loved her and I told you. What more do you want, huh?"

Rashad was getting weary of the conversation. He wanted compassion, not judgment.

"Hmm. That's fine, but I must warn you—marriage ain't a game."

"Says the woman who's on her fourth husband."

Beeva raised her hand and nearly smacked Rashad across his face. "And that is why I am very qualified to tell you that it's *nothing* to play with. It gets *messy*. And *embarrassing*. And *tiring*. Look at Halle Berry. She may be getting a third divorce. Poor thing. People call her crazy and wonder why she can't keep a man. They talked the same shit about me. But I ain't a celebrity. I'm real. And getting it wrong time after time isn't a laughing matter. It *hurts*." There was pain in Beeva's eyes. "I don't want you to make my mistakes, your daddy's mistakes. But hey, what's life without a mistake?"

"A fairy tale," he answered.

In some ways Rashad regretted coming to visit his mother. But he'd really wanted someone to talk to . . . someone who loved him and who understood. He wished he could have gone to Kiara about these issues he was having, but he knew he'd messed up too much to even consider asking her for advice. He felt all alone and wished he'd never done the things that had put him in this position.

Time was flying. He was getting older by the day, and he was sick of the game playing.

If only I had learned to be happy with the good woman that I had. If only I had done the stupid little doable things she asked me to do.

He felt ashamed, like he was a major screwup who wasn't adept at handling his relationships. And he decided that if he didn't have what it took to successfully manage a relationship, then he'd just have to make some tough choices. And even though it needed to be done, he didn't look forward to it.

Rashad had already signed that contract for the house. It was a speedy transaction and they'd be moving in the next day.

"Maybe I should have listened to you, Beeva. But as a man, I thought I could make my own decisions."

"And you can . . . if you can accept the consequences."

"I just want to do the right thing. 'Cause when I look around, barely anyone takes marriage serious anymore. I'm guilty of that myself."

"Hey, it happens. Maybe not intentionally. But we live and learn." Beeva studied her son. "Keep doing the right thing and it may work out. And I'm worried, son, not because you are having second thoughts about this lady. I remember the look in that woman's eyes on your wedding day: like you have the power to save her just by marrying her. Funny thing is, some people believe that marriage lasts forever. But all marriages come to an end one way or another. Question is, how will yours end?"

He couldn't answer his mother, because he honestly had no idea.

Rashad had just left a construction site located in the midtown area. Houston's real estate was booming in spite of the recent oil price crashes. He was amazed to still see the Bayou City filled with mile-high cranes in every direction. One-million-square-foot manufacturing warehouses, luxury apartments, housing developments, and more. And Eason & Son had successfully bid on a higher education project that he hoped would keep his firm busy for the next several years.

As he pondered his future, he was still unsure about Nicole. His new wife wanted to know everything about his business matters: How much is that project? When does it break ground? Did he need her to write up any press releases and send them to local black newspapers and blogs? He appreciated her interest, but he figured that all she saw was dollar signs and she thought money lasted forever. But Rashad knew that riches could vanish as quickly as they came.

Rashad drove down Montrose Street. A streetlight shone upon two men who were walking along the sidewalk. He waited in his sedan with his dark-tinted windows partially ajar and could clearly see that one of the men was Eddison Osborne.

Eddison wore some tight pants and a short-sleeved shirt. Rashad kept staring as he waited for the red light to change. He watched Eddison and his companion enter a gay bar. It was a well-known establishment that Rashad had seen in the news on a few occasions.

"I knew this perfect fucker was too good to be true."

Rashad made a right turn at the light. He hurriedly parked his car and got out. He walked toward the entrance of the bar and decided to go inside. The small corridor was very dark, only a few lights flickering here and there. A long counter could be spotted on the left-hand side of the entrance, and a small stage had been erected on the back wall of the main room. Dark shadows made it hard to see, but Rashad noticed several men dressed in underwear prancing around to "Don't Stop 'Til You Get Enough."

The music was loud and the energy had the customers bobbing their heads as they enjoyed the entertainment.

"Go-go dancers? What the hell?" Rashad tried to remain calm and felt nervous about what else he might find. He soon spotted Eddison and his male companion again. They sat next to each other at a bar. They were handed two drinks. Their heads were close together as they looked like they were talking. Rashad wanted to throw up. How could Kiara be in love with such a man? He stood and watched them awhile longer.

"Hey there, are you looking for anyone?" a white guy in drag sweetly asked as he checked out Rashad.

"Not anymore."

He immediately left the bar, making a note of its name and address. He looked up and down the street, seeing other men whom he assumed were gay as they took their time going in and out of the establishment.

"That down-low dude got Kiara fooled like a big dog. What a fucking loser."

And Rashad couldn't wait to tell her.

"Kiara," he yelled. Rashad called her as soon as he got back in his car.

"What's wrong with you, Rashad? You sound out of breath. Like you've been . . . ugh, never mind."

"It's not who I'm screwing that you should be worried about."

"What's that supposed to mean?"

"Remember I told you everything that glitters ain't gold? Sometimes it's a DLB."

"What in the hell are you talking about?"

"You know. Down-low brother."

Kiara started laughing. "Have you been drinking?"

"No, but your boy has. In fact, he's tossing back a few drinks right now. He probably is consumed with guilt with his fake low-life ass."

Kiara paused in horror. She just knew he wasn't referring to Eddison. No way.

"Your knight in shining armor isn't as shiny as you think he is. At least not in the way you think. Tell me something. Is he with you right now?"

"No, he's not."

"Did he tell you where he was going? You know, since you two have this perfect open relationship."

"Um, Eddison told me he had family business to take care of, that's all."

"Is that what they call it these days?"

"Rashad, you're starting to scare me. What's going on?"

"Your boy Eddison Osborne is gay."

She sighed. Then it sounded like she dropped the phone. She got back on the line. "You are one sick, jealous-ass, delusional son of a bitch, Rashad. Worry about your own household and stop trying to screw up mine."

"Kiara, wait. Think about it. When's the last time you two had sex?"

She thought about it. It had been a while, a week or so. She and Eddison had mutually agreed to stop making love every other day. That's because she was so busy taking care of Jazzy that sometimes Kiara wasn't in the mood to have sex. But she never thought it would be because he was getting it from someone else, especially another man.

"Well, that's none of your business. Your life is yours, and my life is mine. So don't be asking me about me and my man's sex life. My life should not concern you."

And she hung up.

Chapter 7

Nicole managed to smooth things over with Rashad enough to cause him to forget about their most recent stumbling blocks and concentrate on moving into their lovely new house. It had been a whirlwind few days. And Nicole was so exhausted from unpacking boxes and setting up the new house that she was ready to collapse at the end of each day.

"I'm tired as hell. But I'm happier than I've ever been," she told her husband before he went to work. Rashad wanted to put in a few hours that morning, since his daughter's first birthday party would be held later in the afternoon. He stood in the bathroom watching Nicole. She was seated in the Hollywood tub completely immersed in warm, soothing water with white bubbles and surrounded by firelight candles that smelled of vanilla ice cream and caramel.

"I'll admit, you looking hot in that tub." He licked his lips and stared.

Nicole felt like she was starring in a big-budget film and she was the featured celebrity.

"Thank you, babe," she said. She raised a glass of champagne toward Rashad. He smiled down at Nicole's glistening breasts. He quickly removed his clothes so he could join her.

"Damn, you look fine yourself," she told him. "I have the sexiest husband in Houston. Well, make that in all of Sugar Land. We're moving on up." She laughed and sipped from her glass.

"Man, it doesn't take much for you, huh?" he said. He quietly slid into the tub filled with bubbles. The *whoosh* of hot water completely covered him and instantly soothed him. Nicole was sitting in front of Rashad. He reached over and cupped her breasts. His hands were magical and felt so good on her. She maneuvered her body and turned around until she was facing him. She wanted to look Rashad deep in his eyes. The more she stared at him, the more she wanted to pinch herself. No wonder her best friend refused to associate with her. Shyla's actions hurt at first. But Nicole didn't care. Not anymore.

She sighed in contentment and began to clean Rashad's hairy chest with a soapy sponge.

"I finally feel like a queen. And I love you, Rashad Eason."

"Love you, too."

"You're my king, my Santa Claus, my sugar daddy, all rolled into one."

"Oh yeah?" He smiled at her. He liked how that sounded, even if it seemed like she was describing someone else.

"A lot of people dream about having something amazing for years or even their entire lives. And a lot of times that's all it ends up being—a wish. But everything I want is here. It's now. I'm so happy that I'm afraid one day I'll wake up and it's all going to be over, because it was just a five-minute dream I had that felt real. But, no. *This* is my reality." Nicole pressed her lips against his, stuck her tongue in his mouth, and kissed him. She sucked on his tongue and moaned when he lowered his hands and massaged her vagina. Waves of pleasure rolled inside of her. It felt so good she could barely speak. "And I-I'm so grateful and so thankful, because when I—when I think about it, I might not deserve all of this. I probably didn't stay on a straight and narrow path to get everything I have."

"You didn't play your position; you took your position."

"Ouch! That sounds so horrible, as if Kiara was at the top of a mountain and I climbed up next to her and knocked her off."

"But isn't it true?"

"I know one thing. I won't take the entire blame for how we hooked up."

He could only laugh and agree with her. People wanted what they wanted, and at times they didn't care how they went about getting it.

Nicole's voice was quiet and reflective as she splashed more water on Rashad's chest. "Right way, wrong way; point is, I want to hold on to everything I have and never let it go. Because some goal-oriented people might die and never, ever see even a little bit of what they wished could happen during their lifetime."

"Yeah, you are one lucky chick. But every Cinderella has that moment when the clock strikes midnight. The carriage turns back into a pumpkin and her prince has to take back his rented tux."

She tossed her head and laughed. "You're so silly, Rashad. I'll tell you like I told my former best friend. I won't let any negativity rain on my parade. I'm happy. And I plan to stay that way."

She sank deeper into the tub, closed her eyes, and Rashad realized he'd been dismissed.

* * *

Later that afternoon approximately a dozen children gathered at Chuck E. Cheese's. Even though Jazzy wouldn't turn one until the next weekend, Kiara had decided to throw the party ahead of time.

Jazzy, Myles, Kiara, and Eddison arrived first, and from the moment they set foot in the venue, she and Eddison were nearly glued to each other's side. Like true partners, they consulted with the party coordinator and checked on all the details together.

"You're so good at daddy-day-care duties," she told him.

"I'm glad you think so."

"I wish we could have had our own child, sweetie."

"It's not too late for that to happen," he assured her. "Meanwhile I'll have fun treating these kids like my own."

When Rashad and Nicole walked in with Emmy on her hip, she surveyed the room. Kiara had reserved one long table decked out with green, lavender, and pink balloons that nearly bobbed against the ceiling. Numerous party favors were arranged at each child's seat. And a three-layer cake decorated with edible crayons bearing Jazzy's name prominently sat at the middle of the spread.

"Nice job, Kiara," Nicole remarked once she made sure Emmy was seated in the center of the other children. "It's all about the kids today," she said. "Thank God she's only one and she doesn't realize where she's at."

"There is nothing wrong with my daughter having her party at this place."

"Umm, if you say so. But I really thought you'd pick somewhere a bit classier."

"Girl, I'll bet when you turned one, Chuck E. Cheese's would have been an upgrade for your family."

Nicole laughed. "We're not talking about me. It's all about that precious little Jazz and how she's forced to sit at these sticky-topped plastic tables and the non-working video games."

"You are exaggerating. And why would you care where Jazzy has a party?"

"I want her to be happy."

"Why aren't you concerned about your own happiness, Nicole? You schemed your way into getting that man that you were so desperate to have. It seems that nothing else would matter to you after that. But obviously you are the type who is never satisfied."

Nicole was startled by her remarks.

"I don't like what you said. Take it back."

"And I didn't like all the shit that you did by sleeping with my husband. Take *that* back. Oops, I guess it's impossible to do that, because it would mean Emmy would instantly disappear from sight. Like a cheap magic trick."

Nicole glared at Kiara, unable to believe she'd just sunk so low as to target her daughter. Suddenly the joyful squeals of children interrupted them. The kids were laughing, running, and having the time of their lives. She decided to back off.

"I'll ignore your little statement. And just know that I didn't mean harm about this joint. I always thought you were the sophisticated, snobby type and I just thought you'd go all-out—"

"Nicole, I didn't mean what I said about Emmy. I don't like you judging my decisions. The point is, the kids are having a good time, alright? So, please go get yourself some pizza and a beer, and relax for a change. You look really stressed out."

As soon as Kiara turned around, she saw Rashad. And he was headed toward Eddison.

"Damn, if it's not one thing it's another." She quickly approached the men, who'd just engaged in conversation.

"What are you two talking about?" she asked.

"I was just asking Mr. Osborne if he'd been hitting any new bars lately. You know, Houston is always opening up a new place to drink and get your swerve on."

"Rashad, please. I know what you're trying to do, and it's not going to work."

Eddison faced Rashad. "Yeah, man, I heard that you called my lady and implied that I'm down-low, or something to that effect?"

"Are you?" Rashad asked.

"If I was, it definitely wouldn't be any of your business."

"If you were, then you need the shit beat out of you."

"Rashad," Kiara pleaded, "we are here to celebrate our daughter. Not interrogate me and my man. I'm going to have to ask you to leave. Right now."

"I ain't going nowhere. I am here for two reasons: to be with Jazzy . . . and to keep my eyes on this fake P.O.S."

It took everything inside Eddison not to smash Rashad in his face. He came close to losing it, but he held his composure. He avoided Rashad the rest of the night, but he couldn't help but notice the questioning looks that Kiara kept giving him. Looks that made him wonder how much longer he could withhold the words he needed to tell her.

When Rashad had the first opportunity, he pulled Kiara to the side. He grabbed her arm and led her to a corner.

"What are you doing?" she asked.

"I wanted to tell you thank you for organizing this party. I didn't contribute that much."

"Oh, you did. You paid for this and that helped."

"You always know how to get my money, don't you?" He smiled like he was impressed.

"I get what I can get, alright?"

"I like that about you, Kiara. I always have. You're strong, determined. And you look like you are back to your pre-pregnancy weight."

"What it's to you?"

"I like that you're taking care of yourself, managing your life, the kids."

"Oh, well, thanks."

He looked like he wanted to say more but she cut him off. "How's married life, player?"

"I ain't a player."

"Now, that's hard to believe. You cheated on me, a decent woman who really loved you, but you're faithful to that little wench?"

"Hey."

"Hey, nothing. It's true."

"What? Are you still hurt? I-I'm sorry about that, Kiara. I never wanted to hurt you, babe. I know I messed up a good thing."

She could not look him in the eye. It was rare that she allowed herself to display the hurt she had endured from their turbulent marriage. She assumed that she'd gotten stronger from not being around him, and she wanted to always present herself as such.

"Oh well, Rashad. It's all water under your whorish bridge."

Her words stung, and now he was the one feeling emotional. "It's probably too late now, but I'm not the same man, Kiara. I'm a better one. And I have you to thank for that."

"Don't thank me for anything." She shoved his forehead and pushed him against a wall. "Thank yourself for causing the shit that broke us apart. Now, go somewhere, sit in the hoe corner, and think about everything you've done." She left him alone and returned to the party.

Rashad and Jerry were at a construction site installing track lighting into the ceiling of a middle-school gym. Rashad liked to get down in the trenches sometimes and assist with the dirty work. He stood on the seventeen-foot-tall orange extension ladder, his tools gathered in a belt that was secured around his waist. Jerry was standing underneath the ladder attending to other duties.

As Rashad took a big step on the ladder, he tried to reach toward the ceiling at the same time; freakishly, his right foot slipped. Without thinking, instead of gripping the ladder, he shifted backward and lost his balance. He felt himself helplessly falling. Rashad reached out in desperation, trying to grab the ladder but he overreached. His hand barely grazed the step. But it was too late. In no time he was airborne.

Thwack! Thwack! Thwack!

Rashad grunted when his body struck the wooden floor. He'd fallen twelve feet. His legs were tangled like knotted wire. He winced and wailed.

Within seconds Jerry crouched over Rashad.

"Boss Man, are you all right?"

Rashad nodded. Then groaned, "My back."

"Can you sit up?"

He tried. But as soon as he struggled to raise himself, he quickly plunked back on the floor.

"Call my wife," he struggled to tell Jerry. "Hurry. Dial eight-three-two . . ." He weakly recited the other numbers.

Soon Nicole was on the line. Jerry placed her on speaker.

"Hey, Jerry. I was in the middle of doing something. What's up?"

"It's Rashad. He's been hurt."

"What? Hurt how? Is it serious?"

"He's laid out on the floor. He fell off a ladder."

"How the hell did that happen? Did you call an ambulance?"

"He wanted me to call you first."

"Well, that's crazy, call 911," she huffed. "Where exactly is he?"

Jerry provided Nicole with the address. Then the sound of many voices echoed in Jerry's ear as he tried to talk to her.

"Where are you, Nicole?"

"I-I'm taking care of some business."

"Okay . . . how soon can you be here?"

"I, um, I'm on my way," she told him. Then thought, *I need to do something real quick.*

"Where exactly are you?" Jerry asked.

Nicole hesitated, then hung up. She was at the Galleria Mall waiting in line at Neiman Marcus. She was about to buy three pairs of Christian Louboutin shoes that she'd had her eyes on for weeks. And when she learned that the store finally had her size in stock, Nicole grabbed her keys and wallet. On the way to the store, she told herself this purchase was a congratulations gift to herself for convincing Rashad to buy their first home. When she first arrived in the shoe department and told the salesman what she wanted, she trembled when she tried on each pair: a pair of black patent-leather red bottom pumps, scuba studded black leather booties, and beige python-embossed pumps.

The final price would add up to nearly three grand before tax. It would be her first time ever owning a pair of

Loubies. *Yep*, she thought as she caressed the top box of the shoes she was about to purchase. *This shy little girl who used to run around barefoot in Alabama has finally arrived.*

Nicole's excitement rapidly turned to guilt when a nagging feeling tugged at her. She stood behind two other customers who clutched several boxes in their hands.

"Hurry, please hurry. I have an emergency," she said out loud, hoping the sales associate could hear her.

After waiting a brief moment, Nicole was able to swipe the credit card that Rashad had given to her for emergencies. Minutes later she raced out of the store and hopped into her ride.

Nicole expertly hid her purchases behind the driver's seat, covering them with a thick blanket. Finally! She felt ready to perform her wifely duties.

When she arrived at the construction site, the first person she spotted hovering over Rashad was Kiara.

The sight of the woman made Nicole hot with rage. She leaped out of the Jeep and stormed over to the tiny crowd of people that had gathered.

"Mrs. Eason, sorry we're just now getting here. A train got us jammed up," the EMS attendant explained. "Which hospital should we take him to?" He was addressing Kiara, who appeared distressed as she tried not to caress Rashad's shoulder. Eyes closed, he lay there moaning every few seconds. He wasn't talking and hadn't seen her arrive.

"Um, I'm thinking Sugar Land Methodist will work," Kiara blurted without thinking.

"Yes, ma'am."

"Excuse me, sir," Nicole interrupted. "I'm the current Mrs. Eason. You need to go through me, not her."

The man shrugged like it didn't matter. He quietly asked his coworker to help lift Rashad onto a gurney.

"What's going on? Where are you taking him?" Nicole asked.

"We've been consulting with this nice lady since she got here. She said to go to Sugar Land Methodist, so that's what we'll try to do. We'll make sure they have space for him there first, and if they do, you're more than welcome to ride in the vehicle with us or you may follow behind and meet us there."

"Of course I'm going with him. What type of wife do you think I am?"

"You've already shown them what type you are," Kiara wearily answered. She felt distressed and regretful about her ex. "I always warned Rashad that he tried to do way too many things on the job. He feels he has to wear every damn hat at Eason and Son, and he never should have tried to do this type of work."

Kiara told herself that she was no longer in love with Rashad. But all she could think about was Myles and Jazzy. An achy lump developed in her throat. They'd had some rough patches during their years together, but if she stopped acting stubborn, she could admit there'd been more good times than bad.

She pulled herself together and decided to travel to the hospital with Jerry, who had contacted Kiara when it seemed like Nicole wasn't sure when she'd show up.

Kiara climbed into the passenger seat of the company van and slammed the door. She buckled her seat belt and looked around. It had been ages since she'd sat in this vehicle, and she remembered the day she and Rashad drove it home from the dealership.

"Wow, Jerry. We've been through a lot, haven't we? I can't remember one time when you haven't been there for us, Rashad, our family." She warmly patted his hand as he drove toward the hospital. "Thank you so much."

"No! Kiara. Thank *you*. I was scared you'd hang up on me when I called since this really isn't your problem. But you handled the crisis like a true champ." Jerry laughed bitterly. "If Rashad pulls out of this and learns that you were there when he really needed someone . . ." He could barely finish his sentence. Kiara wanted to hug him. They sped along the streets in their quest to be there for Rashad. She knew her ex-husband assumed that she despised him. But moving on didn't always signify hate.

After Rashad was admitted and rolled away to get examined, everyone sat in the waiting room. In time, they were relieved to learn that he wasn't permanently damaged by the accident.

The attending physician provided Nicole with an update: "The muscles surrounding Rashad's spine were sprained."

"What does that mean exactly?" she asked.

"There is no immediate cure for the type of injury he sustained."

"What?" Nicole leaped to her feet, on the verge of flipping out. "I mean, I don't understand. No cure? Is he handicapped?"

"In time he will be back to normal. But he needs to take several anti-inflammatory medications and get plenty of rest. We can also do some icing techniques to ease the pain. And depending on how well he recovers, he might have to go through long-term physical therapy."

"Oh my God, are you serious?" Nicole rubbed her temples and cursed. "It sounds worse than I thought . . . I never expected any of this."

"Welcome to marriage," Kiara calmly told her. "The land of expecting the unexpected." She was standing nearby in the dimly lit hallway and was anxious to hear Rashad's prognosis. She quietly stepped into the room.

Nicole couldn't look Kiara in the face. She was thinking that the woman had to be filled with glee. *She'd* been blessed with the healthier Rashad while Nicole had to deal with his ailing, sickly side.

Nicole turned and begged the doctor, "Are you sure about this? What if it's just a simple backache? My back would hurt like hell when I was pregnant. I'd pop a couple of extra-strength Tylenols and call it a day."

The doctor gave Nicole a stern look. "You can't compare a pregnancy backache with the tragic accident that happened to your husband. Rashad is almost forty. If he's been working hard labor nearly all his life in construction, he may have done damage to his back without realizing it."

"If that's true, then that's messed up. I can't believe this is happening to me."

"What's happening to *you*," the doctor replied, "could be a whole lot worse. At least he doesn't have to have major surgery, young lady, he isn't paralyzed, and he didn't even break one bone . . . or die."

A somber hush fell over the room.

"I'm sorry you seem stressed by the prognosis, young lady, but there has been some damage, Rashad's in a lot of pain, and right now he needs your support."

"Poor thing," Kiara remarked. "I truly hope Rashad pulls out of this. I know he will. He is so active and likes to keep moving. When will he be able to receive visitors?" she asked the doctor.

"Yeah," Nicole spoke up. "I was wondering about that, too, but there was so much confusion and . . ."

The doctor ignored Nicole and began quietly speaking to Kiara.

Outwardly Nicole tried to appear strong and act interested in everything that was going on. But inside she was fuming. And embarrassed. For a rare moment she wished that her mother was by her side. Nicole could use some emotional support, but trying to reach out to Evelyn, or even Shyla, would make her feel stupid and weak. Nicole decided to keep her hurt feelings to herself and prayed for her husband to get better—fast.

That evening Nicole was the first person to visit Rashad. His hospital stay was scheduled to last a couple of days at least.

She held her breath and timidly entered his private room. She almost gasped when she saw him. Propped up against several pillows, Rashad wore a wrinkled blue smock. An IV tube was attached to his arm. His face was ashen, but when he saw Nicole, he managed to crack a weak smile.

"Hi, husband," she said in a tiny voice.

Rashad tried to raise himself up, but quickly slumped back when the task felt too difficult for him.

"Are you crazy, babe? You are in no condition to be trying to sit up. I'm so mad at you I could scream. What were you thinking?"

"It's good to see you, too," he said in a hoarse voice.

Nicole leaned over and kissed his cheek. She'd never seen her man in a state of weakness before. And it scared her. Rashad seemed human. And she quickly realized that what Shyla had told her about marriage was the truth.

"Did you bring my laptop?" he asked.

"What? What are you talking about?"

"I thought I told you, or I told somebody, to bring my laptop up here."

"That sounds crazy. What would you want that for? To try and do some type of work while you're here? Rashad, you are getting to be ridiculous." Fear of the unknown made Nicole agitated. She clutched her purse and repeatedly banged it against her side.

"This is crazy," she continued. "We haven't been married very long at all, and this is what we gotta go through?"

"Excuse me? Did you just call me ridiculous? Do you think I want to be here, Nicole?"

"I, um . . ."

"Listen to yourself and then tell me who's being ridiculous."

And so the arguing began.

"Why'd you even try to climb a damn ladder in the first place?"

"You can't tell me how to do my job. I know what I'm doing."

"Do you realize how stupid you sound? If you really knew what you were doing, you wouldn't have fallen on your ass like a rookie."

He gritted his teeth and tried to sit up and lean over to smack her, but she jumped back in disgust. The more Nicole watched her banged-up husband struggling, the more she felt like she was the one who'd gotten injured.

"If you are so smart, why are you in here looking all pitiful, huh? I'm so mad at you for being careless—"

"Shut it."

"You shut it. The more you talk, the dumber you sound. I don't want to have to worry about your ass every single day that you're gone, Rashad."

Her voice grew louder, which made Rashad attempt to sit up again. But he couldn't.

"I've been doing this type of work for years."

"No one would ever know it by the bandages all over your body."

He sighed. Weakly laughed. What was he doing arguing with her from a hospital bed? "Nicky, these bandages prove the work I've done for years is hard and dangerous, yet I lived to tell about it."

"Oh God! You sound as crazy as you look. I don't want to hear any of that."

"Wow, where's the compassion?"

"I'm too annoyed to be compassionate, you fool. Next time be more careful is all I'm trying to say. Think of me. Think of the kids and take better care of yourself while you're on these *dangerous* and *hard* jobs."

Nicole almost wished she could call a nurse and get her own blood pressure taken. She took a few deep breaths and decided to lighten up. By the way he was wincing, she could see Rashad was still in some discomfort. Perhaps his medication was making him cranky. But she realized that even when her husband was healthy, some days she felt like she was in a war zone. Their arguments were silly, but brief, and always exhausting. Nicole turned her attention to Rashad.

"Babe, time out. Please, let's not fight. It's making me tired. I really just wanted to see you. Make sure you're all in one piece. I hate hospitals. They smell bad. It's depressing to be around sick people. And to be truthful, I am smart enough to realize that your job has safety risks. I-I don't blame you for falling, because accidents can happen to anybody, at any time, no matter how cautious you are." She paused and stared at him. His being hurt made her feel an indescribable pain. The only thing she could do was back off and let her heart slowly refill with love for him. "Babe, you look a hot mess, and I'm probably not making things any better by fussing at you." She leaned over and kissed his dry cheek.

"That's the most truthful thing you've said all day."

She smiled and gently stroked his hair. "How are you really feeling?"

He sighed. "I'm alright, considering what could have happened. Can't wait to get the hell up and out of here."

Nicole nodded. She decided it made no sense to try to win an argument. It was too late to change what happened.

"Rashad, as long as you're here, you might as well enjoy this. At least you can feel good knowing that for twenty-four hours a day, they wait on you hand and foot. I'll give 'em that much credit." She paused and contemplated their future. "I'm assuming you won't be able to go back to work right away. Is that going to affect any of your projects? You know you have critical deadlines coming up."

He said nothing and pretended like he was too busy watching television.

"Did you hear me? Am I right? Will you miss out on any projects because of this?"

"Is that all you care about, wife?"

"Um, well, no—"

"Because from where I'm sitting, you seem to be more concerned about me going back and stacking my papers than you are about me getting better. The company will function even if I'm not there." He took the remote and turned up the TV volume.

She snatched it from his hand and muted the sound.

"Hold up, Rashad, you're taking this all wrong. As long as you're *here* in *this* place, where many people are in great pain, I know that things aren't right, but if they let you out, then it means you're on the mend. The prognosis is good and you'll be returning to your normal life. That's what worries me—"

"Nicole, I found out why you couldn't reach me the second Jerry told you I got injured."

"But I came as soon as I—"

"Believe it or not, I have been able to do some things since I've been here. And when I had a moment to myself, I checked my phone. It took a while for me to get a cell phone signal in here, but I finally got through. I listened to a voice mail from my credit card company. A courtesy security alert. Large purchases were made at Neiman Marcus, which ain't the norm for my Amex. And they wanted to make sure no fraud was going on. I called 'em back and found out someone used my card to buy expensive-ass designer shoes . . ."

Nicole grabbed Rashad's hand, lifted it, and kissed it several times before letting it go. "Babe, I'm so sorry. I know it sounds crazy. But it all happened at a bad time. I swear, the timing was fucked. I was already at the cash register. I couldn't just abandon everything like that. We were almost done," she explained. Her cheeks reddened, which made her feel even more embarrassed. She prayed he'd understand and know that she really did try to get to him as soon as she could. "And you shouldn't have bothered yourself at that moment trying to check a credit card purchase. It wasn't that important." Her voice sounded hollow and empty as her words slid to a strained silence.

Rashad rolled his eyes. "Did you want a marriage . . . to be a ride-and-die partner with me . . . or did you do it just for an expensive wedding . . . and a big pretty house that you wanted to show off to your haters?"

"Oh my God. I can't believe you just asked me that. Because from what I recall, you told me that you were going to spoil me. Remember? You told me that you couldn't make any major purchases for a *girlfriend* at the time because you were still married and going through a divorce. But that when it was all over and you got a *wife*, then you could splurge."

Rashad shook his head. "Nah, I don't remem—"

"The fuck you don't. Your memory must have gotten jacked up along with your back injury. Because I can't forget something like that. And it's very unfair of you to make me think you meant what you said, when you really are el cheapo. I'll bet you bought your bougie ex-wife whatever she wanted and never gave her hell about it."

"Keep Kiara's name out of your mouth." His eyes bulged from his head.

"Why are you looking so crazy, Rashad?"

"Why you talkin' about Kiara?"

"What? I can't believe you actually said that to me!"

"I can't believe you picked some fucking designer shoes over seeing whether your dude was dead or alive after falling off a ladder. That's what has my face messed up from the chest up. Not a fall from a ladder, but the fact that my ride or die put herself first instead of making sure her breadwinner was still alive. And then thinking it was enough to go through a third party like Jerry to check on me. Why didn't you drop everything to make sure I was good? Choosing shoes over me? That shit hurts me way more than my damn back."

Rashad's words hit Nicole like a flinging sledgehammer. She grabbed his hand and shook it. "Babe, I am so sorry for doing that. The shoes aren't more important than you. I'll even take them back to the store and get a refund if that'll make you feel better."

"If that'll make *me* feel better?"

Her eyes lowered to the floor. It felt really bad for her to mess up on this level, especially when she knew that she really did care about him. "Please don't be mad. I can't stand it when you're mad."

He angrily snatched away his hand, pushed the volume

button on the remote, and pointedly stared at the television. *Family Feud* was airing; Steve Harvey was cracking jokes and making faces.

"Babe," she pleaded again. "I don't want you to think I didn't care about you. But in that moment, it didn't sound like a life-or-death situation. And it *wasn't* life or death, or else you wouldn't be here. You're in a doctor's care and you'll be better in time, so try to focus on the good side, not on the worst. I'm so grateful and happy that you're alive, do you understand that?"

Right then a pretty nurse with wide hips, big boobs, and shapely legs sashayed into the room. Rashad's face immediately brightened when he saw her. "Hey there. You decided to come back. I didn't scare you away last time?" he asked.

The nurse and Rashad giggled and smiled as if they shared a private joke.

"I decided to come back because I just had to see what you want to order for your dinner, Rashad Eason." His nurse beamed and handed Rashad a menu. "We have some turkey and dressing that's out of this world. Would you like to add that to your dinner list?"

"Um, his wife can help him pick out his food." Nicole walked over and grabbed the menu from Rashad.

"You need to be eating healthy, babe, and they got a lot of good stuff on here that sounds way healthier than turkey and dressing. Damn, I know you miss my cooking, and I sure wish I could cook for you while you're here. But all that'll change once we get you back home again. I'm going to make sure that you recover really well."

"Is that right? I'd like to see that."

"Stop playing."

The nurse discreetly left them alone.

Nicole sat next to Rashad and eagerly reviewed the menu. She liked how she could feel as if she was doing something to show him that she was concerned.

"Babe, I think you should order some skinless chicken breast and peas, corn, and a nice garden salad. And then you can add a wheat roll and some water, iced tea, and apple juice. How's that sound?"

"It sounds fine. Order for me, will you? Thanks." He suddenly sounded more tired. And right then, Nicole grew sincerely worried. What was going to happen? She thought about the baby, working at her job, dealing with the new house, and not having her best friend to talk to. Life felt like it was too much to handle.

"I can try and call Nadia and see if she can help out while you're gone. Maybe offer her a huge raise or something. And I can take a few days off of work to see about you, Rashad. I know all my sick leave is depleted, but it's okay. We'll get through this somehow. If I'm ride or die like I say I am, I may as well prove it, right?" She tried to laugh. "This isn't going to break us. You will get better and *we* will get better, too."

We just have *to*, she thought and went to find the nurse to let her know everything she wanted her husband to eat for his dinner.

That evening Kiara brought Myles and Jazzy over to Eddison's house. He had invited them to eat dinner and watch a movie.

"You're into Disney movies?" Kiara asked in a teasing voice.

Eddison chuckled as he set up their food on trays in front of the fifty-five-inch TV screen.

"Watching a kids' flick is a nice distraction more than anything. Anything for the kids."

Kiara smiled. "Eddy, I can tell something has been bothering you. Wanna talk?"

She reached inside the baby bag and pulled out Jazzy's binkie.

"Nothing to talk about. Everything is alright. Let's just chill together. I know you could use a little peace and quiet yourself. And this movie will help you to relax."

She nodded, went over to her daughter, and placed a binkie in her mouth. The DVD started playing, but Kiara wasn't in the mood to sit down and watch right then.

Earlier she'd called Eddison and told him what happened to Rashad. It amazed her that it didn't seem to bother him that she'd gone to the hospital to see whether her former hubby was alright.

"I know you may not want to talk in front of the kids. But let's have a brief minute in the kitchen."

"No," Eddison said. His voice was sharp. "I told you there's nothing to talk about. Not right now."

"Oh well, later then for sure, because you're beginning to concern me. This isn't like you, Eddy."

"Who really knows what anyone is like?"

His cryptic remark left Kiara momentarily puzzled. She left him alone and took a seat next to Myles. She set Jazzy on her lap. They let Eddison wait on them hand and foot. He brought out hot plates of food and beverages and neatly arranged everything.

Kiara began to relax and enjoy the detailed attention he gave her. Some parts of him felt different, but the good parts of him felt the same.

After Eddison got through making sure their needs were met, he allowed himself to be yanked on his arm until he was sitting closer to Kiara. Their arms were touching, just like she preferred. She leaned over and gave him a quick kiss.

His lips were warm. Delicious. Soon they were making out. Myles paid no attention. And Jazzy closed her eyes and fell asleep ten minutes into the film.

Kiara stood up and grabbed Eddison by the hand. He followed her into the kitchen. She gave him a wicked look and lifted up her hands like she was a toddler. He obliged by picking her up and setting her on the kitchen counter. She immediately wrapped her arms tight about his neck. She clamped her thighs around the backs of his legs in a warm squeeze. Eddison grinned and pressed his chest against her boobs. They hungrily kissed each other until she began to giggle.

He growled and bit her on her neck.

"Oh, that feels so damn good." She pushed him back and stared at him. "I've missed this. I have missed you."

"I haven't been anywhere. I've been here."

"But you haven't acted the way I'm accustomed to you acting, sweetie. Lately, you've been . . . different."

He stared, nodded. "Kiara, I apologize. I haven't meant to seem that way. And I've tried to make it up to you by cooking you this fabulous meal tonight. Did you enjoy my pot roast?"

"Yes, you're getting pretty good at handling yourself in the kitchen."

"And if I stick with you, I'll be your potbelly stallion."

"You can be my stallion all day long. Fat, skinny, whatever. I don't mind it at all, as long as you stay true and stay mine. I need you, Eddison."

"A lot of people need me," he blurted. Eddison broke eye contact. His eyes glazed over; the disconnect had begun. He quietly pushed himself away from her and returned to the living room to finish watching the movie.

Kiara decided to let it go and kept telling herself, *He's my knight. The armor isn't as shiny as it used to be, but somehow I'll get it to shine for me, for us, again.*

Chapter 8

Kiara brought Myles and Jazzy to see Rashad in the hospital the next day. It was around six o'clock in the evening.

They strolled into the room and discovered Rashad watching *Family Feud*.

"Oh my God. The things we find out about people when we catch them off guard," Kiara said in a teasing manner. She set Jazzy on his hospital bed. The little girl immediately began crawling toward him.

Rashad beamed with pride at his daughter, who climbed on top of her daddy's legs. He waited till she was balancing herself on his stomach, then he managed to sweep the girl into his arms and pepper her cheeks with loving kisses.

"Hi, my little princess." Rashad gazed in her eyes. "You been missing your daddy? You been doing alright since I've been kidnapped into this place and forced to eat this unseasoned food?" Jazzy grabbed his cheeks between her hands and kissed him back. Then the girl started singing the "Happy Birthday" song with a few missing words here and there.

"Dang, I forgot it was my birthday."

"That's 'cause you're getting old," Kiara replied. "That's also why you laying up here in this hospital. You thought you were still young, but you needed a quick reminder that you're double the age you think you are."

Rashad let out the first genuine laugh he'd had in a long time. "This is what I'm talking about. God must have a sense of humor. Because no way I could have predicted I'd have my family back with me like this. And on the day I turn thirty-five. Unreal." He beamed happily at his daughter and winked at Kiara. Then he clicked the remote and turned off the TV. "Steve Harvey can wait. My family is here."

Myles walked over to him.

"Hey, Daddy." He handed him a gift-wrapped present.

"Thanks. How's it going, son? You've been doing well in your classes?"

"I'm doing all right, but I wish you were there to help me with my homework. Mommy has this reminder board set up in my bedroom . . . but sometimes I forget. I can't remember everything. That's why I need you."

Rashad's eyes glistened. "I may not always be there when you need me. But don't forget, standing here in this room is a wonderful woman who can help you out, my son." Rashad stared at Kiara in admiration. "This pretty lady here wants to help you to be your best. And a lot of times I wish I was there to help you with your homework, too."

"Then come back home, Daddy," Myles pleaded. "Just come on back."

Myles's voice tore at Rashad. But his son had no idea what he was talking about. Didn't the boy remember that he had recently married another woman? Couldn't he understand that a remarried man could never just "come on back"? Nevertheless, Rashad liked what Myles suggested. He gave his ex-wife a hopeful look as if to ask, *What do we do now?* She rolled her eyes and pretended to remove a piece of lint from her dress.

Kiara was always told that she could pass for singer Ashanti's twin and she looked as gorgeous as ever. Her hair was stylish, skin clear, makeup impeccable. It stung Rashad to notice his ex appeared so healthy and happy. The worst thing for a man was to know that the woman he dearly loved had moved on and done better without him in her life. Knowing that she was with that guy, Eddison, made his mood grow somber. He wondered how she could look so satisfied if she was sleeping with a man who slept with other men. Would she tell Eddison to return to his gay hoe corner and have a seat?

Rashad sat up in bed and asked Myles to go down the hall and check out the fifty-five-gallon coral-reef tank that was filled with freshwater sharks.

"Just go straight down, look at the fish for a few minutes, and come right back, alright?"

"Okay, Daddy. Even though those fish can't compare to the ones in the Congo River."

Kiara laughed while she stood in the doorway watching Myles. "Our son. He will never change, will he?"

"And that's fine with me, but the question is, why have you changed so much, Kiara? I mean, if we could have given it one last shot, we could have made it, don't you think? My kids love me. I love them."

"As you should."

Rashad frowned. "Kiara, seeing you here reminds me of something I've been thinking about lately. Remember when you used to say to me, 'I love you but you're an ass'? When we were married, you'd tell me that all the time. And it irked the hell out of me. But I-I miss hearing you say that. So as a birthday present to me, tell it to me again. Come on. Do it."

"Rashad, you're weird."

"It's a simple request. Be nice. Say it."

"Please shut up. Weirdo."

"If I am weird, it's just because of the way you make me feel." He looked her straight in the eyes. "Kiara, I-I've been wanting to talk to you. I've been doing some thinking since Jazzy's party. And I need to tell you that I still love—"

"Daddy, those fish were so, so lame," Myles shouted as he returned to the room. His timing was perfect. Kiara didn't want to hear her ex-husband's sentimental ramblings. His words and feelings meant nothing to her now. He wanted to be out there chasing women, so he should be happy with Nicole. But lately he seemed to be yearning for what he'd lost. "Whatever you were trying to tell me, Rashad, just save it."

"I wanted to say that . . . the man you're with now . . . he doesn't deserve you," Rashad said to save face. "You may not want to hear it, but I'm just calling it like I see it."

"Your opinions mean nothing to me. Plus, I didn't come here to talk about my personal business or my man. I remembered what day it was and decided to bring the kids to see you on your birthday and make sure you're alright."

"Thanks for doing that. But we need to have a serious talk about your boy. You need to know he is not all he's cracked up to be."

"You don't know what you're talking about."

"And you don't know who you're living with."

"Please," she huffed. "We don't even live together."

"Not yet. And you need to do a background check on him before you make that decision."

"Enough. You can't tell me what to do anymore. You divorced me, remember?" She trembled as she collected Jazzy from off of his lap. "I don't know why I keep letting you back in a door that should stay closed and locked. I gotta do better," she said, scolding herself.

She sharply ordered Myles, "C'mon, boy. It's time to go. This so-called party is over."

"But Daddy hasn't opened up his birthday present," Myles protested. "And I thought we were going to give him that cake that I forgot and left in the car."

"I'm glad you forgot it." Kiara began gathering Jazzy. "There are some things that just need to be forgotten." She waited for Myles to join her, then steered him by the shoulders and left the room without saying good-bye. Left Rashad to wonder how to magically restore all that had been broken.

The hospital released Rashad two days later. After moping around the house that week, bored out of his mind, he began to suffer from cabin fever; on the spur of the moment he decided to hit the road and pay another visit to his mother that Thursday. He decided to do something random and called a taxi, which drove him along the highway leading to Bryan, Texas. He was still sore and had been warned not to drive himself anywhere, but in this case a driver would do. He paid the fare and walked up to the house; he rang the doorbell and was grateful when his mother's husband, Winston Murphy, greeted him, then disappeared into his bedroom.

"Hey, Beeva, how are things going?"

"Good. The same if not better. And you? Is your back alright?"

"I'm alright. It's getting a little better."

"And how's married life, son? Have things improved?" she said in her no-nonsense way.

Before he knew it, damning words spilled from his mouth.

"I should have listened to you a long time ago, Beeva."

"What are you talking about?"

"I messed up. I'm having serious doubts about Nicole."

"Damn son, it's only been less than a month."

"I know."

"So you're telling me you are just now realizing that chick is wrong for you?"

"That's just it. To be honest, when I said I wanted to marry her, I meant it. I had a couple of doubts, but thought I could still go through with it. Thought things might turn out alright anyway. She loved me so much."

"But did you—"

"Yes, Beeva. Nicole is cool. She's not hard to love. But it doesn't stop things from being hard. I think I rushed into this marriage. Because I find myself accidentally comparing Nicky to Kiara."

"What do you mean?"

"I never told you this, but yeah, I've accidentally called her Kiara to her face."

"How could you do some stupid shit like that, son?"

"It's not hard when the first wife is still on the brain. She and I made it a decade. It takes some adjusting."

"And how'd your second wife react when you called her by the first wife's name?"

"One time she threw her cell phone at me. I ducked, though. It hit the wall, cracked, and guess who ended up having to buy her another eight-hundred-dollar phone?"

"If she broke her own phone and you bought her another one, you can't complain because you're the dummy in that case."

"I felt like it was my fault that she threw it, though."

"That chick needs to control her anger. And if she's throwing phones at you, what's next? A knife? Is she going to get pissed and pull out her gun again?"

Rashad had already told Beeva that Nicole had once threatened Alexis with a gun. She got charged with aggravated assault with a deadly weapon. The case was dropped, but Beeva still felt leery about her daughter-in-law's mental state.

"Well, son. I'm sorry things have gotten worse. But I'm not surprised. As I can recall, that woman chased you. But when the risk becomes greater than the reward, it's time to cut ties."

"What are you talking about?"

"If you don't think you two can work things out, you need to admit you fucked up big-time and get the hell out while you can. It ain't too late."

"Beeva, c'mon, that's crazy."

"What's crazy is that you married that woman at all."

"Yeah, and I owe it to her to at least try harder to work on some things."

"You right. Work on getting that lawyer to help you get a quickie divorce."

"Huh?"

"Check this out. In the state of Texas, you can get your marriage annulled within thirty days. Problem solved. Sure, people gonna talk about you and laugh. But it's better to be laughed at than to hang on to a relationship that you know won't work. Thirty days, and it's like none of it ever happened!"

Rashad's mother was the queen of breaking up with any man she wasn't feeling. But his splitting up so soon from his wife seemed brutal. But Rashad reasoned that maybe it wasn't a bad idea: He could be free, clear his head, and slow himself down from being with this woman, that woman.

"I dunno about that, Beeva. I-I need time to think."

"That's just it. You ain't got time to think. See your lawyer and file those papers, boy. You better hope you can get out of this mess without it hurting you too bad. Only thing is that little gold-digging tramp may stick it to you good for seventeen years since y'all had that baby. But you'll be alright. I know you gonna do right by your kids regardless."

Rashad vigorously rubbed his temples. His mother went on and on about how short life was and how everyone needed to quit faking happiness just to impress other people.

"You don't have to feel ashamed if you made a mistake. It happens every single day of the week. Better to realize you fucked up and move on, than it is to put a Band-Aid on a wound that needs major surgery."

"Tell you what—I'll sleep on it."

"You do that. But at least you learned sooner rather than later. I don't want you to follow in my footsteps. I may be on my fourth husband, but damn it if Winston's not going to be the last one. Like I told you before, true love is not a game."

Rashad stared at his plump-looking mother with her two skinny legs and fat, round waist. She was short, but she could probably arm-wrestle a man twice her height. He couldn't believe how those skinny legs were strong enough to hold up his mother's body. Beeva Reese had been through a lot in life, and he knew each time she spoke, the truth popped out. Maybe that's why Rashad felt so angry. Mostly at himself.

When Rashad told his mother good-bye, he waited on a cab to go back home. He knew he needed to man up and execute a different plan.

A plan that could greatly succeed or drastically fail.

Chapter 9

The next day Rashad woke up, feeling ready to burst. First thing that morning, he took a calculated trip to downtown Houston. By the time he completed his business affairs, there was so much swirling inside of him that he had to let it out. He got in his sedan, pulled out his cell phone, and called Alexis.

"Hi, Skillet. I know this is short notice, but I'm hoping you're available for lunch."

"Maybe. What's up?"

"I want to know if we can meet at our old spot—it's important."

"Our old spot? I don't think so."

"Why not?"

"Old spots can dredge up old memories. I don't want you getting any weird ideas."

She knew how Rashad was and hoped he wasn't planning on dragging her into any of his mess.

"Tell you what," he replied. "You pick the place. I just need to see you."

* * *

"Now I'm really curious. Fine. How about here in Third Ward? There's a little soul food joint that's supposed to have bomb turkey wings."

"Turkey wings, it is," he said, feeling relieved. "See you soon."

Alexis arrived before Rashad did. He rushed through the restaurant, and although the joint was teeming with activity due to the lunch crowd, he spotted Alexis right away. This beautiful woman always stood out in a crowd. She wore her long hair in a high ponytail and was dressed in black jeans and a red tank top.

"You're looking fine as usual." He came and sat next to her. She was seated in a corner booth and was squeezing lemon juice into her glass of ice water. She took a swig of her beverage and talked to him between sips.

"Hey there. Now, what's going on that you had to see me so bad?"

"Damn, I see not much has changed."

"Everything has changed. That's what you're seeing."

"Well, check this out." Rashad leaned in and began to pour out his heart. "This may sound crazy, but um, the wife and I are having a few issues."

She nodded. "Mmm-hmm. I thought it would be something like that."

"And I am not sure about my marriage."

"Seriously? Then why'd you even get with her?"

"I did it because I care about Nicole. Just like she cares about me. But remember, this all happened after Kiara and I were through. I wondered if I even deserved a second chance at love, especially after I could admit to myself that I blew it with Kiara. I wanted to prove to myself I could do this. Be a family man, and a good, faithful husband."

"That's admirable, Rashad." Alexis tried to hide her sarcasm. "If I would have known that you'd mature one day, and act like a real man, maybe I would have stuck around."

He lifted his eyebrow. She burst out laughing. "Sucker! I was just kidding."

"Sure, you were." He stared into space. "A lot of things might have gone different if I had done the right thing at the right time. That's why I'm now at a crossroad. Trying to figure things out. It's crazy, Skillet."

"All kidding aside, I'm glad that you are trusting me with your heart."

He stared at her in amazement. He *was* glad there was at least one female in his life who was easy to talk to. "I'm not very good at this. But yeah, that's what I want to do from now on. Love a woman the right way and follow my heart."

Life could be so odd and uncertain. Every week, it was apparent that his kids were growing up fast. Time waited for no one. And Rashad wanted to make sure that his remaining years were ones that he did not regret.

"Skillet, trust me. I've learned a whole lot about life. And one thing I found out is that there are different kinds of love. The love you have for someone like family; the love for someone who's just a friend and nothing more; the drunken, reckless type of love when you can blame it on the alcohol; and there's that deeper, genuine type of love that causes a man to marry a woman. But even married love can be broken down into different levels."

"I wouldn't know, since no one has ever wifed me."

"You're too independent to get married."

"Whatever," she told him. "Get to the point."

"Listen up. Most of the time, when a man gets married, he is either doing it because he can't live without that woman. Now, that's true love. Or the dude is lonely and just wants someone there because he hates being alone.

And in extreme cases that man wants a domestic, nurturing chick, one who loves him no matter what and he can depend on her to take care of the house, and she can get down in the kitchen every day for his bum ass."

"So are you saying that none of those describes your reason for hooking up with your female Shrek?"

"A combination of the three."

Alexis laughed. "Well, at least you're honest. I think you married that heifer as your rebound chick. You needed some companionship."

"One thing I can admit is that Nicky's a cool companion. She always has something going on. Keeps the energy level up and all of that. But nope, I can't say I married her only for that reason, either."

"But weren't you lonely, Rashad?"

"I thought about it but I ain't had time to be lonely . . . not when I went from one relationship right into another."

"Tell me about it." Alexis interrupted him and asked him to go up to the line and get their food. "I want turkey legs, yams, some of that hot corn bread, some Cajun corn, and a red Kool-Aid."

"Yes, ma'am."

Alexis watched Rashad standing in line. He chitchatted with the other people waiting for their food. He talked to the restaurant workers and made them laugh. He wasn't such a bad guy, she thought. But he'd married a bad woman. And she was happy he was getting away from Nicole, regardless of the reasons he'd married her. Men were such fools. And Alexis was relieved he'd admitted his foolish ways and had decided to do something about it.

Rashad brought Alexis a tray filled with food and set it in front of her. He handed her a fork and a spoon.

"Wow, you such a gentleman. And you even paid for my meal."

"Always, babe."

"Okay, getting back to the inexplicable reason why you legally hooked up with her. Not for love, not companionship. Wait. Let me guess. You wanted your own live-in slave."

"I don't consider a wife a slave. But the truth is, I work more hours than she does. You know that. So that means I don't have tons of time to do shit around the house."

"Especially that big old house I heard you got."

"Yeah. It's a monster."

"But, Rashad, even if that house has to be maintained and kept clean, haven't you ever heard of hiring a maid? You don't have to mess over people and marry a woman just to get housework done. I can't stand Nicole, but if that's why you hooked up with her, then that's whack. And we can already figure out why she married you."

Alexis was right. Rashad knew he'd married Nicole without coming to terms with her true motives. Was her love genuine or manufactured? Did she value money more than him?

"I knew she had some issues before we got married, but it's what you find out afterward that really makes you regret saying yes."

"Like what?"

"This is going to make me sound like an asshole, but she makes this, like, fucked-up crazy sound when she sips her tea. Smacking her lips and shit."

"You gotta be joking. That's so freaking petty."

"I know."

"Rashad, you *are* an asshole."

"Hey, I've been called worse."

He hated the judgmental look that Alexis gave him. So he cleared his throat and threw his wife under the bus as the wheels were rolling.

"Don't defend my 'female Shrek,' as you like to call her. She can be sweet, but she also has a shitty attitude, too. You think I'm petty? What about when I leave facial hair on the bathroom sink? She yells and curses at me and I ignore her. I am rushing, trying to get to work. If she loves me, she can clean up behind me."

"Clean up after your own damn self."

Rashad was just getting started. "Not only that. Why would an honest woman sneak stuff she buys into the house? Expensive shit she doesn't need. What can a woman do with one hundred purses and two hundred pairs of shoes? I swear, it seems like that's how many she's bought since she met me. And she hides the stuff in the back of the Jeep. When she thinks I'm asleep, she sneaks in the garage, brings everything in the house, and stuffs it in the back of the closet. As if I can't go in the closet and see what she's done."

"Do you talk to her about it?" Alexis almost laughed. She had a huge shoe and purse collection herself.

"Naw, I don't say shit."

"Then you've only got yourself to blame. Look, I can understand it if the things she does annoy you. She annoys the hell out of me and I'm so happy I don't have to live with her. But really, Rashad, those minor issues can be worked out if you really wanted to do that. But then again, she is so shady I wouldn't try the bitch. So I can kind of see where you're coming from."

"Okay, alright. Thanks for seeing things my way for a change. And one last thing, Skillet. She tries hard, but she can't suck a dick to save her life."

Alexis spit out her food and watched it fly across the table. "Are you serious? You really think a judge will grant you a quickie divorce because her dick-sucking skills are weak? Rashad, you need to get real. Because your excuses for leaving the mother of your child are as weak as Le-Bron's reasons for losing a championship."

Rashad's face reddened. First of all, he was lying. Nicole was skilled at making love to him in every way. So, why was he making up tales about his own wife? He'd sunk to an all-time low, and he didn't know whether he was coming or going.

"I'm here to tell you everything that's been going on, because it doesn't stop there." Rashad proceeded to inform Alexis of the truthful things that had been happening since that morning. At the urging of his mother, he'd had an emergency consultation with his family law attorney, Lily Tangaro, a few hours ago. Lily had asked him a million questions. She'd listened to his ramblings. And she'd told him what to do but said the final decision was up to him, and she'd warned him to be ready for the fight of his life.

"So, yeah, Skillet. I put in for an annulment today. And that's why I wanted to see you. I had to tell somebody."

"That's crazy. I simply don't believe it."

"And as crazy as it sounds," he said, "my own mama pushing me to get things started before my thirty days are up is what's really pressuring me. She's been on my ass every day."

"Oh, so that's the sudden rush? You allowed your mother to pressure you into making a life-altering decision? Rashad, don't be stupid."

"I'm not trying to be stupid. I just want to be happy."

"Oh, wow, now you're really starting to piss me off."

"Why is that?"

"Number one, you're grown. You've gots to live your own life, not let your mother influence your heart. Do what's in your heart."

"I'm trying to do that. I'm trying to be real, Skillet, and that's why I didn't want to drag this along any further."

"Damn, Rashad. I get that you want to be happy. We all deserve that. But were you really thinking about your happiness when you told her that you'd marry her?"

"I wanted to make her happy."

"You wanted to do that, but you forfeited your own happiness. You shouldn't do things for others if it's not what you really want to do. Nobody would guess that you're almost forty. My goodness."

"Slow your roll, Skillet."

"What? You don't wanna hear the truth? Does it hurt, Rashad? Because you honestly don't care about hurting other people."

"But I didn't do it on purpose." Rashad was feeling very conflicted and wished his truth could be believed and understood. "What about what she's done to me? What about when she played me with her boy, Ajalon? You saw the tape. You saw them fucking on my patio. What about that?"

"If this woman's betrayal pissed you off that bad, then I'm sorry, you should have dumped her and went on with your life." Alexis was so mad she could barely think. "You knew what you were getting from jump street. And to me, when you play with a woman's emotions, especially a crazy chick like Nicole, you can't do certain things without thinking them through. You had doubts early on, and it's like you went into this relationship expecting it to fail. She went in wanting to succeed."

"Hey, I didn't know—"

"You knew exactly what she was like from day one. Men like you get on my nerves. When you were just fucking her, you didn't care about her imperfections, but after you two got married, all of a sudden you can't tolerate her annoying habits anymore?"

"This isn't about me telling you this info so you can attack me, Skillet. I wanted you to hear me out, feel me, because in spite of you trying to be pissed at me, I know you can't be taking up for the same woman who made you call the cops when she pulled that gun on you. So save your sisterhood empowerment speech, all right?"

Ouch! Low blow. Alexis didn't realize how much she was shaking. She tried to quiet down before she responded.

"Look, it's too late for me to tell you what to do, Rashad. But she's going to have a heart attack. All she talked about when she got back from your honeymoon was how happy she was to be married."

Rashad thought about the recent events of his life. He still felt slight pain in his back, and he couldn't believe that he still had to take prescription medicine and make his regular therapy sessions. He never would have imagined that any of these situations would have happened to him.

"I'll be honest with you. I've been blindsided a lot this year. And one thing that shocked the hell out of me is when I looked up and saw my ex-wife in my hospital room. Kiara? Coming to see me? And bringing a gift for my birthday—even though she did it on the slick through Myles?"

"She probably was just as surprised as you by her actions. But that woman has a lot of heart. And I heard that she got to the site of the accident even before your wonderful new wife did."

"I know. And when I think about it, you really don't know what you've got till it's gone." Rashad carefully pondered his words. "Kiara does have a good heart. A stubborn heart, too. Her recent actions showed me a lot. And maybe she's too proud to admit that she still loves me."

"Loves you?" Alexis burst into laughter. "Slow your roll, Rashad, because I do believe you've lost your damn mind. Kiara did the right thing in a crisis. Good for her and good for you. But please, forget all about Kiara loving you. I'm a woman, and I know how these things work."

"So you're saying that you could never love me again, Skillet?"

Alexis held her breath and counted to ten. "I'll pretend you didn't ask me that. This is not about Kiara loving you. It's about Nicole hating Kiara. It's about Nicole despising your ex so much that she brings a negative attitude into your marriage. I hear the things she says around the office to whoever listens. It's disgraceful and unprofessional. She competes with Kiara, and she knows it's a losing battle. That's driving her crazy and driving you away from her. So I'm telling you, Rashad, if you believe that Kiara still loves you with a wifely love, and you leave your current wife for your ex-wife, you might as well call the undertaker, because you'll completely kill that woman once and for all."

"If what you're saying is true, then that's something I will have to consider. But right now I need a big favor because this is where I want you to come in!"

"Me, why me?"

"Because Kiara is your boo."

"I don't want any part of your schemes."

"Just listen to me, please." Rashad took a deep breath. "I need you to convince Kiara that I am still in love with her and I still want her. I need her to know that I want to be the husband I should have been all along. We can try and make things work. Fall in love all over again. And get married again. Raise Myles and Jazzy together. All that."

"You sound like a fool, and you're forgetting one vital detail."

"What's that?"

"Kiara still has Eddison's promise ring."

He threw back his head and laughed. "Promise ring, my ass."

"You are so wrong for that."

"If that Eric Benét look-alike was serious, why didn't he buy Kiara an engagement ring? He's up to something. It's all smoke and mirrors."

"Eddison is not smoke and mirrors, hater. He is perfect."

"No man is perfect. Not even me."

"Rashad, you're too much. Let me hear more about your plans."

"So, if I go to Nicole and tell her that Kiara and I are going to give our relationship one more try . . ."

"You'd hear Nicole scream from here to the moon. I'm serious, Rashad. That child would probably ride an elevator to the top of the Empire State Building, stand on a ledge, and take a flying leap. You know, she's so over the top I wouldn't put it past her."

"I don't know how she will react, but I guess I will find out soon. Right now my mind is on getting my family back. And I think it'll happen. Once Kiara knows that her knight in shining armor is a piece of shit for real, she'll be running back in my arms in no time."

"You really got it bad for her, don't you?"

"What do you think?" he told her. They finally got around to eating their meal, and Rashad couldn't wait to take the next steps that would define the rest of his life.

Part 2

Revenge Is Stronger Than Love

Chapter 10

Rashad paced outside of the church, wincing at times due to his throbbing back pain. He was standing in front of the little stone building where he'd gotten married a month ago. Nicole had asked him to meet her. She was late. And he felt anxious. Although he'd filed the papers for the divorce, he still hadn't told her of his plans.

It was a Monday. Nicole had called in sick and told Rashad she'd be taking Emmy to the doctor. She left him an ambiguous voice mail, and now here he was, wondering what was up.

When he saw his wife's black Jeep swerve to a quick stop in the parking lot, he trudged over to the driver's side.

Nicole pointed behind her and popped the locks. Rashad immediately opened the door and unbuckled his youngest daughter from her car seat.

"Hey, baby girl, are you all right?" He whisked Emmy into his arms.

"Dada. Hi fi." She had recently learned how to say a few words.

Rashad gave Emmy a high five.

"What's supposed to be the matter with her, Nicky, because the baby looks normal to me?"

"You didn't see how she was acting earlier this morning." Nicole came and stood next to her family. "She woke me up, crying her eyes out. She had a high temperature. She was sweaty. She didn't want to eat. I got scared."

"And what did the pediatrician tell you?"

Nicole squirmed and glanced at her feet. "That's the problem. She couldn't find anything wrong."

"No kidding."

"But I don't believe her. She only spent five minutes examining Emmy and then told me the baby simply needs to stay hydrated. Emmy's always got a bottle in her mouth. I don't think the doctor knows what she's talking about."

"Nicky, if you called me way over here for something you could have told me over the phone . . . then I see this as a case of overreacting . . . again."

"You sound angry. And if you think caring about our child is overreacting, then I'm beginning to question your parenting skills."

"Don't even try it. I got experience in this type of thing."

"And I don't? Is that what you're trying to say, Rashad?" When Nicole realized that the volume of her voice had increased, she told herself to calm down. She never wanted to be perceived as crazy. But recently it had been tough to control her emotions. For the past few days, her husband had taken to sleeping in their second master bedroom.

Hmm, he wants me to chase him. I can do that, Nicole had told herself.

So she'd gotten dressed in a sexy red negligée. She'd tiptoed down the hallway to the bedroom. She'd knocked on the door and twisted the knob. Rashad was resting on his stomach with his back turned. Nicole tried not to burst out laughing. Playing sex games was fun to her.

She stood next to the bed and tapped him on the shoulder.

He turned over and squinted.

"I'm sorry, sir, did I wake you?"

"Sir?" he asked.

"C'mon, just play along. Um, I was just passing by and you looked so damn sexy, and so alone in that big bed of yours. May I join you, Daddio?"

Rashad sat up in bed. Much more alert. She crawled onto the bed beside him. But when she tried to place her arms around him, Rashad claimed he wasn't feeling well. His back hurt. His sinuses were bothering him. And he didn't want her to catch what he had. So he asked her to get out of that bed and return to their room. She refused. She argued. And she was downright shocked when he physically pushed her off of the mattress. She plummeted to the floor with a thud. She sat there on the floor for the longest time, expecting him to beg for her forgiveness. To prove to her that he really cared. When he did no such thing, she finally pulled herself up to her feet. She went back to their room. She stared at the ceiling all night, and her mind began to wonder, plot, and scheme.

And now here she was. Waiting in front of the church that she hoped would restore good memories to her husband.

Nicole changed her voice to a sweeter, calmer tone. "Rashad, baby. I know you accuse me of overreacting a lot of times. There's a reason for it. My explanation has to do with the love I hold in my heart. Because when it comes to my family, I'd rather overdo it and be wrong than to underdo it and be sorry later."

"That's cool, but use your common sense. I won't be able to up and run to see what you're yelling about every time you get scared and nervous." He knew his reply sounded lame under the circumstances, but he had to wait till he had found other living arrangements for himself before he could drop the news.

"If you're not willing to rush to my side when I need you, then why'd you even state your marriage vows?"

"Huh?"

Here was her chance to say how she felt. "We made promises to one another, Rashad."

"Oh, alright, so you're telling me that your interpretation of the vows is that I'd up and run to you every time you scream?"

"Well, yeah. Because you are the protector of our family, Rashad. In big or little things. And I am your partner, here to help you protect our baby. When I said my wedding vows, remember I also promised to be the best mother I could be to your children."

Damn, this is awkward. He cleared his throat.

"Um, and I appreciate that, Nicky. But you get too scared over petty shit that you should be able to handle. And now you're losing a day of work when you could have just had Nadia watch Emmy. You told me you don't even have any more sick time."

"I know, right," she replied. "And all of that brings me to this." She paused. "I have no idea what is going to happen when I have to start missing more days . . . because of me having to go to the doctor again in the future."

"Go to the doctor for what? Because of Emmy?"

"Because of me. Your children. All our children."

"I only have one baby with you."

"I know that, but—"

"Nicole, are you trying to tell me you're pregnant?"

"I-I don't know what I am just yet." Then she started pacing. He followed behind Nicole, holding Emmy. "I just don't feel right, Rashad. I've been vomiting. My stomach's all queasy."

"Nicky, please don't play."

"I'm not playing." She came to a stop. "If I was pregnant, how would that make you feel?"

Rashad wanted to explode. The timing couldn't have been worse. But would another baby make him change his plans of leaving her? He'd already filled out an application to lease a two-bedroom apartment and he was waiting to find out if he'd get the unit he requested.

"To be quite frank, I don't know what I feel right now."

"What do you mean?" she cried. "I thought you'd be happy."

"I-I wasn't expecting this."

"But you could handle it, couldn't you?"

"Why would I want another—?" He stared at Emmy, who had begun toying with his ears. She laughed and squeezed his ears between her plump fingers. His precious little girl meant the world to him. He wiped his forehead, which was suddenly beaded with sweat. "Okay, so you may be pregnant. If that's the case, what could I do about it?"

"Nothing at this point. I just wanted to see you in person and let you know what was up."

"Is it mine?"

"What the hell you asking me that for? Are you crazy?"

Alarmed, Emmy wildly squirmed in Rashad's arms. He told her, "It's alright, baby girl. Daddy's here. Daddy got you."

Nicole felt that if Rashad had kicked her in the stomach, it would have felt great compared to the question he just asked.

"Why'd you ask me to come here, Nicole? To this church?" he asked. "Why didn't we just meet at the crib?"

"I-I just thought it would be nice to come back to—"

"The scene of the crime?" he barked. "I know you. And you don't do anything without thinking about it carefully before you do it. This is a safe place for you, right? What type of person do you think I am?"

Nicole said nothing because she already knew the type of person he was. She'd gone through his cell phone last night while he showered. She reviewed his call log and noted unfamiliar numbers, but that didn't mean anything to her. She then looked at his web search history. She noted the saved links for the Web sites of several apartment complexes. As she pondered what it all meant, her gut felt hollow and her heart grew frightened. She found it hard to sleep well last night. It was part of the reason that she'd called in sick. "Rashad, I think you are the type of person who might go postal. I felt better talking to you about this in public."

"You got it all wrong, Nicole."

"Why are you calling me that? I am Nicky to you. Call me Nicky Eason."

"What difference does that make?"

"You just don't understand, Rashad. I feel like from the beginning you haven't really given me a fair chance. And you're not taking me serious. Maybe you feel like we married too quickly and that I wasn't ready to be your wife."

She hesitated, almost appearing as if she really was afraid of Rashad.

"Go on and say what you want to say. Now's your chance."

"Okay, alright. I-I'm beginning to question my skills as a wife . . . as a mother. It's nuts. I don't like feeling this way. I want my happy back. It's too soon for it to be gone."

"Finally, the truth comes out. These tactics you're pulling have nothing to do with the baby being sick, or you being pregnant."

"But I could be—"

"You're not pregnant, Nicky. If you thought you were, you'd just buy an over-the-counter pregnancy kit. So just stop it with the BS and let's get to the root of the problem. You feel insecure and it causes you to act like you do."

"What else am I supposed to do? I-I love you, but I'm not feeling your love anymore."

He handed their daughter back to Nicole.

"There are some things I'm not feeling anymore, either. Take the baby. I've got business to take care of. That's all I have to say. Get some help, though. Some psychological help. And when you're better, I mean, really, really better, then we can talk. I'm out."

"No. Wait, Rashad."

Her cries were met with silence. He calmly returned to his vehicle, started the ignition, and drove away without a second thought.

On the same day that Rashad met up with Nicole, Alexis stopped by Kiara's office. Kiara was busy preparing a financial report to justify several new positions that she wanted to add to her communications department.

"Hold on a sec, Alexis. Let me type something real quick. Our VP is really getting on me about this additional funding I'm requesting. So I really gotta break it down to him in terms he can understand."

"I won't be long. But let me know if you need anything. I can pull up old data if you need me to."

"I might take you up on that." She sighed. "Have a seat. I'll be right with you."

When Kiara finished her document, Alexis casually asked if she would bring Jazzy over to her apartment after work.

"Hayley wants a playdate with her baby sis. They can hang out for an hour, then you can go back home and get your daughter ready for her bath and bed."

"Um, Alexis. How do you know Hayley wants that? Did she tell you?"

"In so many words, yes . . . When we're at home, she kisses Jazzy's baby picture and says, 'Love you'."

"I see. That's so sweet."

"Yeah, so what's your answer, Kiara? Are y'all coming or not?"

"This is an odd request, and normally I'd turn you down, Alexis, but sure. Why not?"

"I really appreciate this. As the mother of a baby, I know doing unscheduled stuff in the middle of the workweek can be hectic."

"That's true," Kiara replied. "But the girls need to bond. We'll pop by, say, around six."

"Great, see you then."

Alexis left work and rushed to pick up Hayley from the day-care center. Then she got home and tried to spruce up her place before Kiara arrived.

Before she knew it, the doorbell was ringing, Hayley was screaming, and Alexis felt ready to pull out her weave.

But she answered the door with an amused smile.

"I swear to God, kids are in control. Not parents. Kids." She warmly invited Kiara and Jazzy into her home.

Kiara walked in with a dazed look on her face. Alexis's place was meticulous and stylishly decorated.

"I can't believe I'm here." Kiara wanted to say that she had never visited a side chick's house before.

"Um, yeah. It's my first-ever apartment. I have a long

way to go. As you can see, I only have a few nice pieces, and of course, I'll need a lot more furniture than what I have, but that will all come much later. I'm in no hurry."

Kiara nodded. "Well, do you. You don't have to entertain me. I always have a magazine stowed away in Jazzy's tote that I can read."

"While the sisters make a big mess as they play and have fun, us two can just sit and talk, okay?"

Kiara said, "Why not?" and Alexis went to grab Hayley. She settled the kids in her daughter's bedroom, where there were lots of dolls and stuffed animals lying around to entertain them. Alexis made sure the door of Hayley's room stood wide open. Then she dragged some dining room chairs into Hayley's room and offered her visitor a seat. Kiara thanked her and rested her leather handbag on the back of the chair.

They watched the girls hug each other and were warmed by their obvious affection for one another.

"You just never know about life," Kiara murmured as she tried to relax. "I'll have to admit something to you. When I first walked into your apartment, all I could think about was whether you and my ex had—"

"No, we did not. Not at all. Please don't think anything like that. What we did way back then was wrong, but it's been over. We are just friends right now."

A year and a half ago, when Kiara had first found out that her administrative assistant had been sleeping with her husband—and they'd even had a secret baby together— she'd almost lost it. The betrayal caused her incredible pain. She wanted both of them dead. But as time went on, she'd learned to forgive and move on. But just because you forgive someone doesn't mean you've forgotten the pain they caused.

"You and Rashad are just friends now? That sounds just

like something a married man would say—'It's nothing, she's just a friend'—but he's steadily trying to get in that so-called friend's panties. I really hope that's not you."

"I told you I have somebody. You've met him."

"Having someone and even meeting the wife hasn't stopped some chicks from sleeping with a married man. It's sickening."

"I understand that, but, Kiara, I'm faithful to my man. And more importantly, he's faithful to me."

"You never know."

"*You* may not have known, but *I'd* know."

"You're so naïve."

When Kiara noticed that Alexis grew stonily quiet, she decided to lighten up.

"I'm glad you believe that you and your man are faithful to each other. What I think isn't important. How is Varnell Brown, by the way?"

"Working like always. He'll be by later tonight."

"Good. I'm happy to hear that you two are still going strong."

"Me too. Relationships can be hard."

"Cosign." Kiara laughed. "If I never get married again, it'll be fine. I just want a happy life for me and the kids."

"Oh, but I didn't hear you mention Eddison. Are y'all still good?"

"Um, yeah, we're great. He is busy himself tonight. Family issues that he has to deal with. But he's still my prince."

Jazzy burst into a wild yell. She rolled around on the floor like she was sweeping the wooden surface with her body. Kiara shook her head in amazement. "This little mama is always doing something to almost give me a heart attack. I can't take my eyes off of her for one second."

"Tell me about it. If we didn't have the support of our

men, our lives would be so much tougher." Alexis paused. "And maybe it's completely none of my business, but our boy Rashad is still feeling you big-time."

"He's what? How do you know that?"

"Um, I just do."

"I thought you and him didn't hang out anymore."

"Oh, we don't. Believe me. It's only regarding Hayley. I told you, I have a man. A very decent man. Um, not to say Rashad isn't decent."

Kiara suddenly sprang to her feet. She grabbed her handbag off the chair. "I don't like how this conversation is going."

"He still cares about you, Kiara. That's all I want to say. Nothing more, nothing less."

"But why do you care about him caring about me? I don't get it."

"*She* shouldn't have him. She *never* should have had him. She doesn't *deserve* him."

"Why did I agree to this, again? I-I gotta go. I feel like this whole thing was a setup." Kiara reached for Jazzy and scooped her up in her arms. The girl was getting heavier. Kiara struggled to hold her. Jazzy squirmed and made protesting sounds like she wasn't ready to go just yet.

"Oh, Kiara. I'm sorry. This meeting was for the kids. These girls love each other and want to be around each other." Alexis pleaded with her boss. "I'm sorry for overstepping boundaries. I should keep out of your personal life."

"Did he put you up to this?"

"Rashad wants you back. And my guess is that he'll do anything to get you back." Alexis shrugged. "Some men find it hard to let go, even if they are the ones who filed for divorce first. It's like a game. A plea for help. I swear to God, if you had wanted to reconcile and not go through with that divorce, you two would still be together now. And the psycho bitch probably would be on her way back to Alabama. Or maybe she would have hooked up with her ex again."

Kiara felt conflicted. She didn't want to talk about Rashad. She wanted to forget, not remember. Thinking of the bad times caused too much pain, even to this day, if she let it. And she thought maybe it was the reason why he constantly implied that Eddison was on the down low.

"That man *will* do anything to get me back. And to be honest, I'm not sure if I appreciate his tactics. They are questionable. He may call it love. But I call it narcissism. After every bad thing he's done to me, why would I still have romantic feelings for him? So please do not try and make me love Rashad Eason again." Kiara shrugged with a sober acceptance of where fate had led her. "Sorry, Boo. Those days are done. And so am I. Good night. See you at work in the morning."

Alexis watched Kiara leave through the door. She could have kicked herself for allowing Rashad to make her part of his poorly thought-out schemes.

"I'm done, too." She vowed to stay out of it and firmly closed the front door.

It was Tuesday afternoon. Rashad knew that each day his daughter Emmy was being cared for by Nadia, if he caught Nicole before she got off work, he could do what he had to do before she got home. Rashad placed a call to his wife and closed his eyes as he spoke to her.

"Hey, what's up?" He paused. "What are you doing? I really need to see you."

"Ooh, you need to see me? I hope it's good news, like you won the fucking lottery or something."

"Um, yeah. Anyway, something has come up and we gotta discuss it."

"I'll be there. Name the place."

"Meet me at LA Fisherman on Highway Six," and he gave her the address, then hung up.

Nicole had no idea what her husband wanted to tell her, but she prayed it would be to declare a truce. She hated fighting with him. She knew that the news of her possible pregnancy had thrown him for a loop.

But now Nicole was ready to play nice with him. She did as he instructed and was waiting for him at a busy crawfish restaurant when he walked in. She was seated in a booth, looking pretty and relaxed. The atmosphere was noisy, with fellow customers talking loudly over the sounds of hip-hop. People were peeling their mudbugs and munching on sweet kernels of corn and red potatoes. It almost seemed celebratory and party-like, but Rashad appeared somber as he sat in front of Nicole. At first she was smiling, but when she noticed his dry-ass expression, her heart began to beat wildly inside her chest.

"We need to talk," he informed her and took a seat.

"Um, hi, hubby. You look nice today."

"That's not why I called you to meet with me, Nicole."

Her face fell. "Babe, alright. You're not in the mood for jokes. But if it's about the tires needing to be rotated and balanced, I swear I will make it happen this weekend." She picked up her smartphone, opened up her calendar, and added the appointment for the tires.

"There," she said. "Done."

"Stop wasting your time, Nicole. This ain't about car maintenance. It's about us."

"Alright. What about us? Like, what do you mean?"

She noticed that he stopped giving her eye contact. She lifted Rashad's chin and made him notice her.

"Talk to me, babe."

"Nicole, I've been thinking . . . and . . . I don't want to do this anymore."

"You don't want to do what anymore?"

"Be together. Be married. To you."

She shook her head as if she'd heard him incorrectly.

"I'm sorry, Nicole, but . . . my attorney has drawn up the legal paperwork."

"Huh? Seriously? Paperwork? Rashad, I know you didn't just say what I think you—"

"We're through."

"What you talking about? How can we be through? It's only been a month."

"I know." He knew she could easily persuade him to change his mind, but he wanted to be firm. "I tried, Nicole. I really did. Tried to be patient, be understanding. But too much has gone down. Maybe it was the accident that did it for me. I had to fall flat on my head to think clearly. And I hate to say this, but I'm not sure you are pregnant. It sounded like a desperate lie. And if you're pretending to be pregnant just to keep me with you, it lets me know you need serious psychological help. That's why I want out."

Nicole was stunned beyond belief. "I thought it was for better or for worse. Not for better or forget it."

"When 'worse' is this bad, I don't want to do it anymore."

"But it's so sudden. Is there anything we can do to work this out?"

"There's nothing to work out because I'm not changing my mind."

"So, Rashad, you're saying you won't even give me one chance to talk about this? I'm sure there has to be something I can do to make our relationship better."

Rashad didn't know how to tell her that he wanted an annulment so it could be as if they'd never been married.

"Um, I don't think so."

"But don't you love me?" she asked.

"Love has nothing to do with it."

"Then what I'm hearing is that you *do* love me?"

"I love Kiara" was what he wanted to say, but he knew his admission would destroy her. He looked at the door and made sure he had an escape route.

"Love can mean many things," he carefully answered. "The ability to love someone is not an easy thing."

"But it should be easy enough, because of the fact that I am your wife."

"It's easier when you're deeply in love with someone. But I don't have those feelings for you."

"What did you just say?"

"I-I'm in love with someone else."

"Who?" Tears quickly filled her eyes. His words hurt her so bad that she felt it must've been some weird joke. Surely Rashad couldn't be serious. How could a husband love any other woman besides his wife?

"All I can say is that you've met her before."

"And who the fuck would that be? One of my coworkers? Or a woman who attended my wedding?"

He quietly watched her reaction.

"Who is she, Rashad?"

"I don't want to say."

"And you're full of shit. I don't believe this. How can you keep that type of information from me?"

"I'm not trying to hurt you."

"That's so considerate of you."

She wondered if it was Remy Davis, a young chick whom he had mentored at one time.

"Rashad, please tell me that you're just being silly."

"I'm being real. It's no joke."

"No, this can't be the real you. I refuse to believe it."

"Nicole, all I can say is that I thought about it and thought about it. I care about you, but we maybe would have been better off as friends. I had fun with you in the beginning, but I honestly can't see myself being with you for the rest of my life. You spend money like it's going out of style."

"Oh, okay. Is that what's bothering you? You're right, babe. I'm a shopaholic, but if that's why you're pissed at me, I can quit right now." Feeling relieved, she opened her purse, dug in her wallet, and slapped her Visa, Amex, Discover, and MasterCard on top of the table. "You can have all these fucking credit cards. Go on, cut them up. I'll stay out of the malls. God knows, I have bought enough things and don't need anything else. But it's the baby I'm mostly concerned about."

"Your shopping sprees have nothing to do with Emmy. She's my heart. Whatever she needs she's still going to get. But, Nicole, can't you see we come from two different backgrounds?"

"Are you judging me? I can't help how I was raised."

"I know that. But we are so different in how we look at things, important things like money and material goods."

"What are you talking about? You act like I worship the almighty dollar or something."

"Some days you do. You act like if you can't have something you'll have a nervous breakdown. I work hard for what I get, and for you to treat it like it's a game and like money is so easy to come by, well, it makes me sick. Now, that's just how I feel about the matter whether you understand it or not. Look at this."

He pulled out credit card statement after credit card

statement from a sheaf of papers that she hadn't noticed he'd been holding when he first walked in.

"I can't believe this is happening," she muttered.

"Look at this. Pages and pages that itemize things you've bought, or ordered online, and tried to hide from me. I feel like I'm a victim of identity theft. You didn't respect me enough to even ask before you went and bought all kinds of stuff."

"Rashad, now I know you're kidding."

"Am I smiling right now, Nicole? Can you face the truth for one day in your life?"

The stack of papers sat on the table in front of her. She had to close her eyes for a moment to help ease the nausea she felt in her belly. Rashad looked angrier than she'd ever seen him. And the party atmosphere had swiftly turned into the cold air of a funeral. As reality set in, Nicole could tell by the weary look in his eyes that her husband meant every word he said. He spoke his truth. But what about the words he'd announced in front of the minister the day they got married? Were those words filled with truth, too?

Just that quick, Nicole began to resent Rashad. Why did it seem he always got his way? And why couldn't she have the husband that she'd always wanted?

This would be Rashad's second divorce in less than a couple of years. Obviously he didn't take marriage seriously. How could this man toy with her heart as if she were a twenty-minute game? Her soul was involved, as well as her pride. She thought of all the people who came to see her at her wedding. My God, she had just finished mailing the thank-you cards for the gifts they received. And part of her ceremony was even loaded up on YouTube; it had gotten thousands of views. Sure, maybe she could have exercised more wisdom and not have uploaded the video clip.

But hell, it was the happiest day of her life, her proof that dreams did come true.

"I'm sorry for anything I've done. It was not intentional. Please, please don't do this."

"I'm sorry, too, Nicole, but I want to go on with my life."

"But what about *my* life? This sudden decision is ridiculous. At least you gave Kiara ten years. Why did I get the ten-minute marriage, huh? This proves that I'm not good enough for you." Tears streamed down her face. "Even that awful Alexis got to deal with you for a few years in secret. But me? Why am I the woman that you discard like trash?"

"Whoa, I'm not calling you trash. It's not that bad. We just don't click as much as I thought we would. Nicole, like I said, I've given this some thought and I didn't go into this marriage lightly. It ain't your fault. Blame me, because I think I rushed into this. Yeah, back then, things were going well. I thought I could handle it, but I can't." He paused. "The love I have for this other person is the kind that I want to have. And I learned that my heart is not big enough for two women. You know this. Side chicks know this shit don't always work—"

"Hush, just be quiet. You're making things even worse than what they already are . . ." She wanted to reach over and slap his face. She wasn't a side chick. She was a wife. And she could not imagine another woman getting the love that she wanted for herself. Rashad was hers. No way he'd love another woman.

"So, who is this woman you're in love with, Rashad? You say I know her? Is it Alexis? Did she connive her way back into your bed? She hates my guts. And if she gave you some pussy, it's only because she wants to hurt me."

He laughed but didn't say a word.

It was almost as if he was hiding something. And the

fact that he was talking to her about loving someone else, she almost wanted to doubt him. Because if the man really loved another woman, why was he still here talking to her?

Rashad quickly stood up. He had gotten everything off his chest. "Nicole, sorry to have to do this, but there is no other option. I suggest you consult an attorney."

"So you're serious?"

"I am. Get yourself some representation."

"If I do, I'm making you pay my attorney fees."

"You can try but it's probably not gonna fly."

"Rashad, how can you be so cruel? I don't have money for an attorney."

"I look at this marriage like I'm the CEO of Eason and Son. My employees are either an asset or a liability. If they're making me lose money, I get rid of them."

"What the fuck? I don't work for you. I'm your wife."

"And as my wife, if you're not adding to me, you're taking away from me."

"That's some cold ass shit, Rashad."

"The world is cold."

"And you're much colder than this fucking shitty world."

By this point a few more people had entered the restaurant. It was time for him to leave before things grew ugly. "Um, Nicole, I thought you should know that some of my stuff is already gone from the house. I had it moved."

"What did you say? Like, why? When? How?"

"I had it done while you were at work today."

"So you moved your shit out behind my back?"

"Nicole, you can be very unpredictable. If I had told you this at the crib, or told you first and then wanted to go back in the house for my stuff, you might've tried something crazy."

"You actually believe I'd set your shit on fire or something like that?"

"Maybe, you never know."

"I wouldn't do that. I don't care about any of that."

She stood up. Hate and love had the same intensity. And as much as she hated him, she knew the love was still there underneath her wounded feelings. But what about him? This man had to have loved her, right?

Every part of her body trembled. She knew she might have sounded and looked pathetic, but she wanted to fight for her marriage. "I-I don't understand why you're acting like this, but I love you, Rashad. I-I may have made mistakes, but why would you go and be with someone else when you know I love you as much as I do?"

He gave her a blank stare, as if love from the wrong woman could never make a difference. He decided he just needed to leave the restaurant. Leave her alone. Leave her to fend for herself. Again.

Rashad had just arrived at Lily Tangaro's office for another consultation. He waited in her office while she tried to end a phone call with another attorney.

As Rashad thought about the morning of his second wedding, he reasoned that his chances of getting an annulment were good. They had to be. Because, right or wrong, he wanted his dignity, his sanity, his money, and everything else that their union had confiscated from him.

On Saturday, March twelfth, the day he was to marry Nicole, Rashad's close friend, Delbert, noticed how Rashad made a trail across the carpeted floor of the hotel room that he'd rented the day before. Rashad had ambled over to the window and stared out over the city. He walked over to the bar and sloshed around a glass of ice water, he then went into the bathroom to stare at his reflection in the mirror. Then he started the process over again.

Finally, he returned to the table filled with fruit and cheese and took a seat.

"Rashad? You good?" Delbert asked.

"Man, I wasn't even this hyped when I married Kiara."

"Yeah, dude. I remember. You were way more chill on that day. So, what's up with you now, running around this room like you on crack?"

"That's just it. I don't know why I can't sit still for long. Nervous energy, maybe?"

Delbert thought Rashad sounded skeptical. "You getting married today, dude. You sure you wanna do this?"

"Yeah, yeah, bro. It's a wrap. This girl is cool. She's an around-the-way girl. Maybe not as seasoned as Kiara. A little young for me to take as a wife, but she's crazy about me and our kid."

"Dammit, Rashad, I'm about to ask you one more time."

"Look, Delbert. I told you I'm good. My little ride or die is the submissive type. I think she will do whatever I say from now on. I need a woman like that. Someone who looks up to me, who openly loves me instead of denying her love."

"Alright, fine. Do you love *her*, though?"

"Ain't no way I'd be here if I didn't feel something for her. I just need to wind down a bit. Then I'll be straight."

Delbert shrugged and asked Rashad to wait a second. He fished around in his pocket and produced a tiny pill.

"What's this?"

"It'll calm you the fuck down. And make you look and act normal, hopefully. 'Cause right now you look like you about to walk down a long, dark hallway to face a firing squad."

"Oh shit, it's that bad?" Rashad laughed. "Yeah, I might as well wash down a pill so I can be ready to make this commitment." He thought for a moment. "I can't believe I'm about to tell a woman who's not Kiara that I want to spend the rest of my life with her."

"Dude, go ahead and take that pill right now. I'm sick of you talking 'bout Kiara. Remember, she can't stand your black ass. She kicked you out your own house. You need to forget her, man. For real, for real."

"I don't know if I can ever forget Kiara. But yeah, I need to focus on the future. Stop chasing a woman who's running away from me. Making Kiara my wife was the happiest day of my life. But the past damn sure ain't trying to repeat itself today." Rashad opened his mouth, shoved the tablet down his throat, and quickly swallowed a shot of vodka. It burned so bad that he began to cough.

"You swear to God that this little pill won't kill me, right?"

"Nah, man. It won't kill you. But see, it's going to make your stomach feel fucked up for a minute, and you might feel as sick as a dog, throw up a little bit, but you'll live. You'll bounce back, though, a little later."

"I hope you're right."

The wedding would begin in two hours. Rashad knew that the effects of the pill would impact him real soon.

"Look, man. I need you to do a good job of recording my ceremony and reception, alright? Get lots of footage from the very beginning to the end. Just follow us around with the camera, getting different shots of us, the vows, the wedding party, the guests, the families' reactions, all of it."

"Sure, I got you."

Delbert kept his promise. He trailed Rashad throughout the wedding, capturing the peculiar way he slurred his words during the vows. Delbert got scared for a second, thinking that the pill had worked a little too good, but it turned out to be alright because before he knew it, Rashad

Eason repeated his vows well enough to earn a new wife. Delbert alternately laughed at Rashad and videotaped him turning up at his reception; Rashad drank like a college freshman, walking around with bloodshot eyes and laughing hysterically. Delbert just figured Rashad was happy to get it over with and was ready to party. Or maybe the man was trying to forget his first wife.

And after becoming a second-time husband, when Rashad realized that his marriage was over and he held his first consultation with Lily, she asked him if he could think of anything that had proved he was under duress at his wedding. That's when he remembered the recordings that Delbert had produced. And Rashad got excited. He told her yes. He brought the DVD to Lily, and she shook her head as she watched.

"My goodness, you were wasted. You could barely stand on your feet."

"And what does that mean for my case?"

"It could mean that you really didn't know what you were doing . . . You were too drunk to actually know what you were agreeing to when you stated your vows. We'll figure out something."

"Good."

"Rashad, it's none of my business—"

"If you want to talk me out of it, don't. I'm trying to regain my life, Lily. I need you to work your legal magic. Get those papers ready so she can be served like she's never been served before."

"As you wish," she said. Rashad hopped up and handed Lily a three-thousand-dollar cashier's check and told her he'd see her soon.

Chapter 11

Nicole couldn't believe it. It was Friday, a few days after Rashad had broken the devastating news to her. Ever since that moment, she felt as if her ship had sunk, and she'd been helplessly drifting at sea and trying to weather the storm without anything solid to grab on to. And last night, she'd found the courage to call her mother.

"Mama," she said, nearly sobbing. "I need you. I-I—"

"Come home, daughter. I'll book you an early flight. Can't wait to see you."

After spending a long evening of tossing and turning, she woke up in the wee hours of the morning. She packed a light bag, grabbed Emmy, and headed out the door. She drove to the airport and hopped on an airplane. It felt like the longest trip in her life as she sat in coach with her child wedged on her lap.

Nicole arrived in her native city within a few hours. Quite frankly, life felt bizarre the moment she realized her feet were back on Alabama soil. She caught a cab from BHM Airport to her old neighborhood, staring at the familiar sights that she knew so well: the high school where she'd decided she wanted to be somebody, and the little church that Evelyn had dragged her and the other girls to when they were teens.

After the cab driver got his cash and drove off, Nicole walked up the concrete steps to the front door of her mother's house. The door was unlocked, and she went inside and stood in the doorway, trembling like she was freezing as she took in the surroundings; the front area was a combination living room and kitchen with a large space for a table and chairs. This was the home where Nicole had spent her teenage years, the time in which she wanted to find herself and discover the meaning of life. It seemed as if nothing had changed. Same furniture, family photos, and dusty drapes. And the notion of life standing still brought about an intense sadness that added to her misery.

Right then, Nicole yearned for her own house back in Texas, the one that she'd chosen for her family to live in, but instead here she was, back at the very place she'd yearned to abandon in the years before she went away to college.

Like a blast of wind, Evelyn Greene breezed into the kitchen. They wordlessly stared at one another. Her mother gave Nicole a heartfelt squeeze that instantly made her feel more at ease.

"Well," Evelyn said, "don't you look prettier than a glob of butter on a stack of wheat cakes?"

The two women burst out laughing. "It's gonna be alright, Nicole. And thank you for taking a cab. I'll pay you back whatever it cost."

"No problem, Mama. I'm just glad you let me come over at such short notice."

Evelyn stole Emmy from Nicole's arms and plastered her fat cheeks with loving pecks. She called out over her shoulder as she shuffled away toward a rear bedroom,

"This precious baby is about to pass out. Bless her heart. I'll get her set up in your old room so she can enjoy a long nap."

"I appreciate that."

Having someone take charge and do something to lighten her load made Nicole feel as if she was being rescued from floating adrift. Her ship might have sunk, but it did not indicate that she was completely doomed. She wearily closed her eyes, still unable to believe she was no longer in Texas with her husband, Rashad.

Soon Evelyn returned. "Give me some sugar," she said. Nicole gave her mom the kiss that she'd been waiting for.

"Welcome back, Nicole. Seeing you here in this house feels good and odd at the same time. Like I'm seeing a ghost."

"You can say that again."

The elderly woman instantly switched into mother mode. They retreated farther inside the kitchen. While Nicole sat at the dinette table, Evelyn rattled back and forth, removing food items from the refrigerator and cabinets, and making lots of noise rattling pots and pans.

"I apologize, but I'm just now getting home after being on my feet all morning. I was hired to fix a fabulous breakfast for the elderly at that senior center around the corner. They're celebrating their fiftieth anniversary. The looks on their faces when they saw my food were priceless—"

Evelyn clamped her mouth shut. She saw the look of despair on Nicole's face and changed the subject.

"How was your flight?"

"I loved it. It felt good to get away."

They engaged in minor conversation about simple topics, ones that Evelyn hoped wouldn't rouse up more pain.

It was nearly lunchtime. Evelyn joyfully got started on a large pot of chicken and dumplings. Then she whipped up the ingredients to make a skillet corn bread. Lastly, she could not wait to cook her daughter a homemade banana pudding.

"I'm not used to this type of treatment. You're spoiling me, Mama."

"That's what good mothers do whenever they can."

"I'll have to remember to be just like you when I grow up." It felt wonderful to feel the love that her mother freely offered to her.

"Since you'll be here for dinner," Evelyn said, "I might as well get started on a slow-cooker stew while I'm at it." She rummaged through the refrigerator and found some leftover meat and vegetables.

Nicole enjoyed sitting back and observing how happy her mother appeared as she dramatically added her special seasonings to the pot. Before long the strange house slowly began to feel like home again, that warm, inviting feeling that makes you feel happy to have a family who loves and accepts you no matter how badly you mess up.

The aroma swiftly carried Nicole back into time. Things might have felt nice and loving right then, but they hadn't always been that easygoing. She clearly remembered the day when she'd decided she was going to leave Alabama and never come back. As usual, they were perched in the kitchen, hands in the dishwater after they'd cleared the dinner table.

"Hey, Mama. I had a telephone interview with a college in Houston."

"Oh, really? So, what are you trying to say?"

"I'm saying that I don't wanna live in the great Vestavia Hills anymore. I'm ready to do something different. Get away from it all. The world is bigger than this place, and I plan to experience it."

"*You're leaving me?*"

"*Leaving you?*"

"*Yes, if you leave this place, you're leaving me. And if you leave me, you are repeating the actions of your dad.*"

"*But wasn't Daddy treating you wrong? Weren't you glad he finally left?*"

"*He left me alone to raise you kids. That's what he did.*"

"*But, Mama, you can't blame the kids for what a grown-up does.*" Her father had been around ever since Nicole was born. But when she was seven, he went away, unable to handle the pressures of life. Overnight everything changed. For years her father had worked as an auto mechanic; he and Evelyn had always split the bills. But two incomes were chopped down to one. Evelyn was shocked when he left. But she couldn't afford to lose her mind or grow bitter. It was time to learn a new skill, take on a second job, and provide for herself and the four girls. Her goal was to take care of the household so well that it would be as if her man had never left. But as much as Evelyn wanted that to happen, things did not turn out that way.

Many times Nicole had to act like the parent when her mom was away earning money. She had to threaten Mimi and her two cousins to do their homework. She had to make sure they completed their chores and put away their toys. Nicole felt like an adult, not a child. But she wasn't getting the benefits of being an adult because she wasn't given an allowance no matter how much she helped around the house. It seemed so unfair.

And after she told her mother of her plans, she

*thought that Evelyn was resentful of Nicole's plans
to leave Alabama and live her own life. Nicole grew
terribly angry at both of her parents. In her mind,
they'd failed her. Failed to properly raise her.
Neglected to shower her with the amount of love, direction, care, and protection that she felt she should
have received while growing up. Instead of her dad
being around to fight her battles, Nicole had to fend
for herself. And she always remembered feeling
alone, even though she had a big family. They could
all be together in one room, but Nicole would be off
by herself, daydreaming, yearning for a happier
life, and feeling completely isolated. She'd want to
cry her eyes out, but instead she'd laugh, crack a
sassy joke, and smile as if everything was fine.
Other times, when she was drained after a long day
of attending high school then coming home to help
out with the girls, she'd lash out at her family and
spew cutting remarks to anyone who got on her
nerves.*

*But later down the road, when she was enrolled
in college, things somewhat changed. That was
when she first met Ajalon and they became a close-
knit couple; all they had was each other and they
somehow created their own happy existence. She
moved out of her mother's house and was living on
campus by then. She went to class, worked, and felt
more independent. Life seemed promising, and
Nicole didn't worry so much anymore about what
her mother thought or did. Ajalon Cantu became
her family, moving in with her and making plans for
their future. They were in love and nothing else mattered. But when her man got caught up in the drug
game and was sentenced to prison, her idyllic life*

rapidly changed. Once again she felt like she was by herself, trying to conquer the world. Their small apartment was lonely, and the bills were mounting. How could Ajalon leave her when she needed him the most? Why did her mother push her so hard to do something with her life, yet not extend a hand to help? Why was life so very hard? So incredibly unfair? Nicole resented people who seemed to have it easy. Women who had loving relationships with their fathers. They were "Daddy's little girl," the "apple of his eye." She wished she could have known how it felt to be loved in that way. She wished that she could have met the right type of guy who would give her the unconditional love that she craved with her very soul. No. Instead Nicole Greene was forced to make her own way in life. Make really hard decisions all by herself. Ordered to act mature when she wanted to be a little girl.

So the day when Nicole felt she really grew up was the day when she decided to accept the job at Texas South West University in Houston. She was shocked she even got the offer. It was a telephone interview, and the second and final interview had been conducted via webcam. So she must have made a decent impression. She was grateful for the opportunity to work as a media coordinator at TSWU. She actually felt her confidence get boosted. Maybe she could have a decent life. That was why she had to tell her mom good-bye. That was why she'd wished her sister, Mimi, well and warned her to be strong. She wanted Mimi to rise up and be a determined, single black woman, just like she was trying to be. And although Nicole felt up to the task, she never abandoned her deepest desire: to do well

and share her life with a good man. But now the
only dream she'd ever entertained was gone.

Finally, their meal was ready. The house smelled like bread, meat, and vegetables, and Nicole was starving. Evelyn fixed her a plate of food, while Nicole sat barefoot at the table thumbing through sales papers from the neighborhood grocery store.

"I can't believe this store is still around the corner."

"Yep, sure is. Some things won't change, while other things are never the same," Evelyn told her.

"But all of this feels so strange. Sitting at your table. About to eat your food again." Nicole wanted to laugh even though her emotions made her want to cry.

"When you think about life, it's not so strange. We all end up back home at some point."

"I never wanted to return like this, though."

"God has his way of getting something to happen in your life that you never thought would happen."

"God has nothing to do with this," Nicole snapped at her mother.

Evelyn laughed till her shoulders shook. She stopped what she was doing and started singing an old gospel song that Nicole remembered hearing as a child.

It sounded depressing, not encouraging at all. But she let her mother continue to sing until she was done.

Evelyn brought Nicole a glass filled with sweet tea and ice cubes, then she finally sat down and rested her aching feet. It felt good to be in the same room with her child and able to do something for her, even if it was just to feed Nicole. The two women bent their heads and said a blessing. Then they took the first bite of their meal and enjoyed their time together. At first things felt homey, but then they grew awkward.

All while she was traveling through the friendly skies, Nicole had worried whether she'd receive a friendly welcome. She prayed and hoped that this trip would do her some good and provide answers to questions that she had. Nicole was relieved to find her mother in a warm and welcoming mood. Yet as Nicole sipped her tea, she felt angry and very helpless.

"I'm not gonna lie, daughter. I was wondering if you'd ever come back here," Evelyn told her.

"Mama, like I told you before, I probably was going to visit you at some point, I guess."

"But troubles get you home quicker than when things are going great, right? Thank God for bad times, or else I might have never seen you again."

Evelyn's words cut with a sharpness that filled Nicole with shame. She prayed the woman would cut her some slack, since Nicole clearly remembered how self-righteous she had acted on her wedding day. She knew her mom assumed that it would be a cold day in hell before she ever saw her again.

Nicole apologized and thanked her mom for her hospitality, especially on short notice.

"As I said last night when I called you, Rashad and I had a bad argument. I was itching to get away, and on the spur of the moment, I told Rashad I wanted to take Emmy home with me for a couple of days and that we'd be back on Sunday."

"How'd he react?"

"He refused to let her go at first."

"Why?"

"Why else do crazy men act crazy over their kids? They think the mother is plotting to kidnap the child and never let him see her again. I was shocked he would even accuse me of doing anything like that."

"So, how did you convince him you aren't a kidnapper?"

"I remained calm. I didn't curse him. I told him that you wanted to see your grandbaby. That you missed us and had offered to pay for us to come see you."

"In other words, you lied about me to get him to let you go?" Evelyn smiled. "I guess I owe you plane fare, too, huh?"

"No, you don't. I had the money for our flights, and yeah, it cost a grip but it's fine. I gave Rashad my itinerary so he would know that I was serious. That I had a scheduled return flight and I'd be home in a couple of days."

"Nicole, don't let the left hand know what the right is doing. I'll bet Rashad doesn't tell you every single move he makes. I'll bet this house he don't do that."

"All I can say is that I'll follow your advice next time, Mama." She sighed heavily. "I needed to get away, clear my head. That's why I'm here."

"I'm glad you're here. You look like someone set your face on fire and beat it out with a logging chain."

"That bad, Mama?"

"That bad. Now, start from the beginning. What happened exactly?"

"My own husband told me that he's done with our relationship. It feels like some sort of sick joke. And no, I don't agree with his decision. It's too rash. And cruel."

"You had no heads-up about him doing this at all?"

"No. He was gone a lot and not talking to me that much this past week, but I thought it was because he wasn't feeling well due to the medications. I never told you that he hurt himself at a construction site, so yeah, he's been pretty moody since then. Or, if it had nothing to do with him being in pain, I was thinking he might be mad at me because he assumed all I cared about was him getting back to work."

"Were you, Nicole? It's hard for a lot of women to see their man in a weak state, especially if she's a hardworking black woman. Did you hate seeing him lie around the house, because you thought it made him look like a bum, but you forgot that he was actually sick?"

"Oh, Mama, please. I knew he needed time to heal and I wanted him to get better. But none of that matters right now. Because if he is serious about opting out, and I believe he is, I hate him, Mama. He's made a fool out of me, especially if he has found someone else already. Some men love to keep a back-burner bitch in their life so if they ever break up with the main chick, they can just take up with the one who's been waiting on the side. She steps right in and he never misses a beat. And if that's what Rashad has done, I want him to pay for the shit he's put me through."

"Isn't that what you did?"

"Yeah? And so?"

Evelyn sighed. "So why is it that you now want to make him pay for what he's done to you?"

"Because it's not fair."

"Unfair things happen to people every day and you know it. That's life."

"But I never wanted my life to be like this. Rashad's marriage was already on death row by the time we met. And I knew he was a good man. He gave me hope. And he made me want to forget Ajalon Cantu and move on to better things. So, for me to get a taste of happiness just to have it all snatched away from me—"

"I understand how you feel."

"Do you?"

"Yes. I've been where you are. When I found out I had

to raise you girls on my own, it's not like I knew six months in advance where my life would be headed."

"Mama, in some ways I feel like I have the right to be mad. In other ways, I question what I did to contribute to my current situation."

"Girl, don't waste your time. It is what it is. Don't sugarcoat anything or else you may end up repeating things you wished you had left alone."

"What do you mean? Help me understand."

Evelyn shook her head and smiled. "When I tell you I have been where you are, I mean it. I have walked in the very path that you're taking. Your daddy left and I hated him. I thought he was just being a selfish bastard and he was acting slicker than owl shit, but then I thought about it. Our life together was beautiful until I came home one day with your two little cousins and told him that they'd be living with us."

"I remember that. We all had to sleep in that one bedroom. You got us bunk beds. At first I had my own bed, but after they came to live with us, I had to sleep with Mimi. I hated it."

"Right. And so I can admit that our life changed because I took in my sister's kids."

"My crackhead aunt Jocelyn?"

"Yes. I didn't want to see these kids stay in a bad situation, with Jocelyn unable to control her habit. They were so unstable they had to enroll in a new school every two weeks. So I went and picked the girls up from my sister and that was that. Your daddy had no heads-up. He wanted a say-so. But at the time, I was like, 'Ain't nothing to think about. These babies are my nieces and I won't have them in the streets.' Oh, we fought like a Komodo dragon attacking a deer. He argued. I shoved him around and accused him of wimping out and acting like we couldn't handle the extra mouths. He tried living with all of us for a month or so. And after a while, he got abusive with his fists. I stood my ground about my nieces, and he acted like he wanted to kill me. And I got sick of the fighting, and we both agreed he had to go."

Nicole finally had the truth about some of her family's history. Now she knew why her mother had made up stories about what really happened when she was a kid. The reality of their situation would have been too much for a young girl to handle.

"Okay. So you blindsided Daddy. And he didn't want to live with all of us under the same roof, and he got the hell out of Dodge. I'm sure you didn't expect him to actually go and never come back. So, how'd you deal with it?"

"I was pissed. I was ready to grab the first iron skillet out the kitchen, hop in my car, find him, and beat his raggedy-weak ass for putting such a hardship on me. I felt we could have compromised, worked something out. But he wasn't having it, and I wanted to bash his head in with a skillet and then kill him. But what good would all that do? I didn't want to give him that much power. I didn't want my anger to cause me to do something I'd regret. So—"

"So you changed your mind about bashing his head in with the frying pan?"

"Yes. I had more important things to do. Like take that skillet home and cook four girls something to eat."

"You're a better woman than I am. I-I've wanted a good life for so long now that it's just part of my soul. My dreams and wishes mean the world to me. Do you know that I was scared Rashad might not even show up at the church on our wedding day? That night before our wedding I had to change pajamas twice. That's how much I sweated on those sheets."

"Sounds like a nightmare and nothing like a dream, Nicole."

"That's what I'm saying. I closed my eyes and pictured myself having everything that I ended up getting. And knowing I could live that way felt so good, so scary, yet so wonderful all at the same time. Mama, I wanted that good feeling to last forever. But it's over and it's not fair. And someone will have to pay."

"Really?" Evelyn laughed. "You sound young."

"I am young, and I am hurt."

"No, listen to me good. When you're still young, you have time to dream again."

"Lots of young people die prematurely all the time. Besides, I don't want to dream again. I want what I've already got. Mama, I don't care how young I am, I'm not ready to start all over, start from the bottom and crawl and fight my way back up to the top. Why would I want to do that when it's taken me so long to get the good things that I've achieved? Rashad is a fool if he thinks I'm going to walk away easily. He promised me a good life, then he acted like I did something wrong. That bastard will pay one way or another."

Nicole's mother listened to her bitter ramblings. Lifelong dreams that were unmercifully snatched away could kill some people. But some dreams were just illusions, unlawfully acquired. And Evelyn knew how Nicole initially got involved with Rashad. She couldn't help but question her, "When you tell me that Rashad has to pay for hurting you, is it the mistress part of you that wants revenge, or the wife?"

"Huh? I don't know what you're asking me."

"You're shocked. Angry. Afraid. A lot of bad things are now happening to you, Nicole. You did not predict this outcome. But you seem to forget about the mess that you put another wife through not too long ago. When you first told me how you and Rashad met, it just sounded bad. I couldn't be totally happy for you because I was afraid of how it might end up. I told you—"

"Mama, I do not want to hear anything else about that karma stuff, alright? You sound like a broken-ass record that keeps getting fixed and then breaks all over again. Enough already."

"Apparently, it ain't enough. Because if you do believe in karma and you're too stupid to take it serious, then you deserve every bad thing that happens to you. Stop being foolish and thinking you can get away with doing wrong. You can accept your punishment and be a woman, walk away from this mess of a marriage, and keep your hands clean, or you can go play around with karma again and find yourself in a deeper mess."

"Now you're exaggerating."

"Am I?" Her mother studied her. "I have no control over how things happen, the bad things that people bring on themselves. And you don't, either. The only way to control the bad is to not do anything to earn the bad."

"I don't wanna hear it. I don't care what I've done, his actions cannot be forgiven, Mama. Rashad wants to divorce me and I don't deserve that. He will not get away with hurting me."

"Your husband wants out. So be it. You can be angry about the truth, Nicole, but it won't change your reality." Feeling angry herself, Evelyn paused to allow her declaration to sink in. "It's not your job to pay him back, sweetie."

"But what am I supposed to do with this anger, then, huh? Am I supposed to just let him dump me like trash and not say a word, just agree with it, just sign away my marriage like it never even happened, and keep my mouth shut

even though I want to scream? If I were to do that, it would
be like I have no say-so in the matter, and that's not right.
Like he counts and I don't. And I do matter—I do." Nicole
had had enough. The situation was too overwhelming. She
wondered whether she would ever feel happiness, but it
did not seem likely. What on earth was she doing in Alabama? She missed her big house. Missed her master bedroom. Missed her life. She sat at the table and began to
weep. Salty tears streamed into her mouth. She could barely
see as water poured from her eyes.

How could someone who knows how much you love
him treat you so badly? How could her own husband treat
her like she was worthless and that her feelings didn't matter? How could he not even give her a second chance?
What about what she wanted? It all seemed so unfair and
so wrong. Rashad had been her anchor, but now he'd
pushed himself away from her. Leaving her to reach out
for him. Leaving her stranded and helplessly going down
on her sinking ship. She just couldn't imagine herself letting Rashad go about his life and leaving her to drown. Her
mother might have changed her mind about punishing her
dad for hurting her, but Nicole vowed to do things differently. No mercy. No regrets.

After enjoying a couple of days wandering through the
Birmingham area and revisiting her old stomping grounds,
Nicole made her way back to Texas. Her mom got out of
the car and said good-bye at the Southwest Airlines passenger drop-off. Evelyn told Emmy she loved her, then she
hugged Nicole and firmly begged her, "Hanging on to hurt
is like swallowing deadly poison. Please don't do that. Letting go of bitterness may give you the strength you need to
get through your divorce."

"There isn't going to be a divorce," Nicole snapped. "He cannot divorce me."

Throughout the flight, she thought about how she was going to handle her problems as she held Emmy on her lap. After her plane landed in Houston, she picked up her Jeep from the airport parking lot and started the long drive home. She pulled up to her and Rashad's house and enjoyed the comfort it gave her. She aimed the garage door opener as she drove up the driveway. Nothing happened. Thinking the battery wasn't working, she smacked the device several times and pressed the button again. The door remained closed.

Nicole got out of the car and walked over to the keypad that was secured next to the garage. She flipped open the lid and punched in the passcode. Nothing!

"The fuck?"

Irritated and exhausted from the trip, Nicole trudged to the front door and inserted her key. It went in halfway, but it was apparent that it no longer fit the keyhole.

She banged her fists against the door and rang the bell. Her cell phone lit up.

"Rashad, I just got back from my trip, and I'm tired as hell. I tried to put my key in the door and it doesn't work. Neither does my passcode to get into the garage."

"Yeah, about the key. There is a new one underneath the welcome mat. It's there for you. Go look."

"Oh, okay, you changed the lock but gave me a new key." She lifted up the rug and got the key, but when she tried to insert it, it didn't fit, either.

"Rashad, what the hell is going on? This key won't work."

"The key that's under the rug is to an apartment. The apartment that I got for you."

"Why'd you get it for me? I don't understand."

"Nicole, at first I was going to live there. But I changed my mind. I don't feel I should have to move out. So while you were out of town, I boxed up your stuff and delivered it all to the apartment that I was going to lease. Now it's your place. It's a nice complex with good amenities. The first three months' rent is already paid."

"Wait a minute—you're actually putting me out? Who the hell do you think you are? I'm your fucking wife, not your child."

"But I told you, we're through."

"Rashad, c'mon, this is too much. I can't take this. How can you do this to me?"

"We can't live together if we're breaking up. Don't worry, you're gonna like this place, Nicole. Go check it out, alright?"

"Rashad . . . I don't even know where this place is."

"It's in a real nice area."

"You dirty-ass motherfucker. How dare you put me out?"

"Nicole, I didn't even have to provide a rent-free apartment for you. I could have literally made you homeless, but I didn't."

Nicole's head was spinning. None of what was happening seemed real.

"What have I ever done to you for you to treat me like shit?"

"Everybody has a right to be happy."

"I get that. But why do me like this when you know how it feels to go through your own breakup? When Kiara kicked you out of your own house, who took you in, Rashad?"

He fell embarrassingly silent. Nicole was right. She did invite him to come and stay with her for as long as he wanted. But that was then.

Rashad was fully aware of how emotional Nicole could

be. And it was better to break things off without letting her negotiate. He knew if she had her way and he let her back in their house, she'd start with a long kiss, then advance to a striptease, she'd suck his dick like it was the last one on earth, and soon they'd be banging each other like two rabbits in a field. She'd skillfully convince him to change his mind and the divorce would be off. But he didn't want Nicole to entertain useless dreams anymore. He knew he'd hurt her with his sudden decision, but the hurt would destroy her heart even if he let her down easy.

"Nicole, you're right about that. And I thank you for helping me out back then, but this is a different situation. I-I can't leave my house. I don't want to. This time around I will be the husband who gets to stay in the house he's paid for. Plus, this place is so big that eventually I plan to sell it. I probably won't even be here that long. I'm starting over. I need a break." He started rambling on and on like he was talking out loud to himself. "And Kiara, my first love, still loves me. I know she does. She might even want to move into this house. And I need space to figure it all out."

"Did you say Kiara? And you? That's who you were talking about?"

Rashad realized he accidentally told her the truth.

"Yes, Nicole."

"And y'all are seriously getting back together? And you're moving that bitch into my fucking house?"

"She's not a bitch."

"You're defending her? Oh God. This is nuts."

"It's not nuts. It's reality. And it's very possible that once Kiara sees the house, she'll want to move in. I'd like that very much. We're taking things one day at a time—"

Nicole pressed the button on her phone and hung up on him while he was still rambling about his future dreams. She couldn't believe what had just transpired.

"How can he give to her what he promised to me? There is no way she will have him, have the house I selected, and get everything I've ever wanted."

She stood back and stared at the beautiful, elegant home that she'd been so proud of the day they'd moved in. Then she stared at her vehicle.

"What if that punk decides to take my car, too?"

Nicole was tempted to call Kiara and tell her off, but that would be the wrong move. She really needed her job and this time her boss might successfully fire her if she overstepped her boundaries. So she swallowed her humiliation and got in her Jeep. Emmy was looking tired and hungry. Although she didn't want to do it, it was time to forget about herself.

Feeling dazed, she put the Jeep into reverse, backed out of the driveway, and drove off.

It felt weird to call another place "home" that twenty-four hours earlier she hadn't known existed. Nicole drove into the parking lot of the apartment complex where Rashad had signed a lease. It was a first-floor unit. She got Emmy out the car, walked to the door, and let herself in. She cautiously inspected the entire place: a tiny living room, a quaint kitchen, an oversized bedroom with two walk-in closets, and a decent-sized bath. Boxes filled with all of her personal belongings were lined up against the wall of the largest bedroom. And to her surprise, the place was fully furnished.

A leather sofa, matching chair, and a rocking chair were nicely arranged in the living room. She even noticed a photo of herself and Emmy sitting in a frame on an end table.

"I don't know whether to be grateful or to call him up and tell him to go to hell."

But she did what she had to do and mentally told herself to get used to living in this place. She literally had nowhere else to go.

Nicole was feeling weak and getting hungry. She went into the kitchen and looked around. She noticed that the refrigerator was stocked with the basics: milk, a carton of eggs, juice, water, fresh vegetables, all the condiments, breakfast meats, and a gallon of sweet tea. The cupboards were full of baby food for her daughter. There was cereal, rice, sugar, pasta, beans, and cornmeal.

It looked like a welcoming committee had set up everything. And when she glanced at the door of the refrigerator and noticed a rectangular magnet with the words "Welcome Home," she burst out laughing. "How fucking thoughtful," she said sarcastically as she glided her finger over its slick surface. "He thinks of everything, doesn't he?"

The fact that he could be so kind to her while kicking her out, but act like a prick to her while she was in his presence, simply amazed her.

Instead of wasting time making sense of Rashad's behavior, Nicole mustered up the mental strength to prepare a quick dinner. She pulled Emmy's bouncy chair into the kitchen and talked to her as she tried to cook.

"It's just me and you, baby. I feel like I've turned into my mother. But that's all right. As long as you love me and I love you, we'll be just fine."

When she was done fixing eggs, sausage, and toast, she placed her daughter in her high chair and filled her sippy cup with juice.

They sat and ate in silence. Nicole fed Emmy with a spoon and made sure she didn't get any eggs in her hair.

Why did her baby have to look so much like her daddy?

Nicole could barely look Emmy in the eyes. She tried not to break down crying. The apartment was so silent and its sterile atmosphere presented a complete contrast to her vision of eating meals together with her family.

Once they were done, Nicole cleaned the kitchen and then decided to pick up a book and read to her daughter. But all of the books seemed to be about happy things—happy families and even happier animals.

"I'm going to have to buy you some new books," she complained and slammed the book shut.

An hour later, when Emmy started pulling on Nicole's leg, repeating the phrase, "Go home. Go home," Nicole began to bawl.

"This is our home now, Emmy. Daddy doesn't want us anymore."

The four walls of the small apartment were closing in on Nicole. She couldn't stand being there a second longer. It reminded her of how far she'd fallen.

So instead of thinking about what she'd lost, she decided to take inventory of what she had.

"I still got my health and my strength. I have a job and food and clothes, even expensive shoes that I can sell if I have to. And I have my precious baby," she said as she wiped the tears from her eyes. "I've been to hell and back. So this annoys me, but I won't let it break me. I have my car and a tank full of gas. And I still have all my joint credit cards."

She fished out all of the credit cards and called each company to see whether the cards were still active. Two were, but two others were now inactivated.

Nicole quickly ended the last call, feeling like she'd been pulled into a boxing ring.

She picked up her cell phone again and immediately dialed a number. When the person did not answer, Nicole grabbed her purse, her keys, her phone, and her daughter, and locked the apartment door behind her. She sped off in her Jeep and was soon on the road. She finally arrived at her destination, turning right at the entrance and slowly creeping past the metal gates so she could park within the complex grounds.

She noticed Ajalon's car and started walking up the steps with Emmy clinging to her waist. The windows of his apartment started vibrating. The bassline of a Drake song began to play.

"Thank God," she said. "Daddy's home."

Ajalon Cantu was her "Clyde" and she was his "Bonnie." The bond they'd shared and the influence he'd had on Nicole could never be broken. His love always felt so intoxicating, and right now she needed to know that a man was in her corner.

As she stood in front of his door, anticipating the look on his face when he saw her, she recalled how good he was at convincing her to do things she did not want to do. It was the way that he talked, the confident way he carried himself. She knew that she, in turn, would have to convince him to help her, just like she had helped him.

It was a cool, breezy night in the middle of autumn. They were at their home in Alabama, kicking it. Ajalon sat on the couch with his legs spread wide open, his big feet lazily perched on top of the coffee table. The volume of the TV was high, and Nicole was content to sit next to her man with her head leaning on his shoulder. A call came through on Ajalon's phone. Once he ended the conversation, he looked at Nicole.

"C'mon, Bella," he said to her. "Come take a ride with me."

"Okay," she said, instantly springing to her feet. "Where are we going?"

"Just trust me. Can you do that? Can you trust me to protect you?"

"You're so adorable it's unreal," she told him. And they were off. Ajalon took the wheel and drove away from the safety of their home, venturing toward a place unknown. They laughed and joked during the ride. She noticed how often he checked his rearview mirror, yet he managed to remain cool and calm.

After they'd traveled less than thirty minutes, he pulled up in front of a two-story flat, and asked her to wait in the car. She told him she would. She let him know that she was hungry, though, so he had to hurry.

"It won't take long. I promise."

Ajalon looked in every direction before exiting the car. Nicole studied him as he walked up to a strange man who was standing on the porch. They greeted one another, then quickly exchanged items. She saw Ajalon slide some cash in his pocket. The two guys laughed and talked for a minute. Then the guy abruptly left, rushing through the doorway and slamming the door shut.

Ajalon returned to the car, whose engine was still running. "Told ya I wouldn't be long. Now, let's go eat."

He didn't say another word. They drove off in silence. And deep inside she realized he was taking care of his business. Trash and discarded debris lined the street. The neighborhood looked old and neglected. A dozen young men hung out on the corner in front of an ancient-looking liquor store. To

Nicole, it seemed like the guys had nothing but time. She never wanted her man to be like one of them.

Nicole shivered and pulled a sweater over her shoulders. "Hurry. Run that red light, don't even stop at that intersection up ahead."

"I-I got to stop," he told her in a nervous voice. He was looking at his rearview. She turned and looked behind her. Saw the patrol car that was now directly behind them. She froze in her seat, feeling hot now instead of cold. Nicole understood why there were times when you couldn't run a red light. They stopped at the corner, obeyed the law, and looked the part of good, law-abiding citizens.

The light turned green. Ajalon slowly drove through the intersection. Maintained his speed until the cop followed behind them for a block, then made a left at a darkened street, then went on its way.

She sighed in relief.

"I never want to go through that again. Don't put me in any more dangerous situations. You hear me?"

"I hear you," he said. And she could've kicked herself for agreeing to accompany him, agreeing to go along with activities that made her uncomfortable and then angry. But Nicole loved Ajalon. And though she did not like what he did, she knew that what had just transpired could happen again. The things that we tend to despise can somehow repeat themselves and make us question ourselves.

During that time of her life, Nicole felt conflicted. She knew Ajalon sold dodi weed and Crissy or glass, the street names for crystal meth. Nicole always felt nervous about what he did, but she went along with it as long as he kept her out of his plans.

Back then she told him, "As long as you know what you're doing, I guess it'll be alright."

"I know what I'm doing," he assured her. Since she refused to accompany him anymore, he'd go on drug runs by himself. Nicole would wait at home and feel scared to death that he'd get caught one day.

"I'm too smart to get caught."

"That's the same thing that the last man said, yet he still got arrested."

Ajalon simply laughed and asked her to trust him. But trusting the man she loved was risky.

There was something intoxicating about Ajalon and this was why she found herself being drawn back to him years later. She stood there on the landing outside of his apartment in Houston, seconds away from knocking on her ex's door. She could have left right then. She could have told herself to leave and stick with her promise to never become involved with him again.

For the memories we leave behind should serve as a warning to leave some people alone. And just before Nicole decided to knock on his door, she recalled how dangerous it felt for her to love him.

Nicole and Ajalon were in Birmingham at his friend's Hosea's apartment. The two lovers were sprawled on the couch, kissing and feeling each other up. He massaged her breasts until her nipples grew as hard as pebbles. She teased his neck with kisses until he begged her to let him make love to her. But she told him she had to use the bathroom. She hopped to her feet and told him she'd be right back . . . Hosea was standing on the second-floor balcony so he wouldn't have to witness Ajalon getting it on with his girlfriend.

While Nicole was hidden away in the bathroom, she found a magazine to read. Meanwhile, she heard a commotion outside the bathroom door. There was shouting and strange voices. It sounded like something big and hard was being thrown against the walls. Fear gripped her heart. She set aside the magazine and was afraid to flush the toilet. But she pulled up her underwear and waited. When it grew eerily quiet, she cautiously opened the door and took a peek. From where she stood, she could see several uniformed police walking back and forth in the living room where she'd just been. She heard the sounds of ringing telephones, shouts, and people talking excitedly. Some were placing drug paraphernalia in clear plastic bags. Nicole quickly escaped down the hall. She ran into Hosea's bedroom and quietly locked the door. She looked around. There was nowhere to hide. He only had a mattress laid out on the floor. The sounds of footsteps approached Hosea's room. Fearing for her life, Nicole ran over to the window. She undid the latch and raised the window. She climbed out of the window and forgot to close it. She was now on Hosea's balcony with a view of a wooded area. Nicole climbed over the metal railing and jumped. She landed and hurt her ankle. She rose to her feet and limped away until she was able to reach the side of the apartment. By then Ajalon and Hosea were in handcuffs and being led away by two state troopers. She was shaking terribly. But she remained there, unseen, watching her man being taken from her. And when

Hosea and Ajalon were eventually charged with the selling of controlled substances, Nicole felt guilty as hell. She knew she could have been arrested, too. That's why Ajalon always reminded her that because of him she had her freedom and could pursue her dreams.

And now that her life was in shambles, Nicole knew she had to turn to Ajalon. She knew the love was still there, and maybe his love for her would be the only thing that could save her.

Nicole took a deep breath, pounded the door with her fists, and rang the bell.

"Hey, Ajalon, it's me. Open the door."

The Drake song that shook the windows stopped playing.

The door swung open. Her ex stood before her, an amused smile stretched across his face. His dark eyes lit up.

"My Bella escaped from her dream world and is now standing in front of me in real life."

She rushed into his arms and pressed her lips against his neck.

"*Ciao*, Ajalon."

Nicole loved being back in Ajalon's arms. He hugged her warmly, and it was as if they'd never parted. He stood back and observed her.

"Nicole, I am surprised to see you standing here. I thought your knight in shining armor had kidnapped you forever. In fact, I was tempted to return to Birmingham. But something compelled me to stay."

"Was it love?"

"Love is the best reason to wait for you."

"Well, whatever the reason, I'm glad you didn't go back."

"Me, too. Because even though I had my doubts, something told me that one day we'd see each other again. I'd bet my life on it."

"You're just too damn confident, Ajalon."

She laughed and stepped inside the apartment. She quickly closed the door. "I honestly didn't think I'd see you again. But things have changed. And that is why I'm here."

Nicole lowered Emmy to the floor, but then picked her up and placed her on the sofa. She handed her daughter a sippy cup filled with a beverage that would soon cause the girl to fall asleep. Nicole didn't want the baby to hear what she was about to say. It was too risky, especially since Emmy liked to repeat words that she heard.

Ajalon also took a seat on his sofa. It had been a good six months since they'd seen each other.

"Ajalon, have you been working out?"

"Oh, you noticed."

"I notice everything about you."

He blushed and told her how he would lift weights and do push-ups every day in his apartment complex's workout room; increasing his strength as if he was preparing for a boxing match.

"Funny you should say that."

Nicole watched Emmy drink from her cup. She waited ten minutes until the child closed her eyes and fell asleep. Then she turned to face Ajalon. He gave her a look of approval as his eyes scanned her body. She wasn't showing a baby bump yet, and she looked good.

"My Bella did not forget me after all."

"I could never forget you nor the fun we had."

"It took you all this time to admit you missed what you used to have?"

"I guess. It's funny how things work out. Because though you crossed my mind here and there, I honestly believed that I'd moved on with my life. What we had seemed like ancient history."

He told her that he understood completely how she felt.

"How is your new husband? Does he know you're over here with me? I think I already know the answer. It doesn't matter, though. You've always belonged to me. Always." He suddenly stood up and pulled Nicole to her feet. He wildly swung Nicole around in his arms. He peppered her cheeks with quick kisses. She laughed and told him to stop, but when he refused to quit she didn't mind.

With their faces drawn close, her lips soon found his. Nicole closed her eyes and let herself get lost once again inside the world of Ajalon Cantu. She moaned as they tongued one another, hungrily exploring each other's mouths with sensual kisses. That old good feeling returned just that quick.

She came up for air as he let her down and she stood solidly on her feet.

"Babe, I just want to tell you I'm sorry how things played out, you know, back when I chose him over you. I-I think I made a mistake. Because right now he's not acting like a good husband. I was crazy about that man. And I always thought that my loyalty would be rewarded."

"What kind of loyalty?" he asked.

"The ride-or-die type of loyalty. The kind of woman who stays with her man even if he's not doing her right. She stays, not because she agrees with his bad behavior but because she believes in him overall. Believes in his potential and his ability to get things right one day."

"Hmm, funny that you should say that, Bella. As I re-call, that is exactly what I wished you would have done for me back in Alabama."

She started pacing. "Here we go again. Why does it seem like everyone close to me wants to keep me glued to a time that is long gone? Birmingham this, Birmingham that. I can-not undo my past. I'm sorry, alright? Plus, I have much big-ger problems that I'm facing as we speak."

Ajalon looked concerned and decided to hear her out. "Come. Sit. Tell me all about it."

Perched beside him, she began to explain at a rapid pace how her brand-new spouse was now demanding an annul-ment.

"He fussed at me and then filed on me. Ajalon. He blindsided me big-time."

"I see."

"We went through all this trouble to be together. It all feels like such a waste. Money. Moving. Everything."

"You moved? Where?"

"From that dump where you found me last August, to my dream home, which I adored. I was finally living the life. But now he wants out, and I just moved into a place he picked out for me."

"And can I have the address of this new place?"

"Let me write it down." She found a sheet of paper and scribbled down her address.

"I'm scared, Ajalon. I will be on my own again. Rents in Houston are so fucking ridiculous. The price of food is out of control. Then there's my car payment, student loans, everything."

"Don't let it stress you."

"Ajalon, you know me. I hate feeling unstable. And it's worse now that I have my daughter. What an awful situation he's put us in. Yet it's real. And the fact that I'm here with you right now? That's crazier than real."

"Hmm, I thought you were glad to be here with me right now."

"Don't get me wrong, I am glad. But I hate how I got to be here. In fact, it feels like I've been tossed into hell."

He gave her a sad look.

"You don't make me feel bad, babe. The man that I thought was good for me makes me feel bad."

"I hate seeing you look so upset. You know how crazy I get when anyone makes you upset. What do you plan to do? Are you here because you want to get back with me again? Is that why you're in my home, eh?"

Nicole hesitated. She cared about him, but she needed him for other reasons besides love and wild sex. But she didn't want to hurt his feelings. She told him, "You know I've always loved you. I never stopped thinking about you. And yes, just like you told me last year, I, too, believe that we can make it this time. We have more in common anyway." She paused as she carefully pondered her words. "Yet, of course, at the same time, I still have feelings . . . for my husband. Is that understandable? I-I was going to try and fight the divorce. And I will fight, in that I plan to take every dime from him that I can. But, Ajalon, getting his money won't be enough." Her voice dropped to almost a whisper. "I need something bad to happen to him."

"Bad, eh? Such as a tragic accident?"

"Yes, a really bad accident. He can't walk away from it and end up in a hospital. He can't make it out alive."

"Nicole, do you . . . do you understand what you're saying?"

"Yes."

"But why?"

"Because sometimes taking the fucking high road is the wrong way to travel. I don't want to just let it go. Do you understand that people treat other people like shit all the time and get away with it? That's not right. I don't deserve it. I don't."

"Alright, okay, calm down. You're angry and you have a right to be. But, Nicole. Think about it. You're mad at him, but you also have his child."

"I know. Yes, it's crazy. But the things he's intentionally doing to me are driving me crazy. So tell me something. Why do I have to think about our child when he obviously isn't thinking about her? If he really cared about Emmy, no way he'd force us out of our home. If he really loved us, he'd put our needs above his, but no. Loving me isn't on his mind. And because of that he needs to leave this earth . . . soon."

Ajalon raised his eyebrows. "How is his 'leaving the earth,' as you say, going to happen?"

"I've been thinking. Construction site accidents happen all the time. In fact, he is recovering from a fall as we speak. It hurt him but it didn't kill him. Next time he needs to go away in a coroner's truck instead of an ambulance."

"I see. Nicole, you don't sound as if you love him. It sounds like hate to me."

"I hate what he's done. In fact, now that I think of it, it explains why Rashad was drunk on our wedding day. He had real bad jitters. Like he wasn't sure he could go through with it. He drank like a fish and my man doesn't even drink that much under normal circumstances. So yeah, he played me for a fool in front of everybody."

She buried her face in her hands. "I'm too damn young to be divorced with a child. It makes me look ghetto."

"You are ghetto. You just don't know it."

She side-eyed him. "Be serious. Life is so weird. You

just never know what can happen. So, Ajalon, let's talk about you. How are things going for you?"

"As you know, I quit my job at Eason and Son. After that I got more temp jobs here and there. Enough to pay rent but not much else."

"So you've kept your hands clean, Ajalon? You ain't messing around with drug dealers, are you?"

"No, Nicole. I'm straight."

"Good. But jobs are tight and you can use some money, right?"

"Always."

"Good. Because thankfully, I still have some cash on hand. I-I have enough to pay you to help me out."

"What does that mean?"

"Ajalon, I will pay you twenty-five hundred to make something bad happen to him."

"That's a lot of money. I could use it, too."

"So, what about it? Can you help me?"

He looked puzzled. "If you love me, why would you want me to do this? To commit a crime and potentially put my life on the line, just to kill your husband? What if something goes wrong? Does he have a gun?"

"I have one, but you definitely can't use mine. He has one, too, but no, you couldn't use that, either. You're going to have to find your own weapon."

"Wait. I thought you said you wanted him to die due to a work accident."

"I've changed my mind. I want him to suffer. I want him to know for a fact that he's dying because someone wants him dead, not because of a freak accident that could happen to anybody."

"Nicole, I'm not sure—"

"But I am. I remember how you told me very specifically you had traveled to Texas to be with me. You sought

me out. You told me you were sorry. You made me feel that
you wanted to prove your love to me. So, this is the way to
make me believe once and for all that you're serious."

Ajalon said nothing. He just stared into space.

"You are still serious about me, right? I mean, we
haven't seen or talked to each other in six months. Have
you been fucking any other bitches since I've been gone?"

"No," he lied. In fact, he and Nadia had hooked up a
couple of times. He'd run into Nicole's nanny one day at
the grocery store. She immediately remembered Ajalon
and slipped him her phone number. He called her the same
day. And when she had a free moment, she stopped by to
visit him. After a little bit of conversation, he sexually de-
voured this woman and thought nothing of it. But their little hookups were only a sex thing, and he knew Nicole
would kill him if she found out. "Of course I haven't been
with anyone else. I've been sitting back waiting on this
day, as a matter of fact. I'm surprised it came so fast. You
came back to me. We returned to each other. Our love is for
real."

"I know that's right."

Ajalon asked, "Can we talk in my bedroom?"

"Sure." She made sure that Emmy was still asleep and
secure on his couch.

He grabbed Nicole by the hand, led her to his room.

"Hi," he said and grinned.

"Hey." She licked her lips.

It didn't take long before every shirt, pair of pants, and
piece of underwear was on the floor. Nipples were massaged into hardness. One wet tongue explored another
tongue. Long, warm legs entwined one another. And piercing screams were heard as Ajalon made love to Nicole with
a ferociousness she'd never experienced before. He almost
seemed like an angry lover. Using his hips, Ajalon banged

Nicole so violently that her vagina felt sore. She loved it. She craved it. The pain hurt like hell, but she felt as if she deserved the hurt. She rocked with Ajalon and pushed him deeper and deeper inside of her. He was wedged so far inside her that, strangely, it felt like they became one person. The closeness was something she never wanted to relinquish.

When they were done he asked, "Can you stay with me tonight?"

"I'd be glad to, except I think I should take Emmy over to Nadia's. Remember her?"

He slowly nodded.

"You want to ride with me to her place? I'll call Nadia and see if she can watch the baby all night for me. Then I'll be clear to stay with you until the morning."

"What if she asks why you need her to watch your child all night? Does she know you and your husband broke up?"

"No. I haven't really told anyone except you and my mother."

"Good. Don't tell her. It's no one's business anyway."

"You're right. So, Ajalon, can you go with me to Nadia's?"

"No, I want to stay right here and wait on you, my love. I'll go to the store. Buy a bottle of wine, some condoms. You go do what you need to do."

"Okay, but that means I'd have to drive back over here in the dark. I still can't stand this place. It freaks me out."

"Welcome to the ghetto," he said, and they fell out laughing.

Chapter 12

It was the next morning. Alexis had just gotten to work. She placed her purse in a drawer and proceeded to the break room to make a pot of coffee. It was early in the morning, and only a few other staff members had arrived.

Her back was turned when she noticed Shyla Perry-Fallender enter the room.

Shyla hesitated. "Hi, Alexis."

"Oh, okay. Hello back at you."

Shyla walked over to the coffeemaker gripping her mug.

"I didn't know you drank coffee." Alexis studied Shyla, whose eyes looked red and moist.

"Oh, please. How can you say that when I'm in here every day, just like everybody else? I'm sure you've seen me in here many times."

Shyla grabbed the coffee creamer and placed a spoonful in her cup.

"Hmm, yeah, you're right. I have noticed you in here every day, several times a day, drinking coffee like it's going out of style."

"Alright, then."

"But you know something else I've noticed? That you and your BFF, Nicole Greene, don't chat and hang out like you used to. In fact, when we had our last staff meeting, you two sat at opposite ends of the room like you didn't even want to look at each other. What's up with that? Y'all fell out?"

"Look, mind your business."

"Oh, oh, okay. The woman that's always in everybody else's business doesn't want anyone in hers. Figures."

"Alexis, please." Shyla had a rare serious expression on her face. Right then Alexis felt convicted, as if she could be more sensitive and friendly to the woman even if she didn't deserve it.

"Hey, I'm not trying to pry or anything, but it's obvious you two had it out. Um, I hope everything works out."

"Highly unlikely. She's a bitch. Always has been a bitch, and I needed to open up my eyes and see Nicole Greene, as you call her, for what she really is. A chick that will sleep with a woman's husband and won't give a damn. So yeah, I can't roll with her anymore. And one day she'll get everything she deserves."

"Shyla, come on now. Whatever has happened, I'm sure you can work it out."

"Slow your roll, peacemaker. She's talked about your ass like a dog ever since she got hired. Don't defend her."

Alexis's voice trembled. "What has she said about me?"

"She told me she could never be like you. You waited until Rashad wanted to marry her before you up and filed for child support. You're trying to get what's rightfully hers. And you're a poor excuse for a mother since you had to adopt your own child."

"She said that?"

"Yes, she did." Instantly Shyla felt guilty for spilling so

much tea and betraying Nicole. "I-I won't tell you everything she said, but yeah, girlfriend, it was nothing nice."

"Hmm. Thanks for the heads-up."

"You're welcome."

"But can you tell me why you two aren't talking anymore?"

"No, I can't. I've already said enough. My mouth is closed." Shyla finished making her cup of coffee and quietly left Alexis alone to think about what had just happened.

Later that day, Alexis was at her desk during her lunch break. She'd missed the deadline to file her income taxes. But it was no big deal; she was getting a refund and the deadline wouldn't matter. She clicked away at her keyboard and began the process of filing electronically. She entered Hayley's Social Security number; an error message popped up. She tried typing the numbers a second time. Soon it was apparent that the IRS was rejecting her attempts to e-file.

"What the hell?" she whispered. "Has someone else already used my baby's Social Security number?"

She rubbed her temples and felt like she needed to drink a cold glass of water. Tax refund fraud was running rampant in Houston. She prayed she wasn't the latest victim.

After feeling hopeless, she quickly grabbed her cell phone and rushed outside, found her car in the staff parking lot, got in, and slammed the door. She called Varnell and explained what had just happened.

"This is really fucked up. I don't know what could have happened, but what if I am the victim of fraud?"

Varnell listened. Then asked, "Have you ever e-filed before? Did you call the IRS? Have you left your tax info or

Social Security number and all that lying around anywhere lately?"

"Hell, no."

"Then it must be something else."

"Like what?"

He hesitated.

"Babe, try calling your child's father. Make sure he didn't already file and use Hayley's Social Security number."

She vigorously shook her head. "No, that's not it. Rashad wouldn't do that. Plus, he told me that he'd let me claim her this year."

"Call him anyway, Alexis."

"I don't want to."

"But you need to."

She practically hung up on Varnell as she rushed to get Rashad on the phone.

"Hey, what's up?" he said.

He sounded normal, nothing close to shady. She wanted to believe this was just a big mistake.

"Rashad, I'm alright, but something weird has happened."

"What's that?"

"I just tried to claim Hayley on my electronic tax return but it wouldn't go through."

"Oh, that. Yeah. I meant to tell you."

"Did you claim her after promising me that I could do it?"

"Yeah, I did. I'm sorry. I forgot."

She closed her eyes and felt like screaming. "Rashad, how could you forget something so important like that? Man, you have no idea how much you just fucked up."

"What do you mean?"

Alexis felt like the world was coming to an end. It seemed like every time she tried to do something good for

her and her daughter's life, it was always like running up
an incline. Making a decent wage, finally being granted
child support, and moving out of her mother's house was
no picnic. Nothing came easy, and now this.

"I was supposed to get back a huge refund. And now you
messed everything up. I-I was counting on that money." Her
throat swelled with pain. She felt a headache coming on.
Soon her cheeks were wet. "And I charged a bunch of shit
on my credit cards thinking that I could pay it all off once
the bill came."

"Damn. That's messed up. You shouldn't have spent
money that you don't even have for sure."

"But I only did it because *you* told me, Rashad, you
promised I could claim Hayley. And now I'll have to do a
paper return, because doing it the other way just won't
work."

"Damn."

"'Damn'? Is that all you have to say?"

"What else am I supposed to say? I'm sorry for forgetting?"

"Negro, you sorry alright. That's what gets me, you
don't give a fuck how your so-called memory loss has put
me in a bad spot."

"No, you spending money you don't have put you there,
not me."

"Rashad, I swear to God, you just don't get it." She let
out a high-pitched scream. "I'm so mad I could kill your
self-centered, reneging ass. You lied to me and now you've
fucked up my money."

"Stop all that screaming like you crazy and calm down.
I suggest you find your receipts and take back the stuff you
bought. You probably don't need it anyway. Like, more
purses and shoes. Women! Just return all that shit and get
the credit put back on your card."

"I can buy whatever I want to buy."

"And that's why you in the jam you're in now. No self-control. Alexis, you can always rebuy everything later. Find your receipts and return that shit today."

"That's easy for you to say. I don't even have the receipts anymore, dummy. They've been tossed away in the garbage. And I'll only get store credit, that's all."

"Oops, you really did it this time."

"Ugh, *I* did it? Is that what you think?"

"That's what it sounds like to me."

"Rashad, I can't believe how selfish you are. You just don't care about anyone but you."

"That's not true, Skillet, and you know it. I still have receipts for all kinds of nice shit that I've bought for both you and our daughter." He heard her crying and it tore him up inside. "Look, calm down, alright? It was an honest mistake. I have so much on my mind these days, I can't think clearly."

"Fuck calming down. You're still a selfish prick with no conscience. You make me sick."

He didn't appreciate Alexis cracking on him, although he could understand her anger. But to call him selfish when he considered himself one of the most generous people she'd ever met made him feel indignant.

"If I am so selfish, why would I pay three months' rent in advance for Nicole to have her own apartment?"

Alexis sniffed. "So you really did that for her?"

"Yeah, I did. And I'm still posted up at our crib."

"That's cold-blooded. Most guys would let the wife get the house."

"I'm not most guys."

"We know that already." Alexis paused. She tried to stay reasonable in dealing with Rashad, but a feeling of dread came over her.

"Look, Rashad, if you are as nice or considerate as you say you are, you'd better find a way to get me some of that money that you got from the government. I mean it. Part of that's mine, and don't you forget it. I am not getting into deeper credit card debt because of you. So, do something about it soon or you'll wish you had."

"Are you actually threatening me? I will answer for you, because I know you're smarter than that."

"You don't know shit."

"Skillet, I told you it was a simple oversight."

She hung up on him when he tried to explain himself. She didn't care anymore. Caring about Rashad never got her anywhere. And she was sick of defending him.

Her emotions clouded her judgment. She grabbed her purse and cell phone and ran out to her car. She started the engine and began to drive.

Soon Alexis had entered the freeway, driving faster than what the law allowed. As she raced down the road, she barely paid attention to the cars she passed. She felt upset and betrayed. And she had no idea how to make sense of what had just happened.

Out the corner of her eye, she noticed a van riding alongside of her; it tried to keep up with her speed. A car horn honked. She saw the Eason & Son logo on the van. Rashad rolled down his driver's-side window. He motioned with his hand. She scowled at him. The sight of this man made her sick. She envisioned herself jerking her steering wheel and swiping his vehicle as hard as she could. Hitting him so forcefully that he'd lose control and the van would roll over with him trapped inside.

Her cell phone rang. It was him. How dare he call her? What did he have to say? Whatever it was Alexis didn't want to hear it. She wanted him to disappear forever. It felt wrong to entertain such dark, brooding thoughts, but at the time she didn't care. She gripped the steering wheel in her hand and gave him a vicious glare. His mouth was moving, but she couldn't make out what he was saying.

She told herself, "Just do it." Alexis clutched the steering wheel tightly between her hands. She pressed her foot against the accelerator and stared into her rearview mirror. A police car swiftly pulled up behind her, its lights flashing. The color drained from Alexis's face. She became confused. Did the police want her for something? But why? Just because she'd thought about doing harm to someone? The police car continued to follow her and flashed its lights again. She pulled over to the shoulder and her tires came to a stop. Rashad, who had slowed down as he observed Alexis, drove over onto the shoulder just ahead of her and parked.

The officer came over to Alexis and she rolled down her window.

"What did I do? Was I going too fast?"

"Yes, ma'am. I clocked you at twenty miles over the speed limit. But something's going on with your car. Didn't you notice all that smoke pouring out of the exhaust?"

"No, I did not."

"Yeah, you may need a diagnostic. It could be a bad fuel pressure regulator, or leaky fuel injectors."

"You sound like a mechanic, not a cop."

"Oh, I'm definitely a cop. May I see your license and insurance, ma'am?"

She cooperated and handed over her info. Rashad had gotten out of his car by then, but he remained at a close distance, quietly watching them. Alexis got cited for speeding. When the officer was done speaking with her and had driven off, Rashad came over to Alexis; she sat behind the wheel looking furious.

"Just more shit to add to my other shit. I gotta go to court and pay this fucking ticket or go to defensive driving and that costs money, too. Plus I gotta go find a mechanic to fix this stupid car."

"I tried to warn you that something was wrong with your car, but you acted like you didn't want to listen when I was waving at you. Don't be this way, Alexis. I'm sorry about the tax thing. I promise to give you some money. In fact, here." Rashad reached into his slacks and pulled out his wallet. He counted out five hundred-dollar bills plus three twenties.

"This should help for now, okay? I'll give you some more later. But be careful. I-I don't want anything bad to happen to you."

Alexis accepted the cash and nodded. At first she couldn't look him in the eyes. She couldn't open her mouth to say anything to him. But soon her eyes told him thank you. Her eyes revealed that as mad as she was, she didn't want anything bad to happen to him, either. And she was glad she'd stopped herself from hurting him.

When shit gets real, there's nothing else to do but deal with it. Legal papers arrived via courier at Nicole's job. Her coworkers gave her odd looks. A couple of times she'd had to take emergency vacation days just to handle her business matters. Change of address, getting utilities placed in her name. Life quickly became overwhelming, and Nicole got to the point where she didn't know what to do.

She had just gotten off work and drove straight home to her new apartment. She changed into a pair of shorts and a T-shirt and slid her feet into some sandals. When she combed her hair and looked in the bathroom mirror, she noticed that her hair was beginning to fall out. Why was this happening to her? No answer she came up with could console her.

Nicole took a deep breath and picked up her cell phone. It had been a while since she'd erased Shyla's info from her address book. But she scrolled through all her text messages until she found her info. She unblocked the number and dialed.

Shyla's number rang one time and went straight into voice mail.

"Blocked," she muttered. Nicole was so upset that she grabbed her purse. She called Nadia.

"Hi there. I know I'm supposed to pick up Emmy, but an emergency has come up. So I will get her later on if that's alright with you."

"So you're not coming to get your daughter soon? Ms. Nicole, I-I had other plans. I was going to go out tonight."

"Nadia, please. I really need your help right now."

"I can reschedule, no problem."

"Thanks so much." Nicole decided to unexpectedly stop by Nadia's. She raced to Nadia's place and rang the doorbell. Nadia answered, looking surprised.

"I'm sorry for this, I'm sorry for the inconvenience." Nicole pressed a fifty in her hand. "Let me handle some business real quick and then you'll be free to do whatever you had planned to do."

"Okay." Nadia smiled and tucked the cash in her bra.

Nicole ran and hopped back in her Jeep. She drove over to Shyla's, but when she saw a lot of cars in the driveway she decided to keep moving. She continued traveling along the streets with no idea what her future held.

At one point Nicole glanced up and saw a huge billboard. It was an advertisement for a church called Solomon's Temple. In the photo, the pastor, London P. Solomon, stood next to a woman whom Nicole assumed was his wife. His hands were outstretched. Soon she found herself driving in the direction of the church.

Once she found its location, she parked, got out of the car, and practically ran to the front entrance. The church felt majestic and appeared white and pristine. She wondered if she looked out of place. Was she dressed properly? She was afraid that she wouldn't fit in when it came to church. But she opened the double doors and went inside anyway.

Nicole wandered around until she came across a directory mounted in the hallway. She decided to go to the administration office. Even though it was a weekday, there was plenty of activity going on. As soon as she entered the offices, a couple of women smiled and greeted her.

"May I help you?" one of them said.

"Yes." She nodded. "I need help."

The woman took one look at Nicole and gently grabbed her hand. She led Nicole inside a suite of offices, where Nicole saw several men and women behind desks answering telephones.

"That's our crisis line room," the woman explained.

She continued past the phone banks and into another area.

"Sit here. Someone will be right with you."

Then she left. Nicole was all by herself in a place she'd never been before. She was tempted to quietly rush out of the church. She rose to her feet. And that's when a woman quietly stepped up next to her and extended her hand.

"Hello, little sister. I'm Sister Zaire."

Nicole reluctantly shook her hand. She sat back down on the edge of the chair. She discreetly touched the bottom of her eyelids and let her fingers absorb the wetness that had gathered there.

"You need a tissue?" Without waiting for Nicole's answer, Sister Zaire handed her a box.

Nicole took it and mumbled thanks.

"Someone told me you said you need help. I'll try my best. What brings you here?"

Nicole's story unfolded in short, awkward sentences. She felt like a fool . . . a stranger pouring out her heart to a stranger. She wanted to run and hide, but the lady seemed so kind and inviting.

"I'm sorry for bothering you, but I have no one else to talk to. Not really. My-my best friend hates my guts. No one at work really likes me. Even my own husband doesn't love me anymore. I'm not sure if he ever did."

Sister Zaire patted Nicole's hand.

"It's going to be alright. Trust and believe."

"Believe?"

She nodded. "Believe even if you can't see. That's what faith is. Blind faith believes when nothing is physically in front of you. I will say this, little sister, God loves you. Believe that."

Nicole wiped her eyes again. The woman wore an Afrocentric dashiki. She looked calm and powerful. Her voice was strong, spirited, and sure. Her head was held high, like she knew who she was and was proud of it.

"Anyway, Sister Zaire, everything in my life is falling apart. And it used to be perfect."

The woman sat back in her swivel chair. "Define 'perfect'."

"I had my man, my house, a good job, a perfect baby who is cute, healthy, funny, and feisty. The man that I loved was my husband, and I was always scared that he might not want me back a while ago. I did some things that could have made him walk away. But he stayed. We got married. I wanted him so bad."

"I see." She studied Nicole with a kindly expression.

"Allow me to say this, little sister. Our definition of perfection is when everything is going exactly the way that we want it to go."

"Yes, I guess you're right."

"But now things in your life aren't going your way. And that doesn't feel good. It feels painful."

"Yes. You described my life perfectly. I wake up in pain, and I go to bed in pain."

"Let me say this about perfection. God's perfect plan can involve pain. Take, for example, when he allowed his only Son to suffer and die on a cross for the sins of the world. A plan that involved pain, so that the world could have joy through the death of his loving Son, Jesus."

Nicole tried not to flinch every time Sister Zaire said "God" or "Jesus." She felt like they were right in the room staring at her, and it made her feel spooked.

"In other words, little sister, perfection may not always feel good, but there can be purpose in the pain."

"I'm not trying to be funny, but I'm not exactly God's best child. So why do I have to feel the pain I'm going through now?"

"I don't know. Maybe it's a wake-up call. Like our bodies can hurt to let us know we need to get something checked out at the doctor due to physical pain we experience. Perhaps the emotional pain is trying to tell you the same thing. It's something you have to figure out. Maybe you need to walk in another direction, make a different decision, and do it until the pain that you feel goes away."

But why did going in another direction have to mean losing her husband? She didn't want that.

"I hear what you're telling me, but this is what I think is happening. I think I made a few bad choices. And the bad choices overwhelmed any of my good choices. Now I'm paying for them big-time."

"Key word. *Choices*. We have free choice. Sometimes that's good, other times it hurts us, as you can probably testify to." Sister Zaire looked as if she wanted to say more, but she grew quiet and simply stared at Nicole.

"Well, certain choices have definitely hurt me, Sister Zaire."

"The good news is that the pain won't last forever, even though it feels that way right now."

"How do you know? Can you guarantee this is going to go away? When will it leave? When will I feel normal again?"

Sister Zaire laughed, her eyes sparkling with kindness, not judgment.

"One day, little sister, all the pain will disappear. That's all I can tell you."

"Oh, like one day when I'm dead and gone?"

"If you're fortunate, you will live to see Him take the pain away."

And she took Nicole's hand and they sat there together in quiet reflection.

It hurt Nicole to keep her mouth shut, but for some reason she felt she needed to sit and remain silent. She thought about all the choices she'd made in her life and hoped that she could do better in the future. Do a million times better.

Chapter 13

It was Friday. Kiara and her man took a day off from work. Myles was out of school too. And Jazzy was being cared for by Mama Flora.

They were all in Eddison's car on their way to some much-needed recreation. Eddison drove into the parking lot of the iFLY building, one of several facilities in the Houston area that offered indoor skydiving.

"What is this?" Kiara asked.

"A surprise. I've always wanted to skydive."

"Eddy, you must be out of your mind. There's no way I'm doing that."

"C'mon, don't knock it until you've tried it."

"I can knock it all day long and I still won't be trying it."

"Mommy, you're a scaredy cat. I'm going to do it. I'm not scared."

"Eddy, please don't let my baby skydive."

"We're all doing it. Including you," he stubbornly told her.

Kiara continued to protest while Eddy tried to convince her that she needed to do something daring for a change.

He pulled on her arm and tried to coax her inside the building, but she remained steadfast in her seat.

"Why are you doing this, Eddy?"

"It's different. It's fun. And it helps you to confront your fears."

"You are a crazy-ass man, and I'll be waiting in the car while you two fools go and try to get yourselves killed."

"No one has ever gotten killed from this."

"That's because they were smart enough to stay outside and wait in the damn car."

Eddison laughed and rolled his eyes. "I thought I had a strong Superwoman who could face anything."

"Oh, that outfit you saw me wearing on Halloween one time is just a costume that looked cute on me. But Superwoman? That's not really me, Eddy."

"You are Superwoman even if you don't think you are."

She smiled. He smiled back. Then she looked angry. "Nice try, babe. Nope, still not going."

After a couple more minutes, Eddison gave up begging. He got out of the car along with Myles, and they headed to the front entrance of the building.

"Have it your way, Kiara," he yelled. "It's hot as hell outside and you'll be waiting, oops, I mean *melting*, for at least an hour."

"You got AC. I ain't worried. Hand over your keys."

He shook his head and tossed her his keys.

While Eddy and Myles went to do their indoor skydiving, Kiara got on the driver's side of the car, turned on the ignition, and flipped on the air. Then she dialed up her girlfriend Adina Davis.

"What up, my Nubian queen?" Adina said when she saw that Kiara was calling.

"So much has been happening. Sorry I haven't been calling you back."

"No problem. I knew you would when you found the time."

"Yes. Time. It seems I have much less of it. And managing my life has gotten so complex." She got Adina caught up on the latest happenings of her complicated life.

"Eddy and I are still good. He's going through some family stuff right now, and all I can do is be there for him."

"That's my girl."

"But, on the other hand, my crazy ex is proving to me that the best decision I ever made was getting away from him."

Adina laughed. "I could have told you that, girl."

"He's a hot mess. He's married to another woman and still hounding me. Not just hounding me, either. He's stooped so low that he has outright lied on my man. Ain't that crazy?"

"That's Rashad."

"Yeah, so I gotta be real careful, because, you know, that's my kids' father. I have to pretend like he's a great man even though I want to wring his neck. I'm tempted to not even let the kids see him sometimes."

"Okay, I can't stand Rashad, but keeping him from his kids would be dead wrong."

"I know. You're right. I'm just so scared, though, that he may plant some weird ideas about Eddy inside Myles's head. He's so good with my kids, and I'm afraid that Rashad may scare the man away."

"I hope Rashad is not that crazy, and I hope you aren't allowing fear to rule your decisions, Kiara."

"No, not at all," Kiara told her and decided not to tell her exactly where she was right then. "I'm going to continue to live my life regardless. And I will do it unafraid," she said as she stared at the skydiving building. "I'm trying not to be scared of anything."

"But remember that time you and Rashad had that boat accident?"

Kiara clearly remembered that day. It was a year after she and Rashad had first been married. She hated taking risks, but early that Saturday morning, he begged her to go with him to ride on one of his friend's boats. They were going to drive down to Kemah Boardwalk and take a sailboat out on the water.

"Rashad, you can't swim."

"It's cool. We'll be wearing our life jackets. It'll be fun."

"I'm shocked you've agreed to do this, but if you insist, I'll tag along."

"Great. I'll let Corey know."

Rashad called up his buddy Corey, and Kiara scrambled to find her bathing suit and packed a light lunch for the two of them. Once she was buckled in their car, she sat back and relaxed. "I'm starting to think this will be fun. It's kind of romantic. I will do anything as long as we're together, baby." Her husband winked at her and sang at the top of his lungs all the way down I-45 toward Galveston. They took the Kemah Boardwalk exit and drove to the parking lot, where they met Corey and his girlfriend at the Seabrook Marina.

Corey allowed the women to step onto the boat and untied the rope that anchored his day sailor.

"Let's go," Corey yelled. "You'll never forget this as long as you live."

At first Kiara's shoulders were clenched and tight. But twenty minutes into the ride, she began to laugh and joke and have a good time with the others. The sky boasted a brilliant-looking blue and there wasn't a cloud in sight.

But thirty minutes later, the fun that they were having had come to a stop.

"Oh shit, water's coming into the boat," Corey yelled.

"What does that mean?" asked Kiara.

"Stand up, and hold on."

She stood up and clutched her life vest against her body. She grabbed her purse. Soon water came over her feet. She was wearing her favorite sandals. It didn't take long for them to get covered and eventually slide off as the water rose higher and higher. Soon she was up to her thighs in water and it was steadily rising.

Kiara was frightened. She could swim, but it was one thing to be in a six-foot-deep pool. Things felt more harrowing out here in the ocean—an ocean that had sharks.

"Rashad," she screamed. During the initial panic, she hadn't noticed that he did not have on his life jacket. Earlier he had complained it was getting in the way of his fun, so he casually took it off and threw it somewhere in the boat.

"Rashad, baby, you can't swim."

The color drained from her husband's face. Corey swam over to Rashad and tried to hold him up. By that time the boat floated on its side. They had all been dumped out of the boat and were treading water in the Gulf of Mexico.

"Sharks," Kiara shouted as the color drained from her face. "What about sharks?"

"Don't say that," screamed Corey's girlfriend.

Although she wore a life vest, the currents made Kiara go under. She closed her eyes and sucked in her breath. The water rushed over her head. The sound of bubbles filled her ears. She rose back up to the top, breaking the surface. She screamed, "Help," and hoped someone could hear her.

Corey struggled to hold Rashad up. Corey was only

five-feet-six and his skinny arms were getting tired. "Don't you dare drop him," Kiara pleaded. She fought hard to stay positive, but it seemed they were doomed.

Thankfully the Coast Guard was nearby and spotted the four people in the water. They were all rescued, Rashad did not come close to drowning, and Kiara felt grateful they made it out alive.

"Now, do you see why I hate taking risks?" she told Rashad once they were safely home. "That whole ordeal scared the shit out of me . . . literally."

"Aw, babe, I didn't mean to scare you like that. I just wanted to show you a good time."

"The best way to show me a good time is to always be safe. I mean it, Rashad. I don't want to lose you to any foolishness."

Ever since then, Kiara hated doing anything that involved tremendously scary risks.

"No more little boats," she'd declared back then. And today during her chat with Adina she wanted to show strength even if it was just in her romantic relationships.

"I'm sure you know how to handle both Eddy and Rashad," Adina told her.

"Yes, I do. I will try to maintain peace between all of us even if it kills me."

"Alrighty then. We will talk later. 'Bye, Kiara."

They hung up.

Waiting in that parking lot of the iFLY building, Kiara continually looked at her watch; she was tempted to run inside the building to make sure Eddison and Myles were alright. But in some ways letting Myles go in there with Eddison was a test. Did she trust her man enough to believe he'd take great care of her son?

"I have to trust this man. I can't be with him if I don't trust him."

* * *

As Kiara continued to wait in her car, her cell phone screen lit up. She picked up. "Hello, Rashad."

"Hey, beautiful."

"Wow, are you even authorized to say something like that to me, ex-husband?"

"I can say whatever I want to you. You know you will always be my heart."

"You know what's funny, Rashad? When we were married, I was dying for you to say nice romantic things to me. But you rarely had time. And now that you've gotten a second wife, it seems you have plenty of time to tell me what you should have told me a long time ago. Why is that?"

"It took losing you to realize how good I had it."

"Is that right?"

"It's true, Kiara. You were a damn good wife. I was so proud of you. You were doing your part. I didn't do mine. And . . . I apologize for failing you."

Kiara was speechless. He'd never been this honest and vulnerable with her. For a moment she wondered what would have happened if she hadn't been so hell-bent on countersuing Rashad for divorce. Maybe she shouldn't have been so stubborn and eager to pay back all the pain he'd given her through his numerous affairs.

"Yeah," he continued. "I've been wanting to say that. To even take you out and have a face-to-face for a while now."

"Oh, really?"

"Yeah, Kiara. You know what? I miss being a family. Coming home to you and Myles. It was just us against the world. We created something great, Kiara, didn't we?"

"Actually, I can't deny that. I can't imagine life without the babies. That's one good thing that happened in the midst of a whole lot of bad."

"Can you ever forget that? Would it be impossible to

start over and do things the way you always wanted them to be done? Look, Kiara. I was a major fuckup. Do you know how hard it is for me to admit that? Even over the phone?"

"No," she murmured. "I cannot imagine. It's hard to see this side of you, Rashad. When I was busy loving you, you were busy acting a fool. Disrespecting me. Locking me out of your heart and pushing me out of your life and your bed."

"I know. Don't remind me."

"I have to remind you, or else you could keep doing it over and over again."

"But that's it. I am not that man anymore. He's dead. I don't want to treat you bad ever again, Kiara. You're my heart. You belong to me, not that lame ass." He couldn't finish. He knew by insulting Eddison, he wouldn't score points with this woman.

"Mrs. Eason. You'll always be Mrs. Eason to me. Can you please find it in your heart to let it go?"

"Rashad, have you ever heard that expression, 'Too little, too late'?"

"I have. But for some things it's never too late to say what's really important. So, for what it's worth, I love you, Kiara Eason. I hope you will always be Kiara Eason. Never marry that corny fake dude you got."

"Leave Eddison out of this."

"You're right. This isn't about him. It's about me, Rashad, and how I feel about you. I love you. I do."

"Rashad, please."

"But it's the truth. Remember how you would always demand the truth from me? So here I am right now, giving it to you, Kiara."

"But it's making me mad."

"That's what truth does, though. I got angry at myself

for realizing I'd lost a good thing, the best woman I've ever known."

She felt herself getting weak. His voice sounded gravelly, so sincere, like he really wanted her to believe him.

"You know how I feel about you, don't you? How do you feel about me?"

"Rashad, I'm about to go!"

"Wait a second, please hear me out. What I've learned is that people push you to be open and honest and to tell them the truth, and when you do tell them the truth, sometimes they get mad at you for doing it. You should never ask for the truth if you cannot handle the truth."

"Rashad, don't you realize the things that you're saying right now is what I needed three years ago? What can I do with what you're telling me today? You always seem to forget that you're a very married man."

"Does that mean if I wasn't married you'd think about reconciling with me and let me be the man that I always should have been for you and the kids?"

A gasp flew out of Kiara's mouth. What was this man doing to her? Why was he pressuring her with his emotional outbursts and forcing her to think about things—awful, painful, complex things that she did not wish to consider?

"Do you still love me, Kiara? Tell the truth."

She stared at her cell phone screen and glanced at the contact photo of her ex-husband, the man who'd stolen her heart over ten years ago. Kiara had an old picture of him in her phone. Yet she knew that he was still extremely handsome. He always took care of himself physically, which was why women were always attracted to Rashad Eason. And she knew his drive to work hard and make his company something to be proud of would never leave him.

That was the man she'd wanted to marry. She had to admit that she'd known what she was getting from day one.

A regretful tear slipped down Kiara's cheek when memories of their good times flashed in her head. Their laughter, the jokes, the amazing lovemaking, and their mutual enjoyment of Myles as he was growing up. Even though Rashad couldn't see her or know what she was thinking, Kiara felt embarrassed. She quietly wiped the tear away. She found her voice and told him that she had to hang up the phone. She promised him that she'd answer his question later.

"Just go on and say it now, Kiara. Please tell me you love me."

"No seriously, I-I have to think about it. I'll hit you up when I can."

He finally gave in and told her that he would hold her to it and she'd better not forget. She told him, "Rashad, I promise. I won't forget. I gotta go."

They hung up the phone.

Little did Kiara know, it was the last time she'd ever speak to him.

Chapter 14

"I can do this," Nicole told herself. "If I can pull it off, it'll be worth it."

With its motor running, Nicole sat behind the wheel of a rental car. It was Friday, around ten in the evening. Her eyes were focused on a two-story house in Fresno, the one where Rashad used to live with Kiara. A radiant full moon hovered overhead. Gray clouds moved across the sky, and Nicole hoped the night looked dark enough to shield her from curious eyes.

Kiara's car sat in the driveway. Nicole hoped that meant the woman was inside. She rummaged through a tote bag and removed a heavy brick and a black permanent marker. She had stolen the brick the other day when she'd passed by a new home development. Dozens of bricks were lying around. The workers were gone for the day. And before Nicole knew it, she got out her car, picked up one brick, and ended up taking it with her.

Nicole flicked on the interior light of the car and scribbled on the side of the brick: LEAVE RASHAD ALONE.

With brick in hand, she quietly got out of the car. It was

a black standard rental. She walked to the rear of the car and knelt beside the trunk. She reached inside her jacket pocket and took out an index card and a roll of invisible tape. She arranged the white card so that it partially hid the two right numbers of her license plate. She applied tape over each edge so that the card would remain secure.

Nicole returned the tape to her pocket and rose up. Both of her hands were hidden inside thin leather gloves. She surveyed the area and didn't notice a single neighbor walking around. Pure quietness surrounded the area except for the sound of the swirling wind. Nicole headed up the path that led to Kiara's front door, then she made a quick left and was soon standing on the side of the huge two-story house.

When she'd secretly scoped out the house the other night, there was ample room between this house and the one next door. Taking a deep breath, Nicole stood right next to the kitchen window. She prayed that Kiara's kids weren't in that room. She drew back her hand and flung the brick with all her might. The brick crashed into the window. She immediately froze when the sound of shattering glass pierced her ears. Several dogs began barking. The yelping sounded like it came from the neighbor's backyard. Startled, Nicole turned around. Her feet quickly moved as she zoomed between the houses and headed for the rental. Wearing brand-new black gym shoes, she cut across the damp grass. She got in the car and closed the door; the engine was still running just as she'd left it. She pulled the lever into reverse and prayed no other car would be driving down the street.

The front porch lights of Kiara's house flicked on.

"Shit."

At the same time, headlights from an approaching vehicle illuminated the street. It was just about to pass Kiara's driveway. Nicole felt trapped as she waited on the older car with the bad muffler.

"Hurry the fuck up," she said, nearly yelling.

A tall figure emerged from inside Kiara's front door. He stood on the porch, then began to approach Nicole. She ducked her head and burnt rubber backing out of the driveway, almost hitting the older car. She put the car in drive; it wildly lurched forward. She heard yelling and looked in her rearview mirror.

Eddison Osborne raced behind her car. "Hey, wait." He waved his hands until he decided to stop running. Nicole watched him in the mirror and felt relieved; she hoped that the little piece of paper she'd used to cover the license plate was still holding up. That little piece of paper would save her.

Soon Eddison's image became smaller and smaller.

Thinking of her plan, she knew it would only work if Kiara Eason got the message loud and clear: "Stop trying to play two men against each other. If you want that stupid-ass Eddison Osborne, keep him, but leave me and Rashad the hell alone."

It was her last small attempt to abandon the idea she'd presented to Ajalon. If she could scare Kiara into leaving Rashad alone, she was sure he'd come to his senses. She could tell Ajalon never mind, there was no need to kill Rashad. But time would tell, and Nicole was running out of it.

Kiara knew something was terribly wrong. She had been enjoying a bath when the loud crash scared her. She asked Eddy to go check things out. After ten minutes, Eddy returned to the bathroom.

"I saw a woman who looked like Nicole backing out of the driveway."

"Are you serious? Are you sure?"

"I could swear it was her. But when I tried to wave her down, she drove off like she'd just robbed a bank."

"But why would she throw something through the window?"

"I don't know, but maybe this will tell you why." Eddy showed Kiara the brick. It was covered with tiny glass particles.

Kiara read the words that asked her to leave Rashad alone.

"What's that all about?" Eddison asked in a clipped voice.

"You already know. That bitch is nuts. I'm going to report her to the police."

"But does she have a good reason to go to these extremes, Kiara?"

"Eddy, she busted my fucking window. I'm going to have to file a claim."

"I see." Eddison studied her curiously. "Is Rashad worth all of this drama?"

"Surely you can't take a brick that she wrote on seriously."

"I don't know how to take it, Kiara. I want to trust you."

"You want to trust me? I can't believe you said that. What about your own mysterious behavior?"

"I have no mysterious—"

"Bullshit. You give me half answers when I question you about parts of your life. I want to trust you, Eddy, God knows, I do, but sometimes I'm not sure."

"But is your reason for sometimes acting like you do because you are still in love with your ex?"

"No," she cried. "That's crazy. You know damn well he and I aren't together."

"You aren't together, but it won't necessarily stop you from loving him."

"Well, you're wrong."

Kiara wanted to tell Eddison about Rashad's recent confession of his love to her. She wanted to tell him that her ex asked her if she still loved him. But she couldn't tell Eddison. Because if she truthfully retold the whole conversation, her man might want to know why she didn't just tell Rashad no. Why couldn't she just tell Rashad that she didn't love him anymore?

Eddy stared at Kiara as if he was trying to see inside her heart.

Kiara sputtered, "Eddy, you know that Nicole Greene is bat-shit crazy. I don't know why she does things like that."

"Nicole Eason, Kiara."

"Huh?"

"Don't forget. She's not Miss Greene anymore."

Kiara nodded miserably and said the words she hated to speak. "Nicole Eason."

"If she's as crazy as you think she is, maybe it's because you're driving Nicole to be that way. She's still not sure that her husband is really her husband. And maybe it's because you have a hard time completely letting go of Rashad."

"What the fuck? Eddison, now you sound nuts. I don't want him any more than the man on the moon."

"I hope not, Kiara." He stared at her with tired eyes. "Look, maybe I should cut out early. Go back to my house and think about things."

Kiara rose up in the water and stood up in the tub. "No, baby, no. Don't let Nicole's insane ways make you think untrue things about my love for you."

Eddison turned around and headed out the door.

"We're still good, aren't we, babe?" she yelled.

The next thing Kiara heard was the loud banging of the door. He'd left her. Kiara couldn't believe it. In that moment she felt so incredibly angry. Things had been going considerably well for her. Lately she had been in a happier space. She had her kids, her health and strength, a great job, but did she still have Eddison? She sat back down in the tub and sank under the warm, soothing bubbles. Her cell phone was sitting near the table close enough to reach. She grabbed it carefully so that it wouldn't fall into the water. She speed-dialed Eddy. Straight to voice mail.

She then texted Rashad with trembling hands.

> **You need to handle your bitch or else I'll be forced to. Why did she come over here and throw a brick in my fucking window talking about leave you the hell alone?**

Kiara thought twice about whether to press SEND or not. Two seconds later she sent it.

She threw her phone to the floor and leaned back against the tub, trembling uncontrollably.

She kept hoping Eddy would call her or come back to the house so they could talk. But he didn't.

Kiara decided that no way was she about to lose the best man that had ever happened to her, due to the worst woman that had ever happened to her.

Distraught, Nicole drove on and on until she saw a Super Walmart. It was twenty minutes till midnight; she still had time to take care of some important business. She unscrewed the cap from the bottled water that she purposely placed in the rental car earlier that day. She took a piece of tissue paper from her purse and poured a tablespoon of water on it. She removed the new gym shoes from her feet and wiped off any mud, grass, and other residue. She placed the shoes inside an empty shopping bag. Then she reached in the backseat, picked up a pair of flip-flops, and put them on her feet. She grabbed her purse and the shopping bag and went into the store.

The customer service department was about to close for the day. Nicole approached the counter, aware that all kinds of cameras were stashed in the ceiling watching her every move. She tried to look calm and act normal. Soon it was her turn.

"Hi, I want to return these shoes. Here's the receipt."

The cashier asked if anything was wrong with the shoes.

"No. I just don't want them. I—" She hushed her mouth, not wanting to say too much.

"Do you want your money back in cash or on a gift card?"

"Huh? I thought I automatically get the cash, right?" She felt annoyed at that point. The lady needed to hurry. Nicole wanted to make another purchase before midnight.

The cashier completed the transaction and finally handed Nicole her refund. She hurried off to the back of the store and picked up a case of beer.

When she returned to the front of the store and stood in line, she felt fine until the cashier carded her.

"I'm over twenty-one," she snapped.

"I know, but by law if you look like you're under forty, I have to ask you for a valid ID."

"That's messed up."

"Don't blame me. I just work here."

"May I see a manager?"

"Sure, but what good will that do?" The cashier glanced at her watch. "You better make up your mind about whether or not you're going to show me ID, because I can't sell any liquor after twelve, whether you're forty years old or a hundred."

"What a joke," Nicole said under her breath. She didn't want this woman to look at her name, see her address, or notice any info that might cause her to remember Nicole.

Reluctantly, Nicole flashed her ID. The salesclerk took a long time to review it. It was as if she was giving Nicole a hard time on purpose.

Nicole snatched back her ID, furious that the entire evening seemed to be going from bad to worse.

But once she left the store and got back in the rental car, she felt happier. At least she was able to return those gym shoes with no problem. She drove on to her apartment. As soon as she got inside, she opened the case of beer. She raised one can to her mouth and took a generous swallow. She finished off one can and quickly popped open another, and alternately drank from a bottle of whiskey that she'd already had but never finished.

Nicole felt out of control and nothing could soothe her right then except the alcohol. Her life was a mess, and regardless of all the advice given by her mother, her former best friend, and even a church woman, she had no idea how to fix things. Just that fast, she felt regretful about the vandalism, but she knew it was too late to take back her reckless actions.

She opened up the music app in her phone and began to play a K. Michelle song titled "Cry," paying special attention to the lyrics.

With the song on repeat, Nicole heard the words in the darkness of her living room. "You understand my feelings," she said, addressing the singer even though she knew the woman could not hear her. "You've been through all kinds of shit with men, just like I have. Hell, I could have written this song."

Nicole felt woozy, like the room was spinning around. She talked to herself. "You gonna suffer for everything you did, Rashad. If you hadn't dogged me out, I wouldn't be here right now." She felt love and hate for him at the same time.

"Don't call me, either, begging for forgiveness." Her words were slurred, but her meaning was clear. "But if you call me in the next ten, fifteen minutes, and apologize to me, we will forget any of this ever happened."

At twelve thirty in the morning, her phone rang. Unlisted number. She thought it might be Rashad or even Ajalon.

She picked up. "Hello."

"You sick-ass bitch."

"Who is this?"

"Nicole, why did you come to my house, causing trouble?"

"Oh, it's you."

"You damn right it's me. You must be out your mother-fucking mind."

"Watch the profanity, boss lady."

Kiara sighed. "You are crossing lines, Nicole, dangerous lines that are about to get you in a world of trouble. Do you want another case? Another arrest? Do you?"

"Look, Kiara." Nicole realized she did not want to get in trouble over a stupid brick. "I am sorry. But blame it on Rashad. He isn't acting normal. And everything that's happening is making me feel insecure." She didn't want Kiara to know that he'd threatened to divorce her. She had to downplay everything. "I had a stupid moment, but only because of the way he's been acting lately."

"I don't care what he's doing. Leave me the hell out of it."

"But you see, he was fucking with my mind and he point-blank told me that he was in love with you."

Kiara felt undone. Why was her ex going around telling people that he loved her? She felt so resentful toward Rashad that she could scream. Why couldn't her ex-husband just remain her ex-husband? The craziness of it all was making her feel stressed.

"And," she heard Nicole continue, "Rashad even said that you two may get back together. He said that he may buy you a bigger house than the one you already have. So, do you understand that when my husband said things to hurt me, I couldn't help myself. Surely you can understand how things like that would make a wife feel."

Kiara was astounded. A side chick who forgets her side-chick ways is doomed to repeat them. Rashad and Nicole truly deserved each other.

"I don't know why he would tell you that, Nicole. That man is not completely stupid, but he does some stupid-ass shit. He's lying. That's all I can say. I don't know his motives. Truly I don't. But you can't take him at his word. Don't let that man drive you crazy and mess up your life. You have your child to think about. And shit, come to think of it, so do I. Nicole, I-I am so sorry for everything that's going on with him, because he's simply not worth it. No man is worth this type of drama. I hope you realize it and stop letting him make you do things that keep you having to apologize for your actions. So, leave me out of your mess, please. Fuck!" she yelled. And Kiara hung up.

Nicole held the phone for a long time afterward. It was an odd but badly needed conversation. So her man was lying to her. Kiara obviously did not care about Rashad, or else she would have fought for him. But she didn't. Good. That meant that Nicole still had one more chance. She wasn't ready to walk away simply because he thought he didn't want her anymore. All because she shopped too much. That was so fucking dumb. If they could calm down and work things out, maybe, just maybe, they could get past the hurt and pain and petty arguing. Maybe they could find a way to love again. Take things slow. Give Nicole her dreams back and be happy again.

But, she thought as she swallowed another shot of tequila, *if the dumb fuck still refuses to make up with me, I must go through with my Plan B*.

By one thirty, Nicole still couldn't fall asleep. She wiped her mouth, went and got a rag from the bathroom, wet it with soap, and wiped the tearstains from her face.

A few days ago she'd paid cash for three separate burner phones. She found her leather gloves in the hall closet. She put on the gloves and retrieved one of the phones from a kitchen drawer.

She had already warned Ajalon that she could be calling him at any time from an unfamiliar number.

At first he did not pick up. But she called him twice more before he answered.

"Hello?"

"Hey, Ajalon, it's me."

Silence.

"I said, it's Nicole. Are you busy?"

"Um, sort of."

"Were you asleep, or did I interrupt you?"

"Um, kind of both."

"I'm sorry. Babe, I can't fall asleep for nothing. I am still trying to figure out what to do, you know, about my situation."

He said nothing.

"And I wanted to talk to you."

"Right now?"

"Yeah, is that all right?" she asked, feeling offended.

"I"—he yawned—"I am sleepy, Ni—"

It sounded as if he was about to say her name, but then he suddenly stopped.

"Are you alright, Ajalon?"

"Just sleepy. I've had a rough night."

"Well, okay, sorry for bothering you. It's just that when you make me feel like I'm something special and I call you with a problem, I don't expect to get blown off."

"I can talk to you much better after I get some sleep. I'm sorry. We'll be in touch."

"But, Ajalon."

"Yes."

"One more thing. I-I still haven't made a final decision about what we talked about. But I think I will give Rashad an ultimatum. That way, based on his behavior, his future is totally up to him. If he forgives me, his life will resume. If he doesn't forgive, his life will change. You know what I'm saying?"

"Uh, yeah. Talk later." Then he hung up.

Nicole sighed and carefully placed the prepaid phone inside a gallon-sized zipper storage bag.

At first she went to her kitchen and tossed the plastic bag inside of a black trash bag that was already filled with garbage. But then she thought about the other items in the trash bag that would point straight at her if the contents were ever discovered: food that she'd cooked but didn't eat, an empty soda can covered with her lipstick stains, credit card receipts that she'd carelessly thrown away, an empty bottle of her prescribed medicine with the label still attached. No. Somehow she must figure out a way to get rid of that cell phone without it being tied to her.

After first contemplating several foolish plans, Nicole ran to her bedroom closet and pulled off all her clothes.

She then fiddled through the clothes on the hangers and found a black active wear top, some black shorts, and a plain navy jacket with two pockets on the side. She laced up her running shoes, put on the leather gloves, grabbed the zipper bag with the phone, and left the apartment and headed outside for the rental car. She stuffed the bag in an interior pocket of her jacket and zipped it carefully so it wouldn't fall out. She took her time and drove over to a big neighborhood park that had a bayou alongside the walking trail. She got out of the car and began to run. She ran and thought about the things she'd do to try to keep the man whom she really loved.

This is nuts. It's insane. But if I can convince Rashad how much I love him, I can slowly return to my right mind. I can be the woman that he needs me to be. He can give me a second chance and I promise not to blow it.

Nicole knew she looked crazy running and wearing leather gloves. But she took a moment to slow down. To her surprise she saw two teenagers standing and talking. What were they doing there? It was so late. The teens didn't pay her any attention. So she felt it was fine to unzip her pocket, take out the plastic bag with the burner phone, and walk to the edge of the bayou. She stood next to the water. It looked deep. So she casually tossed the bag into the water and watched it disappear.

She was trembling by the time she walked back up the small incline and returned to the jogging path. The two teens stared at her curiously. She smiled and waved, then broke into a sprint. She was running again—racing toward the things that she desperately wanted.

Nicole had returned home and gone straight to bed. The next morning, when Rashad showed up outside Nicole's apartment a little before seven, she was ready. She heard her doorbell ring. She ran and looked through the peephole and saw that it was him.

"Oh yeah, give me a minute to freshen up."

"Hurry the fuck up, Nicole."

She begged Rashad to give her a minute. She ran to the closet and got dressed in a red negligée and nothing else. She came and opened her front door, anxious to throw her arms around his neck. But when she saw him, he shoved her to the side and moved past her in a rage.

"You," he said, "need to stop the bullshit. I got this crazy text from my ex about what you did last night. Leave Kiara Eason alone, okay? She's off-limits. My kids are off-limits. Hayley is off-limits. Anything I own is not for you to toy with."

"You *own* them? Are you serious?"

"They all have my name. Leave them alone. You have no right."

"Rashad, I did it because I don't want to let you go."

"I don't give a fuck what you want or don't want."

"But baby—"

"I'm not your baby. Don't you get it? I am done with you, Nicole. Do you really think pulling sorry shit like that would make me want you back? Make me love you?"

"But, Rashad, did you ever love me?"

Now was the time to tell the woman the truth.

"Put it like this. The morning that I was to marry you, Nicole, I felt nervous and unsure of myself. So I drank a lot. I took this pill. It was supposed to clear my head, but it made me feel sick, like I was wasted. I wanted to go straight to the ER, not to that church. But by then it was too late. I had to go through with it. Too much was on the line. So, as bad as it sounds, I married you, Nicole, for the drunken hell of it."

Nicole rushed at Rashad with a raised fist. She had strength enough to clip the bottom of his chin. Her knuckles hit his chin bone. He moaned. Then he reeled back and squeezed her cheeks between his fingers. She watched him with wide-eyed anticipation. Furious, Rashad screamed and rammed her body against a wall. She gasped in surprise.

"Did you forget I'm pregnant?"

"Damn, this shit is messed up. Sorry," he apologized, feeling instantly remorseful. "This isn't even like me. I-I didn't mean to shove you."

"Hit me," she told him. "Since you hate me so much, go ahead and beat my ass."

"No, I'm not going to do that. I-I don't hate you, Nicole. And if you believe that I do, then that's sad."

"Everything is sad."

"Which is why you need to come to your senses. Forget those fantasies you have. Face the reality that we just can't be together."

But Nicole could not hear what he said. "It's all right, Rashad. Let it all out, babe. I have probably stressed you out so much you can't help but want to take things out on me. So, go ahead and hit me. Do it one time only and get it over with."

He threw up his hands and for a rare moment he wished he could cry. But he was too exasperated to shed a single tear. He knew he had to seriously end things with her whether she wanted to accept the situation or not.

"Nicole, I will not hit you. I don't want to. What I want is for you to get yourself some professional help. Hitting you won't solve a thing. Go get help, dammit. Emmy needs you."

Rashad turned and walked away. But before he went through her door one last time, he turned around. "I gave you a chance, Nicole. You blew that chance time and again. So do not blame me for wanting to divorce you. This is as much your fault as anybody's. Yours and that Cornell Cantu's fault or whatever the fuck his name is."

"So you mean to tell me you want to put an end to us because you are holding a grudge against me for supposedly cheating on you?"

"No, it's not that simple. I tried to make it work but it didn't. And everything that happened—even the stuff before we got married—has contributed to the failure of us."

"Rashad, listen to me, please." For once she believed him. In her heart she knew it was over. He stared at her and waited for her to speak.

"Babe, maybe I wasn't perfect, but at least I was sincere. I was your day one. But you, Rashad, it sounds like even before March twelfth, you pretended like you wanted to marry me. I've never heard of anything like this in my life. And I don't quite know how to take it. Why use me for your stupid-ass games? My heart was involved, but you never cared. You hurt me, Rashad, and now you will know how it feels to hurt."

"Wait, what? I did not pretend to marry you. I wanted to do it, but maybe I should have waited and thought things through. Maybe I still had love in my heart for Kiara, and if I failed you in any way, then that's how I did it."

"So you're telling me that you divorced a woman you still loved?"

"I always loved her."

"Stop. You've hurt me long enough. You'll never hurt me again. I promise you that."

He decided to shut up.

Nicole couldn't continue.

She was done. No more pleading words for her uninterested husband. From now on, what she needed to say would be shown—through conclusive actions.

Rashad turned and left.

Her mind was made up. She grabbed a second burner phone from the drawer and placed another call to Ajalon.

"It's me. Do what you gotta do," she said. "*Ciao.*"

Chapter 15

Federico Freddy, aka Slipper, aka the Invisible Man, was ready for his next assignment. He went by many names, but he only had one main mission. Slipper stood five feet two. His mother was of Hispanic origin, and his daddy was African American. Slipper's face was hard and round. It looked like someone took a meat tenderizer and stamped it from one cheek to the next. There were too many pocks and dents to count. He didn't care whether anyone called him ugly, as long as they didn't say it to his face.

Slipper had been running the streets of Houston ever since he was six. There were many days his family couldn't find him. He was tiny and fast. Amongst his friends, he was the best at playing hide-and-seek. His little body could fit in the weirdest of places all around the house and even in the backyard. Slipper's ways of staying undetected followed him into adulthood. Not getting caught was a game to him, and he got paid handsomely for his skills.

And this is how he became a contract killer.

When he was hired to murder Rashad Quintelle Eason, he considered this job to be like most others.

Slipper got specific instructions on who, what, how, and when the murder was to take place. He was told that he'd receive five figures in cash if he pulled off the hit. He could kill him any way he decided, as long as it was successful.

He was given a down payment and the plan was set in motion.

All week long Rashad felt like a flop for the way things had recently played out between him and Nicole. He felt tired, restless, and frustrated. He thought of his accomplishments, Eason & Son, and all his kids. Those were the things that motivated him. And he pondered his failures: his inability to get it together when it came to love. It broke his heart to be going through a second divorce. And although she'd never believe it, he hated himself each time he replayed in his head the vicious words he'd spoken to Nicole. By the tail end of the week, Rashad decided to take Alexis's advice; she'd once told him to put himself in another person's shoes . . . it was only then that you could possibly understand them.

Midday on Friday, he picked up the phone while he was walking around Home Depot. He was by himself and decided to call Beeva.

"Hi there, Beeva."

"Hi, son. How's everything going?"

"A lot of things have been going wrong, and I want to get them right."

"What do you mean by that?"

"I am having second thoughts—again."

"About the marriage?"

"No, about the divorce."

"Why? What happened?"

"I did something stupid. I swallowed my pride and called Kiara. She was nice to me, Beeva, but I could hear the lack of interest in her voice. If I don't keep the topic on the kids, she's not hearing me."

"Are you still chasing her?"

"Um . . ." He couldn't help but tell a white lie. "Nah, Beeva. I don't want her. She don't want me. It's a wrap."

"Ohhh, son. Be strong. I know how hard it can be."

"Yeah, but you lost one husband to natural causes. And two others got on your nerves so bad, you filed those papers. That's why I'm struggling with my decision, Beeva. Especially when I know this other knuckleheaded Mrs. Eason loves me to death."

"Hmm. Nicole loves the size of your wallet."

"And name one person on this earth who doesn't love money. Nicole's no different. She tries hard. She admits her mistakes. She's genuine."

Beeva couldn't say a word. The way her son went on and on made her think that he might have more feelings for Nicole than he realized. Soon he talked loudly into the phone.

"I hurt her bad. And I was wrong, Beeva," his voice bellowed. "Nicky didn't deserve that. I shouldn't have been so harsh, considering I put my wife in that position in the first place. For all I know, I drove her into doing every damn selfish, insane thing she did. Like father, like son."

"Oh well, son. Do what you have to do. I'm sorry for butting in and making you feel like you could end your union if you didn't really want to do it. But I give you advice only because I love you, Rashad."

"Don't blame yourself. And you know what?"

"What?"

"I love you, too, Mama."

*   *   *

It was after midnight on April 28. The weekend was about to begin, and it promised to be a busy one. Rashad hadn't been able to sleep since he got home. The house was empty. No home-cooked meal. No relaxing bubble baths. And definitely no butt-naked sex.

Rashad lay in bed, mindlessly staring at the ceiling. He hadn't spoken to Nicole in a week, since that night he'd showed up at her apartment and told her they were through. He looked at his watch. It was 1:15 a.m. He figured Nicole would be asleep, but what if she wasn't? He impulsively picked up his phone and dialed Nicole's number. The call immediately went to voice mail. He hung up. Waited a few minutes and tried again a couple more times.

He hung up and laughed. It seemed like his calls were being blocked.

"My girl is just being stubborn. If I give her another day to calm down, we'll see where her head is. See if she's still mad at me. Maybe I can try her again tonight after I get off work. Apologize to her for being so unreasonable and not considering her feelings. We can go out for a drink and have a rational conversation. We can see what steps we need to take to make love right again."

Rashad felt good about his decision to make amends with Nicole, because during that entire week when he'd cut himself off from her, he had to admit he did care about her in his own way. Rashad admired Nicole's strength and determination to be happy in life. He knew that he had put her on and in some small ways he'd helped make her dreams come true. And he really liked that she loved him in spite of his tendency to act like an ass. Even Kiara said that. So he knew he needed to cut her some slack.

He'd let her sleep on it and would contact her later. If she was still blocking him, he'd just show up again at her apartment. With flowers, candy, and kisses.

With his mind made up, Rashad texted Lily Tangaro. He typed:

LT, I know this sounds crazy but I've changed my mind about divorce. Call it off. Talk later . . .

Rashad also typed a reminder in his phone. It read: *Call Nicky.* He set it for 7 a.m. the next morning. And he couldn't wait until he got a chance to talk to her again.

Around the same time, Kiara experienced lots of anxiety about the things that had gone down. She hated how Nicole intruded upon her home. And she despised Rashad for making Nicole think that she wanted to reconcile with him. Kiara hated being lied on. And she spent a few restless nights trying to figure out how to handle her ex and his new wife. So when she decided to take Jazz to the park the last Friday afternoon in April, she was eager to get out in the sun and enjoy some fresh air. She pushed the stroller and listened to some music on her headphones. Her walk was pleasant. As time went on she realized she had journeyed a quarter of a mile. The sun was shining brightly, and due to the blazing heat, it wasn't long before little Jazzy fell asleep. Good. That gave Kiara time to think.

As she ventured down the jogging trail, she noticed a man who looked vaguely familiar. She stared at his slight build, light skin, and dark hair. Then it hit her. That was the guy she'd seen on the sex tape. The one in which Nicole Greene was recorded having sex on her backyard patio. Kiara found out later that the guy was Ajalon Cantu. Rashad told her the entire story about who the man was. He angrily revealed that Ajalon had even worked for him at one time, but he did so under a different name.

Kiara was going to walk past the guy and not think any more about it. But she abruptly stopped.

She caught his eye.

"Hello," Kiara said. "Are you Ajalon?"

"Why do you ask?"

"Your ex-girlfriend, Nicole, works for me."

"Oh yeah?"

"Yes."

"You're Kiara?"

"Oh, wow. You know my name?"

"And much more."

Kiara was intrigued. "Got a moment?"

"I sure do."

She and Ajalon began to walk and talk. He seemed like a cool dude. He spilled his story, his background, and let her know that he wasn't doing too well in Houston.

"Truthfully, ma'am, the job market has been up and down, here and there."

"I see. So you need money, right?"

"You hiring?" he asked jokingly.

"Not in my department, no. But I'm sure there's something you can do to make a living."

"I am good at many things," he told her. They stood there, swapping horror stories.

"I haven't always walked a straight path, but it's made me the man that I am today."

"No one gets it right all the time, Ajalon. You aren't alone."

After a while, talking to Kiara felt easy and unstrained. There was something about her that made him want to tell her things he thought she needed to hear.

"My ex-girlfriend doesn't tell the whole truth, for the whole truth would destroy her imaginary perfect world. Nicole loves to call me a criminal. But she doesn't have a perfect history, either."

"Are you serious, Ajalon?" Kiara asked. "Before I hired her, the background check came back clean. Are you sure?"

"Yes. I was there. Ms. Kiara, I am ashamed to admit this, but years ago, I was what they call a drug bunny. If you wanted it, my job was to make sure and get it. And one time, when I couldn't do a job myself, she agreed to deliver a package of white girl for me."

"White girl?"

"Heroin. It was the good shit. She told me not to tell her what was in the package. But she knew it wasn't a bag of groceries."

"I'll bet. Because if it was some food, knowing her she would've opened up that bag."

"Maybe. Maybe not. Anyway, she helped me out one time when I was sick and confined. And this person I was dealing with threatened to slice off my balls and mail them to my parents in Brooklyn if I didn't have his three pounds of white girl, which was valued at a little over one rack."

"One rack?"

"Ten Gs."

"Oh. Go on."

"I told my girl that I needed her more than I ever did. That it was a matter of life or death. I told her, 'Nicolette, if you love someone, sometimes you must do things that you do not understand or like, and I need you to take this package. I need you to go see a man. They call him Rat because he's big, black, short, and fat. Anyway, here is his address. Go to him and give Rat exactly what he wants. And he will hand you something. And you are to bring it back to me. Never ask me what it is, and I won't have to involve you. But if we get married, then you would never have to testify against me and vice versa.'"

"Jesus! How did she respond?"

"She flat-out told me that she couldn't do it. She was scared that this type of 'shady activity,' as she called it, could mess up her college studies. It was almost December. She needed to prepare for finals. She complained and bitched. She questioned why she was involved with me."

"But obviously she did it anyway?"

"She made up a million excuses. But my ride or die went and got in the car and she drove away. I was sick and felt even sicker until the day she got back. She handed to me what Rat gave to her. And I never asked her to do such a thing ever again. But when I got arrested later on, the only thing her eyes spoke to me the first time she came to see me behind bars was, *Do not tell what I did. Leave me out of it.*"

"Nicole left you hanging, Ajalon? That doesn't sound like ride or die."

"Remember, she was almost graduating. She had come too far to blow it on a reckless road trip to see some guy named Rat. She counted up the cost and had a change of heart. She could have said no, but she said yes, and she did me a big favor. Because, as you can see, I still have my balls."

"Alrighty then. I guess that is ride or die."

"I guess."

"But do you feel she should have served time, too?"

Ajalon held his words for a long time before releasing them.

"I-I never completed my college studies. I dropped out of classes and withdrew from school. And she always felt like that was a bad decision. She felt I was hurting my future, our future. She felt like I rebelled against her good advice when she was trying to help me stay on a straighter path."

"Amazing what you can learn about a person from someone else who really knows them."

"Yes. I know her in ways that you don't."

"Like how?"

"Recently, she asked me to kill Rashad. And she gave me some money to do the job."

Kiara stopped walking. "Why would she do that?"

"Because he's hurt her. She wants him dead."

"Oh shit. Are you serious? I don't know that I want to hear this."

"I'm sorry. It's the truth. I cannot keep it inside any longer."

Kiara felt dizzy with surprise. "And so the plot to kill my husband—my ex-husband—it's totally her idea?"

"She's the mastermind. She gave me the what, when, and how. I already knew the why."

"If this has anything to do with her thinking I want him back, she's wrong. What a waste. Because Rashad knows that I would never remarry him. So it's like he deceived Nicole by telling her we were getting back together. I guess he played on her weaknesses."

"And I think he underestimated your strength."

Kiara thought about the hell Rashad had put her through. She, too, wanted him to feel her pain in the same way that he had given her pain.

"How much is Nicole paying you?" she asked.

"Twenty-five hundred total. But the hit man that I found will earn way more than me. I'm just the middle man."

"Um, don't think I'm crazy, but may I pat you down, please?"

"May you what?"

"You're not recording this conversation, are you, Ajalon?"

"No."

"May I see your cell phone?"

"Sure."

Ajalon handed over his phone. Kiara asked him to type in his passcode and unlock the phone. She reviewed his most recent texts and call log. She politely asked him to open the voice recorder. She looked at the previous recordings. None of his log of recordings had been done on that day or during the short time they'd been talking.

"Okay, Ajalon. It doesn't seem like you are trying to act sheisty with me."

"But you saw me and approached me first, remember?"

"Right. Sorry." She paused and looked around to make sure they were alone. "I will double the amount if you do it for me."

"Do it, as in—?"

She nodded.

"You'll pay me five Gs?"

"I will."

"But why would you want to do that when she's already paid me?"

"I dunno. Maybe it's because I'd get to pay my ex back for all the shit he put me through. He's lied to me, lied on me, made me look like an idiot. And the crap he's done to me started many years ago and he's still putting me through hell."

Ajalon gave Kiara's proposal a little more thought. He was almost out of food and other basic necessities. Plus, the other day he received a threatening letter from the electric company due to non-payment. He nodded at Kiara, then said, "I'm in."

Kiara exhaled. She couldn't believe what she'd just asked this man to do. She patted down Ajalon one more time. She returned his cell phone to him. She made sure he had no pen and no paper on him.

She told him what she wanted done.

He agreed to her terms.

They shook hands and she promised to be in touch.

"Don't tell a soul," she told him.

"Your secret is my secret," he said. "I have way more to lose than you."

"Do you really believe that?"

"I do."

He turned around to leave and she instantly stopped him. "Ajalon, I-I've never done anything even remotely close to this. I'm actually quite scared. I'm no saint, but this type of thing is so not me."

"What are you saying?"

"I-I've changed my mind. I don't want you to go through with it."

"You what?"

Unable to help herself, Kiara broke down. She sobbed and tried to muffle the awful sounds by covering her mouth with both hands.

"I've been going through a lot . . . and it's kind of getting to me. But I can't get with this. I just can't."

Kiara continued to cry. Ajalon felt so bad. The lady seemed like a nice woman. She was angry, but definitely not a cold-blooded killer.

She sniffled and pulled herself together. But when she saw Jazzy stirring in her sleep, it brought Kiara to fresh tears.

"Can we please sit down for a second?"

"Sure, Kiara."

"You don't know me very well, Ajalon, but right now I can't help but question why I would allow myself to even go there. How could I even allow myself to—"

"You were angry."

"Angry, yes. Crazy, no! I just contemplated doing something that Nicole would do."

"Are you sure you've changed your mind?"

"Definitely! I hate the stupid shit that Rashad does, but this is the wrong way to go. I mean, who in this world hasn't done wrong? Would death be the payment for all of us who've messed up? Me? You?"

"Not all of us, ma'am. But some people do deserve to die for what their evil ways. That's just how it is."

She regretted ever stopping to talk to Ajalon, and she hoped to God that she could trust him. "Look, Ajalon. Let's forget the whole thing. I had a horrible moment and that's all it was. I-I really hope that you never mention this to anyone. In fact, I-I still think I should pay you. But what if I give you the money, but you tell someone anyway?"

"Lady, you just heard me tell you that Nicole already paid me to find someone to kill your ex. What's stopping you from going to the police yourself?"

"Okay then. Let's look at it like this. If you tell on me, I guess I'd tell on you."

"That sounds like a threat."

"I don't want it to sound that way. But I'm scared. Really scared. The entire thing just sucks. Even if Nicole wants you to do the job, I can't forget that's my kids' father. So please, Ajalon, please don't do it. Return Nicole's money. And I will pay you not to hurt him."

Ajalon was shocked. This scenario was feeling stranger and stranger. He wondered if it was all a setup. Perhaps an unbelievable plot masterminded by Nicole. He wasn't sure about anything anymore. He felt sick to his stomach, and he'd never imagined that coming to Texas would bring more trouble his way. And he had no idea what to do about it.

Chapter 16

Every other Friday, Rashad and Jerry had a strict routine. Together they'd take a drive over to the warehouse and pick up some raw materials that would be needed for the next construction job. But on the evening of Friday, April 28, something came up at the last minute. Jerry wouldn't be able to make the trip.

"I hate to do this to you, Boss Man." Jerry had placed a quick call to Rashad. "Once again, something's going on with my grands. They are running a fever. Can't take any chances. So I gotta go."

"Damn, Jerry, this really puts me out."

"I know. I was supposed to drive over to the warehouse with you."

"I guess I can do it alone. You go on ahead and take care of your business. Hope everything works out with the grandkids."

"Thanks, Rashad. I appreciate this."

"No problem."

"See you in the morning."

"Yeah, 'bye, Jerry."

Rashad hung up. He went to his desk and logged on to his computer to pull a report of the materials that he needed to pick up. It was getting late. Nearly nine o'clock. The new project would begin at seven or eight the next morning.

He made a list and headed out to the Eason & Son van. As he started driving, he made a mental note to try to call Nicole again. Or maybe he could surprise her with a friendly visit. He just wanted to make things right again between the two of them.

After a twenty-minute drive, Rashad arrived at the warehouse location. A two-story building with very few windows, it was sandwiched between two other businesses. A furniture warehouse was on the right, and a gas station was on the left.

The floodlight that normally illuminated the warehouse's entrance was not working.

"I need to let the owners know they gotta get that fixed. I'll call 'em first thing tomorrow," he said. "One more damn thing to remember."

Rashad put a reminder on his calendar, then exited the van. He left the floodlights on so he could see his way into the building. With the driver's-side door still open, Rashad walked to the rear of the van; he opened one of the double doors and retrieved the dolly.

He wheeled the dolly to the garage and punched in a four-digit code; the door squeaked as it opened.

Rashad laughed to himself. "Damn garage needs some WD-40. More shit to remember. This is ridiculous."

He went inside and left the door partially ajar, thinking his task would take only a few minutes.

Rashad went into the building that he'd been inside a hundred times before. It was old, dusty, and dilapidated.

He proceeded inside and headed to the big load of weld-able rebar, steel mesh, lumber, and materials needed to pour concrete. Eason & Son had been contracted to build a five-car detached garage for a house out in the Woodlands and he was excited to do the job.

He piled up a few pieces of lumber and loaded them on the dolly. He then was in the middle of picking up some rebar when he felt a presence behind him. He assumed it was Jerry and figured he had changed his mind.

Without turning his back, he said, "Hey, Jerry. Glad you could make it."

A metal object smacked the back of his head.

Rashad turned around.

A strange man was glaring at him.

Rashad's eyes enlarged. He raised his hands.

"Get on your knees."

Rashad fell to his knees. His lips trembled. His eyes stayed on the gun as he gasped for breath. After a beat, he finally found his voice. For ten to fifteen minutes, he pleaded for his life. But it did no good.

A loud *bang* sounded.

His eyes opened wider but looked at nothing.

The salty taste of blood filled his entire mouth.

Rashad quivered as globs of blood and pink chunks of his brain exploded from his head. Rashad took one final breath. Then he entered into eternal darkness, where no one could hear the screams that burst from his soul.

It was 3:45 a.m., the wee hours of the next morning. Nicole woke up in a cold sweat. Her pajamas clung to her skin. She'd have to wake up in only a few hours because Emmy was about to start attending a new day-care center.

Last night was Emmy's final time being cared for by Nadia. Nicole had invited the nanny over so she could play with her daughter once more. Having a nanny was a luxury that Nicole could no longer afford. "If it wasn't for Rashad, Emmy would still have a nanny. But now my daughter has to be dropped off at a fucking twenty-four-hour day care. The staff is too young and inexperienced. But what else can I do?"

She fought hard to go back to sleep. When she woke up at seven, she showered then prepared breakfast for herself and Emmy. She wanted to turn on the news, but was too afraid. Every time her phone beeped, she jumped. But it was just game notifications. No texts. No calls.

Nicole put on the leather gloves and went and got the last burner phone. She placed it in a storage bag and dropped it in her purse.

An hour and a half later, she and Emmy left the apartment and were on their way. Every time she saw a white van on the street, she froze. And when it seemed as though a police car was following her, she carefully drove until she reached an intersection and then turned the corner. She looked in her rearview. The police weren't following.

Nicole pulled up in front of the child-care facility. Although it was nine in the morning, the parking lot was packed.

"Damn shame that so many single moms have no other alternative than to leave their kids at places like these."

She mustered up a smile and carried Emmy on her hip. She managed to get through the check-in process and had a seat in the lobby.

"Hey there, Nicole," the director said. Her name was

Wendy. "Glad to see you made it out. We'll be happy to spend time with your daughter and make sure she feels comfortable. You're welcome to stick around as long as you like. She's in good hands."

"Thank you."

Wendy led Nicole to the toddler room. "This is where Emmy will spend most of her time."

"Okay, I'll be here for a little while and make sure my daughter feels comfortable. And then I'll sneak away and leave and will check back in a few hours. But I'll be reachable by cell phone if Emmy gets upset."

"I'm sure she'll have so much fun with the other kids she might not even notice you're missing. You go right ahead and leave when you're ready. And I'm so sorry that you and your husband are splitting up."

"What are you talking about? I never told you that. Why would you say something like that?"

Wendy gave Nicole an odd look. "But isn't that what you told me a few days ago? Don't you remember?"

Nicole's face was ashen. "I did? Oh, I don't know why I told you that. I must have been talking about someone else. Not me. My husband and I are fine."

"Oh, okay. Maybe I got it mixed up."

"Yeah, you are very mixed up. Um, is it alright with you if I use the ladies' room? My stomach is hurting."

"Go right ahead. Down that hallway. To the very end, last door on the right."

Nicole practically ran down the hall. She opened and quickly locked the door. She raised the lid and threw up for several minutes. When she was done, she rinsed her mouth out good.

"Oh shit. Why me?"

Deep inside she already knew what a pregnancy test

couldn't tell her. She knew she was going to have another child of Rashad's. But if he was dead, what would happen then? Was it too late to get Ajalon to stop the hit?

Why did she even pay her ex to kill her husband? It felt like a bad dream. She wanted to call Ajalon, but decided to wait. Not knowing what had happened was killing her, and she wanted to delay the inevitable for as long as possible.

Later that morning, even though he did not want to, Jerry placed a call to Nicole. It rang three times before she picked up.

She started to say, "Hey, Jerry," but she simply said, "Hello?"

"Nicole. It's me, Jerry." He never called her Mrs. Eason, and she thought it was so disrespectful.

"Hey, Jerry. What's up?"

"Um. Have you heard from the Boss Man?"

"Uh, not lately," she said. Nicole didn't know how much of their business Rashad told to Jerry. "Why do you ask?"

"I'm out here in the Woodlands. We're supposed to start a garage project, and last night when I talked to Rashad, he told me that he'd meet me out here between seven and eight. I've been waiting since seven fifteen. And three hours later, no Rashad. His phone rings and rings. No answer. No callbacks."

"Um, maybe he overslept."

"Rashad never oversleeps. I've known this man for years and not showing up for work is not like him."

"Well, Jerry, tell you what. I will call him and see what's going on. If I find out anything I'll make sure and call you back. It's probably nothing. He may be at his second home."

"Second home?"

"Home Depot." She laughed. "Or Harbor Freight."

"I dunno. Maybe. When I talked to him last night, he was on his way to the warehouse. Did he mention it when he came home?"

Okay. Jerry does not know that Rashad and I are living separately.

"No. He never mentioned that to me."

"This is nuts. The owners of the house are sitting around looking at me like I'm scoping out their house to rob them. You know how rich people get around strangers."

"I, uh, I wouldn't know, Jerry. Anyway, um, I was kind of busy."

"Sorry to disturb you. Call me back if you hear anything. Otherwise I will tell these people we'll have to reschedule. Waste of time and gas."

"I'll call if I can. 'Bye, Jerry."

She quickly hung up. Damn. It sounded like the hit went off. But she wasn't really sure.

She finished off the bottle of tequila and went to her kitchen. Cooking calmed her down. She threw together a quick lunch and baked a cake.

Suddenly her cell phone rang. It was Myles.

"Oh shit, no, no, I can't do this." She let the call go into voice mail. Soon she saw the icon appear on her notifications. A message had been left.

She pressed "1" to listen.

"Hi, Mom."

Oh shit, he just called me "Mom."

"It's Myles. I drew you a picture. It's of a pretend zoo that I made up. I wanted to send it to you, but I don't know how. Call me back and tell me. My mommy is busy right now talking to Mr. Osborne."

She heard Myles's recorded voice and listened two more times. So Kiara and Eddison were together. That meant that no one had heard about Rashad yet.

She finished eating, then decided to call Rashad's number. Her knees knocked together when his cell rang. She decided not to leave a message.

In her heart she felt that he must've been dead. But why hadn't Ajalon called her?

It had been more then twenty-four hours since anyone had heard from Rashad.

Kiara attempted to call him, but there was no answer. No voice. Only voice mail. When Jerry called Nicole a second time and could get no solid answer from her about his boss's whereabouts, he phoned Kiara.

"I'm worried. This isn't like Rashad at all."

A dreadful feeling gutted Kiara's belly. Had anything bad happened to him? The last time someone had seen him was at Eason and Son. They thought he might have tried to go make a new deposit at the bank. But Jerry doubted that. His boss swore he'd never try that again. In fact, he wanted to come up with some new security measures so that everyone could be safe.

"What about all the construction sites, Jerry? Have you checked with those? I remember when he used to fall asleep at some of those sites. He'd stay all night, then come home."

"Yeah, that man can work so hard that he can't see straight."

"I hope he hasn't had a car wreck. He could be lying in a ditch somewhere."

She said that, but inside she wished that was all that had happened. She hoped that Ajalon Cantu had nothing to do with Rashad's disappearance. She hung up from Jerry and was unable to concentrate. She felt jittery, and negative thoughts punched her mind constantly. But the next evening, not quite a full forty-eight hours had passed, and she still had not heard from Rashad. Kiara felt she needed to take action. She remembered how to get into his Find My Cell Phone account. And when she pulled up the info, she gasped when she saw the blue light flickering on the computer screen. She could barely breathe as she raced to her car with Myles and Jazzy in tow. The address was a warehouse where some of his heavy equipment items were stored.

When Kiara arrived at the warehouse, the entrance gate was wide open. As she drove inside the parking area, she immediately saw Rashad's work van right next to the building.

"Maybe Rashad fell asleep in the van."

Kiara pulled up next to his vehicle and got out of her car. All the doors were closed. When she peered inside the window, he wasn't in the driver's seat. No other cars were in the area.

"Maybe he left the van here and got picked up by someone?"

Kiara dialed Nicole's number, but the woman did not answer the call.

"Hmm."

Kiara decided to go inside the warehouse. She didn't want to leave the kids alone in her car, but she told herself she'd only be gone a couple of minutes.

"Wait here," she instructed Myles. "If I'm not back in two minutes, please come find me."

"Okay, Mommy."

She got out of the car and walked over to the warehouse entrance. She remembered the code to the door and it squeaked as it opened.

"Rashad? Are you here? It's Kiara."

She walked inside and traveled about twenty yards when she encountered an awful smell. It was a sickly sweet, yet sharp odor, similar to pineapples and raspberries. She quickly covered her nose.

A cold chill came over her. Then she looked to the left and spotted a body spread out on the floor. It was lying on its side. Pools of blood surrounded the corpse. Dried blood wildly covered parts of the body. Maggots and flies were descending on top of the corpse. The smell was bad enough to make the last meal she ate rise up in her throat.

She took a closer look. Half of his face was gone, but she knew his body. She could never forget his shape, his hands. He lay facedown, unmoving, and looked as stiff as stone.

"Rashad? Oh my God, noooo."

Kiara heard the ringing of his cell phone, which was abandoned only a few feet away.

That's when Kiara screamed at the top of her lungs.

She refused to believe that it had happened. Did not want to accept that he was gone.

She trembled uncontrollably and she could not think logically for several seconds.

The kids! What if Rashad had gotten killed and the murderer was still nearby or even somewhere inside the warehouse? She had no idea how long he'd been there. Kiara sprinted through the warehouse and stumbled as she ran blindly toward the exit.

She burst through the door, afraid of what she'd discover. But Myles smiled at her through the car window and she'd never been more relieved in her life.

Kiara jumped in the car, quickly locked all the doors, and called 911.

"Hello, there's been a terrible accident. Please hurry."

Chapter 17

Kiara was on the phone with the dispatcher.

"Is anyone hurt?"

"Um, yes. Yes."

"How many are injured?"

"Just one. A man."

"Approximate age?"

"Thirty-five. He just celebrated his birthday not too long ago."

"What type of injuries?"

"Fatal," she whispered.

Myles, who was sitting in the front passenger seat, stared quizzically at his mother.

"Is there a pulse, ma'am?"

"I did not check. His face—" She couldn't bring herself to tell the dispatcher the extent of Rashad's injuries.

"What's the address?"

Kiara told the dispatcher the exact location.

"Um, I am scared to death. I feel like freaking out. Hold on a second, please. Our children are with me." She hesitated, then got out of the car. Myles continued gawking at her. She turned her back to her son.

"Okay, um, it's my ex. He's dead. I think he's been killed. Oh Lord, this is a nightmare."

The dispatcher told Kiara that help was on the way.

"I'm going to hang up." She couldn't bear to talk to a stranger any longer. The woman protested, but Kiara apologized and ended the call. Her phone instantly rang again but Kiara didn't answer.

Myles suddenly sprang from the car and ran to his mother.

"Why did you call 911? Why are you looking so scared? What's wrong, Mommy?"

"Um, Myles, we-we're trying to find out. There's been a terrible accident, and we need the police to come out. Baby, please get back in the car."

"Is my daddy hurt?"

"Get your little ass back in the car. Move it. Now!"

His face twisted up in pain.

"Myles, baby, I'm sorry. I didn't mean to yell. Come here." He raced into Kiara's arms and she held him close, knowing that this hug would be the first of many she'd have to give to him.

"I love you, son. I do. But we're dealing with an emergency. That means your mom may not act like herself right now. I need you to overlook me. You understand?"

"Yes," he said.

"Good. I need you to be a strong boy and get back in the car." Kiara folded her arms and quickly scanned the area. "I have to make some more calls. Please, Myles, help me out and go watch Jazzy and make sure she's okay."

"Yes, ma'am."

As soon as Myles was out of listening range, Kiara's mind was so scattered she had to look through her most recent calls to find Eddison's phone number. Her phone was constantly ringing but she kept rejecting the calls.

She managed to dial her man. "Babe," she told Eddison as soon as she heard his voice.

"Hi there. What's up with you?"

Kiara began gasping for breath.

"What's wrong? You sound like you're about to have a heart attack."

"I think I am, too. I-I found him," she said, unable to say his name. "It looks really bad. My ex is gone, Eddy."

"What?"

The sounds of emergency vehicles filled the streets. In the far distance, she recognized an approaching ambulance and two police cars headed in her direction.

"Babe, please come to me. I'm at the warehouse, and I need you. I really need you."

"I'm on the way."

She gave Eddison the address and he promised to stay on the phone with her until he arrived.

Two officers pulled up; they got out of their vehicles, identified themselves and asked Kiara what happened. They withdrew their weapons and cautiously went inside the building. They came out a short time later.

"It doesn't seem like anyone else is inside, but we will call for backup." The men placed several more phone calls. The EMS personnel arrived and went inside the building toting their equipment. Shortly thereafter, another patrol unit stopped right next to the other vehicles. They taped off the area then went inside the warehouse.

Kiara waited impatiently until Eddison arrived. She rushed into his arms and buried her face in his chest.

"Calm down, Kiara. I'm here for you, babe."

"I know you are, Eddy."

"Did you say Rashad is gone? Like, dead?"

She nodded.

"Damn! What happened?"

"I don't know. I-I'm waiting to find out."

One of the officers asked to see her driver's license. She handed it over and waited for the police to check to see if she had any warrants.

After a while a crime scene unit showed up. Two women, dressed in dark jumpsuits, hurried past Kiara and Eddy. She listened to them talking.

"How's your mom doing?" one of them asked the other.

"She is alright. Just gotta take it easy when she gets in the shower so she won't slip and fall again."

Their casual conversation faded as they disappeared inside the warehouse.

Kiara folded her hands across her chest and watched as she stood next to her car.

Within minutes an unmarked car arrived. A man and a woman stepped out and approached Kiara.

"Hi, ma'am. We need to ask a few questions."

"Okay."

"Were you a witness to this tragedy?"

"No."

"Do you know if there were any witnesses?"

"I dunno. I don't think so. I haven't seen anyone."

"Do you know if the victim wore glasses?"

"No, Rashad had twenty-twenty vision."

"And that van? Is that owned by the victim?"

"Oh my goodness," Kiara said. "Yes, that's the company van and I'm assuming he drove it over here."

"And was this vehicle here when you first arrived?"

"I believe so, but I could be wrong. I don't know what happened, honestly, and I am hoping you guys can tell me something."

She watched them carefully open the door of the Eason & Son van.

The CSU team asked a few more general questions. Kiara finished giving them her statement. They told her she was free to leave.

Eddison led Kiara a few yards away from the commotion. He lifted her chin. "I'm sorry, Kiara."

No words came from her mouth. A terrible dread fell on her and she needed a moment to process everything.

"I need a favor," she told Eddison.

"Anything."

"Call Mama Flora. Call Adina. Just tell them that . . . tell them—"

"I'll do it. Don't you worry about a thing."

Kiara returned to her car and Eddison followed behind her as she made her way back to her house. When she pulled up into the driveway, in some ways she wished that Rashad would greet her. She wished that he'd rush out of the house and yell, "Gotcha" or something equivalent that would let her know that the worst had not just happened.

"You need me to go inside with you?"

"Yes, please do."

Eddison carried Jazzy inside and went upstairs to oversee getting the kids situated. He made phone calls and was ready to do anything else to help.

As soon as she knew the kids were safe and sound, Kiara retreated to her bedroom. There was one other person she wanted to call. At one time the woman had been her enemy. But now she wanted to treat her more like a friend.

She got Alexis on the phone. "Get over here. Now."

"Why? What's going on?"

"Are you driving right now?"

"Yes, I have Hayley with me, and we were going to Baskin-Robbins."

"Don't go. Come to my house. It's an emergency." She burst into tears.

"Kiara, what's wrong?"

"He's . . . Rashad is—" And she hung up.

As soon as Alexis arrived at Kiara's front door, she was immediately yanked on the arm and pulled inside the foyer.

"Excuse me?" Alexis complained. "Hold on a sec. You see, I have Hayley."

"But, Alexis," Kiara pleaded. She took one look at Alexis and whispered, "Rashad is *d-e-a-d*."

"What?" Her purse plunged to the floor. "What the hell did you just say?"

"Your daughter shouldn't be hearing this. Put her in the family room. Never mind. I'll do it. Wait right here." Kiara grabbed the little girl and got her settled in front of the TV, then walked away. She returned to the corridor but it was empty.

"Where'd you go?"

Alexis yelled, "I'm in the kitchen. Because I just know you did not say what I think you said. Are you fucking kidding me, Kiara?"

"No, I'm not," Kiara told her, joining her at the breakfast table. "I don't play when it comes to that. Girl, I found him. He was lying on the ground. It was bad. I didn't want to believe it was him. There was so much blood. I can't get that vision out of my head."

"So he was *killed*?"

"Yes, Alexis."

"That's crazy. Are you sure? How do you know?"

"Because I know what I saw." Kiara's voice was shaking. "I-I saw him lying on that ground. He wasn't m-moving. He didn't respond when I called him."

"But, Kiara, do you think he did it to himself?" Alexis asked.

"No way. Rashad is too fucking vain to put a bullet hole in his own head."

"Oh my God. Rashad Eason, dead?"

"I know. Girl, you look like you're about to go into cardiac arrest. Take deep breaths. Breathe."

Alexis nodded. She slowly breathed in and out until she could find her voice. "Okay, so he was at the warehouse. But how'd you find him?"

"Nobody had heard from Rashad. And I couldn't get in touch with him, either. Then it occurred to me that I could try and find out something through his cell phone. I happened to remember how to log in to his Find My Cell Phone account."

"I wonder how long he was out there. Like, who did this? And why?"

Ajalon's face flashed in Kiara's head. She could not believe he'd go back on his word. Not after she'd paid him. But what if he did do it? And why?

"Who did it? I dunno who. But whoever did it left Rashad alone to bleed to death. I wonder if he could have been saved somehow. I wonder if he tried to call any of us."

"Did you tell Nicole?"

"Actually, before I called you, I was able to get in contact with her. I told her that I had to share some bad news. I told her what happened. And she told me she didn't believe me. She called me a liar. It got nasty. I'm trying to help her out, and all she could do was accuse me of trying to outdo her. As if there is a competition between wives about spreading the news about a husband's death. Just unreal."

"She's a nutcase."

"She is. But it's so ironic and sad that she is the widow, you know. Technically, she is the one who gets to sit in the front pew of the church. And something tells me that she's the type who'd enjoy doing something like that."

"I hate to say this, but I can't stand that bitch. And in some ways I feel like this is all my fault."

"What did you say?" Kiara asked, alarmed. "Why would it be your fault?"

Instead of answering her, Alexis jumped up from her chair. She opened the refrigerator door, then pushed it closed. She flung open a drawer. Then slammed it shut. She cursed and squeezed her temples.

"My God. Are you alright, Alexis? You're making me dizzy."

"I-I just—" Alexis ran into Kiara's bedroom and threw herself on the bed. She closed her eyes and loudly wept. She thought of Glynis and her baby daddy. First her sister died unexpectedly and now this. She could not fathom not being able to see or talk to the people she loved. Why did tragedy have to strike her life time and again? Alexis lay there until it felt like she was being stared at. She opened her eyes. Kiara stood over her with a raised hand.

"Why the fuck are you crying over my husband?" She struck Alexis on top of her head, banging her closed fist on the woman over and over.

"Stop it, Kiara. Stop! What did I do?"

"Why you crying over my husband?"

"But he's not . . ."

Kiara didn't hear a word Alexis said. She got on the bed and reached for the woman's neck. They tussled around on the mattress for a few seconds. Somehow Kiara managed to get Alexis in a chokehold. She pressed both her thumbs against Alexis's windpipe and squeezed.

"Were y'all two still fucking even after you told me you weren't? Are you making a fool out of me again? I'm so sick of you fucking whores I could scream."

Alexis bucked and kicked her legs until Kiara fell off of her. Kiara sprang back, recovered, and climbed on her bed again. She yanked at the frightened woman's strands of hair with all her might. Pulling the hair in between her fingers, Kiara cursed and yelled some more.

"Don't lie to me. Did you fuck again? Did you?"

Alexis shrieked and tried to prevent any more of her weave from being pulled out. But Kiara gripped a few strands and jerked them again. She blankly stared at tracks of hair that were suddenly resting in her palm.

In that brief moment, Alexis reached up and smacked Kiara hard across her face. Kiara reeled back.

"Don't put your hands on me, Kiara. I know you're upset but you acting like a stupid ass wife that wants to beat up the other woman doesn't work for me."

"What?" Kiara asked, clearly stunned that Alexis fought back.

"Even if we did fuck again, take your anger out on the man. He swore up and down what he'd do for you. But I haven't promised you shit."

Kiara closed her eyes and took a few deep breaths. "You're right." She wanted to come to her senses and not be so out of control.

Alexis glanced at herself in the bedroom mirror. "Dammit Kiara. Look what you did to my fucking hair." Alexis's scalp was searing hot, feeling like she'd been doused in boiling grease. She attempted to rub the tiny bald spot.

Kiara glared at Alexis. "All you care about is your stupid-ass hair? I don't give a damn about that. And why did you say 'even if you did' fuck Rashad? I don't like how that sounds. Did you or didn't you?"

"No, *no*, Kiara. Jesus Christ. I haven't had sex with Rashad or any man in I don't know how long. He meant nothing to me. I've told you that shit a million times.

You're going to have to trust me on this one. Please stop believing that I had sex with him. Now, will you let it go? That man is dead." Alexis's voice grew hoarse as she struggled to breathe normally again. Kiara raised her hand again ready to strike her just in case she lied. Alexis yelled, "Please stop it, please!" Kiara looked so out of it that Alexis wondered if she'd have to end up fighting for her life.

Kiara slowly lowered her hand and stood quietly before Alexis. She backed away from her, yet remained in the room as an overpowering presence.

"Why is all of this happening?" Alexis slumped back on the bed and finally wept after getting beat up. The pillow-case got completely soaked with her tears. Her eyelids were puffy. Snot ran from her reddened nose. She felt unattractive for the first time in her life.

"Kiara, I don't understand why you attacked me like that. Why do you keep forgetting that Rashad Eason is not . . . *your* husband . . . anymore."

As Alexis's tears subsided, the room grew eerily quiet. Calmness finally settled over Kiara. "You're right again," she said in a hoarse voice. "Rashad hasn't been mine in a long time, long before we even got divorced. But this situation is unbelievably difficult for me. It's so unreal. And I-I'm truly sorry." Her voice sounded tiny and defeated. "Alexis, you have no idea what I've been through. Finding his body. Feeling so hopeless and powerless. And now my kids . . . I gotta stay strong for my kids. Damn you, Rashad." She meekly returned a handful of hair to Alexis and excused herself.

Alexis didn't appreciate getting smacked upside the head, but she could understand the duress that her boss must have been feeling. Rashad's unexpected death over-whelmed her, too. She stayed in the room thinking about

Hayley and trying to decide how to tell her that her daddy was gone. Her mind grew numb with anguish. And she hoped that whoever had killed Rashad was ready to be punished for their sins.

A short while later Alexis went to get her daughter from the family room. Kiara quietly walked them to the door.

"Again, I apologize, Alexis. I hope you can forgive me."

Alexis was stonily silent. But she nodded, turned around, and left. Kiara's apologies were not her priority right then. All she wanted to do was be with Varnell and seek his comfort.

Eddison returned from upstairs and asked Kiara how she was doing.

"I'm losing it, babe. I don't want to, but it seems like I am. Why am I acting this way?"

"It's part of the grieving process, Kiara."

They retreated to the kitchen.

"I know that this may not sound like much," he told her, "but it's important to do as many normal things as possible. That's why I want you to sit in that chair over there. Don't get up for any reason. Don't take every phone call just because it rings. Your mind has experienced a great shock, and it's going to take a little time for life to feel good again."

"You've been through this when Nina died."

"Right. I know how it feels to lose someone . . . someone who was close to you."

"I did not love him, Eddison, but he is—"

"The father of your children. I know. Anyway, I'm about to fix you some hot tea and I'll put a lot of lemon and honey in it. And I want you to sip that tea and try to relax as much as possible."

"Yes, babe. I will try. God, I'm so glad that you're in my life."

Later that evening, Kiara received a call from a detective. He asked her if she could drive downtown on Travis Street so they could ask her a few questions and she agreed.

When she arrived at the central police station, she identified herself and was escorted to a plain room that held only a simple table and four chairs.

"Hello, I'm sorry we have to meet under these circumstances, but we have a few questions. I understand that you are the one who placed the 911 call this morning. I'm Detective Longfellow. I'm one of the investigators for this case." Suddenly a young woman walked into the room. "And this is Sergeant Humphrey. We will work on this case together."

"Nice to meet you both."

Kiara sat at a table. Sergeant Humphrey pulled out a tape recorder. She said, "Before we get started, please be aware that in this police station there is no expectation of privacy."

"Am I a suspect?"

"Why would you ask that?" said Sergeant Humphrey.

"Because I don't know why else I'd be called down here."

"We just are trying to piece together what happened to Rashad, and we will interview whomever we need to in order to get all the required information," Humphrey replied. "It won't take long."

"Alright."

Detective Longfellow asked, "When's the last time you spoke with the victim?"

"Um, I don't know. It was recently." She was scared to death to say the wrong thing.

"Was it on Friday, or the day before?"

What if the police noticed how nervous she appeared? She knew they were trained to analyze nonverbal behavior.

"I'd have to check my phone," she said, her voice tapering off. She felt around in her purse for her cell phone and prayed they wouldn't ask her for it.

"How'd you find the body again?" asked Sergeant Humphrey.

"I found it through an iPhone app."

"And do you still have Rashad's phone?"

"Um, what?"

"Rashad's phone?" said Detective Longfellow. "It will be considered evidence and we don't want anything to compromise this investigation."

Kiara hesitated and handed it over. She wished she would have carefully looked through his phone when she first found it. But that wasn't on her mind. At the time all Kiara cared about was finding out where he was and hoping that he was all right.

"If you don't mind, I have to be going," she said. "I have to tell my kids that their father is dead."

"I'm so sorry—may I call you Mrs. Eason?" asked Sergeant Humphrey. "Longfellow told me Rashad was your ex and you both still share the same last name."

"Yes, that is true, and yes . . . I don't mind if you call me Mrs. Eason."

"Thank you. Now, do you know whether Rashad had any enemies?"

Kiara paused. "Um, not that I know of." As much as she wanted to implicate Nicole, she resisted the urge. "I could be wrong but I think the current wife would know more than me."

The police took her through a round of questioning that lasted twenty minutes. They thanked her for her time and told her she could leave.

"Please, officers, I want to know what happened. Contact me if you find out any more info."

"Will do. 'Bye, Mrs. Eason."

She had to get in touch with Ajalon. She decided to go see him. She asked him to meet her back in the park, the location where she'd first suggested that he put a hit out on Rashad.

But instead of sitting on the same bench, she waited for him in the parking lot. When she saw him walk over to her, she got out of the car and began to walk. She walked on the jogging trail in the opposite direction of the bench where they'd first met.

"Hi, Kiara. What's up?"

"Rashad is dead."

He nodded like he wasn't surprised.

"So, it really went down?"

"Sounds like it did."

"But did you do it?"

"The hired person did it. And very soon I gotta pay the henchman the rest of the money. And I gotta make sure no one connects the murder to Nicole."

"This is so messed up."

Ajalon appeared super calm.

Kiara told him how she'd found Rashad and saw his dead body with her own eyes.

"Yeah, it's too bad you had to see that. Especially when the woman who took your man is responsible for his death."

Kiara was silent.

She reached in her purse and pulled out a small roll of bills. "Here. You're going to need this."

"What do you mean?"

"I want you to tell me everything—and I mean everything—that happens with her from now on. I need you to keep this completely on the down low, Ajalon, please. I do not know you. And you owe me nothing. But I am begging you to help me."

"Like I'm an informant of some kind?"

"Call it what you want, but I-I need my name to stay clean, very clean. I know we had that discussion and I changed my mind, but still. Once the investigation is complete and they find out who did it, it's possible that someone will pay for her crime. I don't want it to be me. It's likely that she will have to pay. Nicole is responsible for Rashad's death. And I will do whatever it takes to make sure I live to see her get what she deserves."

Kiara was angry, but knew she had to get through this nightmare. She'd help the children to understand and let them know that they still had one parent who loved them. Rashad was gone. And she'd be damned if her kids would lose both parents. From then on, Kiara resolved to be strong, smart, and resilient for the sake of everyone she loved.

Chapter 18

When it came to the death of Rashad Eason, the investigators wanted to deal with the case in the most delicate of manners. They endeavored to capture every piece of data. From the moment they entered the warehouse, they inspected every detail. Did it seem like any of the entrance doors had been tampered with? How about any windows? They examined every inch of the place for hair samples, fingerprints, footprints, gunpowder, shell casings, body part fragments, and more. They impounded the Eason & Son van. They searched Rashad's house. Grilled his neighbors, questioned Jerry, and examined credit card receipts to establish a timeline. They discovered the dead man was fairly prominent in the Houston community. They knew that the recent rash of robberies, burglaries, and murders had happened since the passing of the open carry law. The murderer could have been anybody. Or did he kill himself? How was his mental health? Was he depressed?

When the detectives learned about Nicole Greene Eason's existence on the day Rashad's body was located, they went to her apartment right away. But she was nowhere to be found.

So the next day, when she decided to go to work, they sought her out at her job.

She had been in the break room surrounded by Aisha and Taylor.

"I'm so sorry for your loss," Aisha told her.

"Thanks."

"I guess we ought to go down to Ms. Kiara's office and extend the same condolences," Taylor whispered to Aisha.

"Whatever, Taylor."

Nicole was ready to leave the break room, but she heard the sound of footsteps coming from the hallway. A man and a woman appeared in the doorway; Nicole clutched a tissue and started sniffling.

"Are you Nicole Greene Eason?"

"Yes, I am."

"I'm Detective Longfellow," said the man. "And this is Sergeant Humphrey."

"Are you here about the death of my husband?"

"First of all, we are sorry about what happened to Mr. Eason. And we just want to ask you a couple of questions."

"Of course." Nicole wiped away her tears and sat at the break room table. She kept her hands hidden.

"At least they found the right Mrs. Eason," Taylor remarked as she and Aisha excused themselves.

The detectives started off by asking Nicole the basics.

"When was the last time you saw or heard from Rashad?" That was Humphrey.

"I think it was on a Friday. He came over to my apartment."

"Your apartment?" asked Longfellow. "You didn't live with your husband?"

Nicole hesitated.

Humphrey told her, "Look, let's stop this questioning right now. We can drive you downtown and question you there. We really should not conduct this interview here, Mrs. Eason."

"Of course I will go," Nicole stated. She went to get her purse and texted Kiara that she had to leave but that she'd be back.

Once she got downtown and was taken into the interrogation room, they requested her ID and checked for warrants.

"Boy, that traffic was a mess for this time of day," Humphrey said to Longfellow.

"Tell me about it. I hope it clears up, because I gotta go out to Katy to the Outdoor World and get me some fishing gear later on."

"Lucky you."

Nicole stared at them in amazement. She couldn't believe the casual conversation they were having considering the circumstances, but to them it was just a job.

Sergeant Humphrey applied some lipstick, then turned on her tape recorder.

"Let's start," she said. "We'll be talking about Rashad Eason. Did you know his daily routine, Mrs. Eason?"

"For the most part. Sometimes I didn't, because he would switch things up depending on the type of projects he worked."

"What did he do for a living?"

"He owned a subcontracting business."

"Where was it located?"

She told them.

"Do you have keys to that building?"

"Um, yes."

"And does his office have security cameras?"

"Um, I'm not sure."

Nicole knew that there were cameras. But she was afraid to tell the truth. What if the security cameras showed the hit man who was hired? Even though she did not know his identity, she did not want them to trace the assailant back to her.

The detectives asked a few more questions about Rashad's business dealings: who were his employees, how many did he have, had he recently fired anyone in the past year or two, and had he ever mentioned any conflicts that he had with the people he worked with?

Wow, easy stuff, Nicole thought as she easily provided several factual answers with confidence.

"So you were married to Rashad but not living under the same roof?" That was Longfellow.

"Um, we had been living together up until recently."

"What date did you stop living together?" Humphrey asked.

"I don't know. It's not like I marked it down on my calendar. Living separate was a painful experience that I did not want to think about."

"That's understandable." He monitored her with curiosity, then asked, "Were you legally separated? Had you discussed divorce? Were any papers filed?"

"No. Um, we were trying to work things out. Look, I feel so uncomfortable talking about this topic. It feels weird to answer these questions, knowing he's lying somewhere in a steel box. I loved my husband. I'm sorry he's dead. I wanted us to be together."

"But he wanted out of the relationship?" asked Longfellow.

"Yes. Um, yeah." She shrugged. She was afraid to tell the officers that info, but it didn't automatically mean that she'd killed him. They had no evidence. She didn't even know until after it happened that he'd been killed at the warehouse.

"Will you be the one to come and identify the body?" asked Humphrey.

"Do I have to?"

"Why wouldn't you?"

"I have never done anything like this before. And I don't want to remember Rashad like that."

"Remember him like what?"

"Shot up."

"How'd you know he was shot up?"

"How did I know he was shot? Um, it was on the news. It was on the Internet." She nervously laughed. "The article said he was murdered. I don't know. You're the experts in these things."

"Even so, you may need to go to the coroner's office and sign off on the death certificate, alright?" asked Humphrey.

"Of course."

"Getting back to the interview," said Longfellow. "Where were you at approximately nine twenty-five on the evening of Friday, April twenty-eighth?"

This would be easy. "I was at home with our daughter, Emmy, and with the nanny."

"At home, as in your apartment on Richmond Avenue?" he asked.

"Yes."

"Can you give us the nanny's name and phone number and address if you have it?"

"I'd be glad to."

"Were you home the entire night?"

"Yes." She nodded. "We were watching Netflix. We had a little party, because I could no longer afford my nanny. It was a good-bye party of sorts . . ." Her voice tapered off. She did not want to volunteer too much information.

"Did you leave at any point during that party?"

"No."

"Did the nanny stay at your party during the entire duration?"

"Yes. She never left. And neither did Emmy." She laughed nervously.

"Mrs. Eason, did you try to contact Rashad the next day? Like, had he made any effort to say he wanted to see you that weekend or anytime in the future?"

"Um, not that I can recall. I'm sure we would have hooked up at some point, so he could spend time with Emmy. But no. I—no."

"What time did you go to sleep that night?"

She wanted to say that she'd tossed and turned. But she said, "Um, it probably was around ten or eleven."

"How do you know?"

"I usually go to sleep around that time. I'm assuming it was ten."

"Did he call you that night?"

"Um, I think I got a missed call from him. But I probably didn't because my phone was turned off."

Sergeant Humphrey raised her eyebrows. "You said you turned off your cell phone? Is there any reason why you'd remember that detail?"

"Um, no. I think I turned it off. I don't remember."

Detective Longfellow asked, "Did you hire a divorce lawyer? I'd like to get his or her name."

Sergeant Humphrey added, "And we want the name of Mr. Eason's divorce attorney. If you don't know, we can look it up ourselves."

"Why do you need that info?"

"Mrs. Eason, we're trying to piece together all the info we can so we can find out who placed a gun to your husband's head and killed him. He was also shot in the leg.

Whoever did it seemed very angry. And we plan to find out why."

Nicole said, "Right. Okay."

"Mrs. Eason, thanks for your time. That's enough for now," Sergeant Humphrey said and rose to her feet. "Again, I'm sorry for your loss."

"I am, too," she replied in a sad whisper.

As soon as the officers released Nicole, an HPD patrol officer offered to drive her to the coroner's office, where she was asked to go through the body identification process.

"I'm sorry, but dead bodies freak me out. I really don't want to do it."

"Okay, you're not required to do so, but we will make the process as delicate for you as possible."

Nicole nodded. She was accompanied by an officer and fell into a deep silence all the way over to the coroner's.

When they entered the building, Nicole ran smack into Rashad's mother.

"That's my mother-in-law," she absently said to the officer.

Beeva stared across the room at Nicole. Her eyes were red and she clutched a handkerchief.

"Hi. I was coming over here to identify the body," Nicole said.

"No need. The job has been taken care of." Her mother-in-law raised up her purse and looked like she wanted to hit Nicole.

Kiara emerged from behind Beeva.

"Kiara? What are you doing here?"

"She asked me to come. That's why I'm here. He's dead. His face wasn't identifiable, but I know his hands and I touched them."

"You did not have to do that."

"Oh, but I did. His mother and I did what we had to do, Nicole. Oh, here is a bag of his personal effects, keys to the house, his wallet."

"Thanks, I could have taken care of that," she said lamely.

"Anyway, everything has been handled. No need for you to even go in there now." Kiara started to leave with Beeva Reese. "Oh, by the way, I heard that he was very unhappy in his marriage and was trying to leave you and I'm not surprised."

"How could you twist your mouth to even say anything like that right now, Kiara?" Nicole said and rolled her eyes at her mother-in-law.

"Because it's the truth, that's why."

"Regardless," Nicole replied, "this is not the time or the place. I'll call you later, alright? Um, thanks to both of you."

The two women barely said good-bye and hurried away from Nicole and out the door.

The officer drove Nicole back to her workplace. As soon as she got back to the campus, she fled to her office. With Kiara doing her job at the coroner's, she knew she'd better plan the funeral before the woman took over that task, too. While she briefly sat in front of her computer, she heard a swift knock on her office door and then it swung open. It was Shyla.

"Hi, Nicole."

"Hey there."

Nicole was stunned to see her. She couldn't speak.

"Aren't you going to invite me into your office?"

"I don't know. I'll have to think about it."

Shyla closed the door behind her. "Are you pissed at me?"

"Maybe."

"Don't be. I don't want to do this anymore. I-I shouldn't have been such an ass with you."

Nicole shrugged. "I agree. So, why are you here?"

Shyla came over and embraced her. It was awkward, and Nicole stiffened at her touch. "Okay, alright. I'm sorry, Nicole. I shouldn't have said the whack-ass shit I said to you. It was wrong, I have no real excuse, and I'm sorry about everything."

Nicole knew that trying to remain angry at Shyla would be foolish—because if there was anything she needed right then, it was a real friend.

"Okay, Shyla. I accept your apology."

"Good. Now, I heard about what happened to Rashad. How are you? Are you alright?"

"Yeah. I'm okay. I'm in shock. And I can't believe he's gone. But I'm trying my best to stay sane."

Shyla explained that when she'd first heard the news, there was no way she could keep holding a grudge against her. And more than anything, she wanted to check on Nicole.

"I was surprised when someone informed me that you were here. Why be at the job when you can be out there trying to find the killer?"

"Shyla, I came to work today because I don't want to be home alone."

"I hear you. But at least try to gain access to your house in Missouri City, because you know the scavengers will be there trying to steal shit from y'all like a lot of people try to do when it comes to a rich man."

"Wait. How did you know I don't live at that house anymore?"

"Our wonderful coworkers Taylor and Aisha told me."

"Wow. That sucks. And they swore they wouldn't tell anybody."

"Juicy gossip will always spread. That's all I can say. But look. I'm not here to throw anyone under the bus. I'm here to support you, girl. I love you, I miss you, and the only thing that matters right now is finding out what happened to your husband. And if you need any help whatsoever, let me know."

"Thanks, Shyla." Seeing her friend come support her made Nicole's heart feel less weighed down. "I've been mad at you, but at the same time I wanted to talk to you the way we used to. And I can admit I was scared because I wasn't sure if we'd ever be cool again. It must have taken a lot of guts for you to seek me out. I appreciate that."

"Hmph! Rashad Eason is gone. Life is too short. That's all I can say."

Nicole wanted to open up to Shyla so bad she could scream. Because although Nicole did not want to admit it, in a moment of desperation, she'd gone to lunch with Aisha and Taylor soon after Rashad had told her he wanted out. She needed someone to talk to and thought she could trust the girls.

"I don't plan to be on campus too much longer," Nicole explained. "I have to call my insurance company. Then I'll have to meet with my mother-in-law sometime today, and I really dread it."

"You hate her, and she hates like you."

"Face it, some mother-in-laws aren't very motherly. And then my own mother will arrive today, too. She'll need a ride from the airport."

"Girl, you are losing it. Take care of your business and get the heck away from this job. It's not going anywhere." Shyla placed her hand on the doorknob before opening it. "If you want to talk—really talk—I'm all ears."

"I know you, Shyla. You're all ears, and mouth, and texting and all that."

"Oh, I hear the shade, girl." She fell silent for a moment. "Nicole, girl, I'm sorry, but you don't sound like you're mourning the love of your life if you can make jokes like that."

"With all that I'm going through, I laugh to keep from crying. But to be honest, I am hurting. I've dreaded every minute of this day. All I can think about is Rashad."

"Do you miss him?"

"Um, yeah. Of course. I loved him."

At that Nicole told her friend good-bye. She finished up a few tasks, then closed the door and left. She figured she'd be out the rest of the week, and she wanted to make sure she left no type of paper trail regarding her Internet searches.

"You just never know," she told herself and headed in the opposite direction of the airport. First she had to make another important run. Nicole got in her Jeep and temporarily turned off her cell phone. She knew that if her cell phone was left on, it would track her every movement. She hated that. But she was finally ready to face Ajalon. During the drive to his place, she came to terms with Rashad's death. Nothing could bring him back. And because he'd killed her dreams, she reasoned she'd have to create new dreams, new hopes, and a new life.

By the time Nicole showed up at Ajalon's apartment, she felt ready.

When he opened the door, he greeted her with a wide smile.

"How are you, Ajalon?"

"*Benissimo*. I'm great now that you're here."

"What's that supposed to mean?"

"It means you did not abandon me like I thought you did."

After he let her in, the first thing she asked him was if

he had anything to drink. She meant something like ice-cold water. And she was surprised when he responded.

"I have a lot of things you can drink." He went and got four glasses. He brought back two bottles. One was champagne; the other was wine.

"Which drink do you want, Nicole? Are you celebrating the man as if you want to toast to him, or are you still mourning him and you feel like pouring one out?"

Suddenly she felt frightened. It was possible that she was pregnant with Rashad's child, but she was certain Ajalon would be furious if he found out. The one time when she got pregnant by him, she ended up terminating the pregnancy, something that still made Ajalon unhappy.

"I don't know which drink I want," she said. "It all depends."

"On what?"

"Can you promise me that everything worked out the way we discussed it? Like, was the job done exactly right? Did he earn his money?"

"We all earned our money."

Ajalon poured champagne in two glasses and set them aside. Wine filled up two other glasses. First he handed her the Merlot.

"Here, since you can't decide, why not drink both? Drink the wine and mourn the Negro that took you away from me. And drink the champagne to celebrate the fact that he can't fuck you over anymore."

"Whoa! Sounds like the job was done just right, Ajalon." He waited on her. She hesitated then sniffed her wine. "You didn't put anything in my drink, did you?"

"Don't ask me that. You saw when I poured those drinks."

"But I never saw you purchase these drinks."

"Fine! If you don't trust me, Nicole, bring your own bottles next time."

She laughed, raised the glass, and let her tongue taste a small bit of Merlot. "There won't be a next time. If I make it through the next few months and keep my hands clean, I'm done with the crazy shit, Ajalon. For real." She bowed her head for a moment, and then poured a little bit of wine on his tiled floor.

"Hey, what are you doing?"

"You told me to pour one out for him and that's what I'm doing. Just mop it up."

Before he could further protest, she grabbed the champagne. "You need to get your glass, too. We can celebrate together."

He did as she suggested. They clicked their glasses together. She tilted her neck and pretended to drink. But she never tasted the champagne.

"What does all of this mean?" he asked after he finished.

"It's our new beginning. Maybe we can figure things out one day at a time. I don't want to think too much about it."

"You sound scared, Bella. Like you won't be able to get away with murder."

"Ajalon, as far as I'm concerned, I did nothing wrong. I just didn't want to be in pain anymore. Is that a bad thing? To make something go away that's hurting you?"

"If that's your defense, Nicole, you'll have a hard time convincing a jury of your innocence."

"Please. Don't say that. There won't be a jury. I think everything's okay. I have a solid alibi."

"Which is?"

"Oh yeah. I never told you what I was doing on the night he got killed." She swished the champagne around in her glass.

"I was with . . . Nadia."

He froze.

"And what happened with you two? What did you do?"

"Not much. I made sure we watched a movie. Did something that would be memorable."

"Oh, I see."

"And she acted like she didn't want to be there with me, like she had better things to do, but I made her stick around for as long as possible." Nicole laughed. "I ordered pizza for us and made her play with Emmy for hours. I wanted to crap on myself, waiting around and wondering what was really going on. It was murder."

Ajalon just stared at his ex. Somehow it seemed she'd really changed. Back in the day, she was feisty and fun-loving. But now he saw her in a different light. He still loved Nicole, but he was beginning to lose heart.

"Anyway, I feel pretty good right now, but I still have a few concerns."

"Such as?" he said.

"I wonder how well I did when those two homicide detectives questioned me. They grilled me so much I was scared I'd slip up. But they ended up letting me go. That has to prove I'm not a suspect. But oh, how I wanted to die in that room. I tried my best to play off my nervousness. And these guys study body language. I had to make sure I didn't look like I was lying."

"Are you getting better at lying, Nicole?"

"I don't know. Why?"

"Did you lie about anything?"

"Well, of course. I had to. How the hell could I tell the complete truth? If I did, I wouldn't be with you right now. Plus, I have a daughter to think about. I practically don't have anyone else."

"You have me, Bella." He hoped she believed him.

"I know I have you, and I am going to need you more

than ever. But we have to be careful. No one can know that we are old acquaintances."

"Old acquaintances?"

"Look, once everything clears, I'm hoping you and I can really be together, Ajalon. But I must lie low for a minute. I have a funeral to plan. I'm in mourning. And I have to check on the life insurance and see how much I'm getting."

"Sounds like your hands are full."

"Yeah, they are. But I know for a fact that once I get financially situated, I plan to move again. I don't want to be in Houston anymore. I need a vacation." Her eyes sparkled with excitement. For a minute she looked like the woman he used to know. The one who was game to do something fun and adventurous.

"Ajalon, you and I have never really been on a real vacation together. Let's go away somewhere nice once this is all over. Hawaii, Saint Kitts. Someplace romantic."

There she was. The dreamer had returned. He liked this side of Nicole.

"Ahh, you want us to get away. Make love on a beach."

"Mmm-hmm."

"That means you finally want to be with me? Perhaps as my wife one day?"

"I don't know about all that just yet. I just know I don't feel comfortable in Texas anymore. At first I loved being here, but now?"

"You're sorry you ever left me, not once but twice?"

She was becoming good at lying. "I'm so very sorry for doing that, Ajalon."

"Tell you what. You continue to act normal and do the things that a mourning widow would do."

"I can do it. No problem."

"Then it should be easy to show sorrow upon your face. Get through the funeral, and then we will leave town together. And one day soon, we can really be together the way you wanted to years ago."

"Promise?"

"I promise," he told her and then she kissed him and said good-bye.

The time had come. And Kiara felt stranger than she ever had in her life. With Adina holding her up, she entered the church. Dressed in black from head to toe, she just wanted to get through the wake. Get through it with dignity and calmness. She and Adina went and sat in the middle of a large section on the right side of the sanctuary. The viewing of the body would soon begin. They sat down. Myles said "excuse me" to Adina and planted himself on the other side of his mother.

She squeezed his hand tight. Myles's face appeared thoughtful. It was his first time ever attending this type of ceremony.

"Are you alright, son?" Kiara asked.

"I'm fine. I think."

"Good."

"I-I'm a little bit scared. I'm afraid of dead people."

"Your dad isn't going to hurt you. He loved you. Always remember that."

It hurt so much for Kiara to speak those words to Myles. It all seemed surreal. He was so young and loved his daddy to death. Would the boy grow up and remember the good times he'd had with Rashad? Would he ever feel the same about playing ball or flying the toy helicopters that he dearly loved?

Kiara tried to hush the awful taunting that plagued her mind.

You should have let Rashad spend more time with Myles, instead of acting so evil and selfish and denying a father a right to his own son.

She nodded as if answering the voice in her head. She knew in some ways she had done Rashad wrong. She felt regretful. But it was too little, too late.

As they continued to wait, Adina talked her ears off.

"You know I hated that son of a bitch, but he was alright at the same time."

"Adina, you ought to be ashamed of yourself."

"Now, girl, ain't no use in me acting like Rashad and I was thick as thieves. He was my boy years ago, but the past couple of years, hell to the no. I didn't like how he was treating you."

"I didn't like it either, but that's beside the point. At the end of the day, he wasn't as wicked as I made him out to be."

"Ha. Now I know you're lying. You used to complain about his ass day and night. 'Adina, he's hiding babies. And he's fucking everything that moves.'"

Kiara burst out laughing and couldn't stop. It felt strange to cackle like she was at the comedy club.

"Would you shut up, Adina? I'm not in the mood to hear all those memories."

"Too bad, because I'm just warming up."

"Can you please crack your jokes after the casket is closed?"

"How about I wait till the casket is six feet under and after the ghosts have come to visit him?"

"You wrong for that, girl."

"He was my boy, though, Kiara." The large grin on Adina's face turned upside down. Her voice broke. "All jokes aside, Rashad was my boy. I'm sure gonna miss him."

* * *

They got through the wake and returned to Kiara's home. She saw the kids off to bed and sat around in her family room sipping on a cup of hot tea mixed with honey.

"Is that enough for starters?" Adina asked. "Let me know and I can make another cup." She sat next to her friend on the couch. Adina picked up the clicker and started speeding through television shows: TBS, BET, OWN, prime-time news; she rapidly clicked past the ESPN channels and kept going till she found the movie channels.

"It's a damn shame that people pay an arm and a leg to have these fucking so-called premium stations, yet there's nothing 'premium' about watching ten-year-old movies on a Friday night."

"I know, girl. Cable is a luxury. Definitely not a necessity," Kiara answered.

Finally, Adina stopped clicking when she saw actor Eddie Murphy's face light up the screen.

"We will watch Mr. Murphy. He's old as dirt but is funny and fine. Plus, we could use a good laugh."

"Say that again."

They watched in silence for several minutes, laughing here and there.

Adina frowned. "Look, Kiara, you might want to drink tea, but I am thirsty for something much stronger. I think I'll start by opening up a bottle of wine I saw in your fridge."

"Girl, I don't care. Do you."

Adina left and soon she was back, holding two glasses filled with wine.

"Thanks, Adina." Kiara reached for one glass.

Adina slapped her hand. "Excuse me, but these are for me. You go on and have yourself a good time drinking that tea, girl."

Kiara smiled. "This is insane. I can't believe we're here. Doing this. The day before Rashad's funeral."

"Life's a bitch, Kiara. And right now I feel like pure trash. I mean, hell, he and I rarely saw eye to eye, and our heads bumped more than once. But damn, shit, and fuck. I'd never wish what happened to Rashad on my worst enemy. He did not deserve that. Rashad wasn't so bad. He was a great father."

"But he could have been a much better daddy, if I would have let him. Oh well." Kiara picked up a wineglass and took a long swallow of her drink. She ignored Adina's protests.

"If you need a drink, how much more do I need one?" Kiara wiped her top lip. "Honestly, I've beat myself up about everything, and it's time for the self-condemnation to stop. I apologized to his corpse. I couldn't leave his casket till I felt that he had forgiven me. I felt peace. And it's given me the strength to move on."

"What are your plans, sweetie? I hate to say this, but now that Rashad is forever out of the picture, you can completely concentrate on being with Eddison. Being his wife. Y'all two can truly build a new family. Jazzy is young enough to be raised by this man and never miss a beat. Myles, on the other hand . . ."

As if on cue, Myles was standing before them. Kiara sat up in her chair and set down the wine.

"Are you alright, baby? I thought you were asleep."

"I couldn't sleep, Mommy."

She patted the couch next to her. "Come sit next to me. You want to talk?"

Myles came and sat by Kiara. "I was thinking. I have an idea."

"What is it, son?"

"Can we get some homing pigeons, please, Mommy?"

"Homing pigeons?"

"Yes. My daddy is gone. And I miss him already. I wish he could take me to the zoo, actually to an African safari, but that will never happen."

"I'm sorry about that, Myles. We can still go—"

"Mommy, if you let me buy the pigeons, I can release them in the sky. Because that's where Daddy is, right? In heaven, up in the sky?"

Kiara's lip trembled. She nodded. "I sure hope so."

"So when those pigeons are released, they'll find my daddy. They'll keep him company. And when they get ready, they might come back to me. And if they do, I'll be happy. I'll know that they went to see him and make sure he's all right. That would be great. Wouldn't it?"

"That's the best idea I've ever heard. Yes, we'll make sure and do that. Thanks, son."

He gave his mother a kiss good night and disappeared from the room.

"I must say," Adina replied, "that is one good thing that your ex did. He gave you that incredible human being."

"Didn't he, though? Myles is amazing." Kiara nodded and smiled. "He's gonna be alright. And I will, too."

The day following the funeral, Nicole headed over to Ajalon's. She nearly fell into his arms when he opened his door.

"That was the hardest thing I've ever had to do in my life."

"Why is that?" he asked with a serious look on his face.

"I had to write his obituary. I haven't had to write an obituary since college, and back then it was just to earn a grade. This time it was for real."

"How do you think you did?"

"His mother told me she hated it. She hated the photo that I used for the program. I felt like I couldn't do anything right."

"Get over it. It's over. You can put all of this behind you and start again."

"You're right. Right now I just want to leave. I'll go crazy if I stay here one more day."

They began packing their personal belongings. Nicole just wanted to put the entire nightmare behind her.

Ajalon watched her as she stuffed some of her designer pumps in a duffel bag.

"What would I ever do without you?" Nicole said. "I made a big mistake in not standing by you when you were locked up. I had no idea that you'd be this down for me. You came back to look for me, to regain my love and acceptance. It took a while for everything to come together, but now we can do this. No more distractions." She reached over to hug Ajalon.

"Yeah," he said as he hugged her back. He resumed packing. "So you gonna end up with all your ex's money? If so, how will you get ahold of it if we're leaving town?"

"Oh, don't even worry about that. I have the user names and passwords to Rashad's personal banking accounts. I may still have some of his business checks floating around, too."

"Smart woman. You think of everything."

"I have to."

Once they collected their suitcases and duffel bags and a laptop, Nicole went and bundled up her daughter, Emmy.

"I can't believe she's going to grow up without a father. That's one thing I didn't think through." Nicole felt terrible. "So you're wrong, Ajalon. I don't think of everything.

Because if I'd really been using my head, how could I want her father to die? But he hurt me so bad that I wanted him to feel my pain."

"A lot of us do bad things when we get hurt."

"Yeah, but I shouldn't have went to the extreme. I should have just cussed his ass out and went on one hell of a shopping spree. You know what I mean? Nothing as drastic as hiring a hit man to kill him. Because I did love him."

Ajalon stopped what he was doing. "You are telling me that you actually loved that man who tried to break up with you and ruin you and humiliate you by divorcing you after a month of marriage? You could still love a man who does you like that?"

"True love endures all kinds of things."

"I see."

"True love causes you to forgive a person who treated you so bad that you hated his guts. You wished he was dead. But you only wish it for a minute. You don't really mean it."

"You don't mean it, because true love makes you change your mind? Makes you remember the good things he did instead of all the bad things he did to harm you? Is that what you're telling me?"

"That's exactly what I'm saying. What time is it?" She was eager to get away. Nicole did not plan to go too far, but she reasoned that if they went on a brief road trip, it would help her get her head together. "Well, I'm done packing. Let's go."

Nicole gathered her belongings and let Ajalon carry Emmy out to the Jeep.

"Having my dreams come true might have not lasted that long, but at least I got to experience them even for a short time." She locked up the house and closed the door behind her.

Then she let Ajalon whisk away her luggage and stuff it in the back of her Jeep. She got in the passenger seat and buckled in. She lay back and closed her eyes. She was so drained and mentally exhausted that all she could do was fall asleep. She practically passed out the minute Ajalon hit I-10 going east. She dreamt of nothing while she was asleep. Only darkness filled her mind as she tried to block out all the bad things that had happened in the past few weeks.

An hour later they reached the outskirts of Beaumont. She looked at her surroundings.

"Good. Houston is far behind us. I'm glad. I hated that place."

"Did you quit your job?"

"No, not yet. I have to keep working until I get my hands on that insurance money."

They continued driving until they reached Baton Rouge. Ajalon checked them into a hotel.

Nicole entered the room and set her things on top of a chair. She dropped down to her knees and looked under the bed. She got up and searched behind the curtains. She went into the bathroom and checked for hidden recorders. She opened all the drawers and made sure nothing odd was in them.

"What the fuck are you doing?"

"I heard all about how you gotta check your hotel room when you check in."

"You are paranoid as fuck."

"I won't be forever."

Fifteen minutes later, Nicole asked Ajalon to order a pizza. "Don't use this hotel phone. They have operators who listen to all your conversations."

"Nicole, I thought you wanted to get away so you could relax."

"That's the thing. I'm far away from Houston but I still feel like shit, Ajalon."

"Well, pull yourself together."

"I'll try."

Once the pizza arrived, Nicole toyed with her food. She sat at the round business table and complained that she was bored. Ajalon told her, "Let's watch movies." He turned on the television and began scrolling through channels.

Nothing caught their interest. But then he flipped past a news channel. And there on the screen was a photo of Nicole.

"What the fuck?" she said.

"Why are you on TV?"

"Turn up the volume."

The reporter told how a suspect had been arrested for the murder of Rashad Eason, who was the husband of Nicole Greene, the woman who'd received previous notoriety when a deadly fire happened in Houston.

The photo switched to video footage of Eddison Osborne. His head was hung and he was being led away from his home by the police.

"Wait. What?" Nicole said. "Why in the hell is Eddison in handcuffs?"

"You know him?"

"He works at the university. That's Kiara's man."

"Word?"

"Shhh." She turned up the volume and caught the tail end of the news story.

"They arrested Eddison for murdering Rashad?" She shook her head. "That doesn't make any sense. They're wrong."

"Maybe they're questioning everyone who had a motive."

"Then arrest his employees. Go find Alexis McNeil."

"And both of his wives, eh?"

She wanted to lash out at him, but the words Ajalon spoke made her feel grave with anxiety.

"We should go back," she said.

"Why?"

"I don't want anything to do with this mess, but they need to learn that Eddison would never do anything like that."

"For all you know, Kiara's new man had a reason to smoke Rashad."

"No, it's impossible. And it's not true anyway. It's my fault that he's dead."

"Is that a confession, Nicole?"

She said nothing.

"This so-called road trip is cut short. We got to go back to Houston. Now."

Chapter 19

In the complicated drama that immediately ensued after Rashad's death, Alexis felt that she had been left out and forgotten. People extended condolences to Nicole, and even to Kiara, but barely anyone acknowledged Alexis.

"It's cold-blooded how a baby mama gets done when the father passes away," she told Varnell one morning.

"Hey, take care of your business. Right now, your daughter is the most important thing."

The first chance they got, Alexis and Varnell paid a visit to the child support office in southwest Houston. She rode the elevator up several floors and entered a moderate-sized office filled with men and women. Alexis signed in and took a seat in the back of the room. When her name was finally called, Varnell asked if she needed him to go with her. She told him no. "Cross your fingers," she said and walked through a security door, down a long hallway, and into a child support investigator's office.

"Hello, Alexis. I'm Meicka. What can I do for you today?"

"My baby daddy had recently begun to pay child support. But he unexpectedly passed away."

"Sorry to hear that."

"What happens now?"

"What is his name and Social?"

Alexis gave her the info.

"To be honest," Meicka told her, "once a person who pays child support dies, payments cease."

"What?"

"Yes, that is why the father needed to take out life insurance that names your child as a beneficiary. Do you know whether that was done?"

"I don't know. I have no idea."

"You need to find out. Find out the name of his insurance company and give them a call. How old is your child?"

"Hayley will turn three this year."

"And Rashad was thirty-five. It appears he's been working for decades, so your child might be eligible for Social Security benefits. If I were you, I'd look into it."

"I'm so confused I can't think straight."

"If you are able to get a copy of the death certificate and provide it to this office, that would be helpful. I'm truly sorry for your loss."

"Lost. That's how I feel right now."

"The best thing that can happen is for him to have remembered to get life insurance for your daughter. You two never discussed that?"

"No. Not that I can remember."

Meicka frowned like she wanted to say something, but she thought better of it. "Sorry. In this industry, I see so many tragic cases. So much heartache and heartbreak over young people having sex with anybody and everybody. Young women don't even know the identity of their children's, yes, *children's* fathers. It's a shame. But I just work here and I can't run people's lives."

Alexis slumped in her chair. Her thoughts drowned out

Meicka's ramblings. Somehow she'd have to get some money. No way should Nicole, the black widow, be allowed to benefit from another person's sorrow.

Alexis returned to the lobby, motioned at Varnell, and he followed her back to the first floor. She asked him if she could be excused.

When she dialed Nicole's number, she was surprised that the woman answered.

"Hello, Alexis."

"Oh, I'm listed in your address book?"

"You sure are."

"Alrighty. Um, Nicole, I'm calling you because I have an important business matter to discuss."

"Okay, what is it?"

"Do you know if Rashad ever discussed life insurance policies for the kids? I'm sure you've already looked into it."

"I really can't say, Alexis."

"You can't or you won't?"

"I'm, like, not really feeling this conversation, to be honest. I don't remember you ever sending me any condolences. You avoided me at the funeral. I invited you to the house following the burial but you never responded. Did not show up. And now you have the nerve to call me asking about money?"

Alexis was dumbfounded. Every word that Nicole said was true, but she was shocked that those details would be so important to her right then.

"I-I was in a bad way, Nicole."

"Are you telling me that you were still in love with my husband?"

Alexis said nothing.

"I kind of figured you were, and that's why you always acted so salty toward me once he and I hooked up."

"No, you're wrong."

"I think I'm right. A woman who loses a man will hardly ever admit that she still loved him. She's too proud to admit that. And he's a constant reminder of what she's lost."

"Nicole, wait a second. Why are you talking like this? You do not sound like a mourning widow. I'm starting to believe that—"

"That what?"

"Did you have anything to do with Rashad's murder?" she asked.

"What? Did you see me arrested for his murder?"

"No. Eddison was. And everybody and their mama knows that man wouldn't hurt a soul."

"No one knows what anybody would do. I don't care what they look like."

A cold chill ran through Alexis's veins. "Since you know so much, Nicole, you might want to learn that I know a lot, too. Your husband confided in me. All the time."

"He did not."

"Yes, he did. He told me the shit you were doing that pissed him off. He told me a lot of personal info about you. And I can see why you'd be angry enough at him to blow his head off."

Alexis suddenly wanted to see Nicole's eyes, look deep into them to see if they'd betray her secrets.

"Nicole, I don't know what happened that night when Rashad got killed, but baby mama or not, I swear to God, if you did anything to cause that man to die, I will personally see to it that you get fucked up. I mean that."

When Alexis did not get a response, she was so angry that she ended the call. And the conversation replayed in her head for days.

* * *

When it was determined that Eddison Osborne had nothing to do with Rashad's murder, he was released from jail and issued a halfhearted apology. It was a case of circumstantial evidence. Eddison had a flaky alibi on the night of Rashad's murder and some people felt that he was one of Rashad's enemies. None of it turned out to be true, and he had to be let go.

Kiara came downtown to pick up Eddison. She sat around for hours and the wait was excruciating. But finally he was processed then released.

Kiara looked at the new beard he'd grown and smiled.

"You're looking really good to me right now," she said.

"I'm glad that you can see some type of good still in me."

"Hold on. I knew they arrested the wrong person, Eddison."

"Did you?"

"Of course."

"But you know what? The little good I have done is now ruined. The publicity from this case has caused all kinds of problems."

"Right. It's a shame that people were protesting outside of your home. Some demanded that you lose your job. I'm so sorry that you had to go through all of this."

He said nothing, his jaw rigid with anger. Kiara wanted to hold his hand, but it seemed he wasn't in the mood when she attempted to touch him. They left the jailhouse together and she hurried along the sidewalk far ahead of him.

"Wait, Kiara, hold up. I want you to walk by my side, not far away from me."

"That's what I want to hear from you," she said. "Because, honestly, Eddy, I am here. I've already lost my child's father, and I refuse to lose you, too."

"I know, love. I hate that you had to go through all of this."

They openly hugged. He smelled like sweat, but she did not care. She just wanted to feel the connection again that she'd once enjoyed with this man.

"Eddison, we have to talk. I mean, really talk, with no secrets between us. If you want to tell me everything you went through in there, go right ahead. But I feel there's also something else you need to talk to me about."

"What is it?"

"Long ago Rashad kept insisting that you're—"

"On the down low?"

She nodded.

"Do you believe him, Kiara?"

"I . . . um."

"You do believe him." Eddison's voice was filled with sorrow. She could have kicked herself. This was not the reconciliation she hoped to have with him.

"Babe, wait a minute. Please don't accuse me of believing what Rashad said. I knew that he could have been making it up, because it's no secret that he wanted us to still be a family. But I can't help that. I did not try to encourage him. I was with you, Eddy, happily with you. Do you believe me?"

It took him a long time to answer. "I've always believed you, Kiara."

She sank in his arms, grateful that faith and trust and love had been restored.

"I'm glad we had this talk."

"Me too," he stated. "But there is one other thing that I've hidden from you, Kiara."

Her heart nearly stopped. "Go on please. Just tell me."

"There's one thing that Rashad told you that really was the truth." He paused. "Yes, Rashad saw me at the gay bar that night."

Suddenly her joy disappeared. "So, Eddy, you lied to

me about being there? Are you serious? You had me thinking one thing when it was really another?"

"Kiara, please—"

She felt foolish and wanted to leave him right there in
the parking lot.

"What the fuck were you doing there, Eddy? Straight
men don't visit gay bars."

"Some do."

"But what are you?"

"I'm straight, babe. I was there to support my brother."

"What?"

"I-I have a brother. His name is Desmond. He wanted to
break the news to me that night that he was coming out. He
wrestled with his decision. He didn't know how the family
would respond. He was contemplating suicide. I had to talk
him out of it. He suggested that I go in there with him. And
I did. I-I care about him, and everything was so—"

Her cheeks reddened. She hated herself for overreacting
and didn't want him to think she was unhinged. "Oh, wow.
That's deep, Eddy. You could have told me."

"I could have, but I didn't. Not back then. Desmond
coming out wasn't anything I ever expected. So I was still
struggling with it myself. I wanted to be the peacemaker
for my family. I wanted to be there for my brother. And the
whole thing forced me to deal with all sorts of feelings that
I didn't know I had. So, I'm sorry I shut you out."

She was glad that he finally told her what was up, but
she still had more questions.

"Eddy, um, I want you to be honest with me."

"Alright."

"Have you ever slept with another man?"

"No."

"Have you ever thought about sleeping with another
man?"

He looked horrified. "Hell no."

"Alright, I just wanted to be sure."

He studied Kiara then replied, "Let me ask you some questions. Have you ever slept with a woman?"

"No, I haven't."

"Have you ever wondered what it would be like to sleep with a woman? Do you watch lesbian porn?"

"No, and no, and let me throw in a third no in case you have any more dumb questions." She sighed and wearily told him, "Eddison Osborne, you know what I love. I'm your woman. You've been there for me. Let me be there for you, too."

"I'm glad to hear all of this; glad we talked," he said. "I love you more than ever, Kiara. Now, let's go home."

She quickly nodded and they got in the car and drove away. Far away to better days.

It had been four weeks since Rashad had been killed. After Eddison was no longer a suspect, the authorities appealed to the public for help. They released surveillance video that spotted a vehicle leaving the scene around the time when Rashad was killed. And a five-thousand-dollar reward was offered for any tips that led to the arrest of his killer. Lots of tips were received, but none proved to be helpful.

It was quickly determined that Rashad did not take his own life. And that was a winning moment for Nicole, for if he had committed suicide, she would have been denied any insurance money. Nicole hadn't been contacted by the police for further questioning. And she wanted to forget everything that happened and move on with her life.

On that Friday morning, she received a phone call from

a number that popped up as Allstate on her work phone. Excellent! This was the call she'd been waiting for.

"Hello," she said in a breathless voice.

"Hi, Mrs. Eason. It's me, Mrs. Canterbury. Remember, I'm the agent with the insurance company?"

"Oh, I could never forget you. How are you doing today, ma'am?"

"I'm excited," she said in her little-old-lady, raspy voice. "This is the last day of work for me before I go on a twenty-three-day cruise on the *Silver Explorer*."

"Oh, really? Where are you going?" Nicole asked even though she didn't care one bit.

"My husband, Wally, and I will be visiting Cape Town. That's in South Africa, you know."

"I had no idea."

"And we'll be traveling along the Indian Ocean. It's been a lifelong dream for us. Let's see, we'll go to Dakar and Senegal. We might even see a voodoo priestess. We had to save up a lot of money to afford this trip."

"Sounds exciting. Speaking of money, did you call me to talk about my life insurance check?"

"Oh, yes, Mrs. Eason. I'm so sorry. I'm so excited about my trip that I forgot all about telling you that you should meet me at my office today. I have an opening at four thirty. So, are you able to make it?"

"Sure," Nicole said in a chirping voice. "I get off at three, so I can definitely meet you by four thirty." She paused. "Can you tell me right now how much the payout is?"

"Yes, let me grab the check."

Mrs. Canterbury made a lot of noise that sounded like she was shuffling through some papers. It took so long that Nicole started biting her fingernails. What was taking the old lady so long?

It took five minutes before the woman picked up her phone again. "Hello?" she said. "Are you still there?"

Will you just get with it, lady? I want my damn money.

"Yes, ma'am. I'm still here. How much?"

"The check is for—" Then the line went dead.

"What the hell?" Nicole scrambled to call Mrs. Canterbury back, but the number she dialed was busy.

"A busy tone? How the hell does she get a busy tone?"

Nicole tried to call the woman back three more times before giving up. "I'll just see the little old scatterbrained lady at four thirty. Bitch better have my money."

For the rest of the workday, Nicole envisioned herself getting her hands on the check. It was the money that Rashad had left to her as his widow. She wanted to laugh as she sat at her desk and worked, but a laughing widow would present the wrong image. No one yet knew who killed Rashad, so Nicole had to keep boxes of tissue on her desk so she could wipe her eyes every few minutes.

But when she was alone with her thoughts, she imagined how she'd spend her fortune. Paying off her Jeep and buying herself a Lexus. Tossing out her current clothes and getting a brand new wardrobe, something she'd been dying to do for a while. Emmy needed some new furniture and clothes. And it was way past time for them to move out of her apartment. Next time she moved she wanted to hand-pick a home big enough for herself, Emmy, and Ajalon to comfortably live in.

Nicole picked up her phone and called Ajalon. "Hey, baby! What are you doing?"

"I'm working. Working my ass off."

"Good, I'm glad. That's what I like to hear."

"What's up with you?"

"I-I have to go to . . ." Then her voice drifted off.

"Huh? What did you say, Nicole?"

"I'll tell you about it later. Too many ears are around here."

"Alright, call me later."

"Will do. Love you."

She hung up. And when three o'clock came around, she left the office with a tiny smirk on her face. *The next time y'all haters see me, you will really have something to hate on.*

Nicole really wished things had never come to this. She was sad that Rashad was dead. But he got what he had coming to him. He'd treated her with such disrespect that she could no longer coexist on the same planet with him. And now she was in a daze knowing that she could financially capitalize from being married to the man.

"Thanks, Rashad," she whispered. "You put me through pure hell, but it's going to pay off soon." Nicole raced home and changed into a different, more conservative outfit. She called the day care center and told Wendy that she'd be picking up Emmy later that day.

At four thirty sharp, Nicole arrived at the insurance office. She stepped through the doorway. The receptionist desk was empty. Her heart panicked. Did Mrs. Canterbury forget about their appointment?

"Hello?" she cried.

No one responded.

Nicole went past the receptionist desk and walked about the suite of offices, looking inside each open door until she heard a sound coming from one of the rooms. She stepped through another doorway.

There was the little old lady, staring at her computer monitor and smiling.

"Hey, Mrs. Canterbury."

"Oh, you scared me. You are Nicole Eason?"

"Yes. I'm here to . . . to see you."

"Yes, my dear. Have a seat."

Nicole sat on the edge of her chair. She pretended like she didn't just catch the woman looking at the cruise line Web site. She engaged Mrs. Canterbury in general conversation to make her feel at ease. And for the next fifteen minutes the two women looked over the insurance policy papers.

It was 4:50 by the time the old woman finished explaining the particulars. She picked up the check. "First of all, I want to say I am so sorry about the loss of your husband. It's so sad that you two weren't married that long. But at least he was diligent enough to think about you and your child and leave you with a nice policy. That's a good man for you."

"Yes, Rashad was something else."

"Here it is, Mrs. Eason."

Nicole looked at the check. It was a good amount of money, and her eyes glazed over as she thought about all the things she could buy with that type of cash.

"Okay, this is wonderful . . . except you spelled my name wrong. Would that cause a problem if I try to deposit it?"

It was now 4:54.

"I'm not sure, but tell you what. I will make a small modification on the check to correct your name and it should be fine. Your bank should know you anyway, as long as you have proper ID." The old woman picked up her fancy pen and noted something on the check.

Then she stood up and handed it to Nicole.

"Good luck, young lady."

Nicole stood up, too, and tried not to smile. "Yeah, I'm going to need it."

She started to walk out of the office. "Oh, do you need to make a copy of this for your files?"

"Yes, good idea." Mrs. Canterbury snatched the check from Nicole's hand. She disappeared from her office. Nicole could hear a copier machine making noises. Then she returned and handed Nicole an envelope.

"There you go. I'm sorry, I must be leaving now. I have a flight to catch, and I don't want to miss it. You take care, Mrs. Eason."

"Yes, ma'am, have a great trip. Be safe."

Nicole's knees were shaking as she walked down the hall and out the front door of the Allstate office.

Nicole hopped in her Jeep and finally let out a loud scream. "Lord, have mercy, I was about to pee on myself up in there. That old lady is a hot mess, God bless her soul." She buckled her seat belt and drove away. She still had time to deposit the check at her bank. Twenty minutes later, when Nicole reached the drive-through, she found a pen and filled out a deposit slip. She decided she wanted to withdraw five hundred dollars up front, and she was sure the bank would place a seven-day hold on the rest of the money since it was such a large amount.

When she reached in her purse and got the envelope that Mrs. Canterbury had handed to her, she pulled out what she thought would be her check. But all she found was the photocopy of the check.

"Fuck!"

Nicole couldn't believe it. She knew it was hopeless at that point. That little old lady was on her way to Africa, and there wasn't a damn thing Nicole could do about it.

That evening she finally got the call she'd been waiting on.

"Bella," he said when she answered.

"Ajalon. What's going on?"

"I need you to get that ten grand that is supposed to go

to my henchman. He actually gave me thirty days' grace, which is unheard of, but now I must pay up."

"Um, I don't have it."

"You what?"

"I said, I don't have it. I did not get the insurance money. The lady I was dealing with accidentally gave me a copy of the check instead of the real thing."

"Well, get in touch with her. We need that money. I must have it by ten o'clock tonight."

"What?"

"If you don't give me all of the cash, a bounty will be put on my head. These guys don't play, Nicole."

"Well, I don't know what to do, Ajalon. The insurance company is closed. It's Friday night. They won't open again until Monday morning."

"Those goons don't want to hear that." She heard absolute fear in Ajalon's voice. "You don't understand how serious this is, Nicole. They have already threatened my family in Brooklyn."

"But how did they know—"

"They know, Nicole. They know everything."

"Even about me?"

He paused. "No. The hit was set up by me, and I left your name totally out of it."

"Oh good." She sighed.

"So, what are we going to do? Do you have access to any other money?"

"No, not that much."

"What about the GoFundMe account? How much is left in there?"

"A thousand," she lied. In actuality, Nicole still had five grand. But she refused to hand over all of her money to Ajalon. She needed cash to live on for the next few weeks. She knew that when she did actually get her hands on the insurance check, they'd place a seven-day hold on most of the funds. So she had to protect herself and her daughter. She already had a thousand dollars hidden away inside her apartment. She never knew if she'd have to flee or rent a car, or fly out of town really quickly.

Fear made Nicole do things she'd never before thought of doing. Fear made her even afraid of Ajalon, something she didn't think could ever happen.

"Are you still there?" she asked.

"Yes. But for how much longer, I don't know." He paused. "Listen to this." There was silence at first. Then Nicole heard the sound of a bloodcurdling scream. It was the voice of a woman pleading for her life. She yelled for Jesus so many times that Nicole lost count. The woman pleaded over and over. Then Nicole heard what sounded like a whip cracking. After that, total and utter silence.

Nicole was spellbound. "What was that?"

"A video that my henchman sent me. It was footage of someone else that he'd killed. Someone who told him she did not have his money. Two days later the woman was dead. Pushed off a ledge and found with a rope hung around her neck. Vultures ate most of her remains before she could be found. My henchman told me she was married. He said she had four beautiful kids. He told me she was a VP at an oil and gas company in Katy. He told me she was only thirty-eight years old."

"Oh my God, Ajalon."

"The man who I owe money to told me that the woman he killed was his first cousin, Nicole. A chick he grew up with."

"Lord, no." She wanted to throw up. She wanted to help Ajalon, but she was more concerned about herself. "Ajalon, that's a horrible situation, and right now I don't know what to do. I'll try and think of something."

She hung up.

Ajalon waited and waited for her to call him back. By ten minutes to midnight, he knew she wasn't going to help him. His ride or die did not care if he lived or died. And that's when he made a decision. Ajalon quickly left the house. He drove for miles and miles until he was on the other side of town. He sweated bullets and hoped that no one was following him. He found a truck store where he knew there would be a good chance to come across a pay phone. He inserted two quarters into the slot and dialed the Houston Crime Stoppers phone number. Ajalon told the police he had a tip on who had murdered Rashad Eason. He gave them Slipper's name. And he told them that Nicole Greene Eason, the murdered man's wife, was the one who'd solicited his murder and agreed to pay funds to the contract killer.

When he hung up the phone, he wanted to hang himself. But Ajalon decided to stick around and see what happened. He had enough money to rent a hotel room. He never wanted to return to his apartment ever again.

The police responded right away. They needed to verify the information that they got from the anonymous tip. Several credible informants agreed to take lie detector tests. The details were amazing. A neighbor was courageous enough to tell the police that a little man had asked him to discard of a leather wallet that looked like it was used. The neighbor handed over the wallet to the police. It had Rashad's fingerprints all over it.

And one of the little man's ex-girlfriends remembered how he beat the shit out of her one time. She worked as a nurse, and he loved to make her put on her uniform and then make sweet love to her afterward. They still stayed in touch. And when he showed up to her house in the wee hours of the morning the night that Rashad got killed, she thought it was strange that he wanted to come see her and post up at her place. She let him in. He got undressed, and she noticed the scars on his head, the scratches on his body. She made love to him until he fell asleep. She made sure he was sound asleep and then went poking around in his pockets. She had always been told you could learn all you need to know about a man by going through his pockets. She found his car keys and went out to his car. She felt underneath the car seat and found one black men's sock and a voice disguiser device. The sock wasn't his size. She took the sock out of his car and hid it in the bushes outside her apartment. He woke up an hour later and never realized the sock was missing. She described the man to the police from head to toe, and they reviewed some video footage of the gas station that was next to the warehouse. This time they compared the description to the video. It seemed like a good match.

After reviewing the tapes slowly and carefully, they were able to identify the vehicle that had been spotted in the area that night: a low-to-the-ground two-door dark Nissan. The tape showed that the sporty-looking vehicle drove through the gas station lot. It did not stop at a pump, but they saw the vehicle park a few yards away from one of the pumps. A door opened. A short man, maybe five-foot-three, emerged. He wore dark clothing and a hat. He was seen emptying an unidentifiable object in a trash can. The guy seemed like he was trying to stuff the item deep into the can. Then he got back in the car and drove away. It was only a few seconds of footage, but enough for the police to see the plates and run them.

The owner of the vehicle turned out to be Federico Slipper Cuevas. The SWAT team began to search for Slipper. A cousin of his alerted the police that he was spotted on his street. He was playing basketball with a few of his cousin's friends. Without him knowing, the police set up a perimeter. The second he noticed a canine unit, Freddy dropped the basketball. He ran to hide behind a car. Then he crawled underneath the car, scrambling to get away until he got situated under a truck. He maneuvered his body, but the undercarriage of the vehicle placed big holes in his shirt and punctured his skin.

The German shepherd barked and Freddy heard the sounds of footsteps getting closer.

"Federico, come out and give up. Put your hands behind your head."

Freddy ignored their orders. He rolled from under a pickup and saw an escape. He lifted the top of a manhole and leaped inside. Slipper's reputation preceded him. For all the HPD knew, sneaking into manholes was his specialty. He always frustrated the police, because he was able to stay three steps ahead of the sheriffs, deputies, and the Texas Rangers. He was proud of his legendary reputation. Tonight he did not appreciate the cops getting so close to him. This had never happened before. How did they know he was on this street? Who told on him?

Freddy was just about to pull the lid over his head and hide on the block for however long it took. But he heard a scraping sound. The lid was partially lifted. Then he heard another warning.

"Cousin, don't do this anymore. Give it up, man."

He recognized the voice. The brother of the female cousin that he'd killed. Freddy was heated with anger. He did not move. He took deep breaths as he sweated profusely, still inside the manhole. They called him to come out again.

He did not respond to them.

He heard someone yell, "If you have any weapons, throw them to us and get your ass out of that hole."

Freddy thought of his mother. He whispered that he was sorry. He made the sign of the cross.

Soon multiple gunshots were heard . . . then silence.

The police carefully approached the manhole and lifted the lid.

The notorious shooter had put his own gun to his head. The police finally had Slipper exactly where they wanted him. The fifteen-year manhunt was over.

The following evening, Nicole was sitting in bed watching a movie on Netflix. Emmy was in bed next to her, snoring away. She had not heard from Ajalon since the last time they spoke. The apartment was quiet. Nicole's eyes were on the movie, but her thoughts were on her life. She had no idea what her future held, and she could have kicked herself for not being prudent enough to check the envelope that Mrs. Canterbury had given her to make sure the insurance check was inside. She'd called the insurance company and explained what happened but they told her to wait until their coworker returned to the office.

As she sat in bed, the doorbell rang, and she heard persistent knocking. She got up and walked to the door. When she looked through the peephole, she saw the police.

She took a deep breath and opened it.

"Are you Nicole Greene Eason?"

"Yes."

"What is your date of birth?"

The color drained from her face.

"Yes, I am Nicole. Please. Don't hurt me."

"I know you're thinking about what you've read in the newspaper, what you've seen on TV. Not all cops are bad."

"I know, but I'm still afraid. I don't want to resist arrest, but I don't want to do this, sir." She thought if she could reason with him and not act like a typical thug, maybe he'd take it easy on her.

"I'm still going to take you in."

"But why? How could I hurt him? I loved him."

The deputy sheriff looked at Nicole and shrugged. "Like I read in a book one time: 'A thousand times more crimes have been committed in the name of love than in the name of hate.'"

"Oh. That's crazy."

"Yeah, it is, isn't it?"

Within ten minutes, she had been read her rights and was on her way to jail to get charged for the murder of Rashad Quintelle Eason.

"But my baby . . ." was the only protest she made.

"CPS will get custody of the baby until we notify your next of kin; that person can pick her up."

"But I don't have any kin. I don't have . . . anybody." Nicole was handcuffed and placed in the back of the squad car. Everything was happening so fast. She slumped in the seat and closed her eyes. Life couldn't get any worse for her.

Later on, Nicole was booked and fingerprinted, and took a mug shot in which she refused to look directly into the camera.

After she was placed in a holding cell, it took four hours for her to be able to make a phone call. But she couldn't remember Ajalon's phone number. He'd recently gotten it changed and she kept inverting the digits. She hung up after five attempts to call him.

Please, baby, please be in sync with me enough to real-
ize what happened. Please come to my arraignment and
get me out of here. Don't hold my past against me, because
I actually did support you for months before I decided to
give up.

Nicole felt like shit when she remembered the times
when she'd refused to accept Ajalon's phone calls from jail
after being willing to hear from him in the beginning of his
imprisonment.

She wondered if he'd ever come see her or if he'd forget
all about her and leave her alone to rot. This was the state
of Texas. They hated murderers. And they seemed to love
to kill those on death row. But she refused to think the worst.
She did not kill Rashad. That was a fact. And she had no
idea who the murderer was, so she couldn't be caught lying
about that, either, when her trial came up. She tried to remain positive, but in that bleak atmosphere it was almost
impossible.

Her attorney, Lloyd Johnson, told her he'd do his best to
defend her.

"Did you kill your husband?"

"No, I did not," she said.

"Did you pay someone else to do it?"

"No," she said. They couldn't prove it.

"As I am your attorney, you have to tell me everything."

"And I *have* told you everything."

"Why was there a major withdrawal from your Go-
FundMe account around April twenty-fourth, four days before the murder?"

"I had some business to take care of."

"What kind of business?"

"Bills, shit."

"Specifically?"

"Like car note, rent, gas, food, doctor bills, student loans, cell phone bill, Pampers, child care—happy now?"

"Nicole, I'm trying to help you. Make my job easier by cooperating, please."

She apologized. She began to chew on her nails, biting on them until bits of nail were in her mouth. Attorney Johnson watched Nicole with unsurprised eyes.

He explained the process of collecting info for her case. Then he told her, "When it comes to committing a crime, a lot of people say they are innocent. That they did nothing wrong. That is their perception. But, Nicole, according to the law, in my field we have something we call 'culpable mental state'."

"What?"

"Let's say that you *did* pay someone to kill your husband. Five dollars, five grand, doesn't matter. Money was exchanged, and a deed was done that caused him to die. Poisoned Kool-Aid, an accidental drowning in the tub, or even the occasional gunshot. If you knowingly and willingly asked someone to kill your spouse, you can be found guilty. But let me go back a second. There are four mental states of being when it comes to culpable mental state. You can act intentionally, knowingly, recklessly, or with criminal negligence. If I do my job defending you against any of these things, you will be found not guilty. If not, we have an issue, and a jury or judge will decide which of these was your mental state of being."

" 'Recklessly,' you say? What is that?"

"Here's an example. You were driving down the street because you have diarrhea. You just want to make it home before you have an accident in the family car. In doing so, you are speeding through your neighborhood, where the speed limit is twenty miles an hour. But you were going forty-five. And you end up hitting someone, a pedestrian who was crossing the street. Now, you knew that you never meant to hit anyone with your car. You did not plan to murder that old man. But you did. That's a reckless mental state. Do you get what I'm saying?"

"I'm not culpable, sir, not responsible, not anything, okay? Now, please leave me alone."

But she knew he'd never leave her alone, for this was just the beginning of her sorrows.

In time, Nicole's fate was sealed. She was charged with capital murder. Bail was set at two million dollars. She nearly shrieked when she heard what the judge said.

Lloyd Johnson placed his hand on her shoulder.

She could only hope that between Ajalon and her mother, she'd get to see the light of day again.

After the bail hearing, she was led back with shackles on her feet to her cell. Her eyes cast downward, she couldn't bear to look at the faces of all the awful criminals as she shuffled her way down the hall. There were tall women who looked like they could have played for the WNBA. There were nonchalant women who acted like they didn't give a damn about living somewhere with a jailhouse address. There were a few, a very few, who looked like they didn't belong. They seem fresh-faced, somewhat intelligent, spoke the king's English, and daily thought of all the strategies their attorneys could use to get them out of there.

Then there were others. Cold-blooded killers. One woman she met had thrown kerosene on her man when she caught him fucking her sister. She lit a cigarette lighter and laughed as her man screamed and yelled, racing around the house, going outside and running down the street, lit up like a Christmas tree as the flames overtook him. And Nicole also met a woman, a girl barely eighteen, who'd put twelve bullets into her father, a man who had snuck into her bedroom every night for years to fondle her vagina, kiss on her little body, and stick his penis where it did not belong. "I did it so he couldn't do that to my baby sister. He had to go," she said unapologetically. "He got twelve bullets, one for each year he did that to me. He destroyed my life, but at least I won't have to feel his nasty, sweaty hands and his disgusting, sweaty balls on me ever again. Deuces."

Nicole nodded in wide-eyed horror as some of the other women shared their stories. Some were true nutcases. Women who had been institutionalized for so long that causing uproar through fistfights and loud arguments didn't faze them. Or they were schizophrenics, spending their time accusing others of things they never did. She stayed far away from those women, for there was no predicting what they would do to her. But there was one female whom she got to know.

"Hey, my name is Viv. What's yours?" Viv's hair was a buzz cut that made her eyes look big and scary.

Nicole shrugged and turned away from the woman, whose face was devoid of makeup but whose sparkling smile made up for it.

"It must be your first time, huh? It ain't so bad. You get used to it after a while."

"No way I will ever get used to this."

"The thing that makes it better, sweet thang, is when you get visitors from the outside. That helps to make the time pass."

"Nobody will come see me." Nicole's voice sounded like a whisper. "Nobody."

But the next afternoon, she was surprised when a prison guard called her.

"You've got a visitor. Follow me down this hall. You have fifteen minutes."

Nicole didn't feel excited. It was probably just going to be her lawyer, the man she couldn't afford to pay.

She slowly walked down the narrow hallway behind the guard. He let her into a visitor room, which held a series of benches inside of little booths. Glass partitions divided the prisoner from his or her guest.

When Nicole sat down, at first she saw no one. Moments later Ajalon's handsome face popped up in the window as he slid onto the round metal seat.

He leaned toward the glass, as close as he could get, and pressed his mouth against the speaker. "How's it going, Bella?"

"You son of a bitch. What are you doing here?"

"I wanted to see how you were holding up." He wore a slick smile on his face.

Nicole felt numb at first. She now knew that Ajalon had sold her out. She knew he was the one who had snitched on her and told the cops that she'd solicited her husband's murder. And she knew that the henchman had been betrayed, too, and that was why he'd ended up taking his own life.

"*You* should be in this horrible place, Ajalon. Not me."

"I have no idea what you're talking about. Do you think they got the wrong person?" He had a look of innocence on his face. But she knew he was mocking her and there was nothing she could do about it.

Nicole couldn't help it. It was like a pipe burst, and angry tears streamed from her eyes.

"How could you do this to me?"

"You know why."

"So, this is about money? I offered you money."

"Someone else beat your price."

"What do you mean by that?"

"Your husband must have pissed off a lot of people, because someone else offered to pay for his death. So I took your money and that person's money, too."

"But how could you go behind my back and accept an offer from someone else?"

"Remember, a long time ago, you told me, once a criminal always a criminal? I didn't want to believe it. It hurt me and I didn't believe your words described me. So I fought against that label. Then I stopped fighting. Getting a regular man's job was too hard. And the streets kept calling me. So when you came up with the idea to make money doing dirty work, I jumped at it. And when a second opportunity arose, hey, I couldn't help myself. Because, you know, it's in my blood. Besides, Bella, haven't you heard that anyone who can be bought once can be bought twice?"

It was the moment Alexis McNeil had been waiting on for a long time. She was preparing to walk through the metal detector. She acknowledged the guard, who stared at her with a silly grin. She wore a fedora and was asked to remove it and she complied. After searching her, the guard discovered there was no contraband hidden inside of her hat. He told her she could put it back on. Alexis knew she stood out among all the other visitors coming to see inmates. But she wore the hat to make a point. She had on a sleeveless polka-dot blouse and black silk pants. Three strands of pearls rested against her neck. Alexis looked calm and strikingly beautiful. She felt good on the inside, too.

Once she passed security, she rode the elevator to the fifth floor of the Harris County Jail. She checked in at the window and took a seat at a hard bench as she waited for Nicole to come out.

I can't wait to see the look on that tramp bitch's face.

Alexis didn't have to wait long.

The second Nicole saw her visitor, she scowled, and she was about to twirl back around and go back to her stall.

But Alexis yelled, her voice loud enough to be heard through the thick glass window, "Wait, Nicole, it's about Emmy."

Nicole faced Alexis and slowly sat down on the round swivel seat.

"What about my baby?"

"Emmy's fabulous. I went to see her."

"You went to see her? How?"

"I've kept in touch with your mother, Evelyn, and your sister, Mimi. They had to come to the workplace to pick up your personal belongings. So we talked. We talked a long time."

"Stay away from my family."

Alexis looked surprised. "Is that a threat?"

"Leave my daughter alone."

"I'd think you'd be happy that I was around Emmy. Remember that time that you reminded me that our daughters are sisters? Well, regardless of what's happened to you, they will always be family; and they have a lot in common, Nicole. And I think that they may need each other one day."

"You're getting a big kick out of this, aren't you?"

"Not as much as you think but, then again it does feel like poetic justice. You tried to pull a gun on me. But you got off easy. Yet I knew that one day you'd pay for all the trouble you've caused ever since you arrived in Houston."

"Oh, really? You're not completely innocent, either, Alexis. You're the original side bitch, remember? I guess that's why you always acted so salty toward me. You wanted to be me."

"No, Female Shrek, I never, ever wanted to be like you. In fact, when I met you and saw how hard you were chasing after Rashad, it made me want to do better. And thank you for that one thing, Nicole. Because I learned my lesson and kept it moving. The side-chick business is not for me."

"Oh, please, you are no better now than you were when you were secretly fucking him."

Alexis came to the jail to have a little bit of fun with Nicole. But now she bristled with anger. She flashed her left hand. "Anyway, I thought you'd want to know that my man proposed to me."

Nicole gave Alexis a stony, miserable look. "Wearing a ring means nothing. You could have bought your own engagement ring."

"Oh, I don't have to do things like that. A woman whose man really feels her doesn't need to buy her own ring or coerce him into making things legal."

"Whatever Alexis. I don't care."

"I've really been blessed. It feels good to be a reformed side chick. But you, Nicole, you were always a mistress."

"What the fuck are you talking about? I was a wife."

"No, sweetie. Unless you feel regret about sleeping with a married man and change your scandalous ways, even if you convince the fool to marry you, the mistress mentality will always be in your head; the woman that the man must hide because she's not legitimately his. That lifestyle sucks because the woman never wins." Alexis thought about how she almost fell into the exact same trap that Nicole did. She used to dream about being with Rashad permanently. But she was happy that her wake-up call forced her to change her life. "I had to find my own man. Well, actually he found me. Our love was created the right way."

"Sounds like you are feeling yourself, Alexis. Yet you

seem to forget that you had a baby with your married man. Way to go," Nicole said sarcastically.

"Yes, I did have his child. It wasn't right but I owned up to that. But you?" Alexis glared at Nicole. "You may have gotten him to marry you, but you never were a wife. And deep inside Rashad despised you because you reminded him of how much he fucked up. You thought your dream wedding was just the beginning, but girl, it was the beginning of the end."

"Get the hell out of here. And don't ever come back," Nicole shrieked.

Alexis stood up, gave Nicole one last stare, and started to walk away. She stopped, turned around, and shouted, "Mistress!" And then she left Nicole alone to go back to her cell.

Chapter 20

Weeks later, on a beautiful, late summer day, Eddison and Kiara drove out to his property in Katy. Myles and Jazzy were seated in the back of the car, both talking over one another as they enjoyed the pleasant ride. Eddison had popped in a CD by world-renowned composer and pianist Brian Crain. "One Morning in June," a beautiful piano and cello duet, was playing softly in the background.

"Oh my God, this music is amazing," she told him. "It is so peaceful. Everything I need and want." Kiara relaxed in her seat and couldn't have been happier. Life had been tough going for a while, but things were looking up.

"What does the music make you think of?" Eddison asked as he drove.

"Being free, letting go."

"Good. That's the effect I wanted it to have."

"You're a clever man. You know just what to do." Kiara was so content that she felt a little guilty. Ever since her ex was killed, she'd experienced a myriad of emotions: anger, sadness, and her brain flushed with so many memories. Things she wanted to forget, but she knew she had to remember, for through her recollections his memory would go on for her children's sake.

Once they arrived in Katy, they got out of the car and walked the grounds. Together they reviewed the floor plan of the dream house they planned to build.

Kiara stood on top of the grass near the front of the land.

"Okay, this is where Myles's room will go, and Jazzy gotta be right next to him so they can drive each other crazy," Kiara said.

"Yes. And I think Hayley won't mind bunking with her sister."

"I agree. Kids need to share bedrooms and not always have their own."

"Unless it's a little infant, a newborn who needs its own room," Eddison gently told her. She looked up at him and smiled.

"Wow! I agree with you two times within one minute. You're good, Eddy."

They both decided that they wanted to have a baby together. And Kiara was so happy that although at one time she thought she'd get her tubes tied, she decided not to. She would be honored to have this man's child.

"I love you to the moon and back, Eddison Osborne. You have proven yourself over and over again. I feel like I don't deserve you sometimes."

"You are the best woman ever. The best mother. The best everything."

"Oh, you exaggerate. But I love it." She sighed with contentment. But he had one more thing to tell her. "I just wish you'd change your mind about—"

"Eddy, I think we can be happy without that piece of paper. So many people will do anything to get the piece of paper, but it doesn't guarantee their happily-ever-after."

"I understand but—"

"But nothing, sweetheart. I feel blessed to have you right now, right here, and I know I will always love you. I don't want anything to mess that up. I'm afraid of marriage, but I'll take another chance on *good* love, Eddy."

"Marriage provides much more security than simply living together. Don't you want that?"

"I'm secure in that I love myself. I adore my children. I know that you are a good man, the best man I've ever met, and I feel confident you will always do the right thing and make sure that I'm okay. That's enough for now. Anything else would be a bonus." Kiara Eason knew that she wanted to love again, but this time she was determined to get it through her own terms. Whether Eddison thought she was copping out on him didn't matter. Her heart must be protected. No matter what it took.

Evelyn and Mimi came to see Nicole one Friday evening in early October.

At first mother and daughter grimly stared at each other through the big, thick glass partition. Finally, Nicole spoke.

"I should have listened to you."

"Most adult kids stop listening to their parents. And all we can do is to try our best to raise you."

"Who is going to tell Emmy what she should and shouldn't do? Damn, I really messed up. Things got way out of hand. But I feel like I'm innocent. I was set up. My lawyers will prove my innocence. And that bastard Ajalon will pay for what he did."

Evelyn raised an eyebrow. "Oh, really?"

"Yes, Mama! He committed the ultimate betrayal. Ajalon took me to the cleaners and I didn't even know my pants were off. When I get done with him, he'll wish he could walk to the cleaners. I know people."

Evelyn laughed. "You still don't get it, do you, Nicole? When will you learn that you can't keep trying to pay someone back for hurting you? Your husband tried to do that, and look where it got him. Let it go, baby. Or else the cycle will continue . . . until another person ends up dead."

"It won't be me."

"But you never know how things will turn out. I never thought you'd end up here."

"For once, I agree with you, Mama." Her voice trembled as she poured out her heart. "I hate it here. I think I might seriously go insane. And the food they serve to us . . . I could get better tasting food from a garbage Dumpster."

Evelyn felt so sorry for her child. Compared to how she existed now, she was sure Nicole would give anything to go back to Alabama, and eat her mom's cooking and live in the tiny one-story house that she couldn't wait to escape.

Nicole stared into space and continued. "I've been thinking a lot. And every day I ask myself, is it my fault for wanting the nice, normal things I've wanted, even if I made the wrong choices in trying to get them? I didn't mean for all that crazy shit to happen. So what is it about me, that I can't get what so many other women have? The Kiara Easons of the world. The beautiful, successful women who were easily handed the good life? Ever since I can remember, it's like God has had it out for me, but why?" She sniffed and looked to her mother, who had no answer. "You know what, Mama? If there's nothing else I've learned, it's that I finally understand why some people become criminals. They may have tried to do the right thing, but bad still happened. So what else could they do except do things differently? They know their way is risky, but they roll the dice anyway. Mama, if you know what it's like to lose all your life, what more do you have to lose?" Memories of what Nicole gained and lost flashed through her mind. "I-I felt I had nothing left to lose. And by being here, it looks like I've proven that. But I never wanted to prove anything except that I could have a good husband, a child, a nice home. Normal shit." She sneered as she looked around. "And now all I have is this fucking miserable, unreal existence."

"That sounds like a confession to me, daughter."

"You know what I confess to? You asked me a question a while ago. Which part of me wanted revenge? Well, my wise mother, the wife part of me loved Rashad and could never hurt him. But the revenge side of me is the mistress. She is the one who is given a shitload of broken promises. She is the one whom a married man builds up with his false dreams. His 'I love yous' that don't mean a thing. That's the part of me that Rashad let down. Yes, I've been a wife. But the mistress part of me, that I wish I could totally get rid of; she wanted him dead and now I wish she were dead."

Nicole broke down and began to sob. She covered her eyes and wept as the sorrow of her reality overwhelmed her entire soul. Evelyn wished she could reach through the glass and comfort Nicole, but what had her advice ever done for her daughter? For a minute Evelyn hated Rashad. And the only thing she could do right then was cry silently with Nicole and mourn the past.

Kiara was comfortably sitting on the lawn chair on the patio. She was browsing through a fashion magazine and sipping on iced tea. Myles suddenly burst through the door, holding her cell phone.

"Mommy, your phone is ringing."

"Well, gee, thanks, Myles, for bringing me the phone. I'm shocked you don't know how to answer it."

She flipped back her hair and answered. It was an unrecognizable number.

"Hello?"

"Hi, is this Kiara Eason?"

"Who's speaking?"

"My name is Patrice Grant. I'm calling from MetLife."

Kiara's heart dropped. "Is there anything wrong?"

"No. I just wanted to inform you about an insurance policy."

"Oh. Not interested. Good-bye."

"Hold on. Don't hang up. Um, this has to do with the death of Rashad Eason."

Kiara hesitated. "What about it?"

"We are sorry for taking months to contact you. But someone had been going through a lockbox that he had at a bank, and they found a life insurance policy that apparently the people close to him didn't know existed. I wanted you to know that Rashad listed you as his beneficiary."

"What? We aren't—"

"And we have a check ready for you to pick up. Bring your driver's license."

"Oh. Alright. How much?"

When Patrice told her, she nearly hung up on the woman.

"Okay, Ms. Grant. Thanks for the call. I'll be in to your offices. Very soon. Good-bye."

Kiara stared into space, feeling as if she was dreaming. Could it be possible that this man really had cared for her after all? Sure, some of his reckless and selfish behavior had led to so much confusion in their lives that she'd had no choice but to want better for herself. She thought that he might have forgotten to change his beneficiary from her to Nicole when he got remarried. But something told her that he left her on the policy on purpose. Maybe in his own peculiar way, Rashad's enduring love for Kiara and his family had caused him to look out for her even when she might not have deserved it.

"You crazy-ass man." She fussed at him as if he were in the room. Memories flooded her heart and mind. And the pain of his absence threatened to cause her to cry fresh tears. But she had made peace with him and did not want to cry anymore. Kiara wiped the corner of her eye and said out loud, "You're not going to believe this, but guess what? I loved you. Period." And she realized she did.

She remembered the ups, downs, highs, and lows, and she knew that nothing or no one could cause her to ever forget the love and the life that she shared with Rashad Quintelle Eason.

Chapter 21

One year later, Nicole was as restless as a caged animal as she tried to grow accustomed to the life of an imprisoned murderer. Although she'd been sentenced to life without parole, she told herself that one day this nightmare would end.

Each day she woke up at four in the morning. But the morning felt exactly like the evening. Time meant nothing in prison.

She spent her days playing dominoes, working out, and hoping that someone would come to visit her. Once a month, Evelyn and Mimi stopped by. Twice a month, Shyla showed her face.

But Nicole never wanted to see Ajalon Cantu again. She closed up her heart to his memory, and after a while it almost felt like he never existed.

One particular day in the fall, she went to the yard. A game of volleyball was about to begin. It was the black team versus the white team. The black team wore black T-shirts. They rolled up their sleeves. The white team didn't.

Three minutes into the game, Nicole was hit hard by an ugly, almost six-foot-tall woman with the thickest arms she'd ever seen. She braced herself, for Viv had warned her how things could pop off any second.

The thick-armed woman hit Nicole so hard she fell to the floor. Soon three other females pulled Nicole's shoulders to the ground, keeping her from being able to get up.

"Move," she screamed. "Get the fuck off of me."

"Shut up," said one of the women.

Another chick said, "Get her."

Nicole's eyes enlarged with horror. She was dragged by the arms into a corner of the yard. The rubber surface of the floor made it feel like her skin was on fire.

As the three women pressed her back hard down on the floor, she started to yell. But one other chick came out of nowhere and held her hand over Nicole's lips. Some sheets were shoved into her mouth, making it difficult for her moans to be heard.

The big, tall chick, with a thick neck in addition to her huge arms, walked over to Nicole and bent over her. The lady was just about to kick her in her stomach. This reminded her of the last time she got kicked. Nicole screamed, "Don't, please!"

In a rare moment, the woman simply laughed and walked away. The violent kick that was planned for Nicole never happened. The women all abandoned her, and she was relieved.

As she lay alone on the ground quivering from fear, she wondered if that would just be the last time that she'd be targeted. And her helpless feeling made her want to remain on the ground and not get up.

Nicole prayed that one day Karma would leave her alone, but she knew in her heart it may not happen until the day she died.

* * *

On that same day in the late afternoon, Kiara Eason met up with Ajalon Cantu at a fancy Italian restaurant in the Montrose area.

They sat in a private booth far away from all the other diners and ordered their entrées and drinks.

"Do you have any news for me?" she finally asked.

"Yes. Nothing has changed. She's not doing too well. She got back-doored this morning."

Ajalon had taught Kiara prison terminology and she knew exactly what he meant. She gave him a blank stare, then finally muttered, "I would have given anything to see a video of her getting attacked. And it's a damn shame that she lost her baby last year. Having a miscarriage in jail must have been a nightmare. Or maybe not," she concluded. Kiara took a tiny sip of champagne.

Ajalon continued and exaggerated his report. "From what I was told, someone gave her an ass whipping she'll never forget. 'Her jaw turned to jelly' is the quote I was given. I think she'd tried to make a friend or two in there, but that won't be happening. Nicole always told me she didn't trust anyone. Too bad she learned she can never trust an inmate. Once a criminal, always a criminal."

"Ain't that the truth? You definitely can't trust anybody and everybody. Not in this crazy-ass world." After they ate their delicious pasta meal, Kiara reached in her purse and left a thick pile of cash on their table.

"This money will pay for the meal plus there's a bonus for the waitress. There are two tips, actually. Thirty percent for her, and the rest is for you."

"Thanks, as usual. I appreciate that."

Kiara got up, sweetly told Ajalon good-bye, and quickly left the restaurant. She reached for her cell phone and placed an immediate call to Alexis.

"Hey there, Mrs. Alexis Brown. I have something crazy to tell you. I heard that some lesbians treated her like she was a piece of hamburger and they were the brass meat tenderizer."

Meanwhile, back in the restaurant, Ajalon took another long sip of his bubbly champagne. He felt a teensy bit of regret about what happened to Nicole. At one time he loved her with all of his heart. But love made a fool out of him and left him a broken man. Ajalon shrugged and grabbed the generous tip money that Kiara had set aside. He counted off the bills and decided to skip out on paying for their meal. He looked both ways and pocketed all of the money.

He'd already decided not to meet with Kiara anymore to inform her about Nicole. Ajalon reached down and lifted a suitcase that Kiara never noticed. It was filled with all of his belongings. He calmly walked past the other diners until he had exited the restaurant. He stood outside and glanced up at the sky.

Ajalon was on his way to the Greyhound bus station. For he no longer wanted to be involved with the criminal life, or with love and all of its tragic revenge.

A CONVERSATION WITH AUTHOR CYDNEY RAX

Cydney Rax has been published since 2004 and brings with her a wealth of knowledge through her experiences as a novelist who primarily writes about infidelity and forbidden love triangles. Here she gives us her thoughts about her writing process and what she went through for two years in penning the Love & Revenge series.

How did you feel about writing your first-ever fictional series? At first I wasn't sure if I could pull it off. It is very challenging to develop continual storylines using the same characters for three books, or using 240,000 words. But the more I wrote, the more I got into it. By the time I was writing the final book, I was hooked. I became very involved with all of my characters. They invaded my mind and captured my imagination more than any other characters that I've written about.

Where do you get your ideas for plot twists and storylines? Believe it or not, as I wrote these stories, sometimes when I was driving to work at my day job, ideas would suddenly pop into my head. And I would open up the recorder app on my smartphone, and I would just talk into the recorder, describing the new ideas that had been developed. It was a very involved and amazing process.

How do you come up with the titles for your books? I must say that the title selection process is incredibly important. Thankfully, IF YOUR WIFE ONLY KNEW was the perfect title for the leading novel in this series. It was so fitting, and basically it was chosen because it is catchy and memorable. A title for this type of series should be juicy and maybe even scandalous. So MY MARRIED BOYFRIEND was perfect. Simple and to the point. I have become known for these titles—it's what makes readers pick up my books in the first place (along with their amazing book covers).

Why did you feature Birmingham, Alabama, in the Love & Revenge series? This probably happened subconsciously. I just mentioned the city and it kept coming back for return appearances. I think one reason is because I knew that Nicole Greene was going to be a Southern girl. And I've been to Birmingham a few times, so it made sense to include that city in the novel.

What are your goals when you write a novel? I want to write a story that has a plot with a beginning, a middle, and an ending. I want to take my readers on an emotional journey. I want to make the readers *feel* something. There's nothing worse than reading a novel and you never felt anything at all. I want you to laugh, be angry, be disgusted, to think, and either agree or disagree with a character's philosophy or attitude. I want my characters to be flawed, never perfect. Like someone said, "Perfect people make horrible art." And lastly, I never try to write the absolute perfect book. Don't get me wrong, I will write the best story that I can, but it's never my goal to try to be completely perfect, to be completely politically correct, and to try to do something that I think everyone will like or agree with. That's not me at all. If my characters spark an emotion within a reader that hits close to home, I think I've done my job. And I want to be unique in having my own style. Although I admire many talented authors, I do not wish to write like any other novelist. My desire is for readers to like me for me.

Do you feel a need to rescue your characters when they get themselves into trouble? Why or why not? I definitely feel some type of sympathy for some of my characters regarding the trouble they find themselves in. And I hope they eventually get it together. But like someone said in one of my books, "You just never know."

Overall, how do you feel about the entire Love & Revenge series? Why should readers get involved with these books? If you love juicy, scandalous fiction involving insane love triangles, this is the series for you. I had a fun time writing these novels. They pushed me out of my comfort zone, believe it or not. I had to explore topics that I'd never written about before. So, yeah, I am in love with these books. And I hope that the readers will get a kick out of the Love & Revenge series, as well.